Blockade Runner

David Kent-Lemon

First published in Great Britain in 2012 by
CLAYMORE PRESS
An imprint of
Pen & Sword Books Ltd
47 Church Street
Barnsley
South Yorkshire
S70 2AS

978-1-78159-064-5

A CIP catalogue record for this book is
available from the British Library

Printed and bound in England
By CPI Group (UK) Ltd, Croydon, CRO 4YY

Pen & Sword Books Ltd incorporates the Imprints of Claymore Press, Pen
& Sword Aviation, Pen & Sword Family History, Pen & Sword Maritime,
Pen & Sword Military, Wharncliffe Local History, Pen & Sword Select,
Pen & Sword Military Classics, Leo Cooper, Remember When, Seaforth
Publishing and Frontline Publishing

For a complete list of Pen & Sword titles please contact
PEN & SWORD BOOKS LIMITED
47 Church Street, Barnsley, South Yorkshire, S70 2AS, England
E-mail: enquiries@pen-and-sword.co.uk
Website: www.pen-and-sword.co.uk

Blockade Runner

To Jeanette, Adele, Nichola and Allan with love.

Chapter One
Fire on a Steamship

"Me sir, me, I'll go!"

My hand shot up as if I was an enthusiastic schoolboy wanting to answer a question in class.

Mr Pembroke looked at me dismissively, and then glanced round the rest of the general office. The clerks had their heads down, studying their ledgers. It seemed that no one else was prepared to sacrifice his evening to act as one of the night watchmen on the *Messalina*. The owners had been let down by the shipyard. We were brokers for the ship, and Mr Pembroke had been asked to remedy the problem.

His severe glance swung back to me. As he stood in the doorway to the partners' office, he pushed back the tails of his frock coat, stuffed his hands into his pockets and rocked backwards and forwards as if in thought. Then his bearded chin jutted.

"So be it, Wells. Get yourself down to Lungleys and report to John Reynolds."

He paused.

"And don't make a mess of it. Remember the firm's reputation. I can't see how you can bungle it, but I don't want to hear of any more of your bull-at-a-gate nonsense."

He swung round and strode into the partners' office, firmly closing the door behind him. My friend David Hardcastle, the most junior clerk, sniggered.

"And make sure you're on the right ship!"

I flushed. He was referring to an episode where in my haste, I had come back to the office with the cargo capacity details for the *Caroline* in mistake for the *Carolina*. I felt that my reputation had been sullied unfairly. As a distant relation of Mr Pembroke's I had been lucky to get my place as an office boy at Stringer, Pembroke and I had been determined to prove myself. Through an excess of misplaced zeal, I had made mistakes.

Sheepishly I put my papers away, closed the lid of my desk and left the office. The wind tore at my clothes as I hurried across London Bridge to take the train to Deptford. Little did I realise that this was the start of one of the most dramatic evenings of my life, triggering a chain of events that would transform everything for me.

The evening started quietly enough. The gale that had been blowing all day had now died down and the *Messalina* was lying almost motionless at her moorings off Deptford. The Thames was at high water. The *Messalina* was an elegant sight, low and sleek against the evening sky. She was a big ship, wooden built in New York, and nearly two hundred and fifty feet long. She was a three-masted steamship, driven by two huge side wheels. She had been built as a passenger ship for the Atlantic crossing, but now her new owner was converting her for cargo. It was unusual in those days to use steamships as merchantmen, as the coal usage was too expensive. I could only imagine that she was destined to be an exceptionally large mail ship.

To me the sleek, gleaming elegance of the *Messalina* struck a strange contrast with the prosaic grime of Deptford itself. Charles Lungley & Co. had finished their work on the ship some days earlier, and had transferred her back to the owners. As I lived nearby, I had seen the ship in Lungley's shipyard; I had even watched cargo being loaded on board from lighters coming up from Woolwich.

I was excited at the prospect of spending a night on the ship. Mr Reynolds, the other night watchman, was an experienced seaman, and a local Deptford character. He claimed to have served as a cabin boy with Admiral Nelson on the *Theseus* at Santa Cruz; it was there that Nelson had lost his right arm, and Reynolds was rumoured to have Nelson's right hand in a jar of rum in his room. Reynolds was rough but engaging, and I liked him.

The light was just beginning to fail as John Reynolds and I rowed across to the *Messalina* to relieve the shipkeeper. Reynolds was at the oars. During the day, that stretch of the Thames at Deptford would have been as busy as Piccadilly, but late in the evening there was hardly a soul about. In the height of summer the Thames stank of London's effluent, but it was early June, and the smell was just tolerable. Reynolds was a wizened little man in his sixties, and his sharp eyes scanned the Thames as he pulled us across towards the ship. He was wearing the untidy clothes of a retired seaman, with a peaked nautical cap partly covering his long grey locks.

"What are they doing Tom?"

Reynolds gave a jerk of his head towards three men in a small rowing boat moored against a buoy.

"Fishing?"

Reynolds sniffed the air and laughed.

"It won't be a fish they'll be catching here. Half the sewage in London's in the river, it joins the other half at Greenwich. I'm going to ask them. Take the oars a moment, lad."

He stood up in the skiff to call out to the other boat. We rocked a little as Reynolds steadied himself. He cupped his hands.

"Ahoy there! Need any help?"

"We're waiting for the *Rebecca*," a gruff voice replied, "she sure is late. Should have been here an hour back."

"Good luck!" called Reynolds, and he sat down.

"I'll take them oars again, Tom."

He paused and said reflectively,

"E's not from these parts that fellow. Where d'you think 'e comes from?"

"Sounds American, but it could be anywhere, Mr Reynolds," I said, "half the sailors in the world seem to come to Deptford to join their ships, don't they?"

"True enough. Look Tom, when we gets to the ship we'll go over 'er together. Our duties are simple enough, so you'll be able to get some sleep later. I knows what you young lads are for needing sleep!"

"What do we have to do?"

"It's easy, Tom. Once we've checked the ship, we must just make sure that the lanterns stay lit at each end of 'er, and watch out for other ships – who knows whether the *Rebecca* may not come galumphing through the gloom and go smack damn right straight into 'er. And with 'er cargo, that could be the bloody end of us."

I have to admit that I blushed at Reynolds' coarse language. My widowed mother had brought me up very strictly, and I found his words offensive. He gave an amused smile.

"You've gone as pink as a girl, Tom, what's the matter? It's only sailors' talk."

I looked down at my feet. No lad of my age likes being accused of being girlish, but I could think of no smart response.

"What's her cargo, Mr Reynolds?"

"They've been bringing boxes up from Woolwich."

He could see the blank expression on my face, and he smiled.

"The Arsenal's at Woolwich, Tom. It's cases of rifles and ammunition. Rumour is the *Messalina's* to be a blockade-runner. You know, smuggling stuff to the rebels in the Southern States."

The Civil War in America had started a few months earlier with Lincoln's presidential victory in 1860. The London papers were full of it. South Carolina had seceded, and many of the other Southern States soon followed. I had heard that some London shipowners were involved in running Lincoln's blockade of the Southern ports, but this was the first evidence I had seen of it. I stared at the *Messalina* with new interest.

Despite his modest size, John Reynolds was remarkably proficient with the oars. Soon we had arrived at the ship, and we were making fast at the stern. We were surprised to see that there was no other boat tied up there. We joined Mr Brown, the shipkeeper, who was a rotund friendly man whose deeply tanned, chubby face seemed permanently wreathed in smiles.

"Where's your boat, Alfred?" was Reynolds first question.

"You don't miss nothing do you?" Brown replied, "one of the Lungley's engineers was on board – something to do with the boilers. He asked if he could take my boat back. Can you take me across John? The Missus won't be too pleased if I don't turn up. She'll think I'm spending the night at the Anchor again!"

"I'll do it if you'll buy me a pint, but we'll go over the ship first. You don't mind standing first watch do you Tom? You're a sensible lad aren't you? I'm sure you can look after things. I'll only be away for an hour. All you'll have to do is inspect the lanterns every quarter of an hour or so, and keep an eye out for shipping."

I was surprised and rather pleased at the request to look after the *Messalina* on my own. Responsibility was coming to me slowly at Stringer, Pembroke and I wanted to take on more. I liked to have a go at things, even if I regretted it afterwards. Besides, I felt that I could hardly refuse, especially if it meant more accusations of a lack of manliness.

"I'll do it Mr Reynolds."

"Good lad."

Brown and Reynolds knew each other well, and they chatted amiably as we checked the ship from bow to stern. Our brief was to make sure that all fires were extinguished, and that the only external lights were the lanterns fore and aft. By half past nine we were satisfied with the state of the ship. Brown and Reynolds clambered down into the skiff and Reynolds gave me a cheery wave before he spun the boat round and headed towards the quay at Lungley's shipyard.

"Don't fall asleep 'till I get back Tom!" he shouted, as he pulled away, and I could hear the two of them laughing and joking as they headed towards Deptford.

Now that I was alone on the ship, I felt almost as though I was the captain. I suppose at eighteen I should have been more nervous, but at the start it was pride that filled my head, although as darkness crept up, I have to admit that my responsibilities seemed to grow in size as the light diminished. It was quiet, but someone must have been working late in Deptford, as I could hear a carpenter sawing in the distance. There was the gentle lap of the water against the *Messalina's* hull, and the occasional sounds of distant laughter and shouting. Soon the public houses would be closing. I thought wistfully of the cheery light and laughter in the public bar of the Anchor and Crown and the short walk back to my widowed mother's tiny house in Deptford.

I shivered. The day had been warm enough, but now the light breeze off the Thames was chilly.

Mr Reynolds and I had decided to have our headquarters in the saloon. I made my way there in the gathering gloom, and I turned up the lamps. Whilst this made the saloon bright and cosy, it enhanced the darkness of the night. The reflections of the lamplight in the saloon windows made it hard to see anything outside, although I could see the glow of fashionable London to the west. The gloom made me edgy, but I told myself that I had to make my inspections of the warning lanterns, and make sure that we were not in any danger from shipping. There was a chronometer in the saloon; I used this to set the time for my promised quarter hour inspections. It was now just gone half past nine, and I calculated that I would probably only have to make three before Mr Reynolds returned.

I confess that in the periods between those first inspections I was too restless to sit down and make myself comfortable. I paced up and down, glancing frequently at the chronometer. Often I would go to the saloon windows to check for any approaching ships, but I saw nothing. The inspections themselves were reassuring. The river was quiet, and the *Messalina* rode serenely at her moorings. Each time I left the saloon I found it difficult to adjust my eyes to the darkness, but eventually I could see enough to ensure that we were in no danger. Creaking and scuffling sounds came from the ship, but nothing that seemed unusual to me.

After my third inspection, I finally sat down at the saloon table and felt in my jacket pocket for the book I was carrying - Wilkie Collins' latest. Somehow the words didn't sink in. My imagination was filled with thoughts about the *Messalina's* rumoured purpose. If the gossip was correct, soon she would be crossing the Atlantic and dodging Union warships as she tried to get through to New Orleans or Charleston, in support of the Southern cause. There seemed to be something very romantic and dashing about the brave stand being taken by the Southern States. I had read about the brave souls who were risking their lives to run through Lincoln's blockade fleet. Was this ship really going to be going on adventures like that?

Suddenly I was wrenched back to reality by the sound of something heavy scraping along the starboard side of the ship. A glance at the chronometer showed me that it was nearly half past ten, and I realised that it must be Reynolds returning to the ship. I stuffed *The Woman in White* back into my pocket and raced out onto the deck.

"Is that you Mr Reynolds?" I shouted.

The scraping sound had ceased now, but I thought I could hear the sound of oars dipping into the water. There was no reply to my shout.

"Mr Reynolds, where are you?" I called out again, "do you need a hand?"

I wondered what could have caused the scraping sound. Was there a ship or something equally heavy adrift in the Thames? There was a smell of burning wood and paraffin, which I assumed to be coming from somewhere on shore. I ran to the stern of the *Messalina*, but there was no sign of anything sinister. I ran anxiously down the other side of the ship towards the bow, and then I could see the shadowy outline of a boat being rowed quickly away from the ship. Could this be Reynolds, having lost sight of the *Messalina*? I shouted again at the top of my voice.

"Mr Reynolds, I'm over here!"

Finally a voice came from the rowing boat.

"We're not Reynolds, we're the tender to the *Rebecca*," and then more quietly, "pull on those oars, Fraser."

It was the same gruff American voice that we had heard earlier in the evening.

I was relieved to have found an explanation for what had happened, and I was comforted by the thought that they weren't big enough to have caused any damage. But I was puzzled by their actions. If they had barged into us by mistake, why had they not tried to apologise or explain? They were now a fair distance away, so I went back to the stern of the *Messalina* and looked towards Deptford to see if I could see Reynolds and his boat. I looked as hard as I could into the gloom, and in a few moments I was relieved to see his slight figure plying the oars of his skiff. Every minute or so he would glance over his shoulder towards the ship to make sure he was heading in the right direction. It seemed to me that he was rowing with increasing urgency. As he got closer he caught sight of me.

"Stand by Tom," he shouted.

When he reached the ship, he pulled sideways on to me and threw me a rope. As he scrambled on board he asked sharply,

"What was that shouting? Was that you?"

"Yes, Mr Reynolds, I..."

"We've got no time for that now. There's a light showing through one of the portholes where there damn well shouldn't be. Follow me!"

He ran along the deck to the saloon.

"Wait there!" he cried.

He dashed in and grabbed one of the lamps. Then we were running along the deck again, and he jerked open a door behind the port paddlewheel box.

"Hold that!"

He passed me the lamp and scrambled down a ladder into the ship's hold.

"Pass the lamp down!"

I placed the lamp by the top of the ladder, and clambered halfway down. Then I passed the lamp to Reynolds, and jumped the last few rungs to join him.

He ran along a shadowy corridor to a door, I reached to open it, but he pushed me aside to open it himself. We were greeted by darkness. He ran to another door. This time when the door was opened we were met by a blaze of light and the crackle of flames. There was the acrid smell of smoke, and a strong reek of lamp oil. My heart sank in the realisation that this fire must have started whilst I was on sole watch. But what had I done wrong? I had followed Reynolds' instructions to the letter. He closed the door again quickly, and turned to me.

"It's the lamp room Tom ... no steam pressure for the pumps, dammit ... we'll have to get water from over the side. Get those buckets there!"

Every wooden ship at that time was plentifully supplied with fire buckets, as fire was one of the hazards most feared by seamen and shipowners. Reynolds' wiry frame was seized with energy. He put down the lamp, and fitting the buckets inside one another we grabbed all we could see, and Reynolds sprang for the ladder to get back up to the deck level. I followed him as fast as I could. Reynolds found a length of rope, and then he was filling the buckets from the Thames with impressive speed. I watched as he tipped the buckets onto their sides and pulled them against the current to fill them. Soon the sleeves of Reynolds' jacket were wringing wet from the rope as he pulled the buckets up onto the deck. As each bucket was filled I lugged it to the top of the ladder, trying not to spill any water. When the last one was filled, Reynolds carried it over to the others, and we started the difficult process of getting them down into the hold and along to the lamp room door.

Reynolds put his hand on the door handle. Then he turned sharply to me.

"Stand back Tom!"

He had to struggle to open the door, as it must have warped with the heat. When it finally opened he leapt back, and it was fortunate that he did so. Heat and smoke billowed out of the opening. The fire was far worse than before, and soon we were both choking from the smoke. Reynolds ripped two pieces of material from his shirt, and soaked them with water from one of the buckets.

"Tie that round your nose and mouth!" he shouted.

Then we feverishly dashed the contents of bucket after bucket through the doorway and over the flames, but the water seemed to have little effect. Reynolds tried to shut the door again, but it was too distorted to close. We collected up the empty buckets and rushed back for the deck.

"It's bad Tom," Reynolds said as he filled the buckets again, "we'll give it one more try. If we can't get a grip of it, we must go for the engines."

He never seemed to tire as he hauled the buckets of water out of the Thames and onto the deck. I offered to help.

"You do your part, and I'll do mine," was all he said.

Getting the buckets down to the hold again was increasingly difficult in the smoke and heat. The fire was spreading towards the lamp room doorway. We flung the water as close to the fire as we could, and then we scrambled up to the deck again.

"We'll go for the engines, get to the stern!" shouted Reynolds.

"Shouldn't one of us stay? Don't we need to keep the fire under control?"

Reynolds looked at me keenly.

"How are you with the oars?"

"Not really..."

14

"Then we'll both have to go. I'm not leaving you here; it's too dangerous. Come on Tom!"

How can I explain the decision I made then? Was it because of Mr Pembroke's warning not to make a mess of my assignment? Or was it just my own impetuous temperament? Perhaps it was a combination of the two. But whatever the reason, I refused to leave the ship.

"Have it your own way Tom," said Reynolds, "I can't stand here arguing, but *stay on deck!* Get as much water as you can through that doorway. Don't go down the ladder. I'm off! I'll be back as quick as I can."

And with that he sprinted along the deck to the stern, flung himself into the skiff and rowed powerfully towards Deptford. I watched him for a moment with a sinking heart, but the smell and crackle of the fire galvanised me into action, and then I was filling those buckets as fast as I could.

Reynolds had made it look easy, but at first all that the buckets would do for me was to float on the surface of the Thames. Feverishly I tried to learn the knack of filling them and finally I achieved it. Then I was able to collect them together by the door to the hold. I ignored the instruction to stay on deck, and somehow I managed to manhandle the buckets down the ladder. The passageway was filling with thick black pungent smoke, but I got to the lamp room. I could see the fire was worse as I emptied the buckets; it was the paraffin that seemed to make it spread so fast. I raced back on deck again with the buckets.

Twice I repeated the process, until finally the smoke was too thick for me to be able to get down the ladder. I emptied the buckets down into the hold, and stood exhausted on the deck. I glanced towards Deptford to see if there was any sign of the floating fire engines. Disappointed, I turned towards the saloon. There was the flicker of fire. One of the windows was scorched and broken and the flames and sparks were beginning to lick upwards into the night sky.

Somehow the fire must have worked its way up into the cabins and through to the saloon. They all seemed to be burning. Until then my fear had concentrated on the risk of being blamed for

15

allowing the fire to start, and I hadn't worried too much for my own safety. But now I could see that I was in imminent danger. It was clear that the fire was not far from breaking out all over the ship.

Already it was no longer possible to get to the stern of the *Messalina*, so I made my way anxiously to the bow. I tried to work out what to do as the fire intensified; I had never learned to swim, but frankly that made little difference at Deptford. The water there was so dirty that you stood little chance of life if you were unlucky enough to drink any of it. The prospect was dire. Even in that moment of virtual despair I checked my pocket to make sure that my precious library book was still there. I almost thought of it as a talisman to get me through this hour of trial. Then I turned my mind to escape.

Eventually I calculated that my best chance would be to shin along the bow rope to the mooring buoy. It was going to be dangerous, but maybe it was my best chance of survival.

I waited as long as I could.

Finally I felt that I must make the attempt, but just as I was bracing myself to start, I heard the sound of a steam whistle. I looked towards Deptford, and my heart lifted as I saw the two Deptford floating fire engines steaming towards the ship. I had seen them moored off Deptford so many times, but I had never imagined that the first time I would see them in action would be when they were coming to my rescue! Relief flooded through me.

Moments later the leading engine was crashing alongside the *Messalina* and I was dragged over the rail to safety before the two ships parted again.

I must have looked a strange sight, with my face, hands and clothing blackened with smoke from the hold; much of me was soaked with water from the buckets, but everyone was far too busy to notice it. Reynolds ran over to me, and soon he was wringing my hand, and thanking me for staying with the ship.

The steam pumps were fired up, and soon we were flooding the fire with water from the Thames. It took a full hour for the flames to be extinguished.

I was in a state of shock, and coughing badly by the time they got me to Deptford. The smoke seemed to have got right down into my lungs. I half remember offering to stay, but they put me ashore and got me home. A large crowd of idlers had collected to watch the fire, and one of them offered to run to the railway station to find a cab. Soon I was at home, with a doctor tending to me.

Even though the fire had been put out, the *Messalina's* cargo was considered too dangerous to allow her to stay where she was. She was towed out to the mouth of the Thames, and it was only after her cargo was removed that she was brought back to Dudgeon's for repair.

The police never traced the three men who we assumed had started the fire. Despite all attempts to find them, they seemed to have disappeared like ghosts in the dawn. The *Rebecca* also proved to be a phantom, and failed to make an appearance. Reynolds was voluble in his praise of me to anyone who would listen. I received the heartfelt thanks of the *Messalina's* owners and a ten pound reward for my part in saving the ship.

Two days after the fire I was fully recovered and back in the office of my employers Stringer, Pembroke, in the City of London. Mr Pembroke was in Liverpool that day, but late in the morning his partner Edgar Stringer made an appearance. He was a tall, fair-haired, handsome man, elegantly dressed, with a gardenia in the buttonhole of his fashionable frock coat. He was wearing a beautifully brushed tall silk hat. He stopped at my desk before going through to the partners' office. There was a faint smell of expensive hair oil as he stood close to me.

"Pembroke tells me you're a hero, Wells," he said languidly in his aristocratic voice, "congratulations old fellow. No after effects I trust?"

"I'm fine sir,"

"Damn tricky business though," he continued, "Pembroke thinks that those characters in the rowing boat you spotted could have been President Lincoln's agents. He thinks that the *Messalina's* owner was preparing her to run the blockade into the Southern States. If those chaps set fire to her, then Lincoln's arm is getting far too damned long. By-the-by, if they did get on board it was damn lucky you didn't come across them. You'd have been a gonner if you had."

He turned to go into his office.

In truth I was still worried that I might get some of the blame for the fire, even though I had followed Reynolds' instructions. Mr Stringer's comments gave me reassurance.

A couple of minutes later he came out of his office again and flung a copy of *The Times* newspaper towards me.

"Here, read about yourself! They call it 'Fire on a Steamship'; Pembroke tells me that half of it's wrong as usual. Look old fellow, we're very grateful for what you did. Pembroke and I would like to find some new opportunities for you."

"Thank you, Mr Stringer."

Chapter Two
The Whispering Gallery

When Mr Pembroke returned to London the following day, I received his thanks for my efforts on the *Messalina*, and he also promised new opportunities. I was impatient, and to me they seemed to come slowly. My pay was less than a pound a week in those days, and by the time I had paid my train fare and given something to my mother, there was very little left. But I said nothing, and tried to be patient.

The Stringer, Pembroke offices were at Austin Friars in the City of London, a quiet little road off Old Broad Street, conveniently close to the Baltic Exchange and the Bank of England. The Baltic was where the shipbrokers did most of their business, but my position was far too lowly to gain entry there. My friend David Hardcastle and I were keen as mustard to get on, and often we were there by eight in the morning. Usually we were the first into the office, to be greeted by the familiar dingy, gas-lit rooms, and the smell of ink, sea coal fires and wooden floors damp from scrubbing.

A week after the dramatic events on the *Messalina* I arrived in the office to find that David was already there. He was as short as I was tall, and his elfin face was sharp eyed and full of fun. There was almost a competition between us to arrive first, and as usual David made a joke of it.

"You're late Tom. Another crash on the Deptford line? How many killed?"

"No," I said, "this time it was a herd of giraffes on the track, escaped from the Zoological Gardens. I think Stringer will be eating giraffe haunch at his club today."

"Ah, the elegant gentleman!" exclaimed David wistfully, "how on earth did he ever become a partner in this firm? I think he must know the secrets of Lord Pembroke's past life. Which is he, trunk murderer or railway share swindler?"

"We can only dream of Stringer's life of luxury," I said.

I closed my eyes.

"I have been at my country house in Surrey … had lunch at my club … a snooze in the billiard room … dinner at Willis's … I'm on my way to a ball at Buckingham Palace …"

I opened my eyes again.

"Then I wake up in my third class carriage on my way back to my mother's boarding house in Deptford."

"With a giraffe sitting on the seat opposite," said David.

We both laughed.

"At least Mr Pembroke generates business for us," I said.

"Yes," responded Hardcastle with a groan, "and now I must get on with entering all these ships' tonnages in the charter ledger, or his lordship will give me one of his set-downs."

We were sitting on high stools at raised desks in the Stringer, Pembroke general office. Hardcastle was now making painstaking entries in a massive leather-bound ledger with his quill pen. I was sorting the mail. The general office looked out over Austin Friars. At that time of the morning clerks were hurrying to their offices, and pages and office boys were scurrying about on errands. But Mr Pembroke was always early into the office, and soon we could see him walking up Austin Friars with his brisk stride. Although he was still just short of thirty, he was already balding, but this was concealed under his tall hat. He invariably wore the same unfashionable, elderly frock coat, but otherwise he was tidily dressed. He glanced sharply at us as he came up the stairs, and I knew that look. He ran a tight ship; he wanted to be sure we were at our tasks.

Then the office door flew open, and there was Pembroke's bearded face peering into the room.

"Good morning to you both. Will you be in the office tomorrow, Wells?" he asked, in his abrupt style of speech.

"Yes, Mr Pembroke."

"Mr Blair is visiting us. He brings his sister Mrs Munro and her daughter. They were caught in Paris when the hostilities started in America. They are returning to Wilmington. The ladies wish to visit St. Paul's. I will be at the Baltic with Mr Blair. Will you be a guide to them? Richard will take the party in my Brougham."

I agreed, and Mr Pembroke went on to explain that Mr Blair and the Munros were staying with Mr Lindsay, the retired founder of our firm, whilst they tried to find trans-Atlantic passages on a steamship.

I noticed that Mr Pembroke was looking at me critically.

"Can you try to look a bit more respectable, Wells? Those trousers are too short. Your legs are sticking out like bean poles."

I blushed at his criticism of my appearance. My father had been tall, and I was too. I knew that my linen was old and worn, and my jacket cut too short, but I had hoped that all of this was not too obvious. I assured him that I would be wearing my Sunday best, and would not let the office down.

"Ah, the duties of the office boy," said Hardcastle when Mr Pembroke had left, "now do you regret being Mr Pembroke's cousin? A fine fool you'll look showing two fat old trouts round the cathedral."

"I'm only a distant relation; but I wouldn't have got this job otherwise. I don't think Mr Pembroke would have taken me on for my school reports."

The following day I appeared in the office as respectably dressed as I could, in my Sunday frock coat, lightly checked trousers and with a well brushed tall hat. I had suffered some taunts and jeers on my journey in the third class carriage on the train from Deptford, and my sufferings did not end there. Hardcastle was already in the office when I came in.

"Excuse me, sir," he said, with a stately bow, "I think you have come to the wrong address. Piccadilly is a short ride in a hansom from here, and St. James's Street is easy to find."

"Hardcastle! You know perfectly well why I'm dressed up like this."

"Just make sure that the two old birds don't faint when they see you in all your glory," he sniggered.

My answer to Hardcastle was a clip round the ear. After a short scuffle we settled down to our work. Both of us were making ledger entries and we worked carefully. The quill pen was an unforgiving instrument, and blotches often led to pages having to be re-written. Suddenly a whistle from Hardcastle broke my concentration.

"I spy strangers! Take a look at the young lady old tubby Blair has with him!"

Mr Blair and his party had arrived in a four-wheeler. He was a stout man and very fond of his food. I could see the two ladies he was escorting to the front door, and the younger one was a beauty. We could hear the sounds of them being ushered into Mr Pembroke's office.

"Why didn't his lordship choose me to take them round?" moaned Hardcastle.

"Perhaps he thought they might end up at the Music Hall, rather than the cathedral?" I answered.

He grinned, and we went on scratching away with our pens. Soon there was a knock on the general office door, and Mr Pembroke appeared with Mr Blair and the two ladies.

"Mrs Munro, Miss Munro, may I introduce Mr Tom Wells and Mr David Hardcastle to you both? My cousin Mr Wells will be your guide at St. Paul's."

Mrs Munro was a stout lady who walked with the help of a stick. But of the two it was her daughter who immediately caught the eye. She was slim with dark brown hair and brown eyes. She was petite, and wonderfully attractive, but she had a quiet look and appeared to be totally unconscious of the impression she was having on Hardcastle and myself. Both ladies were dressed in the height of fashion – it seemed that they had used their time in Europe well. They were wearing short tailored jackets above their crinolined dresses, and both had brightly coloured Indian shawls draped over their shoulders.

"Mr Wells," said Mrs Munro, "my daughter Amy and I are grateful that you can spare us the time to show us round the cathedral. We have some fine buildings in Wilmington and Charleston, but everyone says that we shouldn't miss St. Paul's. John Ellis, he's the governor of North Carolina you know, particularly recommended it."

She spoke with the soft drawl of the Southern States, which sounded pompous when used by her brother, but charming both for her and her daughter. I did not tell her that Mr Pembroke had virtually instructed me to accompany them. The obvious distinction of these two ladies made me nervous. Not only that, I had little experience of women. I was an only child, and I had been at a school that was only for boys. Beautiful young ladies like Miss Munro were longed-for but inaccessible delights for me. Up to now I had only been able to admire them at a distance. Somehow I managed to stutter out a reply.

"I, I am delighted to be able to be of assistance to you and your daughter, Mrs Munro."

Richard Kelley, Mr Pembroke's coachman, had been called, and was waiting with his carriage outside the office. Soon we were on our way. I sat opposite the two ladies and I tried my hardest to look at Mrs Munro rather than her daughter, but Miss Munro's appeal was irresistible. Her mother kept up a constant flow of conversation, which made me more relaxed. She mainly seemed to want to mention the important people she knew in North Carolina, and the big houses she had visited in and around London with Mr Lindsay. As she chattered on I seemed to detect the occasional gleam of sympathy from under Miss Munro's demure eyelashes.

Eventually Mrs Munro broke her monologue to ask me a question.

"Amy and I are just delighted to be here in London on our way back to North Carolina. You have so many beautiful old buildings. Do tell us about the history of the cathedral Mr Wells. We simply adore old architecture, and we would love to know all about it."

I could not help noticing a small unspoken plea from Miss Munro to keep the history short. I had researched St. Paul's as much as I could in the very limited time I had been given. Fortunately the vicar of our local church in Deptford was a student of church architecture, and he had lent me a history of St. Paul's. Now I had good reason to keep my story to the minimum. I started nervously, but gradually got into my stride.

"Well, you may not know that the current cathedral is… is actually the fifth to be built on the site. The first cathedral was built in six hundred and something, I think. It was built on top of a Roman temple dedicated to Diana, the moon goddess. So perhaps the cathedral is a little more pagan than people realise."

Miss Munro gave a gentle but enchanting smile.

"I think you are teasing us Mr Wells."

"No, really it was. But the four cathedrals built before this one all had very bad luck, so maybe we should be worrying about the latest one. The first cathedral was built of wood, and burned down after only seventy-five years. It was re-built, but then the Vikings came and destroyed that one.

"The Saxons then built a third cathedral, and that burnt down like the first one. Then the Normans built the fourth, and that lasted until 1666."

"We surely know what happened to that one Mr Wells," said Mrs Munro, "it burned down too, in the great fire, did it not?"

I was getting into my stride now, and I was feeling less shy.

"Yes, the Norman cathedral had been repaired and patched up many times, but Cromwell's soldiers did the most damage in our Civil War. In fact Christopher Wren, the architect for the new cathedral, had wanted to knock down the old one, but wasn't allowed to do it. He was told to patch it up instead, but the great fire came just in time and his problem was solved."

Mrs Munro looked surprised.

"I think my daughter is right, you are teasing us!"

"No, that's what really happened. Then Wren submitted his designs for the new cathedral, and he wanted to build in the Italian style. But the Church Commissioners insisted he built a traditional gothic cathedral, and eventually Wren agreed. Then he covered the whole site in scaffolding and built the Italian cathedral anyway."

Now both of them were smiling.

"Surely you do not expect us to believe all that do you?" asked Mrs Munro.

"I assure you it's true, so you can hardly describe the history of the cathedral as being boring."

Miss Munro gave me a grateful look.

"As far as the architecture is concerned," I continued, "I am certainly no expert, so I would be happy if you could explain it to me. I do know that the most successful part of the design was the Whispering Gallery. If you go up into the dome, it was so cleverly built that if you whisper on one side of the dome, you can be heard on the other. I've never been up there myself, but I was hoping that you would help me to put it to the test today."

"I think there will be two tests Mr Wells," said Mrs Munro, with a friendly smile, "one will be the whispering, and the other will be whether you have made up the whole story. If the whispering is true, maybe we will believe the rest of your historical romance."

"I will accept the test," I said, pleased that I had been able to overcome my shyness.

Miss Munro was now glancing keenly out of the carriage window as we made our way up Poultry towards Cheapside and the cathedral. Some of the buildings were being renovated, and twice we had to stop for carts of wooden scaffolding poles being unloaded at building sites. The pavements were busy with clerks, errand boys and smartly dressed city grandees, but there were also the usual street sellers, loungers and beggars. The Crimean War had been good for our business, but many of the beggars in this part of London were Crimea veterans who had lost limbs in the war. As we progressed up Poultry there was the pervasive smell of horse dung and coal smoke, and frequently Mrs Munro held a scented handkerchief to her nose to protect against the odours. Sometimes the noise of carriage wheels and the cries of street sellers made conversation difficult, even though the windows of the Brougham were closed.

Suddenly Miss Munro looked at me with an urgent appeal in her eyes, and asked me if I could stop the carriage. I lowered my window and shouted to Richard, and soon we had pulled to the side of the road – much to the disgust of an omnibus driver who was close behind us. He had the greatest difficulty manoeuvring his horses round us, and the air was blue with his curses. Miss Munro took no notice, slipped out of the carriage and hurried over to a diminutive flower seller who was standing with her tray, leaning against some church railings.

"*What* is that girl doing now?" asked Mrs Munro in disapproving tones.

She pulled down her carriage window and called out to her daughter to come back into the carriage. Miss Munro was talking earnestly to the flower seller, and seemed not to hear her mother. Finally Mrs Munro turned to me.

"Mr Wells, would you be so good as to get down and make sure my daughter comes to no harm?"

As I came up to Miss Munro, she was still deep in conversation with the flower seller, who was a sad, thin-looking little girl, very poorly dressed. I saw Miss Munro pass a gold coin to the little girl, who started crying. The girl handed Miss Munro a bunch of miniature roses from her tray, and soon we were back in the carriage. With a solemn look Miss Munro handed the flowers to her mother.

"I thought these would look nice with your shawl, Mother."

"Amy!" said Mrs Munro, sternly, "I know perfectly well what you were doing, but you cannot befriend every waif and stray you see here."

Miss Munro made no reply, looking demurely but a little defiantly down into her lap. Until then she had just seemed a pretty and hopelessly unobtainable girl to me. But that defiant look somehow infinitely increased her appeal. Miss Munro was clearly no drawing room shrinking violet.

Now we were getting close to the cathedral. We could hear Richard Kelley talking to the horses as he pulled the carriage to a halt. The horses' hooves clopped against the cobbles as they struggled to hold the carriage stationary on the slight downward slope. Then Richard was down from the box, and opening the carriage door by the steps to the cathedral. Mrs Munro clambered down from the carriage with difficulty, and looked anxiously at the array of white stone steps leading up to the magnificent front entrance.

"Oh, this wretched leg, I am afraid that I am going to have to ask you two to assist me up those steps," she said.

By taking an arm each we managed to make the trip up into the cathedral, but then all she wanted to do was to take a chair and sit down.

"Mr Wells, would you kindly escort my daughter round the cathedral? I think I will just sit here and enjoy St. Paul's quietly. Perhaps you could find someone to explain it all to me sitting here."

I have to confess that my heart leapt when I realized that I was going to have the chance to be alone with Miss Munro.

"Mother, are you sure you would not prefer us to stay with you here?" Amy's question made me fearful that my hopes would be in vain.

"No dear, you go with Mr Wells. Remember, we have to put his historical nonsense to the whispering test. You two go along, but you must be back here in half an hour."

She gave Amy a stern look.

We found an usher to come and give his lecture on the cathedral to Mrs Munro, and then we set off down the nave towards the area under the dome. My heart was racing with the excitement of being alone with this beautiful girl, but I was anxious too. My knowledge of girls was restricted to admiring them as I walked mostly alone or sometimes with my mother on Blackheath. Although my female acquaintance was slight, that didn't prevent my thoughts and dreams being filled with imaginary encounters with beautiful girls such as the one by my side at that moment. In my imaginary meetings I had no difficulty in engaging those lovely creatures in conversation. Now that the prospect was real I found myself completely tongue-tied. It was Miss Munro who broke the silence. She turned to me with a confiding look.

"I have to confess Mr Wells that my interest in architecture is not quite so deep as my mother's. Thank you for keeping the history lesson so short. Was it all nonsense?"

Her sweet look seemed to loosen my tongue.

"Well in fact most of it was true I think, but I learned it all yesterday when I heard I was to accompany you here."

"Oh Mr Wells," she said, putting her gloved hand on my sleeve for a moment, and sending a thrill of pleasure through me, "I hope we are not too much of a trial to you. What would you be doing if you weren't here with us, do you have very important work to do?"

"I think that even the architecture of the cathedral might be more interesting to you than that. I'm one of the most junior people in Mr Pembroke's office. I'm sure you know that Stringer, Pembroke are ship brokers, and I find information for the partners, I take letters to ship owners, run errands, check cargo measurements and all that kind of thing. They engage in the important business of buying, selling and chartering ships, and finding cargoes for their owners."

"Yes, I think I agree with you, Mr Wells," said Miss Munro with an amused look, "the cathedral architecture was *much* more interesting."

"Thank you, Miss Munro! I promise I won't talk about the office any more. May I ask you something?"

She nodded.

"Did I see you give a guinea to that flower seller? That would be more money than she sees in a month!"

"Oh I felt so sorry for her, she looked so small and thin. Did you know she is only twelve? She says she lives in the Rookeries by St. Giles. Her mother is ill, so she has to get up at four in the morning to buy her flowers in the market, and then she stands there all day to sell them. It is so sad."

She looked up at me with her beautiful brown eyes.

"But please don't tell Mother about the guinea, I'll tell her it was a sixpence," her eyes twinkled, "fortunately my mother doesn't understand your English money – she will never notice."

"I will guard your secret with my life!" I said, smiling back at her admiringly, "but the Rookeries is the most awful place, Miss Munro. It's the worst slum in London, and a den of thieves into the bargain. It seems to me that you're more interested in London's slums than our cathedrals. Can *that* be why you are over here Miss Munro?"

Her pretty face took on a solemn look again.

"No Mr Wells."

She hesitated for a moment, as if wondering whether to share a confidence, and then she continued.

"My uncle, Mr Blair, needed to come to England for his business affairs. My mother said she wanted me to acquire some European sophistication. She thinks I spend too much time worrying about the welfare of the Negroes on our plantation. She asked my uncle whether we could come with him, and she persuaded him to take us to Paris and Rome too. He was not so keen, but my mother can be very persuasive."

28

"I'm sure you can be persuasive too, Miss Munro."

She smiled, and once again my heart seemed to surge. There was something infinitely appealing in this beautiful girl, with her modest look, her caring nature and that hint of steel lurking underneath. But she was not always solemn; she seemed to have a sense of fun too. I felt that with the huge difference in our social positions my admiration for her was hopeless, but at least I could spend half an hour alone with her, and that would be paradise.

"We came over to France on the *Fulton* in March," Miss Munro's face took on a solemn look, "and we went straight to Paris. Mother hurt her leg in a dreadful carriage accident there, and we were stuck in Paris for six weeks. Then we heard about all the difficulties back at home, and we decided to cut our holiday short. My uncle is hoping to book passages on a trans-Atlantic steamship today."

As we were talking we had reached the end of the nave and we could look up and see the magnificent dome. We stood in silence for a moment, and then Amy turned to me again.

"Is that the whispering gallery up there? Should we go up and see how much nonsense you were talking earlier?" she giggled. "I just can not believe that my mother is allowing me to be alone with a young man. Normally she is so strict. Perhaps she thinks that Englishmen are safer than the young men from North Carolina…"

This seemed almost like a challenge.

We found the stairs, and started walking up towards the gallery. As Amy walked ahead of me up the shallow, winding, wooden steps, I could catch an intriguing glimpse of the pantalets she was wearing. As we walked up, I wondered if I would ever be able to bring myself to express to Miss Munro some of the admiration I felt for her. The fact that she felt able to share confidences with me gave me some hope, and her innocent sweet look was encouraging too.

We talked as we walked up the stairs. I longed to know more about her and her life in America.

"Is your father here in Europe too?"

"It's Marion, our plantation, Mr Wells. He always finds it difficult to spend too much time away. He said that with the politics the way they were in America he could not come anyway. But now with the war … there was a letter from him when we arrived in London telling us to return immediately. He has rejoined the army, and my brothers have volunteered too."

"You must be so worried. The whole thought of civil war seems strange to us here, the sort of thing that only happens in history books, or maybe in France or Italy…"

Miss Munro smiled and then hesitated before answering.

"Well it seems strange to me too, but it is all about protecting our way of life. They just do not understand us in the North. We need Negro slaves to run our plantations and they want to sweep it all away."

I didn't mention to her that I had read Miss Stowe's book about Uncle Tom, and so I understood a little bit about the disapproval felt in the Northern States for slavery in the South.

"Living in England it's hard to understand what life must be like on a plantation."

"Well we always think that life in the South is fine. I have visited cousins near New York, and it is so cold and smoky up there."

"But, if you'll forgive me for asking, what is it like with so many Negroes living and working all around you?"

"Well," said Amy, "we were really brought up by our Negro servants, and they are just wonderful. Sometimes the field hands seem a bit… well I get a bit nervous at times. But their life is difficult, and it is understandable that they do not always have affection for us. But when this war is over you ought to see the South for yourself. Will your work take you there?"

"I don't think so," I said, a little wistfully.

We were continuing to wind our way up the stairs, and soon we could see the light coming through from the Whispering Gallery. We had reached the top. Rather than dwell upon my lowly position in Stringer, Pembroke, and the remote chance of a visit to the Southern American States, I changed the subject again.

"How are you enjoying visiting London, Miss Munro? Have you met interesting people?"

"We are staying with Mr Lindsay whilst my uncle finds us places on a steamship. Mr Lindsay is an invalid as you know, and he lives way out of London in Shepperton. The only people who seem to come to his house are people in politics, or business. Mr

Lindsay has a fine chef who prepares wonderful dinners, so my uncle just loves staying there."

We both smiled.

"My mother is content enough," she said, "but I would have liked to meet people of my own age. I am sure you understand. Do you think Mr Lindsay would invite you and your friends out to Shepperton?"

There was an appeal in her look that made me yearn to say yes, but I knew that it would make no sense to say so. Socially there was a gulf as wide as St. Paul's itself between Mr Lindsay and me. He was a wealthy member of parliament, and I was the son of a poor widow in Deptford who had to take in lodgers to make ends meet. Mr Lindsay was as likely to invite a crossing sweeper and his friends to his house as to invite me.

"No, even though I am a relative of Mr Pembroke's, Mr Lindsay would not consider inviting me to his house. All I am to him is an office boy in his old firm. I think I would have to rescue him from a carriage accident, or save him from drowning before he would even recognise me outside the office."

"Now you are joking again, but my mother will never forgive me if I do not find out about the whispering. How do we do it?"

"What they say is that if I whisper against the wall here, you will be able to hear what I am saying on the far side of the gallery. Normally we would look awfully foolish trying it out, but fortunately nobody else seems to have wanted to tackle the stairs today."

"This is so exciting," said Amy, "now we shall find out!"

She almost ran round to the other side of the gallery. She had her back to me as she hurried round, and her figure was shown to its best possible advantage. Her graceful neck and shoulders and her narrow waist contrasted intriguingly with the flare of her dress over her crinoline, concealing the rest of her figure. I caught my breath at the pretty picture she made. When she reached the far side she smiled and waved to me to start the experiment.

What is it about whispering that makes one indiscreet? So many confidences are shared when one can whisper them to a friend, and things that might be considered forward are more acceptable in a whisper. Was it that which made me say what I did?

"I love your brown eyes, Miss Munro," I whispered.

"Mr Wells, I can hear you perfectly, but I am not sure that I ought to be listening to you," she giggled, "are you flirting with me?"

"It's not every day that I have the chance to whisper to a beautiful girl, so I am making the most of it!"

"You are flattering me, Mr Wells. You have said so much nonsense today, you are just teasing me."

"No, I was never more serious in my life," I whispered, "as soon as I met you this morning, I knew I would never meet anyone as beautiful in my life again."

This time there was silence from the other side of the gallery. Then eventually Amy whispered back in amused tones.

"I think you *are* serious, Mr Wells but I must be strict with you, and stop all this whispering nonsense."

We started walking towards each other round the gallery. When we came together, Amy looked up to me. She looked shy, but also I could see a little bit of the admiration I felt for her in her expression too. I was frightened that I had said too much, and that she would be angry with me, but that sweet expression gave me hope.

"I'm sorry Miss Munro, I startled you. Somehow I seemed to be able to say the things I have been thinking ever since I first saw you, when I was whispering. But I am serious when I say that you are beautiful."

Amy's little gloved hands were folded gently together, and somehow seemed to touch mine for an instant, and I felt a rush of happiness through me. Was it possible that she might feel some of the same affection that I did?

"Mr Wells," she said quietly, "this is not possible. We will be sailing for America soon. You say that we cannot meet socially here in England. You say that you will probably never come to America. How can there be any future in this? I really think we ought to go down and see how my mother is getting on."

But she was still looking up into my eyes, and she made no attempt to move towards the stairs. I tried to be even more courageous.

"What I am trying to say, Miss Munro, is that I admire you and I would love to see you again. But ... but if you would rather not, let's say no more about it, and go down to see your mother."

Amy smiled.

"Yes, I would like to see you, but I don't think my mother would approve."

A sweet solemn expression came over her charming youthful face as she seemed to pause for thought, and excitement coursed through me as I realised that she might be thinking of how she could see me again. Part of me knew that it was impossible that this beautiful elegant girl could possibly like me enough to arrange an assignation, but part of me hoped and longed for it.

"Could you come to Shepperton on Sunday, Mr Wells? If you were to come to St. Nicholas Church at twelve, I'll find an excuse to walk back on my own to Mr Lindsay's house along the river after the service. Wait until you see the others leave in the carriage, and then meet me in the porch. But please don't say a word to anyone."

Breathlessly I agreed, and Miss Munro sealed the bargain by giving me one of her little gloved hands to kiss, and with a shy conspiratorial smile she turned to walk towards the stairs down from the gallery and I followed her almost in a trance. All too soon we were back with her mother again. Mrs Munro turned in her chair to speak to me.

"Mr Wells, the usher tells me that it is true about the Whispering Gallery, and he even agrees with your stories about the history of the cathedral. But he did not tell it in quite such a sensational way! Amy, have you enjoyed your excursion? Has Mr Wells been looking after you?"

"Yes mother, Mr Wells has been most attentive, and has been telling me the most fascinating things – just as he did in the carriage."

She gave me a quick, happy look under her lashes as she said this. I was nervous that she might say more, but she was discretion itself.

"I think we ought to get back to the carriage, Mrs Munro," I said, "as I believe Mr Pembroke is inviting both of you ladies, and Mr Blair to luncheon."

The carriage journey back to Austin Friars seemed to pass far too quickly. Once again Amy and I were able to exchange quick glances, which meant the world to me, but of course we could not speak as we had in the Whispering Gallery. When I was back in the office I hugged myself in the knowledge that I was going to see Amy again on Sunday.

In those days we worked a full day on Saturdays at Stringer, Pembroke, so the next few days gave me the distraction of ceaseless office work, although Amy still filled my thoughts. True to his promise, Mr Pembroke was giving me some additional tasks, and on one of those days he sent me to Bristol to see a shipowner on his behalf. Finally Sunday dawned, and I took the train to Shepperton. As I had promised, I said nothing to my mother of the true nature of my assignation, but I hinted that I was on a confidential mission for my employers. She was disappointed that I would not be attending church with her, but she always approved of anything in connection with my work for Mr Pembroke.

At St. Nicholas Church I could see a group of carriages waiting to take their wealthy owners back to their houses after Matins, and I could hear hymns being sung in the church. I thought of Miss Munro with her mother and Mr Lindsay, and I smiled at the thought that they were unaware of Miss Munro's secret tryst with me. I thought it might be possible that Mr Lindsay's coachman might recognise me. So, as it was a fine day, I waited in the churchyard and stood concealed behind some trees.

At last the service ended. Smartly dressed people started to come out of the church. The vicar was chatting to his congregation, and slowly those with carriages started to leave, whilst others were walking back to their houses in the village. Then to my shock I saw Miss Munro, her mother and Mr Lindsay getting into their carriage and setting off. In a daze I walked slowly to the church, and sat down in the porch. Either Amy had forgotten about our arrangement, or somehow her mother had found out about it, and had refused to let her stay. I sat with my head in my hands as the last few people left the church. They looked curiously at me, but said nothing.

Then, just as I was deciding that I had better walk back to the station and take the train back to London, I heard light steps coming up to the church. I looked up, and there was Amy, smiling at me with sympathy in her beautiful eyes!

"Mr Wells, did you think I had let you down? I am so sorry. I decided to leave something in the church, and I asked Mr Lindsay to let me down from the carriage to go back and collect it. I told them I would walk back to the house…"

We walked together back into the church, where Amy collected her prayer book from her pew and slipped it into a pocket. Then we walked outside again. I was speechless with the relief of being with her after the disappointment of seeing her disappear in the carriage. She made a beautiful picture. She was wearing an elegant green and white dress, trimmed with lace that swept enticingly over her narrow crinoline. Her hat was green and white too, she was carrying a white parasol, and she was wearing white gloves. Her charming innocent look made the picture complete.

"You are very quiet, Mr Wells," she said as we stood outside the church, "not at all like the person I met at St. Paul's Cathedral. Mr Lindsay lives on the other side of the village. The grounds of his house are on the river, shall we walk that way?"

"Yes, yes of course Miss Munro. I am sorry too. To be honest, it was the shock of seeing you leaving in the carriage; I had been so looking forward to seeing you…"

Gradually the power of speech began to return to me. Miss Munro told me that they now had passages booked on the *Great Eastern* on Tuesday to return to New York. She said that she was worried about getting through to North Carolina from the Northern States, but they had been told that civilians could pass through in relative safety. She told me of her life at Marion, their plantation on the Cape Fear River, and I told her about my life in London, and my hopes for the future. As we walked slowly towards Mr Lindsay's house, so our conversation became increasing intimate. She confessed to her discomfort with the oppression of the slaves on her father's plantation, and I admitted to my shame about my humble home circumstances. I also told her of my admiration for the way that my mother had coped with the difficulties following my father's early death. For the moment we spoke not a word about any possible connection between the two of us, but I think both of us felt that sense of intimacy that begins to grow between two people who are gradually falling in love.

I walked with Miss Munro hardly noticing my surroundings. As we neared Mr Lindsay's house we were walking along a beautiful stretch of the river. The June sun was glinting on the rippled water and the trees were swaying in the slight breeze in their full summer glory. We stopped in silence to admire the scene. Then Amy pointed out Mr Lindsay's house through the trees on the riverbank, and she told me that she was expected, and must return to her mother.

"Miss Munro," I said, "I can't tell you how much this walk has meant to me, and how much I shall treasure the memory of it. Is there any chance that you might come back to London, and that I might see you again?"

"No, Mr Wells," she said sadly, and she squeezed my hand with one of her little gloved ones. "I think it must be you who should come out to North Carolina, and see us in Wilmington or at Marion. I believe in you, and your longing to do so well in your business. Surely you can persuade your employers to allow you to make that journey?"

I promised her that I would make every effort to get to North Carolina, but in my heart I knew that the possibility must be remote in the extreme. She could see the sadness in my face as I contemplated the difficulties.

"Will you write to me, Mr Wells?" she asked with her sweet smile.

I promised her fervently that I would, and then I felt that I had to express my feelings for her, even if I was to risk a rebuff or even a reprimand.

"Miss Munro, will you allow me to say how much I admire you, and long to see you again?"

I hesitated, expecting to be told that I was too forward, and that I should be more respectful, but Amy just looked at me as if wanting me to continue. Boldly I took both of her hands in mine, and went on.

"I know it is too early to talk of love, but I am sure you can see those feelings in me. Can I just say that I will do everything I can to succeed in the shipping business, and earn the right to say those words that I long to say?"

"Yes Mr Wells, yes I hope and pray that you will."

And with that she quickly kissed me on the cheek, and ran through the trees towards Mr Lindsay's house. Sadly I watched her light elegant figure as she hurried out of my sight, and I wondered if I would ever see her again.

The following day a letter from Miss Munro came to me in the office.

Dear Mr Wells,

Or may I call you Tom? I write this in haste as we leave for Southampton to take the steamer for New York early tomorrow morning. Will you write to me in North Carolina?

Our address is:

Marion Plantation

Fayetteville

Please address me as Miss Amy Munro, or my sister Louise may open the letter. I never told you that I have a sister (Louise) who is fourteen, and my two older brothers are called Jack and Preston.

I am writing this in Mr Lindsay's drawing room, and they think I am writing my diary! I do not want my mother to know that I am writing to you.

Please write to me soon, as I long to hear from you, dear Tom, My love, Amy.

I wrote immediately to Amy at Marion, and I continued to write every Sunday. I received a further letter from her, posted in New York, but then there was a long gap. Mr Blair and his party were making their way to Wilmington at the same time as Lincoln's new army under General Scott was advancing through Virginia in their first attempt to re-unify the states. I scanned the London papers with increasing anxiety. In late July I read of Beauregard and Johnston's stunning victory for the South, defeating McDowell's troops at Bull Run, close to Manassas Junction. It seemed to me that this could hardly be far away from Amy's route to Wilmington.

Finally in August a letter came from her telling me of a dramatic journey by train, hired carriage and even a farmer's wagon, which had indeed taken them close to the Manassas battlefield. But she was now safely back at Marion.

As the Civil War progressed, Amy's letters came in fits and starts as the vagaries of the wartime postal system increased. She told of her anxiety for her father and her brothers in the Confederate Army, and her mother's attempts to match her to the few remaining eligible young men in the area. In her later letters Amy mentioned a particular suitor who had made an offer for her, and her parents were pressing her to accept. She gave his name as Hamilton Douglas. His parents lived near Charleston in South Carolina, and they had a large plantation on the Ashley River. Hamilton Douglas was a major in the Confederate Army and he was a distant cousin of the Munros. He had visited Marion when he was inspecting the munitions depot in Fayetteville, and it seemed that he had fallen for Amy as I had. Although Amy had rejected his offer, he continued to write to her. Her parents were pressing his suit. This development filled me with anxiety.

The long months of our separation did nothing to dampen my ardour for Amy, and my thoughts were filled with those magical moments in the Whispering Gallery and our happy walk at Shepperton.

Chapter Three
The Clara

Amy's letters told of the privations being suffered in the Southern States as the Civil War grasped their lives with its ruthless steel fingers, but we too were suffering from some of the impact at Stringer, Pembroke. First the South itself put the squeeze on the cotton trade by stopping their exports. This strangled Britain's cotton mills in an attempt to persuade us to come into the war on the Southern side. Then the Northern blockade of the Southern ports started to bite in earnest. Although we placed some cargoes into Savannah and Wilmington in the early months, insurance became difficult, and ship owners were reluctant to risk losing their ships and cargoes. The South was desperate for munitions but shipowners held back; if they could have loaded with cotton for the return voyage they might have been more willing. Since shipbrokers were going through difficult times, we juniors had to work extra hard to ensure that we didn't lose our places. Happily Mr Pembroke and his partner Edgar Stringer seemed to be satisfied with my work, and they continued to increase my responsibilities.

In the summer of 1862 Mr Pembroke gave me an important new task. There was a shortage of materials, factories and skilled men in the Southern States and the Confederates were finding it difficult to build their ironclad warships, and their commerce raiders. They decided to have ships built in Britain, and the *Alabama* and the *Florida* were under construction in Liverpool. Mr Pembroke was contacted by a Confederate agent, George Sinclair, and he was invited to undertake the construction of a further Confederate warship, the *Canton*, in Glasgow. The ship would be paid for by cotton certificates, which would entitle the bearer to lift cotton at highly subsidised prices at Southern States ports. Sinclair needed to follow the progress of the ship's construction, but he was known to be a Confederate agent, and so he could have no overt contact with the shipbuilders. An intermediary was needed, and this was the task that Mr Pembroke gave me.

Sinclair took lodgings in Glasgow, and it was my responsibility to pass his instructions to the shipbuilders, and report to him on their progress with the ship. This proved to be intricate and interesting work, and I spent many weeks in Glasgow, but by November the secret was out, an intermediary was no longer needed, and my dealings with the *Canton* came to an end.

I learned afterwards that I had been fortunate to escape further involvement with the ship. The *Florida* and the *Alabama* both wreaked havoc with Union shipping, capturing or sinking over a hundred Northern merchant vessels between them. Lincoln put huge pressure on the British Government, and they stopped the *Canton* putting to sea; she was only released from port at the end of the war.

In November of 1862, Mr Pembroke and I took the train to Glasgow for a meeting to put Lieutenant Sinclair directly in touch with the shipbuilders. On our return journey we secured a railway compartment to ourselves. I was excited to learn that Mr Pembroke wanted to offer me a new post that would give me much increased responsibilities, and a very considerable increase to my remuneration.

We had corner seats opposite each other by the window. It was dark outside, but as the express rushed southwards through the night we could see the lights of small towns, villages and the smaller railway stations as we flashed through without stopping. Mr Pembroke was sitting very upright and was looking at me keenly as he started to outline what he had in mind for me.

"You proved yourself in that difficult affair of the *Messalina*," he said, "and I am grateful for your work with the *Canton*. You can be headstrong, but you handled yourself well. I now have another proposal for you, but I will fully understand if you cannot accept. Please listen carefully to what I propose, and ask what questions you like. Once you understand my proposal, take twenty-four hours to think it over. I hope you will give me your reply tomorrow."

Mr Pembroke was silent, and all I could hear was the clatter of the train as we sped south. I was curious to learn why he thought I might reject what he was about to offer. He leant forward in his seat and continued.

"I think you are aware that the Confederates have run out of convertible currency and Sinclair is paying us with cotton certificates for the *Canton*."

"Yes."

"I could sell them of course," he said, "but it's much more advantageous to use them. I've decided to go into the blockade-running business myself, with the financial participation of some fellow investors. We are currently investing in five ships. Three are new. The *Flora* and the *Clara* are being built in London, and the *Granite City* in Dumbarton. I have also purchased two older ships, the *Calypso* and the *Giraffe*. None of the ships will be operated out of London.

"They are specialist ships, and my intention is to base them in Nassau, in the Bahamas. They will do the fast shuttle from there to Charleston, Wilmington or Savannah, whichever suits best. They'll be supplied in Nassau by bigger merchant vessels from London or Liverpool."

I was stunned. I thought I knew Mr Pembroke's business pretty well, but this came as a thunderbolt. But there were other thoughts going through my mind as well. Why was he telling me this? And the mention of Wilmington gave me a faint gleam of hope that this new venture could bring me closer to Amy. He was looking at me intently, almost as if he was reading my mind.

"We have a reliable agent in Bermuda as you know, George Murchison. But I need a representative based in Nassau to manage the commercial side for me there. You would be my agent on board one of my ships, supercargo in fact. You would travel backwards and forwards from Nassau to Charleston and Wilmington to transact my business there. You're energetic and you know how our business works. You've also met Mr Blair, my agent in Wilmington. In Europe I can rely on the telegraph to manage my affairs, but for this I must have a man out there I can trust. I want that person to be you."

He sat further back in his seat.

"I can see that you are bursting to ask questions, but before you do so, I want to outline the benefits you would enjoy. For risks of this kind you could normally expect almost ten times your current salary. Because of the additional responsibilities you have had with the *Canton*, your salary has been sixty pounds per annum. This would increase to five hundred pounds. You would also be paid a bonus for each successful run.

"In addition I would allow you up to five percent of the cargo capacity of your ship to trade on your own account. I would advance you five hundred pounds for this purpose."

He looked me in the eye.

"Fire away!"

Now that he had put forward his proposition, Mr Pembroke seemed to relax, and he sat back more comfortably in his seat. His beard hid most of the expression on his face, but I could see from his eyes that he was intensely interested in my response. Whilst *he* was more relaxed, I was being pulled in different directions by what he had proposed. I was thrilled and ecstatic to be offered the opportunity to get near Amy, also I could see that this was a golden chance for a dramatic uplift to my career. I have to admit that in those days the moral side of the Civil War meant little or nothing to me; almost my sole interest was advancement and financial success. But I was curious about the hazards he had hinted at.

"What *are* the risks, Mr Pembroke?"

"I will not hide from you that there are serious risks. Your ship could be sunk, or you could be captured. As long as our ships do not fire back at the Northern blockading ships, then the crew are not treated as pirates or belligerents. I do not have to say that my captains will be ordered *never* to return fire. If your ship were to be captured then you would risk being imprisoned for a short while somewhere in the Northern States – probably New York. But most captains will try their best to get through, and take the risk of being attacked by gunfire. In that case a ship could be sunk or damaged.

"There would also be the financial risk if you were to choose the wrong cargo, or if the cargo was lost."

"When would I start, sir?"

Mr Pembroke smiled at the indication of my interest.

"As I said, I have two ships under construction in London. I expect the *Clara* to be complete early in December. You would sail on her. That's in about four weeks."

This was far sooner than I was expecting, and it brought the risks more fully into focus.

"Can you give me any idea of the chances of getting through the blockade, sir?" I asked.

He looked uncomfortable.

"That's a fair question, but difficult to answer. ... It was reasonably easy at first, and almost any old tub could get through. The blockade was thin and badly coordinated. It's more difficult now. But you will see that the ships being used to run the blockade are fast and manoeuvrable. I think that with a good crew the chance of being caught must be no worse than one in twenty ... perhaps one in fifteen. We will use Charleston and Wilmington as our ports, but I am told that Wilmington can be the easier."

"You don't think me too young for the post, sir?"

"You are just twenty years old, Wells, and I was twenty-one when Mr Lindsay made me a partner. No, I am confident that you are the right man for the task."

The mention of Mr Lindsay made me think of Mr Pembroke's partner, Edgar Stringer.

"You haven't mentioned Mr Stringer, sir. Is he investing in these ships too?"

Again Mr Pembroke looked uncomfortable.

"No, Wells. He considers a direct investment like this too risky. This will not be in the partnership. Stringer tells me he would only consider investing as a shareholder in a company like Anglo Confederate, where his risk would be widely spread. He accepts that you would now be working for me alone."

"I understand," I said.

Mr Pembroke was looking at me quizzically, and was obviously expecting more questions, but I felt I knew enough. He had accused me of being impetuous in the past, and now I was about to prove him right again.

"I think I have made..."

But he held up his hand and stopped me.

"No, don't answer me now. I know that you like to make decisions quickly, sometimes *too* quickly," and he gave me a stern look.

"Think about it tonight, and give me your answer tomorrow. Do you need to discuss it with Mrs Wells? I quite understand if you do, but she *must* be discreet."

I have to confess that I hadn't even considered my mother's reactions, and this brought me back to earth with a jolt. She was a widow, and I was her only child. I knew that I was very precious to her – perhaps the most important thing in her life.

"I will have to think about that," I said. "I don't think my mother would want to stop my advancement, but she does have a tendency to gossip with her acquaintances about what I am doing. I think I will just tell her that the post would involve some risk, but I won't tell her of the details."

"I would be grateful," he said.

We spoke little for the rest of the journey. I was thinking deeply about Mr Pembroke's proposal, and Pembroke himself was working on some papers he had brought with him. When we arrived in London we went our separate ways, Mr Pembroke to his grand house in Tulse Hill, and I to our cramped little terraced house in Deptford.

By the time I reached home my mind was made up. This was my opportunity to break away from my humble origins and make my fortune. As I look back I find it ironic that as my age increases my inclination to take risks reduces. At twenty, with all my life ahead of me, I did not hesitate. Also in my thoughts was Amy Munro. When would I ever have such an opportunity to see her again? No, the decision was easy to make.

After supper I finally found the courage to speak to my mother about Mr Pembroke's proposition. We were sitting at a small table in the tiny parlour next to our basement kitchen. My mother was wearing her apron, and she had just picked up some plates and was taking them into the kitchen.

"Mother, wait just a moment, there is something I need to speak to you about."

My mother turned round anxiously to listen to what I was saying.

"Mr Pembroke has offered me the position of supercargo on one of his ships. I would manage the financial side of the ship and I would be his agent in the Bahamas. This would mean a huge increase in salary. Of course there are risks, as there always are with ships. I want to take the post, but only if you are happy about it. How would you get on without me here?"

She moved nervously towards the table again, almost dropping the plates, and looked at me with fear in her eyes. She took a moment to reply, but then she surprised me:

"Tom, if Mr Pembroke wants you to take the post, I am sure it's the right thing for you. I will worry my silly old head all the time and I will miss you terribly, but you must take your chance to get on. Father would have wished it. I will manage perfectly well. There is Aunt Lillian in Greenwich who I can always turn to."

She put the plates back on the table, and sat down again. She smiled bravely.

"When do you start Tom?"

"Thank you mother!" I cried, "You don't know how much this means to me. We will start next month, when the ship is completed."

She sighed.

"Oh Tom, are you to cross the Atlantic in the winter? Well I suppose it's safe enough these days. Which ship will it be?"

"Mr Pembroke will make everything clear tomorrow. I believe she will be a newly built steamship. As far as money is concerned, I will contribute to the household as before."

Only then did my mother start clearing the table again, and we both went through to the kitchen, and continued our conversation there. I was pleased but surprised that it had all been agreed so quickly. I felt guilty about leaving my mother alone, but I knew that chances like this were not two a penny and I desperately wanted to seize the opportunity. I was thrilled and grateful to have my mother's agreement.

That night I wrote to Amy, telling her that I hoped to be in America before long. I said that I would write again when I knew more, but I suggested that she should leave a letter for me with her uncle in Wilmington. I knew that there was a good chance that my letter would not get through, but I wanted to do my best to let her know that I was coming.

The following day I met Mr Pembroke again, but this time in his office. Stringer was out that day at a race meeting in Newmarket, and so we had Mr Pembroke's office to ourselves. I was only rarely invited into the office that he shared with Mr Stringer. Its size and grandeur, and the fine models and pictures of ships decorating the room always impressed me. There was a distinctive smell of leather chairs and Stringer's expensive cigars. Mr Pembroke asked me to sit down, and immediately wanted to know whether I had been able to reach a decision. He looked anxious, and I was flattered that he seemed to consider me to be such a key part of his plans

"Yes, sir," I replied, "I will take the post. My mother accepts – although I have to confess that I did not tell her too much about the risks. You will be pleased to know that I didn't say that we will be running the blockade."

Mr Pembroke smiled, and sat back in his chair. He seemed relieved.

"Excellent Wells, I am pleased you will take this on. I'm sure you will make a great success of it. Although I accept that the risks are much greater than the normal risks at sea, so are the rewards! The next thing is for you to see the *Clara* at Dudgeon's in Limehouse. James Donald will captain the *Clara* – he is American, and a very reliable man. I will contact him and make arrangements for you to visit the ship."

"What's she like, Mr Pembroke?"

"I think you should see her for yourself and form your own impression. All I will tell you is that she is of the very latest design. She has an iron hull, and twin screw propellers. If any ship can get through the blockade, it is she."

"Twin screw propellers?" Single screw was a relatively new means of propulsion then, and I had never heard of a ship with two propellers.

He got up from his chair, and walked over to one of the ships' models to illustrate what he was saying.

"Yes. Single propeller ships like this one are just not fast enough, and they cannot manoeuvre quickly. Dudgeon's have come up with a new design where the ship is driven by two propellers. I have concluded that although they may not be quite as fast as ships with side paddles, they will be less vulnerable."

I had to wait until the following week until I could see the *Clara*. Then Mr Pembroke told me to get myself down to the Isle of Dogs, and ask for Lieutenant Mansell at Dudgeon's shipyard. It seemed that the captain was away that week, and I would be shown the ship by the first officer. He gave me a letter of introduction for Mansell. There was tight security at Dudgeon's as Mr Pembroke wanted to ensure that no Northern States' agent could get access to the *Clara*.

I had been down to Limehouse before for Mr Pembroke, so the area was not strange to me. J & W Dudgeon's yard was close to where John Scott Russell had built Brunel's *Great Eastern* five years before and Russell had gone bankrupt in the process. I thought of Amy's voyage across the Atlantic on that great ship eighteen months previously. At Dudgeon's yard I asked for Lieutenant Mansell, and a tall confident man not much older than myself soon faced me. He was a fair haired and pleasant-looking man; clean-shaven, and with a keen and intelligent look.

"Wells?"

I nodded a little nervously, and handed him Mr Pembroke's letter. He studied it and then smiled a greeting.

"I'm Harry Mansell," he said, "have you been on a merchantman before?"

"On short voyages."

"Trials, was it?"

"Yes, mainly," I said.

"Well I guess you'll never have seen anything like the *Clara* . I'm Royal Navy myself, and I have to admit I was astonished. Come along! She was launched two weeks ago, and she's being fitted out."

Then he led the way to where the *Clara* was lying. She was in a very secluded part of the shipyard, and it was obvious that every possible measure was being taken to avoid her being seen. There was nothing illegal about building, owning or running a ship of her type outside American waters, but we knew that Union spies were trying to track down the construction and movement of blockade-runners. Once they had been identified and located they could then be trapped and captured by Union warships even on their voyages out to the waters off the Southern States. There was also the suspicion that Lincoln's agents had been involved in the attempt to destroy the *Messalina*.

As Mansell had suggested, I was stunned by the appearance of the *Clara*. The merchantmen I was used to were tall sailing ships, usually stout, timber built and designed for maximum cargo. In those days steam engines were inefficient and merchant ships could not justify carrying the huge amount of coal needed to propel a steamship long distances. Ocean-going steamships tended to be built as passenger ships, like the *Great Eastern*, or mail ships; ships with high value cargoes, which needed to travel quickly and punctually. The *Great Eastern* herself, in order to achieve her twelve knots, needed both paddles and a screw propeller. Even if they were designed to be able to travel entirely under steam, they were still rigged for sails. This meant that if the engines, the boilers or any of the propulsion mechanics were to fail, the ship could still be moved under sail.

The *Clara* was long, low and narrow, like a silver eel. Her masts were short, and her funnel seemed to be in sections like a telescope. Her hull was iron, and her deck was virtually flush except for a curious mound on her bow. She was painted a silver-grey colour, almost white.

"Christ!" I exclaimed, "how will we get across the Atlantic on that? And where will we put the cargo?"

"Surprised, eh?" said Mansell, "and what do you think of the turtleback on her bow?"

"You mean that strange hump?"

"Yes, you see she lies so low in the water that in rough seas the water can sweep from bow to stern over the deck, and the turtleback prevents that."

"But is she seaworthy?"

Mansell laughed.

"I can see we have a landlubber here! She will not be the first ship of this shape to cross the Atlantic, nor will she be the last. She will roll a bit, but she's seaworthy enough. As for the cargo, you'll find she's pretty roomy below. They've built the cargo space into compartments making her safer – especially if a Yankee warship were to put a hole in her side! But don't think Mr Pembroke has paid for compartments to protect the crew. It's the cargo *he's* worried about!"

"The masts are short," I said.

"Yes. Everything is designed to give the ship maximum concealment from the blockading warships. The masts are shorter than usual, and they can even be lowered flat to the deck. The funnel can be telescoped down, and her colour makes her almost invisible to other shipping. Quite a piece of work! Come on board and have a look about."

Mansell was a tall man, about my height, but on board he was surprisingly nimble, I had difficulty keeping up with him as he ducked and weaved his way around the ship. The *Clara* was far from finished, but you could already see what she was going to be like. We looked at the cabins first. There were only three smaller ones, one for the captain, one for the pilot, and one for me to share with Harry Mansell.

"It'll be cramped, but the bunks will be fitted in that corner, so we'll manage."

We had a look at the wheelhouse and the saloon, and then we went down to the engine room, and we could see a figure hunched over the machinery.

"Mr McNab!" called Mansell.

The figure straightened and turned towards us. He was a small, middle-aged man, clean-shaven and dark-haired. He was stocky, and his face and hands were somewhat blackened with oil and soot from the engines.

"Let me introduce our supercargo, Tom Wells. Fraser McNab is our chief engineer."

"Verra pleased to meet ye," said McNab.

He came towards me wiping his hands with a cloth. We shook hands, but his remarks were abrupt, almost to the point of rudeness.

"I hope ye'll forgive me if I continue with ma work. Welcome aboard. She's a braw ship, but there's a gae amount of work to be done before we sail."

We moved on to have a look at the rest of the ship.

"I'm not sure I understood every word that Mr McNab said, but there were few enough of them…"

"Well he's Scotch and verra broad," mimicked Mansell, "but he knows what he's doing. It's not everyone who can understand these new engines, and the twin-screw arrangement. It's certainly all a mystery to me."

When we had completed our tour, we walked through the shipyard to a high point by the side of the Thames. Harry Mansell pointed along the riverside.

"There's our next task, a pint at the Prospect! It's on your way back to the city."

"I don't think I can…"

"*I* know, 'Mr Pembroke needs me at the office'. Well, Mr Pembroke is going to wait. We are going to be shipmates, and we're going to get to know each other. Besides, we can get luncheon there, and I'm starving."

Soon I found myself sitting opposite Harry Mansell in the parlour of the Prospect of Whitby. The opinion I formed of him then never changed, and we were destined to become close friends. He was an engaging, carefree character, who seemed to be totally fearless. Fortunately for me, he seemed to take a liking to me – something I could never understand. He was the son of a gentleman farmer in Lincolnshire. He had gone to a private boarding school, but had run off to join the Navy at the time of the Crimean War. He had joined as a common sailor, but had worked his way up to lieutenant in his early twenties. Life was one big adventure story for him, and blockade running was the new chapter.

First he told me about himself, and what he had done before joining the *Clara*. We were sitting at a scrubbed wooden table, and Mansell was moving things around on the table to illustrate where he had been, and what had happened to him. As he lost himself in the excitements and dramas of his career to date, his lively face took on an almost boyish look. He lost some of the cynicism that sometimes lurked in his conversation. I felt drawn to his enthusiasm and the friendliness he showed towards me. Soon he started to describe how he had become involved in blockade running.

"We've hit a dead patch now that the war in the Crimea is well and truly over," he said, "a lot of the fellows from the fleet have gone onto half pay to join the blockade runners and I'm doing the same; but I'm thinking of leaving the Navy. Mr Pembroke has promised me a command of my own when I've got some experience under my belt. But what about you? What's calling Tom Wells to a life of adventure?"

I explained my desire to get ahead and break out of my humble circumstances.

"I don't believe you," he said, "there's more to it than that. I don't think that Tom Wells would go adventuring just for the money. Out with it! You've fought a duel, or you've had a tragic love affair, which is it? Or maybe you've run off with the church funds. Come on, tell all!"

I hesitated and blushed as I thought of Amy. He smiled as he looked at me.

"It's a girl isn't it?"

I had never told anyone, even my mother, of my passion for Amy Munro. I don't know whether it was the effect of the liquor, or Mansell's attractive personality which made me tell him, but soon I was letting slip my hopes and dreams for Amy. He looked more serious, and leant forward to speak more quietly.

"I will keep your confidence," he said. "I was only larking when I said you might have other reasons. But we will pull together in this. If you need help, Harry Mansell is your man. Here, let's shake hands on it."

He toasted Amy and me with his beer.

"But you've probably got more questions for me," he continued, "what else would you like to know about the ship?"

"Well, yes there is something, although not about the ship exactly. You said you're thinking of leaving the Navy. What would you do when the Americans settle their differences?"

"Oh, I don't know. That depends on how much money I've accumulated – probably precious little the way I go through it.

Maybe I'll join Garibaldi, or go gold prospecting in Australia."

This all sounded very exotic to me, and I found myself bringing matters back to the *Clara*.

"I haven't met the captain yet, what's he like?"

"He's American – but you probably know that already. He's a very experienced man, and he's worked with steamships - mainly riverboats - and ocean-going merchantmen. He also knows the Southern States' coast pretty well, although he has mainly worked out of New York ... but I'm not telling you what he's like..."

He put his glass of beer down and studied it thoughtfully.

"Well he can be a bit rough, but that's not such a bad thing in a captain. He would not necessarily be on my list to be the head of a charm academy. But let's not worry about that. I think cheese would go down well – especially with a bumper of port."

It was late in the afternoon when I got back to our offices in Austin Friars. As I sobered up at my desk, I came back to the realization that only too soon I would be crossing the perilous Atlantic on the *Clara*. That elegant but frail vessel would have to cope not only with the inevitable winter storms but also the Yankee blockade.

Chapter Four
Madeira and the Atlantic

The next three weeks were a time of feverish activity. I had little hand in completing the fitting out of the *Clara*, but I worked with Mr Pembroke on her cargo. He was wary of putting military stores on board, such as rifles or uniforms as the *Clara* was so obviously designed as a blockade-runner. If she were to be challenged by a Northern cruiser even on the Atlantic, it was not worth the risk to have incriminating cargo. So we concentrated on the more neutral stores needed by the Confederates – brushes, thread, horse blankets, and even whisky and tea. The military stores were being shipped out to Nassau separately in larger trading vessels. We were carrying extra coal for the long ocean crossing. This would be topped up at Madeira. The military stores would be added in Nassau.

For my own section of the cargo I took advice from Amy's letters. She had written to me of the difficulty of obtaining the small luxuries of life. I concentrated more on fancy items such as candles, lamp oil and high quality muslins, silks and lace. This all had to be packed very carefully to avoid damage at sea. I also spent some time on my own clothing. I was determined to give a good appearance if I was to meet Amy's family. Harry Mansell was very helpful in providing the names of good tailors, shirt makers and boot makers.

Finally the time came to leave, and I made my farewells to my family and friends. This was made all the more difficult as I had no idea when I would be back in England again. The parting with my mother was the most difficult and sad – she was fearful of the dangers facing me, and she was terrified that she would never see me again. She shed many tears on the days leading up to my departure. Her concerns affected me deeply. Hardcastle also seemed genuinely sad to see me go. He said that the office would be boring without me. I assured him that no office with him in it could ever be dull.

I spent many hours with Mr Pembroke getting his final instructions on the direction of his business in Nassau, Wilmington and Charleston. He told me that he had already made the decision to sell the *Giraffe* to the Confederates, but the other ships would be retained.

On the day of our departure he came down to Dudgeon's, and joined the *Clara's* captain James Donald and myself in Donald's cabin to give some final instructions. Donald was large and burly. His hair and beard were black and he had piercing blue eyes. I had already heard that he insisted on strict discipline with the crew, and was liable to back this up with his fists. He was respectful to Mr Pembroke, but all the time we were talking I could see his sharp gaze on the movements of the ship's crew, making sure that everything was going smoothly. Mr Pembroke opened the conversation brusquely, as was his habit.

"I was at the Baltic yesterday. Two other shipowners were there who are engaged in the same business. They tell me that the Northern blockade is becoming more and more effective. You probably know that Wilkes – the same fellow who seized the two Confederate ambassadors in the *Trent* affair – has been appointed admiral of the North's Gulf Blockading Squadron. Ever since he was appointed, he has been making a nuisance of himself in the Bahamas and Bermuda. He has even entered their harbours. I'm afraid you can't be too careful there. I'm surprised that they've appointed Wilkes. He stirred up a hornets' nest with the *Trent*, and our government's only just got over it. If Wilkes was prepared to seize Southern States' ambassadors from a perfectly innocent British merchant ship like the *Trent* off the Bahamas, it proves he will stop at nothing.

"The Northern navy has also taken to lurking around European ports too, especially off Portugal and Ireland. Be on your guard as soon as you leave the Thames, Donald."

"We will do that, sir," said Captain Donald, "but the trials have proved that the *Clara* is a fine ship, and at fourteen knots I reckon she will be able to outrun any Northern warship."

"That's all very well," said Mr Pembroke, "but you would be wise to keep steam up at sea wherever you are, despite the additional cost. Apparently one blockade-runner was caught under sail. By the time she had sufficient steam pressure it was too late."

"Yes, we will take your advice, sir," muttered Donald, with a roll of his eyes to me.

"I have explained to both of you the separation of your responsibilities. I will state it again for clarity. Mr Wells has full power to take all decisions on my behalf at Nassau, Wilmington or Charleston. Only whilst at sea, and for a nautical decision does he come under your command Captain Donald. Is this clear?"

We both said it was clear enough.

"Then I wish you every success, gentlemen," said Pembroke; "I have just heard that the *Flora* has arrived safely in Bermuda, and that she had an excellent passage. I'm sure that bodes well for you both."

The *Clara* already had steam up, and almost as soon as Mr Pembroke left the ship we were under weigh.

Before this Atlantic crossing, my furthest sea voyage had been on a steam packet from Bristol to Liverpool, I was excited, but I was nervous too. I had very little idea of what to expect on an ocean voyage. I had been on board the *Clara* for one of her sea trials in the Channel, and I knew that she was a very fast and handy ship, but I think we were all a little anxious about her behaviour in the big Atlantic swells.

We had a total crew of about thirty, including three engineers and fifteen firemen. Nearly all of them were British; in fact I think that Captain Donald, as an American, was the only foreigner on board. Everyone was being very well paid. Donald had been able to hand-pick some fine men.

He set a course for the Island of Madeira, which would be our only stop before the Atlantic crossing. By going down to Madeira's latitude we would pick up the prevailing easterly trade winds to help us across the Atlantic. The weather in the Channel was calm enough, but as we started to cross the Bay of Biscay a strong westerly gale set in, and the motion of the ship began to be extremely unpleasant. Everything on board seemed to be wet, and our clothes became stiff with the salt water. I had never suffered from seasickness before, but now I was sick as a dog.

"She rolls and pitches doesn't she?" said Mansell, coming into our cabin, "but I think if you weren't sick in the Channel you'll soon find your sea legs."

"The only legs I need are the ones that get me to the water closet," I muttered.

"I'll leave you to your agonies," he said, smiling, "but I think you'll find that you would manage better if you had things to do. Come up to the wheelhouse when you feel a little stronger."

Half an hour later I followed his advice and joined him there with Captain Donald.

"You're looking mighty pale," said Donald, "shape up, we don't want to lose our supercargo so early in the voyage."

The ship was pitching in the massive seas, and despite the turtleback, the bigger seas were washing over the deck from bow to stern. The seamen were gripping the ropes running horizontally between the shrouds to avoid being washed overboard. The *Clara* was under canvas, and I could hear no noise from the engines.

"Are we under steam, Captain Donald?"

He was standing with his feet wide apart staring ahead into the storm lashed horizon. His black-bearded chin was jutting aggressively.

"The furnaces are alight Mr Wells, as Pembroke advised," he said sharply, without turning to look at me, "but they're little use in this blow."

There was an ugly gap in the conversation after Donald had uttered these cryptic remarks. Then Mansell chipped in.

"You see the sails give us some stability, and the screws can be out of the water at times when she's really pitching."

"We need to keep a sharp eye out for other shipping," said Donald, "another pair of eyes will do no harm."

He pointed to the side of the wheelhouse.

"Wells, there is a spare telescope in that locker. Sing out if you see anything suspicious. Lieutenant, Mr McNab is on duty in the engine room. Make your way down and check that none of this green stuff is getting through to his equipment."

"Aye, aye, sir," said Mansell, and he made his way out of the wheelhouse.

Donald and I stood for a while casting our eyes round the horizon. The motion was severe. As the *Clara* lurched I often had difficulty keeping my footing. I was still feeling nauseous although, as Mansell had suggested, getting out of our cabin had brought some relief. My anxiety intensified as I saw that the seas were higher than the ship's masts, and the strong gale was whipping spray off their crests and against the wheelhouse windows. I felt that the ship must be in danger from the storm, but Captain Donald looked calm and confident, so I said nothing, and kept my fears to myself. Occasionally the captain would give a sharp order to the man at the wheel.

Donald turned to me. I imagined that he would say something about the state of the ship. I couldn't have been more wrong.

"You're mighty young to be taking on Mr Pembroke's work at Nassau."

I found myself haltingly answering his questions.

"Yes ... I'm very fortunate to have his trust."

"Have you been there before?"

"No, this will be my first time across the Atlantic."

"Well, I guess you'll have plenty to learn there. Which agent will you use?"

This was not the sort of information that Mr Pembroke wanted me to discuss too freely, but I felt that I could hardly fail to respond to Captain Donald's question.

"We have used Henry Adderly in the past, and they have proved reliable enough."

"How about Fraser, Trenholm?" he asked.

"Well they're good too. I believe that Adderly does a lot of work for them."

I felt that I would rather focus the conversation on Donald himself than reveal too many of Mr Pembroke's secrets.

"Have you been to Nassau, Captain Donald?"

"Yup. Didn't Mr Pembroke tell you that I've been in this game before?"

"Yes, he did say that you had experience in blockade running, but he didn't say where you operated from. Is it right that you have operated out of New York? Was that in the riverboat business?"

"Yup, I was the captain of a paddleboat on the Hudson for a year or so."

"Do you come from that area?"

"Well my folks were all over when I was a kid, but we did spend some time in New York State. Say, you're looking a little green, how's that stomach?"

I muttered that I was feeling well enough, but in truth my stomach was still turning.

"I understand that we will mainly be running to Wilmington," said Donald.

"Yes. Mr Pembroke has an agent there he trusts, Angus Blair, and Pembroke's been told that Wilmington is the least risky port to use. We'll be going to Charleston too."

"Charleston's more difficult," said Donald, "it's like Savannah, both have narrow single entrance channels – they're easy to blockade. Wilmington has two entrances. That makes our job easier. It's a shame the Yankees have closed New Orleans – that's the best of them."

"What's Charleston like?"

"Pleasant enough," said Donald gruffly, and he turned away to the chart.

As we were talking I was feeling increasingly nauseous, and I asked to be excused. I lay down in my cabin, but this proved disastrous for my condition, so after a few minutes I went back up to the wheelhouse, and Mansell was coming up too. We both had some difficulty keeping upright with the ship's movement. When we were in the wheelhouse Captain Donald asked Mansell to take over control of the *Clara* for a few minutes, and he went to his cabin, leaving me the chance to talk quietly to Mansell.

"Captain Donald isn't giving much away," I said, "did you know he comes partly from the North?"

"He told me that he has lived both north and south of the Mason-Dixon line; but don't start getting your suspicions about him," said Mansell, "just because he's a bit abrupt, doesn't make him a sinister character. He's got the ship to worry about."

Donald was back almost immediately.

"What's cooking in the engine room, lieutenant?" asked Donald.

"All shipshape, sir. Fraser McNab is happy with his precious boilers, and there's no water coming in. He says that a real sea in the Atlantic will be the true test, but for the moment he's as content as a gloomy Scotsman can be."

The mention of a real sea made me feel queasy again, and I didn't stay long at my post; but once we had cleared the Bay of Biscay the swell died down a bit, and I felt more comfortable. The whole voyage to Madeira took nearly two weeks. By the time we docked the queasiness was gone. I was fortunate enough not to suffer from seasickness again on that voyage.

We came into Funchal harbour from the east, and steamed in against a stiff westerly breeze, which was unusual for that latitude. We had a warm welcome, as this was a traditional route for blockade-runners preparing to cross the Atlantic. The locals knew that we would have plenty of money to spend. Captain Donald was determined to leave quickly, and he told us that we only had twenty-four hours to relax and recover from the rigours of our trip across the Bay of Biscay. Our coal bunkers had to be topped up, and fresh supplies of food and water taken on.

Since I was not required for provisioning the ship, I decided to take a walk in the town and visit the main sights. I was also anxious to buy some Madeira wine for Mr Blair, as I knew he had a passion for it. I was returning from the cathedral towards the *Clara*, when I found myself in the company of Mr McNab, who was also walking towards the ship. He was unshaven and haggard from long nights in the engine room.

"I suppose the last ten days have been a fair test of the engines, Mr McNab," I said.

"Aye, a fair test, and I have tae admit I'm muir than saitisfied, and wie the boilers too."

"But you do look a bit worried."

"Weel, I have tae say that I'm nae saitisfied wie the coal that we've taken on."

"What's wrong with it?"

"It's gae damp and puir quality, it'll slow us doon wie'out a doot."

I questioned him more about it, but that was all he would say.

When we were back on the ship I mentioned what he had said to Mansell.

"Yes, he's said the same thing to me and Donald. He and the captain have agreed that the best thing to do is to burn the new coal first, rather than risk using it close to Nassau. I don't think there's much chance of meeting a Union warship on this side of the Atlantic."

I couldn't help thinking of Mr Pembroke's words of warning, but I said nothing to Mansell, as I didn't wish to appear jumpy. The voyage across the Bay of Biscay had tested the ship and it had tested me too. I felt that I had acquitted myself reasonably well, but I was keen to make a good impression on Donald, Mansell and all the *Clara's* crew. I was feeling some pangs of homesickness for London and our little house in Deptford, and I had some anxiety about how I would cope with the new challenges in Nassau and running the blockade, but I kept these thoughts to myself.

In the end we had a further twenty-four hours in Madeira, as McNab needed some time to make adjustments to the boilers. We would be leaving Funchal straight into a westerly breeze, so there was no chance to work on the boilers under sail. This gave Mansell and me a chance to sample the delights of the taverns in Funchal, and although we tried to persuade Donald to join us, he would not leave the ship. Nigel Fenton, one of the two junior officers – both Navy men – was only too delighted to take his place. Fenton was quite a contrast to Mansell. Where Mansell was tall, he was short and stocky, and Mansell's light heartedness contrasted with Fenton's serious nature. Fenton had not joined the *Clara* for adventure. He was newly married and he was desperate to build up capital to finance his family and his first house. His wife had a child on the way, and that worried him too. All he wanted to talk about was the risks and rewards of blockade running, and soon Mansell and I were tired of it. We drank deep, and we were back on board quite late. The following day we had headaches to remind us of our evening.

When steam was up we left Funchal harbour and worked our way round the coast towards the Atlantic. Captain Donald, Nigel Fenton and I were in the wheelhouse. The wind was still from the west, so we were using the engines. Heavy white smoke was coming from the funnel from the effect of the damp coal. Fenton and Donald were deep in conversation about a technicality to do with the *Clara's* rigging, which meant little or nothing to me.

Then, as we came round the Camara da Lobos headland, suddenly we could see the masts and sails of a sizeable ship.

"Get your telescopes on that!" shouted Donald. Then he spoke down the tube to McNab in the engine room. "Chief, I'll need full steam as quick as you can."

I grabbed a telescope from the locker in the wheelhouse, but dropped it in my nervousness. I managed to save it from breaking by catching it partly on my foot, and I looked round sheepishly.

"What are you doing Wells?" yelled Donald, "that's a precision instrument, not a football!"

As he spoke the ship came into full view. Fenton had his glass on her.

"She's a Yankee cruiser, Captain," he said, urgently, "she's flying Union colours."

She had the advantage of the wind and had steam up. She was coming down on us fast. Captain Donald called down to the engine room and the man at the wheel to turn the *Clara* away from the cruiser, making the turn southwards. The crew had the sails up quickly, and soon we were showing our stern to the cruiser. The three of us made our way up to the flying bridge, an open deck space on the roof of the wheelhouse, linked to the engine room and the wheelhouse by speaking tubes. The *Clara* could be directed more easily from there.

The moment that I was first to be tested in action had come early. It was with some trepidation that I followed them up to the flying bridge.

"I think she may be the *Kearsarge*," said Fenton, "I've seen her once before. She's a Mohican class sloop, and well armed – four thirty-two pounders I think."

"And a couple of eleven pounders," added Captain Donald. "She's gaining on us. With her screw she can do at least twelve knots. Dammit, we should be on maximum by now, what's happening?"

He called down to McNab.

"Why can't you give us full speed, chief?"

"It's that coal!" came his reply from the speaking tube, "but we're daeing our best!"

"Well do better!" shouted Donald.

He had his telescope on the cruiser.

"What's she going to do?"

As he spoke, the cruiser herself answered the question. We could see puffs of smoke and hear the noise of gunfire. There were big splashes as her shots landed in the water close to the *Clara's* stern.

"We're still in Portuguese waters aren't we?" asked Fenton urgently, "Christ they're taking a risk."

"Yup," said Donald grimly, "they don't give a pig's nose whose waters they're in. We'll work our way southwards. With her spread of sail our best chance against her is into the wind. If we can get some distance we'll turn westwards again. Let's hope we get the chance!"

At this point Mansell arrived on the flying bridge.

"What can I do, Captain?" he asked.

"Get down to the engine room and see what McNab's problem is! We're well short of full speed."

Donald turned to me.

"It's clear the cruiser wants us to haul-too. I guess we could, as our cargo is not incriminating, and our papers show our destination as Nassau. But for the moment we'll manoeuvre, and see if we can get away."

He started directing the helmsman to vary our course. For the moment we managed to avoid the shells from the cruiser, although they were uncomfortably close. Even though I was suffering with nervousness myself, I couldn't help being impressed by the coolness of the officers and crew under fire, and a little bit of that coolness began to rub off on me. But when I tried to focus on the *Kearsarge* through my telescope, my hands were shaking too much for me to get any useful view of her. Donald must have noticed something for he turned to me.

"Difficult ain't it, when you have no job to do?"

He turned back to give another order to the helmsman, and then to me again.

"I would suggest you go below, but I may need you up here. Damn, she's still gaining on us."

Our funnel was belching huge quantities of white smoke, but this seemed to be having no effect on our speed. Donald began pacing nervously backwards and forwards as he gave his orders to the helmsman. Suddenly there was a crash from the stern, as one of the cruiser's shells put a hole in the pilot's cabin.

"This is getting uncomfortable," said Donald, "Fenton, get aft and see what the damage is."

He paused, and looked intently at the Union cruiser through his telescope.

"Wells, you need to be part of this decision. What would Pembroke want us to do? Two or three more shots like that, and we could lose the ship. Should we haul-to?"

I was surprised that Donald wanted any involvement from me in this decision. I thought carefully. My nerves were screaming for me to agree to surrender, but my head was telling me otherwise.

"I know that we might get away with an inspection," I said, "but I don't think Mr Pembroke would want us to risk it. I think he would want us to do everything to get away."

At this point Mansell reappeared on the flying bridge.

"What's going on down there, lieutenant?" asked Donald searchingly.

"It's the damp coal," said Mansell, "but now the firemen are shovelling in dry coal like the foul fiend, and I think it's taking effect."

It was true that the smoke from the funnel seemed darker and thinner, and even as we looked, the *Clara* seemed to surge forward. Donald continued to direct the helmsman to make frequent small course changes, and we started to edge away from the cruiser. We had several more tense minutes whilst we were still in range, but gradually the shots from the *Kearsarge* were fewer and further away.

Soon Fenton returned from checking the damage to the ship, and asked Donald if he could make his report.

"It's only the pilot's cabin," he said, "the shell smashed a big hole in one side, and it must have passed clean through. There's no fire thank God. The cabin's unusable at the moment. I suppose McNab will have to sleep elsewhere for a while."

Donald laughed.

"Serve him right for getting the engines going so slowly! We'll have a pilot on board after Nassau, and he'll have to move then anyway. We won't risk going in to Funchal again for repairs. Albert can fix it up."

Albert was the crewmember who acted as ship's carpenter.

By this time we were far enough away from the Northern cruiser to be able to swing south and then take a long course round to the west to get away from her.

That afternoon I sat talking to Mansell in our cabin. He was off watch, and we sat together on one of the bunks. My nervousness was gone now, indeed I was exhilarated by our escape, but I was puzzled at Donald's behaviour with the *Kearsarge*.

"I think Captain Donald might have surrendered to the cruiser," I said, "I was amazed when he asked my view. I suppose he may have been right. It was difficult for me to judge the risks. Certainly our increased speed came at the right time."

"I agree that it's strange," Mansell responded with a grin, "but it makes you look like a hero! We'd all have looked foolish and a little damp if she'd put a couple of holes in our hull. By the way, can you swim?"

I admitted I could not.

"Another strange thing," Mansell continued, "is that he agreed to use the damp coal coming out of Funchal harbour. Well the captain knows best, and we are well out of our problems now."

Mansell's carefree attitude had little effect on my doubts. Was it possible that Captain Donald was in league with the North? He had been evasive on the question about where he was brought up, so perhaps his sympathies lay with the Yankees. Maybe he had managed to get in contact with Northern agents in Funchal. I turned these problems around in my mind as we progressed towards the Bahamas. When we were in Nassau the problem would be mine. I would have to make the decision whether to retain Donald as a captain of one of Mr Pembroke's ships. As my suspicions grew I decided to say nothing more about it to Mansell. It was hardly fair to create suspicions in his mind about his captain.

The wind soon changed to the prevailing easterly, and we made good progress. Over the first couple of days after leaving Madeira there was the constant sound of hammering as Albert patched up the pilot's cabin. At first the weather was reasonable, but then gales set in and we were back to pitching and rolling. Everyone on the ship was busy and I leant a hand as best I could. I have to admit that I never offered to help the firemen with keeping the furnaces stoked, but I learned about the engines from McNab, and I tried to help with the sails. Donald, Mansell and the other officers generously gave their time to show me something of navigation and the general management of the ship.

To conserve coal stocks, we mainly used our sails for the Atlantic crossing, and it took us three weeks. The swell was even more vicious than we had experienced in the Bay of Biscay, but the *Clara* coped well. At first I found it difficult to get used to the mountainous seas, far higher than our masts, but the others seemed to take it in their stride. Eventually I did so too. We saw no Union ships after our encounter with the *Kearsarge*.

As we approached the Bahamas the weather improved, and the ship took on a more relaxed appearance. The sailors off watch took to playing cards in quiet corners of the deck. Lines were thrown over the side to catch fish, and Donald even permitted the men's wet clothing to be hung in the shrouds to dry. Often shoals of dolphins accompanied the ship, and their antics were a delight to all of us. As we neared the tropics I saw my first flying fish, and, as the *Clara* rode low in the water, occasionally they would land on deck.

One day when we were in calmer waters, Fenton and I were sitting on the forward cargo hatch watching the dolphins. He had been telling me of his hopes for his family, and his constant worry about his wife's pregnancy.

"Are you married, Wells?" he asked.

"No, but I have hopes."

"Stay single, that's my advice," he said, "you've no idea how expensive it is. My father's a captain in the Navy, but he's never been well off. There are six of us children, and he can hardly spare us any money. Donald tells me I'll be paid a hundred and fifty pounds for every blockade run. How many runs can we make in a year?"

"I'm told that it's difficult to make more than one trip a month," I answered, "most captains want to make the run in and out of the Southern ports on moonless nights. Then you've got discharge and loading at either end. The autumn months are difficult because that's the hurricane season. Perhaps you could count on ten in a year unless we get caught."

There was silence whilst Fenton made his calculations.

"I'll have to be out here for two years at least," he said mournfully, "supposing I was chief officer like Mansell, what would I be paid then?"

"Well it's no secret. Captains get as much as a thousand per trip, and chief officers two fifty. How about trying out for pilot? They get seven hundred and fifty!"

"There's no point in joking about it," he said, "it takes almost a lifetime of experience to be a pilot. You have to know every inch of the harbour *and* its approaches. You might just as well ask me to be an engineer."

"Chief engineers get five hundred."

"Don't torture me," said Fenton, "I'll just have to be content with second officer. At least I'll get ten times more than I would in the Navy if all goes well."

That night I relayed my conversation with Fenton to Mansell, who was highly amused.

"No one could ever accuse Fenton of not taking life seriously enough. And if happiness depends on money, Fenton is on course to be a very contented man. Let's just hope that Mr Lincoln's plans coincide with ours. He needs to keep the war going, and not put too many ships on the blockade."

This was an unpleasant reminder that we could not expect every voyage to go smoothly. But we were fortunate for the rest of the present one. I continued to help with the ship as best I could. After we had passed through the entrance to the Northeast Providence

66

Channel, and New Providence was finally on the horizon, I was feeling that at least I could contribute to the running of the ship. I had learned something about myself on that long voyage, and if it hadn't been for my worries about the captain, I would have been a contented man as Nassau came into sight.

Chapter Five
Nassau

Mr Pembroke had warned us that Wilkes' Gulf Blockading Squadron could give us trouble on the way into New Providence. We had a lookout in the cross-trees at the top of the foremast, and Captain Donald and his officers were on the flying bridge as we headed towards Nassau. Fortunately our fears were groundless, and no Northern cruisers were lurking in the approaches.

Nassau lies on the northern side of New Providence Island, and Hog Island, a long narrow islet, shelters the harbour. Donald guided the *Clara* into port past numerous merchant ships. There were three or four obvious blockade-runners looking much like the *Clara*. But the harbour was thronged with other ships too, ranging from big merchant sailing ships to schooners, sloops and even brigs. I was soon to learn that specially built steamships didn't form the majority of the blockade-running fleet. At that time many merchants and their captains were still prepared to run the gauntlet of the blockade with fast sailing ships.

We tied up in the beautiful clear, almost apple green water of the harbour, and I caught my first sight of Nassau. It was a fine sunny day, and the brilliance of the scene made a huge impression on me. The town lies on a hill sloping gently down to the harbour. The houses and most of the public buildings are constructed of dazzling white limestone. Government House, Fort Fincastle and the magnificent new Royal Victoria Hotel, lie along the crest of the hill. But what immediately caught my eye was the huge number of Negroes on the quays, streets and squares. The women were dressed in brilliant colours, and the men lounged, chatted, and sold all sorts of goods, mostly sugar cane sticks, roots and nuts. Down by the harbour there were one-horse barouches waiting for custom, and their Negro drivers were wearing red waistcoats and battered silk hats. Negroes were rare in London, so I was astonished to see that in Nassau they seemed to make up most of the population.

Arrangements had been made for the ship's officers and me to stay in the Royal Victoria Hotel. Captain Donald had work to do with customs and the harbour master, but soon Mansell and I hailed one of the barouches and asked to be taken to the hotel.

Although the day was hot and a little steamy, it made a pleasant contrast to the January cold and fog of London. Mansell was glancing keenly about him.

"The place is transformed!" he exclaimed. "I was here three years ago, and it was quiet as the tomb. There are new buildings everywhere, and judging by those fellows - rum is flowing. What do you think of the weather?"

"I thought it was supposed to be winter here."

"You wait and see what the summer's like! When I was last here it was a place for invalids, but they only came from November to May. After that the place almost closed down. In the summer you can *really* feel the heat. That's when they get the Yellow Jack."

"What's that?"

"Haven't you heard of yellow fever? It's a filthy disease, turns you yellow, and attacks the liver. Thoroughly nasty and can be fatal – don't get it! But you don't have to worry about it at this time of the year, old fellow."

"I'm glad they're building here," I said, "I'll be looking for an office with some bedrooms above it. Mr Pembroke suggested that we rent a house here. If it's large enough it'll give us somewhere to stay when the *Clara*'s in port. This afternoon I'll be visiting our contact in Nassau to see if he can help."

"Well I have other plans," said Mansell, "let's meet for dinner tonight in the Victoria."

The barouche took us along Bay Street and then up Parliament Street towards the hotel. I saw little Negro girls selling flowers by the side of the road, and I thought of Amy and her concern for the little flower seller on our way to St. Paul's. But these little girls were happy and smiling – quite a contrast to the sad, hungry-looking street sellers in London. Less attractive were the groups of drunken, swaggering sailors who we saw jostling their way along Bay Street.

Finally our barouche pulled up under the covered court in front of the hotel, and our bags were whisked away by the waiting Negro servants. I wondered what the poor invalids would feel if they could see the hotel now. The fine, wide, four storey, limestone structure, with its wide piazzas on the first three floors, was now bursting with blockade-runners, merchants and speculators taking advantage of Nassau's new trade. I was shown to a luxurious large room on the third floor, with French casements opening out onto a wide veranda. It had wonderful views of the harbour. It was a relief to feel the solid hotel under my feet after weeks of being tossed about on the *Clara*.

That afternoon I visited Henry Adderly, Mr Pembroke's contact, and started the process of getting the *Clara*'s cargo prepared for our first run through the blockade. Adderly also gave me advice on renting a property in Nassau, and I made plans to visit houses the following day.

Then I made my way back to the *Clara* to see Captain Donald. I had still not made up my mind what to do about Donald, but after the dramas of Funchal everything had gone smoothly, so I was inclined to give him the benefit of the doubt.

On the *Clara* Captain Donald was arranging for the repairs to be made to the pilot's cabin.

"How long will it take?" I asked.

"A week is what they say," said Donald, "and I'll be here to make real sure they're right. We were mighty lucky to come away from that encounter with so little damage. I sure do blame myself for agreeing to burn that damp coal. Anyways, we got rid of the rest of it coming over here, so that's that."

Then I told him of the arrangements I had made with Adderly on the rest of the cargo. We agreed that the ship would be fully coaled up and the cargo loaded at the same time that the cabin repairs were due for completion.

"There was a letter for me with Mr Adderly from Mr Blair in Wilmington," I said, "it seems that he is going to be in Charleston in January and early February, and he wants us to make our first run there."

"Charleston, eh?" responded Donald reflectively, "well that will be a mighty good test for the *Clara*."

"I understand that we will need to find a pilot for Charleston," I said, "Adderly says that Louis Heyliger can make a recommendation, do you know him?"

"Sure!" said Donald, "I became acquainted with Heyliger in September, when I made my last run to Wilmington. Let's take a walk over to his place later on."

So that afternoon we met Heyliger, who was the representative for the Southern States in Nassau. He found us our pilot, Isaac Jones. Heyliger was also able to tell us the rates of pay that the pilot could expect. This was higher than Mr Pembroke had indicated, but the risks were increasing all the time. Even now the rates seem incredibly inflated – he told us that Jones would be expecting to be paid £850 for a round trip.

The day had been a full one, so I was looking forward to my evening with Mansell. The hotel was seething with blockade-runners with money to spend, and the saloons were buzzing. We prepared for our dinner with cocktails, meeting a number of friends of Mansell's from the Navy. Then the two of us went to our table in the dining room. I was unused to alcohol at that time, and I have to admit that I was already a little unsteady on my feet.

"You said you had 'other plans' this afternoon," I said, "how did they go?"

"I was making plans for you, old chum."

I laughed.

"And what evil were you cooking up?"

"Well you are doing the hard part, and getting the good ship *Clara* stoked up for our next adventure, so I thought I would work on the recreational side. I have made two plans. Item one, to find a tropical beach where I can teach you to swim; item two, to find a suitable house of pleasure for our nocturnal escapades. How does that sound, Thomas Wells?"

I blushed.

"Well I am grateful for your thoughtfulness on the swimming, that does worry me. Item one accepted."

I paused.

"I'm not sure about item two. I have never… I mean, Amy means a lot to me, and I don't want to do something that she wouldn't like."

Mansell laughed.

"She wouldn't like? Of course she's going to like it, only she's going to like it a lot more if you know what you're doing. You're hinting that you have no experience in that direction. My father always used to tell me that lack of experience can be fatal in a marriage. Anyway, I think I have found the perfect place, and it would be a pity to waste it!

"One of the Navy fellows told me that Mrs Dalrymple on Mackey Street runs the sweetest and cleanest house in Nassau. I called there this afternoon and it looks promising. She's very discreet, and she tells me that if the girls don't appeal, there's no obligation. Anyway I said that we'd call round this evening."

He hesitated.

"I am not detecting the level of enthusiasm I usually get for my plans, has someone blundered?"

The rum cocktails we were drinking were blurring my judgement, and I was being torn in two directions. One side of me was saying yes, this is what I have wanted to do ever since I had moved into my adolescence. This is an opportunity to learn about life in the company of a friend who will stop me making a fool of myself.

The other side of me was doubtful. I was sure that Amy saw me as upright and moral, how could I act so much against her view of me? Surely this was hardly sticking to the strict moral code that had been such a part of my upbringing. I was apprehensive too, as one often is of something that is to be done for the first time.

"Well let's finish our dinner and make up our minds then," said Mansell.

So we talked of other things as we finished the excellent dinner provided by the Royal Victoria. Finally Mansell stood up.

"Let's go for a stroll. We'll walk towards Mrs Dalrymple's, and you can decide when we get there. After a month at sea the choice is easy for me. I'm going in."

We soon came to Mackey Street. Mansell pointed towards a large tidy-looking house, discreetly lit. Like so many of the Nassau houses, it was limestone, and had a two-storey piazza round it.

"There she blows, bliss beckons. Let me go inside first and make sure we can be private. It wouldn't do for Mr Pembroke's agent to be on display to Nassau society in this place. Wait here."

Before I could remonstrate, Mansell went forward and knocked on the door. A large, smartly dressed Negro answered, and let him in. There was silence. I began to realise that events were taking over, and morality was being left behind; but the rum was telling me that I had nothing to lose by going in - nothing except my virginity. Although I was nervous and doubtful, I was excited too. The wait seemed forever.

I have no excuses for what happened that night, and certainly intoxication hardly counts. Like the scenes in Hogarth prints, it was just the first step in a chain of events that led inexorably downwards.

But any thoughts of compunction were forgotten that night when the front door opened and Mansell reappeared.

"The preparations are complete."

We went inside.

"We have a private parlour," he said, "we can have cocktails there. Mrs Dalrymple says that various girls will come in and offer us refreshment. If one of them takes your fancy, place a coin on her tray, and Mrs Dalrymple will arrange the rest. She says that for reasons of privacy they will only use our Christian names here."

The parlour was luxurious, the lights were soft and we sat in comfort on red velvet plush chairs. A middle-aged woman, very respectably dressed, came in with our cocktails. Mansell stood.

"Tom, may I introduce Mrs Dalrymple?"

"It's a pleasure to meet a friend of Harry's," she said. "I have made everything ready, and I'm sure you gentlemen will enjoy your evening. Let me just say that we are not the cheapest house in Nassau, as I'm sure you know, but I think we are the best. Harry has kindly settled the finances in advance, and has paid for the whole night. Anton, our chef, cooks a wonderful breakfast."

She rustled out.

"Mansell, you shouldn't have…"

"No," he interrupted, "tonight is at my expense. I have more than enough of Mr Pembroke's excellent gold coins jingling in my pockets to finance that. I told you that money doesn't stick to me long. The next evening will be for your own account, old fellow."

As we were speaking, the first of the girls came in with a small tray of refreshments. She was tall and fair, and she was wearing a full starched and ruffled apron. It was low over her breasts and then came down nearly to her knees. It seemed to cover her dress completely. Her legs were long and inviting. She smiled.

"Mrs Dalrymple has sent these cakes for you gentlemen, would you like some?"

She came forward to offer them to us, then she turned round to walk back to the door. There was no dress underneath the apron. Peeping out from the back, where the two sides failed to come together was her naked, beautiful and shapely bottom.

"Madonna," exclaimed Mansell, "these are refreshments indeed!"

"Mrs Dalrymple likes to please," she said, "my name is Lucia, I will be back later with more if you would like that."

"Tom?" asked Mansell.

"I … I think I would like to see what other refreshments Mrs Dalrymple is offering."

"Well," he said, "Lucia is refreshment enough for me!"

He sprang out of his chair and walked over to her. He placed a coin on her little tray, and gave her posterior a caressing slap as she left the room. She turned her head and gave him an inviting smile.

A couple of moments later the same Negro who had opened the front door for Mansell knocked and came into the room

"Miss Lucia, she ready, sah. Would the gen'mun like to follow me?"

Mansell stood up and walked towards the door, then he turned.

"See you at breakfast!"

Three more girls came in to offer refreshments. Mrs Dalrymple seemed to specialise in tall, fair girls. They were all beautiful and charming, but somehow none of them quite had the appeal for me. Each was wearing the same uniform, and their naked posteriors shone and beckoned as they moved away.

Then the fifth girl knocked and came in. She was smaller and had dark brown hair. Her olive skin implied a touch of Spanish or even Negro blood. She was young and looked as though she was only seventeen or eighteen. She gave a charming, alluring smile as she came in. There seemed to be passion, excitement and adventure lurking in her beautiful dark brown eyes.

"May I offer you refreshment, sir?" she asked, "I am call' Susan."

As she said this she leant forward to offer me the tray; as she bent down I caught my breath.

"Y … you are lovely, Susan," I said.

Her reply was a sweet irresistible smile. As she turned to walk back towards the door I could see that she was also wearing nothing under her apron. The sway of her body and the movement of her charming posterior had me beguiled and enchanted. Somehow she made her body move in a way that was infinitely more attractive to me than the other girls.

"Wait," I said, and I walked over to put a coin on her tray.

She turned round and for a moment there was almost a triumphant look on her pretty face, as if I was the one she wanted, and she had secured me in front of the others. Then she smiled, and the look was gone.

"Thank you sir, I'll see you in a momen'."

She went through the doorway and with another sway of her charming body she closed the door behind her.

The next few minutes passed in a fever for me, but soon the solemn Negro reappeared.

"Follow me, sah."

We went up some stairs and down a corridor. He paused at a door and knocked.

"Are you ready, Miss Susan?"

"Yes," said a low melodic voice.

The Negro held the door open for me, and I went in. Susan was standing in front of a large, comfortable-looking feather bed. She was still wearing her ruffled apron, but her hands were behind her back as if she was untying the apron strings. She was leaning forward and my senses thrilled at the swell of her breasts, revealed by the low cut over her starched apron.

"May I call you Tom?" she asked.

"Yes, Susan."

"Our maid always does these aprons up so tightly, can you help me Tom?"

She looked at me appealingly as she turned round, and I could see that the strings were tied awkwardly. Her beautiful body tensed as she tried to undo the knot.

I stepped forward to help her, and as I untied the strings my hands brushed against her soft skin. My blood raced. Finally it was undone, and her bottom brushed against me, almost as if by chance, as she moved to pull off her apron. She seemed like a cat stroking its soft coat against me to persuade me to its will. Then she looked at me demurely.

"Mrs Dalrymple tol' me you are plannin' to get married, and you wan' to know the best ways to please a girl."

I started to explain my situation, but she put her finger to her lips.

"Come here Tom," she said softly.

So began an interlude of exquisite passion and pleasure lasting late into the night. All my doubts and fears were soothed and forgotten as I gave myself up to the wonders of love. Morality had left me completely in that comfortable lamp-lit room, and was replaced by a gratification that should have felt shameful, but at the time was pure delight. Finally I fell into a deep and dreamless sleep.

I was woken by a low knock at the door. Slowly my mind dragged back through feelings of delicious languor into consciousness. The last time I had woken up had been on the *Clara*, and it seemed to take forever for me to realise where I was. Then the reason for this feeling of rapturous contentment came back to me. I turned to look for Susan, but she was gone. I pulled the covers over me and called out.

"Come in!"

A Negro servant entered and pulled the curtains back, letting in some light. The windows were discreetly covered with a lacy gauze. The room had been tidied, and my clothes neatly folded.

"Massah Harry he wan' to know if you like to breakfast with him, sah."

"Yes, I'll come down in a minute."

"I'll wait outside, sah. Mrs Dalrymple said to say dat that you and Massah Harry, you de only guests."

When I was dressed the Negro servant escorted me downstairs to a charming terrace, where breakfast was laid out on a long table. The terrace looked out over a bright but secluded garden, full of scented tropical plants, and surrounded by a high stone wall. Tall coconut palms with feathery tops partly shaded the garden, and humming birds darted about between the flowers.

Mansell was seated at a round table, eating from a plate of pineapple and oranges. He smiled a welcome.

"Help yourself Tom, it's all there."

"How was Lucia?" I asked.

"Secrets of the confessional, old fellow, secrets of the confessional. All I will say is that I think Mrs Dalrymple is to be congratulated on running such an excellent establishment. I am sorry to have had you woken, but I think you said that you had appointments today, and I am expected on the *Clara*."

"Thank you Harry..." I began.

He held his hand up.

"Don't say it, Tom. We are shipmates, and that is all there is to say about it."

"My appointments are for later in the morning, Harry," I said, "but I do need to get to the hotel to sort some things out - and also to shave and change!"

"My feelings exactly," said Mansell.

We ate our breakfast in comradely silence, but accompanied by the sounds of the birds in the garden, and an old Negro brushing the paths. Just as we were getting up to leave, Mrs Dalrymple came onto the terrace.

"I hope we shall have the pleasure of seeing you two gentlemen again," she said, "if you would like a particular girl to attend to you, perhaps you would be good enough to send a note round earlier in the day. I will do my best to oblige you."

We thanked her, she let us out by a garden door and we made our way back to the hotel. Now that I was sober I was feeling guilty about the night's adventures. No matter how intriguing and sweet Susan had been, my passion was for Amy. I found myself holding two thoughts in my mind; one was the excitement and pleasure of my night with Susan and the other was my love and longing for Amy. Eventually it was my love for Amy that predominated and I was filled with remorse. But I kept my thoughts to myself. Although I already considered Mansell a close friend, I felt he would not understand the way I was thinking

The rest of the day was hectic for me. I looked at three houses with an agent, and agreed to take a three-month lease of one of them. We had an option to extend if the house suited us. With Heyliger's help I engaged a clerk, Tobias Johnson, to assist me with the administration of Mr Pembroke's ships. He would mind the shop whilst I was at sea, or at the Southern States' ports. In the evening I went to a reception at Government House. Heyliger had insisted that I should meet the Governor of New Providence, and had made the arrangements. I had already sent round a letter of introduction provided by Mr Pembroke. I was thankful that I had spent some time improving my wardrobe before the voyage out.

All this meant that I had no time to visit the *Clara* that day, and I didn't see Mansell. During the afternoon I sent a message to Donald saying I would like to see him on the *Clara* the following morning.

At breakfast in the Royal Victoria Mansell joined me.

"You are a busy man, Wells," he said, "what are your plans today?"

"Well, I'll be on the *Clara* this morning, then I have a meeting with the owner of the house we are going to rent. Mr Pembroke has sent out most of the cargo we need, but we still have spare capacity, and I will be talking to Fraser, Trenholm about buying some more munitions. I think they may be cheaper than Adderly, and a bit more reliable."

"When will you finish?"

"I hope to be clear by three o'clock."

"Right!" said Mansell, "the day is fine, and I have found the perfect beach in one of the coves on Hog Island. It's sheltered, so swimming is easy there. Let's meet in the lobby at half past three."

His engaging smile and his enthusiasm were persuasive. I wasn't sure whether I would really have the time, but I couldn't resist it.

"Agreed!" I exclaimed.

I made my way down to the *Clara*. I had found Captain Donald easier as I got to know him. He seemed to be making an effort to be pleasant to me. He and I had many things to discuss about the cargo and the crew. Donald wanted to take on extra firemen as we would need to keep full steam up for long periods, and I agreed. Whilst we were making the cargo arrangements, there was a knock at Donald's cabin door. It was McNab. Donald smiled a greeting, and gestured at a vacant chair for McNab to sit down.

"Say Chief. What can we do for you? We're mighty busy here, but we've always got time for our chief engineer!"

McNab settled himself into a chair but he looked uncomfortable and restless.

"Aye sair, and I'm graitful. I need to sort out some things fuir the engines, and time wull be tight. Can ye tell me exactly when you would like tae leave?"

Captain Donald looked at me.

"It's a fair request," he said, "if we are to have a good shot at getting to Charleston, discharge our cargo, load the new cargo and get away when the nights are moonless, we must leave Tuesday. Can you be ready in five days, Chief?"

McNab smiled and looked more at ease.

"Aye, I think I can sair. Wull that be in the muirning?"

"This is my schedule," said Donald, "the *Clara* must be loaded, everyone must be on board and the engines ready Monday night. If you agree Mr Wells, we will sail soon after midday Tuesday when I have made a full inspection of the ship."

I was a little surprised that Donald wanted to leave in the middle of the day, and I asked him why. Wouldn't we risk being trapped by a Union warship?

"Any Yankee cruisers can be seen from the harbour," he said, "the tricky point Tuesday will be the passage between Great Abaco and Eleuthera. The *Clara* will be headed into the wind – that's a great chance for a cruiser to pick us up. I aim to hit the channel just before dusk. That gives us a real good chance to slip through on the sly."

"I understand," I said. Mr McNab nodded too.

"That's fine, I'll be getting back to ma engines. We'll be ready on Monday night."

He got up from his chair and left the cabin.

Captain Donald looked at me.

"What's your impression of McNab, Mr Wells?"

"From what I've seen he's a hard worker. He keeps himself to himself and gets on with the job. Apart from that coal problem, his engines have been working perfectly."

I hesitated.

"Why do you ask me?"

"Well I guess I don't know. Sure he works hard, but he's kind of sullen. It would be great to see him smile once in a while…"

"If that's our only problem with him, let's celebrate," I said.

We both laughed, but afterwards Donald looked pensive.

I took one of the barouches waiting at the quayside and set off for my meeting in East Street. I was due to meet the owner at the house I planned to rent. I was pleased with it. There were two rooms downstairs which would make excellent offices, and four main rooms upstairs, one would be a sitting room, and the others bedrooms. There was also accommodation for two servants. The house was cool with its wide piazzas and thick limestone walls. The owner, an enormously fat middle-aged Bavarian called Herr Kohler, assured me that he would work with Johnson to get everything ready by mid February.

"Haff no conzerns," he said, "if I say all vill be ready, zen it is zo, yes?"

I told him that I had heard that building work was unreliable on New Providence. He looked at me sharply, as he mopped his purple face with a large bandana handkerchief.

"Nein! Zay do not verk vor me who such nonsense do. I haff been here five years now, and I know who to trust."

He waddled angrily away fanning his face with his straw hat.

I managed to finish my work that afternoon in time to meet Mansell at the Victoria, and we made our way to the beach at Hog Island. The sea was warm and clear, and the beach was charming. In the end it took me several weeks to learn, although this was largely to do with blockade-running interruptions. But the exercise and the soothing effect of the beach and the sea made a pleasant end to days of office tedium.

We all worked hard over the next few days to make sure that the *Clara* was ready for our first attempt on Charleston. I think all of us had some apprehension about the dangers to come, but the hard work was a distraction. I was disappointed that our first voyage was not to Wilmington, as I knew that it would have been easier to get to the Marion plantation from there. Somehow my guilty interlude with Susan made me even more eager to see Amy. Perhaps sometime to enjoy with Amy what I had learned in Susan's arms. A dark cloud was Amy's suitor Hamilton Douglas. I worried that I had spent too much time separated from her and that her family's wishes might have prevailed.

Mansell and I made one more visit to Mrs Dalrymple before we set out on the *Clara*. Despite my guilt, Susan's charms were addictive and I told myself that just one more night would make no difference. I promised myself that this would be the last time I would see her. I had made my request in advance, but when we reached Mackey Street, Mrs Dalrymple told me that Susan was no longer with her.

"I am really sorry sir," she said, "I am as disappointed as you are. She had only been here for three months, but I could see that she was perfect. She's a professional. She seemed to have that amazing ability to find what would please her clients best. I never had any complaints, and they always wanted to come back to her."

I have to confess that I was indeed deeply disappointed. I no longer wanted to stay at Mrs Dalrymple's, and I walked thoughtfully back to my solitary bed in the Royal Victoria Hotel.

Chapter Six
The Run to Charleston

On that Monday evening we were all on board the *Clara*, making the final preparations for our voyage. The masts were taken down to their lowest level, with no yards across them. There was a small crow's nest on the foremast for observation. The ship's boats were lowered to deck level. The funnel was telescopic, and this was also lowered. All of these measures made the ship's profile as low and insignificant as possible, in the hope of avoiding being sighted by Union warships. The cargo was stowed. We were carrying mainly Welsh coal, although we had about fifteen tons of Pennsylvanian anthracite coal, smuggled out for us through Canada. This we were assured would reduce visible smoke from our funnel to virtually nothing. I had sent a report to Mr Pembroke in London by that day's mail steamer, and I had given my final instructions to Tobias Johnson on everything that had to be done in my absence. I felt that we were as ready as we could be.

I tried to put my thoughts of Amy and Susan behind me, to concentrate on the voyage ahead. Nassau was full of stories about blockade-running ships being captured or sunk by Northern naval ships, or even being wrecked by storms in the treacherous Atlantic. I was anxious, but I knew that the *Clara* had a good a chance of getting through the blockade.

She was a classic blockade running steamship, if perhaps on the small side. She was one hundred and sixty feet long by twenty-three in the beam, with a draft of only ten feet fully laden. Her displacement tonnage was three hundred and fifty. Dudgeon's had said that she could carry two hundred and fifty tons of cargo, but we exceeded that. Her full speed well laden was an absolute maximum of fourteen knots if her engines and boilers were in perfect condition. Captain Donald calculated on thirteen knots. This was pretty fast, but the fastest Northern cruisers under sail could threaten her.

In our hold were cases of Enfield rifles, cartridges, percussion caps, uniforms, cavalry swords, barrels of gunpowder and other military paraphernalia. We had added all these to the more neutral items we already had on board.

In my report to Mr Pembroke I mentioned my suspicions of Donald, but I said that as the evidence against him was slight, I did not think I could countermand his appointment and replace him. I took full responsibility if my judgement turned out to be faulty. Early on that Monday evening I was thinking of this when there was a knock at my cabin door, and there was Captain Donald's burly figure.

"Wells, would you spare me two minutes in my cabin?"

We walked round, he closed the door and we both sat down. Donald's burly black-bearded figure always gave an impression of strength and fearlessness, so I was surprised to see him looking tense and almost nervous. He drummed his fingers on the cabin table and looked at me questioningly a couple of times before he started to speak.

"I have something strange to tell you," he said, in quiet tones, "and I must ask you to hear me out."

"Fire away," I said.

"You remember that business with the damp coal in Madeira?"

"Of course."

"Well I have my suspicions that it was no accident we were so nearly caught by the *Kearsarge*."

He paused but I said nothing. I was amazed that he was raising this now and I waited to see where it was leading.

"You see it was McNab who suggested that we burned the damp coal first. Then he asked me to delay our departure for a day – some business to do with the boilers. I questioned Mansell about the coal afterwards. Even after we had sighted the *Kearsarge*, McNab continued to load the furnaces with the damp coal. Now maybe he was just being dumb, but I don't read McNab like that."

"But why are you telling me this now?" I asked, "if you wanted to replace him, why didn't you just do it?"

"I guess I didn't feel I had enough evidence."

This was echoing my own thoughts on Donald himself.

"So I've set a sort of a trap," he said. "I thought it was mighty strange that he wanted to know exactly when we were sailing tomorrow, so I told him midday. You were surprised too, but I hope I managed to fool you both. If you agree, I will now tell the crew that we're going to leave at dawn. I'll watch McNab to see what he does. If I'm right, he'll try to get a message to a Yankee agent tonight.

"In all events," he said, "changing our plan reduces the risk of a Union cruiser waiting for us, and dawn is a better time to leave. The sun will be behind any ship waiting for us outside the Northeast Providence Channel. I doubt they would spot the *Clara*."

"I agree," I responded, "I have to admit I had my suspicions in Madeira too, but I couldn't make out where the blame might lie."

"You thought it was me, right? You asked me some strange questions. That's what got *me* wondering."

I nodded.

"Well, let's see if we can catch a different fish tonight," he said.

So Captain Donald called all the officers and crew together and told them that we would now be starting just before dawn. He asked McNab to be sure that steam would be up half an hour before that.

I went to my cabin and lay down fully clothed on my bunk. Mansell was puzzled, but I said that I was restless and wanted to be able to walk about on deck during the night.

"Don't be nervous, old fellow," he said, "we've a good ship and a good crew. Get some sleep, you'll need it tomorrow."

"Good night," I replied.

As I lay on my bunk, I wrestled with the new suspicions that Captain Donald had raised. Fraser McNab seemed such an ordinary, quiet individual; I really could not imagine what possible motive he might have to damage our enterprise. I still felt that Donald was more likely to be the culprit if there was one. I even toyed with the idea that Donald could be using McNab as a decoy to allay my suspicions. In the end I found that my mind could only come up with a limited permutation of possible motives and culprits. Gradually I drifted off into a light uneasy sleep. A distant shout woke me at about one in the morning. Immediately I was fully awake and I sprang out of my bunk. Mansell was still asleep. I was out on the deck in a moment. Captain Donald was standing at the rail looking out over the quay. He was shouting down to a small shadowy figure walking quickly away from us.

"Mr McNab! Will you come here? I need a word with you!"

The figure turned, and we could see in the lamplight that it was indeed McNab's dark haired, clean-shaven face that was staring anxiously back at us. He stopped, walked back reluctantly towards us and came up the companionway.

"Let's not disturb everyone," said Donald, "we'll talk in my cabin."

Captain Donald and I both sat on chairs, but McNab stood nervously by the cabin door. The light from the oil lamp in the cabin was low, and it was difficult to see the expression on McNab's face, but even so he looked furtive.

Donald produced a pistol.

"Turn out your pockets!" he said.

McNab stood sullenly looking at us, but did nothing.

"Right Wells, turn them out for him!"

"There's no need," said McNab.

He reached into a side pocket, pulled out an envelope, and before we could stop him, he rapidly tore it up.

"Was it you who slowed us up out of Funchal?" I asked.

"Aye, and they'd have had you too if that interfering fellow Mansell hadn't made me switch to the dry coal!"

"But what have you got against us?"

"Have ye heard of the Anti-Slavery Society? Well I support their aims, and I'm prepared to risk ma life tae help the cause!"

"But we're not a slaver!" shouted Donald.

"Aye, but you're supporting the rebels in the South, and that's reason enough for me."

"There's going to be no future in this," said Donald, "let's turn him over to the authorities here and see what they make of him."

He called a sailor in, and asked him to collect McNab's belongings from his cabin.

"We'll turn everything over to them. I'll be mighty glad to be shot of him."

Between us we wrote a note describing what had happened, and we sent this, along with McNab's possessions and McNab himself, to the West-India Army barracks. We explained that we were leaving at dawn and would provide any further evidence they needed on our return. McNab had left in the company of Fenton and two stout seamen, I was watching him as he was hustled back down the companionway. Suddenly his head twisted round, and he shot me a glance of pure malevolence.

"Don't think ye'll get away with this," he shouted, "I'll make trouble for ye yet!"

Fenton clamped a hand over McNab's mouth, and we heard no more from him as he was marched across the quay. I shivered as I felt the bitterness and anger of his words, but then Captain Donald's friendly hand was on my shoulder as he invited me back into his cabin. He seemed unaffected by McNab's barbed comment. He clearly wanted to get things moving again.

"There's nothing he can do now," he said, "but I'm mighty sore anyways. The main thing is to make sure that his antics don't ruin our plans. We only have two engineers now, but they're both good men - I picked them myself. They won't be the same colour as McNab. I vote we risk it, and make sail at dawn as we planned. What do you say?"

Donald poured himself a brandy, and poured me one too.

"If you think we can manage like that, that's fine with me," I said, "but I have an apology to make. I thought you could have been the spy, and I even wrote to Mr Pembroke to say so. Can you forgive me?"

"Sure, all's well that ends well, as your poet says. Let's drink to a successful voyage!"

We clinked our glasses and toasted the *Clara*.

"Now you must get some sleep," he said, "you sure must be tired. I'll stow the pistol back in the hold; we can't risk being caught with it up here."

I went back to my cabin, but sleep did not come easily. As I turned the events of the night over in my mind I couldn't help being relieved that the Madeiran mystery had been solved, even if it had made me look a fool. I felt disgusted at McNab's knavery, but also a sneaking sympathy for a man who could live up to his principles as he had. I was also wondering whether Fraser McNab was the same Fraser who had been one of the party lurking near the *Messalina*, that night on the Thames when she had been so damaged by fire. A shiver went through me as I thought of McNab's bitter parting words. Could he make more trouble for us? Surely the Nassau authorities would put a stop to that.

Eventually I got to sleep, but it seemed like only a moment later that Mansell was shaking me to say that I should get up and see the dawn. Steam was up, and we were on our way.

By the time we made our first blockade-run attempt at the end of January 1863, the North had built up their navy, and there were plenty of Union Navy cruisers on the Atlantic between the Bahamas and Charleston. We saw nothing as we went through the passage, but at about midday our lookout shouted from the crow's nest that he could see sails to the west. Captain Donald immediately altered course to steam east, and this was the pattern for the day. The *Clara* had the legs to avoid Yankee shipping if we were vigilant. The lookout was given a reward of five pounds for every ship he sighted, but lost five pounds if it was sighted from the deck first. By nightfall we had avoided everything and we were able to take a direct course towards Charleston. The same pattern was followed the next day, and that afternoon Captain Donald called the officers, Isaac Jones the pilot and myself into his cabin.

"Early tomorrow morning I expect to be off Charleston," he said. "Jones and I have made our plans, and this is what we intend. The blockading ships will be in a semi-circle around the entrance to the harbour, and we will make our approach at dawn. Jones reckons the northern channel is our best bet, and we will line up on that. I aim to be some fifteen miles off the coast just before dawn, and Jones will con us to the channel in the early light.

"Tonight we will make sure that there are no lights showing, even the men's pipes, and we'll steam quietly into position."

He looked over to the pilot, "Mr Jones?"

"We'll have to take soundings as we get close to the harbour mouth."

"Sure, I'll put a good man on the lead. Then once we get close to the two forts at the entrance, we'll be under the protection of their guns. Well, that's the plan, sounds mighty easy doesn't it? Well I guess we'll just have to wait and see where it goes wrong gentlemen!"

My hands tremble even now as I remember those prophetic words.

As planned, we steamed north as the gloom of the evening turned to the darkness of the night. There was quite a heavy sea running; the *Clara* was pitching steeply as we progressed. On the flying bridge we were swaying with the motion of the ship and being gradually soaked by the spray from our bows. We watched around us intently. The sky was partly cloudy. Although there was no moon, the stars gave some faint light. The man in the crow's nest was supported by crewmembers at the *Clara's* bow and stern, all on constant alert for Yankee ships. We knew that we would soon be at the outer edge of the semi-circular blockade. The risks were increasing by the moment.

The crew were told to stay as quiet as possible. Even if a Yankee ship were to be sighted, they had to inform the captain quietly. Donald, Fenton and I were on the flying bridge, and although Mansell was off watch he joined us there too. Hot coffee was keeping us alert as we peered into the gloom looking for lights or dark shapes that would warn us of Northern vessels. We were also listening intently for the sounds of other ships.

I was nervous. I still doubted my ability to react calmly in the event of another encounter with a Northern warship. As the tension on the flying bridge grew, so did my anxiety. The others, although extremely vigilant, seemed to take the situation in their stride. I suppose that our successful evasion of the *Kearsarge* off Madeira should have made me feel less anxious, but somehow the darkness heightened my fears. I started to say something to Mansell, but I found Donald's vicelike grip on my arm.

"Stow it, or go below," he whispered.

Then there was a long period of silence on the flying bridge, only occasionally punctuated by Donald's quiet instructions through the speaking tubes to the engine room or the man at the wheel. It seemed strange to me that we had to maintain silence even though the ship was pitching and tossing in the heavy seas.

Surely there would be little chance of anything being heard. But I kept my thoughts to myself and scanned the dark horizon. I told myself that since we could hardly see more than two or three hundred yards from the ship in the inky gloom, we ourselves must be virtually invisible.

Suddenly Fenton spoke quietly.

"What's that on our bow?"

We peered into the blackness and then we could see the outline of a Northern cruiser not two hundred yards from our port bow. My heart sank, but I held my breath, hoping desperately that she wouldn't see us. Whispered warnings came from the lookouts. At first we seemed to be creeping forwards unnoticed, but then a loud shout came from the cruiser.

"Heave-to or I'll sink you!"

We turned to Captain Donald, who shrugged and moved to the engine room speaking tube.

"Stop the engines."

Then he shouted to the cruiser, "Aye, we're stopped!"

It took me a few seconds to take in what was happening. Then I was devastated. This was my first attempt, and we hadn't even reached Charleston. Instead of having a chance to meet Amy, I would soon be heading for a Northern jail, and an ignominious trip home. Virtually all my savings and the money lent to me by Mr Pembroke were tied up in my portion of the *Clara's* cargo. It was an awful prospect.

I felt a hand on my arm, and I could see Fenton standing alongside me. His face was a picture of gloom and despair.

"We're right underneath their guns," he muttered grimly, "there's no way out. There go my hopes and dreams. What rotten luck, why is she lurking here so far from Charleston? If this was a Navy ship at least we could try to shoot our way out."

I had no words of comfort for him. He was echoing my own thoughts. We both of us stood wretchedly looking at the cruiser.

The news of our imminent capture spread around the *Clara*. Soon dejected seamen were standing by the rails, also looking mournfully at the shadowy figure of the Yankee cruiser. All of us had long faces in anticipation of rough treatment and Northern captivity. Soon we could hear the captain of the cruiser again.

"Lower those boats away!"

"They're too damned close," grumbled Donald. "Wells, do you have any papers you need to destroy? You only have a few minutes."

I rushed to my cabin, and started to stuff all my most incriminating documents into a canvas bag. When I returned to the flying bridge I found that Donald had done the same. He had weights to make sure that they would sink when we threw them over the side.

Now we could make out three or four large rowing boats crammed with heavily armed Northern sailors making towards us as fast as they could. They were shouting and laughing, no doubt celebrating in advance the prizes they would enjoy. The heavy seas hampered their progress, but soon they were almost alongside. As I was making ready to throw my papers overboard, Captain Donald grabbed my wrist to prevent me.

"What are you doing?" I asked.

"We're not done yet," he said grimly.

He leant forward to the speaking tube again.

"Full ahead both engines. Give her everything!"

The *Clara* bolted forward like a hare out of the grass. We waited for the inevitable shots from the cruiser, but amazingly none came. Cries of rage and surprise came from the cruiser and the boats, and yells of delight from the men on the *Clara*. My own mind was in turmoil. One minute my suspicions of Captain Donald had been reawakened when he prevented me from jettisoning my papers, the next we were speeding away apparently unscathed. A huge grin spread across Mansell's face.

"Captain Donald, you've humbugged them!" he shouted, "why didn't I think of it? They didn't want to risk their own boats by firing at us did they? And I guess that they may have put some of their guns' crews into their boats."

"We can't celebrate yet," said Donald calmly, "she'll be after us as soon as she's got those boats' crews aboard."

As he said this, a rocket went up from the cruiser, and the sea was lit up as bright as day. We could see their crew scrambling on board, and then they were after us, guns firing. We had half a mile's start, but we were not out of danger yet.

Donald altered course sharply every few minutes to confuse the cruiser's gunners. We could see the almost continuous flashes from the muzzles of her guns and we could hear splashes around us as they tried to find our range. The cruiser sent up rockets every minute or so to pinpoint our position.

The *Clara* was the faster ship. Gradually our lead extended, and I was beginning to be more confident that we would get away. Then suddenly there was a tremendous crash on the flying bridge. A large piece of the wheelhouse, which formed the platform for the bridge, was blown away, taking a section of the rail with it. The *Clara* started to swing round towards the east, still at full speed.

I was stunned and dazed, and at first all I could do was stare at the jagged, twisted hole that had appeared in the flying bridge as I gripped what was left of the rail. Then my heart lurched when I realised that it was the area where Donald had been standing with one of the lookouts. Mansell must have seen it at the same moment, and he ran across to find out what had happened. He called out to them, but there was no reply.

"Wells! Fenton!" he shouted, "I must stay here and take control of the ship. You go down to the wheelhouse and look for the captain and Peters. If they're overboard we must heave to and look for them."

Harry shouted down the speaking tube to the engine room to find out whether they had sustained any damage, and Fenton rushed down the ladder to the wheelhouse. I was unable to move with the shock of what had happened. Harry came over and gripped me by the arm.

"We have to keep going Tom," he said firmly, "every minute is vital. You must get down there and help Fenton. He's got medical knowledge and can help the wounded. Are you hurt yourself Tom?"

I shook my head, then I managed to get myself going. When I got down to the wheelhouse there was no sign of Fenton, but I could see that the man at the wheel had been wounded, and was trying to bind up a gash in his arm. I went over to help him. The ship was no longer being steered, which explained our drift to the east as she was pushed off course by the wind. I could still hear occasional shots from the cruiser and there were flashes of light from her rockets, but we sustained no more hits. There was no sign of Donald or the lookout. When I had finished helping the sailor I took hold of the wheel, and shouted up to Mansell.

"The helmsman's been wounded, Harry. There's no sign of Donald or Peters. What course shall I steer?"

"Keep her as she is, where's Fenton?"

At that moment Fenton came into the damaged wheelhouse looking grim.

"They're both dead, Wells. They were both lying on the fore deck. There's nothing I can do for them. I've detailed two of the sailors to take them below. I've checked the rest of the crew. There's nobody missing."

I pointed out the injured sailor by the wheel, and Fenton went over to check his wound. Then he took over from me at the wheel and asked me to go up and tell Harry what had happened to poor Donald and Peters.

When I broke the news to him, Harry looked grim. Then he seemed to get hold of himself and he turned towards me.

"Bad as it is, we owe it to the crew to do our best to get out of this. Two deaths are terrible, but thirty would be worse. We have to be thankful for one thing. All the damage seems to be to the wheelhouse and to the bridge, there's no damage to the working parts of the ship. For the moment we seem to be out of range of that bloody cruiser."

He paused.

"Christ it's ironic, first Donald gets us out of the deepest hole I've ever been in, and then he pays for it with his own life.

"What should we do Tom?" he asked, "turn back for Nassau or head for Charleston? Do you want to flip a coin?" he added bitterly.

At first I found it hard to bring myself to address the future. The two deaths were not only shocking in themselves, but I also have to confess that they were yet another reminder to me of my own mortality. Eventually I found myself able to reply.

"We must see those poor fellows decently buried. I had the

92

greatest respect for Donald, and I feel terrible about my suspicions of him at the beginning. He was a first rate captain. For me that rules out the Nassau option. I can't help thinking too that the nearest doctor for our helmsman's going to be in Charleston. I vote that we stick to Donald's plan."

"Agreed," said Mansell.

After another quarter of an hour we seemed to be out of sight of the cruiser, and we saw no more rockets. Mansell set a course to take us back towards Charleston, avoiding the area where we last saw the cruiser; he worked with the pilot to make for the harbour entrance. I was deeply impressed with Mansell that night. His experience with the Royal Navy must have helped him. Despite his obvious distress at Donald's death, he worked calmly and purposefully. The crew responded to him immediately. They knew that he had a more light-hearted approach, quite a contrast to Donald's rigid discipline, but it seemed to be equally effective. I checked with Mansell if he needed me for anything, and went below. Fenton had found a replacement at the wheel, and he was treating our helmsman. We were fortunate that his wounds were relatively slight. He had cuts from the broken glass from the wheelhouse windows, and slight concussion. I went back to the bridge.

We saw no more Northern ships during the night. They would certainly have been searching for us, but we must have found one of the gaps in the blockade. Just before dawn Mansell and the pilot were convinced that we were close to the harbour mouth. A man at the bows was casting the lead forwards and then pulling the line in hand over hand. Softly he called out the depths, and occasionally the pilot would check samples of sand from where the lead had scraped them up from the sea bottom. Then as the light came up we could see the silhouettes of Fort Wagner to the south and Fort Moultrie to the north. We were under their guns, and we were safe.

There was no quarantine in operation for yellow fever in the winter, and we were able to make our way directly across the harbour towards the city. The entrance was narrow, but then the harbour expanded, dividing into the two rivers flowing on either side of the city. We could see the huge brick structure of Fort

Sumter on our left as we made our way towards Charleston. This was where the first action of the Civil War had been fought. There were cheers from the men standing on the barbette tier of the fort as they saw the battered *Clara* coming past. We found it hard to respond.

We needed the skills of our pilot. The Confederates had strewn the harbour with mines and obstructions as a protection against incursions from the Union Navy. But we threaded our way safely through. Soon we could see the splendid mansions lining the southern corner of the city. Eventually we were tied up at one of the wharves opposite Shute's Folly Island. This was my first time on American soil, but although the sights and sounds were strange to me, I hardly took them in for those first few days. I was still shocked from the terrible events of our voyage.

I was able to contact Mr Blair through his agent in Charleston, George Somerville, and I was directed to Blair's lodgings in Meeting Street. He couldn't have been more helpful. He was the same fat, fussy bachelor I had got to know when he had visited our offices in London. He had a kindly heart, and he got down to work immediately. He found a doctor for our wounded helmsman; he helped me to make the funeral arrangements for Donald and Peters, and he assisted with the arrangements for repairing the *Clara*.

Two days later the combined funerals took place at St. Philip's church, and the entire company of the *Clara* was present. The ship's crew were tough, experienced sailors, but the funeral affected them all deeply. Peters had been a popular crewmember, and all of them had respected Captain Donald. As we sang the sad funeral hymns, some of the crew were openly shedding tears. The funeral affected me deeply too. As Mr Pembroke's representative I felt some responsibility for what had happened, and this filled me with guilt as well as sadness. I was also wondering whether this was a taste of the future for our enterprise. Maybe the blockade was becoming too tight to give ships like ours a reasonable chance to get through. Would I have more blood on my hands over the coming months? It was a gloomy prospect.

Finally the service came to an end, and the two coffins were carried outside and placed in a funeral carriage to be taken through the narrow Charleston streets to the Magnolia Cemetery. We all walked behind it, and I found myself next to Mansell.

"I feel awful about Donald being buried here away from his family," he said, "it's just unimaginable that his wife doesn't even know that he's dead. He was a fine captain, and the *Clara* will not be the same without him."

He paused.

"Donald was married, but I'm not sure about Peters, what do you think Mr Pembroke will do for their families?"

"As soon as we're back in Nassau," I said, "I'll write to Mr Pembroke. Of course we all knew that there would be risks in this blockade running business, and we even knew there was risk to our lives. Despite that I'm afraid I never discussed with Mr Pembroke the financial consequences of the death of a crewmember, but I'm sure he'll be generous.

"Leave it to me," I continued, "I'll make sure their families don't suffer. As far as the *Clara* is concerned, I am Mr Pembroke's representative, and I'm appointing you as her captain now. Let's hope and pray that her luck improves. The last forty-eight hours have been the worst of my life. I'm not sure I could go through that again."

We walked in silence for a while. Then Mansell turned to me.

"I can't imagine a worse way to become captain," he said gloomily, "don't get me wrong Tom, of course I'll do the best I can for the owner and the crew, but I'd give anything to turn the clock back and have Donald and Peters alive again."

Finally we came to the cemetery. It was one where many Confederate soldiers were buried, and there were fresh graves, flowers, and one or two sad black-clad figures standing by the graves. We gathered round two new graves to see Donald and Peters buried. I had made a commitment to Mansell that I would ensure that their two families would be well looked after, and at that moment I swore to myself that I would honour that commitment. Fortunately my trust in Mr Pembroke was well founded. He dealt with their families very generously.

Chapter Seven
General Beauregard

Two days after the funeral I spent the morning selling my own portion of the *Clara's* cargo. As soon as we had arrived, there had been merchants desperate to get on board to purchase anything we had. They were a mixed bunch, ranging from respectable locals to renegade Northerners and European merchant adventurers. The goods we had shipped for Mr Pembroke were sold through Angus Blair, but I sold my own portion of the cargo separately. I was astonished at the prices I could achieve; soon I was feeling like a rich man. I also questioned them closely about the items that were in short supply in the South. Amongst other things they told me that local ladies were clamouring for cotton thread, needles, buttons and all the paraphernalia needed for the making and repair of clothes. These were all things that had mainly been purchased from the North before the war or imported from Europe.

In the afternoon I made my way to the office Mr Blair shared with Mr Somerville in Meeting Street. I was used to the chaotic jumble of streets and lanes in London, so Charleston's orderly grid system came as a pleasant surprise. I found my way easily past the fine houses as yet untouched by the siege that was soon to come. Less pleasant were the parties of downcast Negro slaves under the watchful eyes of their white overseers, often made to stand aside whilst the white citizens walked past. It was my first taste of the effects of slavery, and I found it distressing.

In the rush of events following our sad arrival in Charleston, I had not yet had the chance to speak to Blair about Amy and her family, and this was foremost in my thoughts as I went up the stairs to his office.

Mr Blair was alone, seated at a large desk. I could see that he was scanning papers comparing the cargo manifests and prices, with the 'prices current' and the recent auction prices listed in the local papers. It was a fine room looking out over Meeting Street, and there was a fire burning in the grate. As soon as he saw me, he sprang up to come over and shake my hand.

"My dear fellow, please forgive me, but we only have a few minutes for our business. We are having dinner with George Somerville and General Beauregard in the Mills House Hotel. I have made the arrangements, and I am anxious to make sure that the dinner goes well. The chef at the hotel is excellent, but supplies are difficult, so don't raise your expectations too high."

He sighed.

"I only wish they could give us some of the dishes that I relished so much in London, but I trust you will not be disappointed."

I had already met Mr Somerville, Blair's agent in Charleston, but I was astonished to be invited to meet General Beauregard.

"Beauregard? Isn't he the general who secured the victory with Johnston at Manassas? What's he doing in Charleston?"

Blair looked at me sharply.

"He's had some difficulties since then. President Davis took him out of the front line after the retreat from Corinth in Mississippi, and replaced him by that wretched man Bragg. Beauregard is in command of our coastal defences in this region now. Davis still blames Beauregard for our failure to defeat Grant at Shiloh."

"What's he like, Mr Blair? Are you sure you want me with you tonight?"

"My dear chap, he knows that you are going to be with us. He's a friend of George Somerville's. Beauregard's a charming fellow. The *Clara* is quite famous in Charleston, you know. You might say that one of his main tasks is keeping the harbour open for blockade runners, and we don't often see them arriving with as much damage as you had."

We conducted our business as swiftly as we could, with Blair frequently glancing at the clock in his office. Then he stood up and indicated that it was time for us to make our way towards the hotel. At first we were walking past elegant shops and houses, but as we got closer to the hotel we started to come into an area that had been badly damaged by a fire a year earlier. Many of the buildings were still under repair. Now at least I had the opportunity to raise the topic closest to my heart.

"How are Mrs Munro and Miss Amy? Do you have any news of

them?"

Blair frowned as we hurried along.

"I am worried about them, but that is beside the point. You probably know that Colonel Munro owns a large plantation near Fayetteville. That's about a hundred miles north of Wilmington. The plantation has been in his family for a long time, and it is well established. But the war has been very difficult for them."

He waved perfunctorily at an acquaintance on the other side of the street, and then continued.

"The story is not a happy one. Both of their sons joined the army as soon as they could. Jack went missing last August in the second battle at Manassas, and we have just heard that Preston was killed at Fredericksburg in December. We have tried in every way we can to get news of Jack, but there just seems no trace of him.

"Colonel Munro was with Johnston, but after Shiloh he was transferred to General Jackson's staff. Even with what has happened to his sons, he feels he must stay with the army. Did you know that Amy has a younger sister?"

"Louise?" I asked.

"Yes. At least all is well with her. She was married in October to the son of one of the Munros' Fayetteville neighbours. With Colonel Munro still with Jackson, that means that my sister and Amy are alone at the Marion plantation. I was there in December, and you can imagine that it is a sorrowful place."

I expressed my sympathy.

Mr Blair glanced sideways at me.

"Amy has confided in me that you and she have taken a liking to each other, young man."

I nodded.

"Colonel and Mrs Munro are aware that you have been writing to each other. They think that may be the reason why Amy shows no interest in the other young men whom she meets. I believe that one of Amy's cousins has made an offer for her, and the Munros are very disappointed that my niece has refused him. They are concerned about Amy, but of course they have other things on their minds just now."

This was confirmation about the offer from Hamilton Douglas

that Amy had mentioned in her letters. I was secretly pleased to hear from Mr Blair that Amy had turned him down.

"I'm so sorry about Jack and Preston," I said, "these difficulties must be hard for you to bear too. This war must have caused so many tragedies. My heart goes out for Miss Munro and her family."

Blair stopped and turned to me. He was puffing slightly from the walk.

"Yes. It has been terrible. They will appreciate your concern. They know that you are visiting me, and they have extended an invitation for you to see them at Marion. Would you have time whilst your ship is being repaired?"

My heart lifted.

"We're told that it will take nearly three weeks, so I would like to."

Mr Blair looked pensive.

"Now that the *Clara* is here and being discharged, I plan to travel to Marion myself in two days time. Why don't you come with me? If you agree, I'll get a message to my sister letting her know that you will be coming."

I was delighted with this proposal, and I agreed immediately. He went through the arrangements we would have to make to travel to Fayetteville, and we started walking again.

Mr Somerville and General Beauregard were already at the hotel. We went into the dining room to join them. There couldn't have been a greater contrast between the two men. Somerville was a huge man, towering over all of us, whereas the general was short and dapper, with a swarthy Creole complexion, dark hair and moustaches. Somerville was a jolly, boisterous character and Beauregard was, as Mr Blair had promised, suave and polite.

The dining room was filling up, and many of the diners knew either Beauregard or Somerville, and wanted to come up and make themselves known. General Beauregard was always punctilious in introducing me, and he was charm itself to those who came up to our table, especially the ladies.

Mr Blair was the host, and he had ordered the dinner in advance. Soon he was on his favourite topic, much to the amusement of the other two.

"I hope you will accept simple fare, gentlemen. As you know, decent food is hard to get in Charleston these days, but the chef here does his best. I hope you will find our local dishes to your liking Mr Wells. But with the shortages of sugar, coffee, cocoa, spices... ah well, let's see what he can do."

"Well let's hope the dinner won't be burnt, Blair," said Beauregard, smiling, "that's what happened when General Lee came to the hotel a year ago!"

The others laughed, but Blair could see that I was puzzled.

"General Lee happened to be staying in the hotel in December '61, Mr Wells" he said, "at the time of the terrible fire in Charleston. Don't listen to them, I'm sure that the dinner will be perfectly prepared..."

"Good heavens," exclaimed Somerville, "I'm sure Mr Wells has been eating royally on the *Clara*, surely he can accept a little austerity whilst he's here in Charleston. But I know you'll never be satisfied with our limited supplies here Angus. Wells, why don't you bring him in some delicacies on your next voyage?"

"Well we did bring in one or two things..."

"Don't encourage him, Somerville," interjected Beauregard, "we want their ships filled to the brim with munitions, don't we? I was sorry to hear of the casualties you took on your voyage in Mr Wells. We get used to them here I'm afraid, but it always grieves me when I hear of civilians dying in our cause."

At this point the first dish was brought in, and Mr Blair's eyes lit up.

"Oyster pie, Mr Wells," he said, "a Southern speciality, I hope you enjoy it."

"Would you tell us of your voyage," asked Beauregard politely, "I gather that your ship was badly damaged."

Haltingly I told them of all we had been through, and the difficult moments we had experienced. As my story progressed I became more confident, and hopefully my tale was fluent enough. I mentioned our surprise that we had found the Northern navy so far out from the entrance to Charleston harbour.

"Well you were unlucky there, my dear fellow," said Somerville, with an amused glance at the general, "Beauregard here had just had a major engagement with the Yankee blockading fleet. Two of our ironclads, the *Palmetto State* and the *Chicora*, slipped out of the harbour and gave them a heavy battering a few nights ago. The Yankees were probably further offshore than they usually are. You made quite a mess of some of their ships didn't you Beauregard?"

He looked across at the general.

"Quite a feather in your cap, let's hope Davis gives you the credit for it!"

Beauregard looked modestly down at his plate, and said nothing. There was a small silence, so eventually I felt compelled to say something:

"I was wondering whether I could ask your views on the progress of the war. Our owner, Mr Pembroke, has asked me to seek advice on the latest developments. He is wondering whether to make further investments in blockade running ships."

Whilst I was asking this, waiters were clearing away the remnants of the oyster pie, and bringing in a pork dish. The aroma was inviting.

"Help yourselves, gentlemen," said Blair, "chicken and pork, the Southern staples, Mr Wells... but I think you will find that the chef here is an artist in his own way."

He was right. I soon found that the pork dish was delicious.

"What do you think," Blair continued, "who wants to answer Mr Wells' question? I have great respect for Mr Pembroke and his firm, so I feel we ought to give him an objective view."

"Could you accept the views of a humble amateur like myself?" asked Somerville, "I am no expert like Beauregard here, but I do follow the war very closely with my son Charlie."

Beauregard smiled his assent.

"I am sure you know, Mr Wells, that General Lee, with Jackson and Johnston, has had outstanding victories in the east. The general here," he nodded respectfully towards Beauregard, "with Joe Johnston licked them at Manassas, and we've had great success since then. There's been quite a cost to us in lives and material, but the Yankees have suffered even more damage.

"I am happy to say that President Lincoln can only be described as an idiot, as he keeps picking stupid generals. When they fail, he

101

replaces them with even worse ones. Scott and McClellan have gone, and now we hear that Burnside has been replaced by Hooker."

"That's true," interjected Blair, "but in the west the Yankees have been more successful and they are working their way through Missouri and along the Mississippi. What is President Davis going to do about that? We depend upon armaments and supplies being brought through the blockade, here and into Wilmington and Savannah, won't these ports be at risk? We can get the imports at the moment, but what will happen in the longer term? Isn't there a risk that we could be ground down in the end, Beauregard?"

"Nonsense, Blair!" exclaimed Somerville, and one or two heads turned towards us in the dining room. He lowered his voice again.

"Where do you get these extraordinary ideas from? Good Heavens, it's bad enough fighting the Yankees without having doubters on our own side."

"Well in a way he's right, George," said Beauregard diplomatically, "it's all a question of strategy. If we allow the Yankees to dictate the course of the war, there is a risk that they could predominate with their superior numbers and wealth of materials. We need to play to our strengths, and I am sure Davis appreciates that. Our troops are superior. Knowing that our cause is just, inspires them. The Yankee army has many units composed of immigrants straight off the boat from Hamburg, and that saps their courage.

"But as you say, Somerville, our generals are better. We must take the fight into the North again, and knock them out there. It's the only way. We must defeat them before they can build up their strength."

"And before Lincoln stops appointing bad generals, and finds a good one," said Somerville.

His remark caused laughter around the table, and relieved the tension. At this moment a young soldier came into the dining room and scanned the tables. When he saw General Beauregard he came over to our table and passed him a note. Beauregard read it, and stood up.

"Gentlemen, I must apologise, duty calls. Thank you for the

dinner, Blair, I'm glad I was at least able to eat some of that delicious pork. Goodbye Mr Wells. I hope you make plenty more voyages into our ports, and you take no more casualties. I'll see you on Saturday Somerville."

With that he left the dining room with the young soldier.

Somerville turned to Angus Blair.

"Good God, Angus, you were taking a risk there! I do believe that people have been shot for remarks half as defeatist as yours!"

Blair smiled and replied quietly.

"I think it is only fair to Mr Wells to give him as clear a picture as we can. In my opinion there are only two realistic outcomes, either the Yankees will get tired of constant defeats and loss of life and they will come to a settlement, or, in the end, through superior numbers and better supply of material, they will grind us down."

Somerville thumped the table, the glasses and plates rattled, and once more heads were turning in the dining room.

"And what about a military victory, pray? Surely Beauregard is right. General Lee could smash them in a month if he was sent north by Davis!"

"I wish I could believe that," responded Blair softly, "up until now all the fighting has been on our own soil, or just over the border in Pennsylvania. With all their resources I cannot believe that the Yankees would ever surrender to our armies in their own territory. A negotiated settlement perhaps, surrender would be politically impossible for them."

There was silence at the table, and I pondered what this meant for our enterprise. Somerville looked pensive, but Mr Blair was piling his plate again from the fine savoury pork dish.

"Which of your two outcomes do you think more likely," I asked, "settlement or failure Mr Blair?"

Once again he paused before replying.

"Defeat is an ugly word, and I hate the thought of it, but I do not believe that the Yankees will try for a settlement under Lincoln. They say that McClellan will run against him in the 'sixty-four Northern presidential election. McClellan would have a chance of winning if the Yankees continue to suffer so many defeats. They say that he might try to settle the war, but is that realistic?

Personally I have my doubts. Both sides believe their cause to be just, and neither side will give in easily. I think we have to face up to the fact that the North could win … eventually."

Somerville was scowling, and his great frame was hunched over the table, but he did not disagree.

"But what does that mean for Mr Pembroke?" I asked.

"Make hay whilst the sun shines," Blair replied, "but do not put your profits into Confederate money or bonds… and do have some more of the pork."

"Well I'm amazed at you, Angus," said Somerville; "all I can suggest is that you keep your views to yourself in future. I think you're more likely to be lynched than thanked for them…"

The rest of the meal was taken up with a more general discussion on the progress of the war. The pork was followed by a salad, and then we had a jelly cake, made with what must have been virtually the last chocolate in the South. Mr Blair seemed in part to regret the pronouncements he had made, but he didn't go back on what he had said, despite being repeatedly challenged by Somerville. Finally it was time for us to leave, and Somerville left first. I thanked Mr Blair for his hospitality, and praised the dinner.

"Thank you. I am afraid it was nothing in comparison with those wonderful dinners in London," he said mournfully, "but I must put my memories of turbot with lobster sauce, pigeon pie, roast hare, saddle of mutton, meringues and almond cheesecake behind me."

Then he started, as if suddenly remembering something, and he thrust his hand into an inside pocket of his frock coat.

"I do apologise, I was distracted by our meeting with Beauregard. I have a letter for you. I am not sure that Colonel Munro would approve of this, but Amy sent it to me."

He handed over an envelope addressed to me in Amy's familiar handwriting.

Then he said that he would shortly be in touch with me on the *Clara* for the final arrangements for our journey to Marion.

The *Clara* had not yet been put into the shipyard for repairs, and I was still staying on board. As soon as I was back I read Amy's letter. It was dated in December, and it had obviously been sent before the news of Preston's death had reached Marion.

Marion Plantation

15th December 1862

Dearest Tom,

How wonderful it is to know that you are coming to America. I am sending this letter to wait for you at my uncle's house in Wilmington, and I pray that you will be reading it soon. I think of you so much, and I long to see you.

There is still no news of Jack. My parents have tried every possible way to find out what has happened to him, but all we know is that he was missing after the second day of the battle at Manassas at the end of August. He was in General Longstreet's force, and father knows the general. He assures father that Jack was not among those poor souls recovered from the battlefield. That must mean that he was captured and taken away by the Yankees on their retreat. But try as we may we cannot get any news of him.

Preston and father are still with General Jackson's army, and we pray for them every day. Our army is doing so well, but the cost is terrible. Almost every family in our neighbourhood has lost someone, either captured or killed, and many have been wounded.

The house is very quiet with just mother and me here. Louise used to share my room, but now she has moved to Sandy Plains and I miss her so much, she is always so cheerful and light-hearted. Jack and Preston have the room next to mine, and I could hear them shouting and laughing. It used to annoy me sometimes, but now I would give anything to hear them again!!

Mother and I do our best to look after the plantation whilst father is away, but it is not easy. Our latest problem is that one of our Negroes escaped! Father bought Ralph for one thousand three hundred dollars, three years ago. That is a very high price for a slave – it must be more than two hundred and fifty of your pounds! Ralph is a good worker, and father was very pleased to have bought him. When Louise was married there was a big party at Marion, and Ralph met Betsy, one of the house slaves from Sandy

Plains. They wanted to marry, and father and Mr Scott agreed. They 'jumped the broom' at Marion, that is how Negroes get married here. Betsy was still needed at Sandy Plains, and father would not part with Ralph, so he had to stay here in our slave quarters, but Betsy comes to visit once a month. Ralph asked me to try to persuade my father to sell him to Mr Scott, but father would not do it.

Then Ralph ran away. He left during the slaves' prayer meeting one Sunday evening, and was not missed for several hours. It is very difficult for slaves to travel at night unless they have a pass. There are patrols (the Negroes call them paterrollers!), which usually catch them. But Ralph eluded them. One of our neighbours has bloodhounds, and so these were sent after him. Eventually he was found in a swamp by the river, and brought back to the plantation. He had to be punished, and since my father is away, our overseer sent him to the slave market in Fayetteville to be whipped. When he came back I went down to his cabin to treat him. He told me he had been whipped for two hours! He is very weak, but I did my best for him. He told me he ran away to see Betsy who is going to have their child. I suppose they must have been planning to run away together to the North. Mother says that he must be made an example to stop other slaves thinking of running away, but it is very hard.

Even though it is quite cold now, the cotton harvest is still going on. Our overseer runs competitions between the slaves to see who can pick the most in a day. Ralph holds the record with over 300 pounds, but they cannot pick that much at the moment. Ralph was out picking yesterday, but he is too weak to pick very much.

Please do not think that everything is gloomy here! Last week there was a big party for the Negroes at Marion. We give two parties every year, one on the Fourth of July, and one on my father's birthday. No work is done, and a big feast is held. In the summer there are long tables down by the river, but in the winter it is held in one of the cotton barns. The Negroes dig long trenches out in the open, and they are filled with wood and bark. When these have burnt down to hot coals, a whole pig and a whole sheep are roast over the coals on spits, and basted with a special butter. This year two enormous apple cobblers were made for sweetmeats. They were made in great big earthenware bowls. First a layer of pastry goes in the bottom of the bowl, then a layer of apples, then a thick layer of sugar, and then another double layer of pastry. The bowls are then placed in big ovens over the hot coals.

On father's birthday the Negroes were highly excited by their feast. There was a lot of laughing and joking. The barbequed meats were cut up, and heaped onto plates in the barn. There was almost silence whilst this was being eaten, as they enjoyed it so much. Then the excitement mounted again as the apple cobblers were brought in. They were served onto plates, and once again the Negroes were smiling and laughing, but not for long! I am sure you can never guess what had happened! The cooks had used salt instead of sugar in the cobblers! It seems that they were told to take it from a box with an 'S' at the beginning of the label, and nobody thought that salt begins with 'S' too! (Of course the Negroes cannot read and write). Some tried to go on eating, claiming that it made no difference, but soon all agreed that it was uneatable. There were some very sad faces until my mother had cakes brought down from our house, and soon they were happy again. Only my mother was upset by the sad waste of salt, which is very hard to get these days.

I hope I am not boring you with all of these tales of the plantation. It must seem very dull compared to your exciting life as a blockade-runner! But please be careful Tom. My uncle often tells us of the terrible risks they run.

I have spoken to mother, and she has agreed that I can invite you to come to visit us at Marion. My uncle has offered to bring you himself, so please come and see us as soon as you can!

Your loving Amy.

Chapter Eight
Marion

Travelling by rail in those days was difficult and unpleasant. The tracks were poorly maintained, trains moved slowly and derailments were not uncommon. There were trains packed with troops moving to the different areas of conflict, and they were always given priority. Carriages were often so crowded that passengers had to resort to travelling on the roofs. Journeys that would normally take a day often took three or even more. Angus Blair had planned that we would travel by train to Wilmington, and then take passage on a steamboat up the Cape Fear River to Fayetteville.

The journey to Wilmington was indeed unpleasant. Fortunately Blair was taking despatches from General Beauregard to General Whiting in Wilmington, and we had special passes. I was also carrying bottles of brandy from the *Clara*. By judicious bribery we managed to obtain places in the conductor's car. Even so, the carriage was ridiculously full.

Three days later we reached Wilmington. Mr Blair delivered the despatches, and I looked for places on a steamboat bound for Fayetteville. In the end we obtained passage on a munitions boat that was travelling there directly, and would be returning with a cargo of turpentine and cotton.

The steamship was driven by a paddlewheel at the stern, and its draft was shallow to cope with the shoals and mudflats of the river. The trip took us two days, and we travelled in some discomfort. The ship was not designed for passengers, and we slept huddled in chairs in the saloon. The train had been too crowded for private conversation, but now I was eager to ask questions about the Munro household. As we neared Fayetteville I was getting more and more anxious about my reception at Marion. We were seated on cane chairs in the saloon when I began to ask Mr Blair about Amy's family. First I asked him about Colonel Munro.

"I think you will find that the colonel is at Marion," said Blair, "I know he has requested furlough from General Lee, as he wants to give my sister some help with the management of the plantation. The armies are in their winter encampments, and it probably will not be until April that the spring campaigns will start. He must be thankful to get away from the dreadful camp food. I am told they live entirely on pork and beans – terribly unhealthy."

"Can you tell me something about him?" I asked anxiously. Mr Blair smiled.

"He is very much the Southern gentleman, and I am sure he will be the soul of hospitality to you as a visitor. Nothing to worry about there, my dear fellow."

"And as a suitor for Amy?" I asked.

"Goodness, I can hardly answer that!" said Blair, laughing, "I will have to leave him to speak for himself. Did I tell you that they now have news of Jack? I was told at the depot in Wilmington that he is in a Yankee prison in New York called Fort Lafayette – ironic is it not?"

"Strange that the name should be the same as his home town, is there a reason?"

"Of course there is, but as an Englishman you would not know about it! General de la Fayette was a Frenchman who was one of our generals in our War of Independence; didn't they teach you about him in school?"

"No, they only taught us about the wars we won; the War of American Independence was carefully brushed under the carpet. For that period we were only told about our victories in Canada and India – not about our losses here!"

"Well that's the reason why there are so many places called Lafayette in America. Fort Lafayette has a bad reputation. Early in the war there were a number of deaths there from typhoid fever, so the Munros are very worried about him. They are trying to get him exchanged, but that is very difficult now."

"How is Miss Munro?"

"She has been very much affected by Preston's death, and the worry about Jack, but she is fine - as beautiful as ever," he said, with a twinkle in his eye.

We reached Fayetteville in the morning, and Mr Blair hired a buggy to take us out to Marion. It was a cool January day, cloudy but dry. The road to Marion took us past a number of other plantations. Some of them were small, with quite humble looking cottages for the owners, but we passed two or three quite sizeable properties with grand carriage drives and large elegant plantation houses. One of these Mr Blair pointed out as Sandy Plains, the plantation belonging to Amy's sister's parents-in-law. After about an hour we came to the long drive taking us to the Marion plantation house. I was getting more and more nervous. It was nearly two years since I had seen Amy and her mother, but so much had happened in the interim. How would I feel about Amy now? What would her feelings be for me? And what would her family think of me? All these questions were turning in my head as we passed through the cotton fields. As we neared the house I could see that it was partly screened by the inevitable pine trees of the region. The house itself was a handsome white two-storey structure, with white-pillared piazzas at the front and back. Beyond the house I could see that there was a fine view across fields sloping down to the river. As we pulled up in front of the house, two Negro servants came out to help us down from the buggy, and carry our baggage into the house.

There was a wide hall, lit from a skylight at the top of the house. A broad sweeping staircase wound its way elegantly round the hall to the upper floor, with twisted columns giving support.

Angus Blair turned to the butler.

"Where are the family, Dixon?" he asked.

Dixon was a tall elderly Negro with white hair. His face had a kindly expression.

"They are in the drawing room Mister Blair," he said, "Miss Amy, she's out riding."

He led the way to the drawing room where colonel and Mrs Munro were standing by the windows talking. As we came in Mrs Munro turned and limped over to us, supported by her stick.

"Angus, Mr Wells, welcome to Marion. Mr Wells, may I introduce my husband. Dearest, this is Mr Wells who showed us round St. Paul's Cathedral when we were in London. It seems an age ago."

Colonel Munro strode forward and shook my hand. He was a tall man with dark hair and a sweeping cavalry moustache. His face was burnt brown from his time in the army. He had the strict look of a man used to command. He also seemed to be examining me intently as we spoke.

"You are very welcome Mr Wells," he said, "Amy will be here shortly, I will send one of the servants out to find her. Dixon, can you send Joe for Miss Amy?"

"How was your journey?" asked Mrs Munro.

"Well it was easy enough coming up from Wilmington on the munitions boat," I said, "but the train journey from Charleston was very slow and crowded."

"It certainly was," said Blair, "but Mr Wells' passage from Nassau was even more unpleasant. Beauregard chased some Yankee cruisers away from the Charleston blockade ten days ago, and Mr Wells' ship had the misfortune to run into them. Beauregard was almost apologetic when Wells and I had dinner with him last week!"

Colonel Munro looked at me with new respect, hearing of our dinner with the general, and he asked me what had happened.

"Yes, we ran into trouble with a Yankee cruiser, and we suffered a tragedy. They managed to hit us with one of their shells, and we had two men killed, including our captain."

"I am very sorry to hear that," said Colonel Munro, with a sympathetic look, "I'm sure it must have affected you all deeply."

He paused.

"What were you carrying?"

"Mainly munitions and uniforms."

"I am glad to hear it, sir, glad to hear it. I have heard it said that too many of those ships come in with silk and lace."

"Well it's true that for us blockade running is a commercial enterprise, but Mr Pembroke, our owner, is a supporter of the South, and he likes to ensure that most of our cargo is military. If we are under fire from a cruiser, we wish we had more silk, and less gunpowder."

They laughed, and the conversation moved onto other topics. Eventually Mrs Munro turned to Mr Blair and myself.

"After your unpleasant voyage on the munitions boat, I am sure you would both like to wash and change. Dixon will show you to your rooms. Shall we meet here again at quarter to one?"

She pulled the bell rope, and Dixon led the way upstairs.

I was shown into a fine large bedroom, with beautiful views across the plantation. My valise was already unpacked, and a Negro maid brought a large basin of hot water. She showed me where to leave any clothes I would like to have washed. I was soon feeling much more comfortable in a clean shirt. It was half past twelve, and I was wondering whether to go downstairs, when I heard the sound of soft footsteps and the rustle of a woman's dress outside my door. There was a quiet knock. I went over and opened the door, and there was Amy. She slipped inside and closed the door.

"I couldn't wait until you came downstairs, I had to see you!" she said.

She was as beautiful as ever, and my heart lifted.

"Amy!" I exclaimed, and soon we were hugging and kissing each other, and she was crying.

"Oh, it has been forever!" she said, "I thought you would never come."

"It wasn't easy, Amy, and I don't think either of us could have imagined everything that's happened since we first met. But it's so wonderful to see you, I can't believe it's finally happening. I have thought of you so much. But how are you? I am so pleased to hear that Jack is safe, and I'm so sorry about Preston."

Her expression changed to one of great sadness.

"Thank you for your sympathy Tom, I do not think we shall ever get over Preston's death, and we worry so about Jack. Father still has some contacts in the North and we have been trying to get Jack exchanged for a Yankee officer held here, but it seems hopeless at the moment."

"At least it must be wonderful to know he's alive."

"Yes," she said, wistfully.

"Tom, we only have a few moments before we must go down. I just wanted to say how much I still love you. I have been worrying so much about you too, and it seems like a dream to be standing

112

here holding your hands."

We kissed again, then Amy broke away.

"I must go down, and nobody must know that I have been here. Can you look outside the door and make sure that there is no one there?"

Soon she was gone, and I prepared to go down. In those few moments I was convinced that Amy was the person I wanted to be with for the rest of my life. Before I left Marion I was determined that I would ask her to marry me. The sight of Amy's pure beautiful face, and the evidence of her sweet loyalty to me, was making me bitterly regret my shameful episode with Susan.

We met again in the drawing room. Mrs Munro was a charming hostess and made me feel very welcome. Colonel Munro was also a gracious host but he had strong views on the war which he expressed vigorously, and which he defended almost to the point of rudeness. Mrs Munro was eager to make our visit comfortable.

"How long can you both stay?" she asked.

"Two days at the most," Mr Blair replied, "I have business to conduct in Fayetteville on Monday morning. Tomorrow is Sunday; may we both stay here then? At the moment we have our places booked on a boat returning to Wilmington on Monday afternoon. Mr Wells tells me he must be back in Charleston by the end of the week."

"The repairs to our ship are due to be completed then," I said, "we must be ready to sail immediately if we are to have a chance of getting back through the blockade."

"You are both welcome to stay as long as you like," said Colonel Munro, "but if you must leave on Monday, well there it is. Far be it from me to stop Mr Wells from bringing munitions back into the South!"

"Father!" exclaimed Amy, "it sounds as though you are almost encouraging Mr Wells to risk his life for us."

"Nearly all of us are risking our lives for the Southern Cause in one way or another," he said, "as we know to our cost."

There was an uncomfortable silence, eventually broken by Mrs Munro.

"Louise and her parents-in-law have asked us all over to Sandy

Plains for dinner later this afternoon."

She turned to me.

"Louise is our other daughter Mr Wells. She is married to the son of one of our neighbours. Her husband James is with the army."

"That sounds delightful," exclaimed Blair, "the Scotts have a cook who is a legend in this area, Wells. Let us hope the dinner will blank out memories of that pork on the munitions boat."

In the afternoon, Colonel Munro and Amy showed me round the plantation. The colonel drove us round in a buggy. He told me that the plantation extended to close to a thousand acres, which was large for the area. It seemed to be split half and half between pine forest and open fields. I had seen slaves working in Charleston on the wharves and in houses, but seeing them in the fields was a shock. Colonel Munro had nearly a hundred slaves, and sixty or seventy of them were hoeing mechanically in the fields between the rows of cotton plants. Many were women, and male black foremen were supervising them. Some of the slaves were singing, but mainly they looked tired and dejected. Apparently they had started working at six, and even at three in the afternoon they were still working on. Colonel Munro was proud of his plantation and seemed totally impervious to the inequities and cruelty of the system. He spent much of the time listing instances of laziness in his workforce, and the difficulties of selling his crops during the war. I knew I needed to keep him on my side, so I kept my counsel.

As we came back to the house we came past the primitive cabins where most of the slaves lived. Amy began to look a little agitated. Eventually she touched Colonel Munro on the arm.

"Father, could you stop the buggy for a moment. I have something here for Rosa's little sister."

Colonel Munro flushed and set his teeth.

"This has to stop Amy. What is it this time?"

"Cough medicine, father. I called to see little Tina when I was out riding this morning. She's really sick. We must try to help her."

Colonel Munro stopped the buggy, but he was frowning deeply, and looking furious.

"We'll say no more about this now, go ahead, but I expect you to be back in two minutes."

He pulled his fob watch out of his breeches' pocket, and stared at it as I handed Amy down from the buggy.

"Wait here Mr Wells," she said, "they'll be frightened if they see you too."

With that she slipped into one of the cabins. I stood waiting for her as Colonel Munro sat angrily in the buggy. Soon she came out, and I handed her back up again.

"Thank you father," she said.

Colonel Munro made no reply, but whipped up the horse and we set off back towards the house. When we were back, Amy went on ahead to Sandy Plains to help her sister prepare for the evening.

Mr Blair and I went over to the Scott plantation with the Munros in their carriage in the late afternoon. Louise Scott lived with her parents-in-law. She was expecting her first child, and she was full of the preparations for the longed-for first grandchild of both sets of parents. James was the only child of Mr and Mrs Scott, and they were torn between the happiness surrounding the expected birth, and their worry about James in the army. Before dinner Louise offered to show me round their house, which gave us the opportunity to talk. She was a much more high-spirited and light-hearted person than Amy, and she found the idea of my semi-secret relationship with Amy very thrilling. As we talked I found myself liking her more and more. Soon we were exchanging confidences.

"Amy has told me all about you, Mr Wells," she said breathlessly, "and I think that it is all very exciting, have you told my parents anything yet?"

"No," I replied, "there's nothing formal between us, although I would like there to be. If Amy accepts me, I'll talk to Colonel Munro then."

"Well I declare, you are mighty slow. James and I decided to marry in a couple of weeks! Full speed ahead Mr Wells!"

"Mrs Scott, Amy and I have only met twice! We've written to each other often, it's true, but that's not the same. Do you think Amy would accept me?"

"Well you are very handsome Mr Wells, certainly that part of

115

what she told me was true. She says that you have changed. You have become more serious and more like the man of destiny. Test your destiny, try asking her!"

"I will," I said, "if she accepts me, do you think your parents will approve?"

"It's my father you have to worry about, he makes the decisions at Marion! But why should he object, surely anyone would want a handsome pirate like you for a son-in-law?"

I could see that I was going to get no serious advice from Louise, so I didn't ask her any more about it. At dinner the Scotts were full of questions about blockade running, which they seemed to find very exciting and glamorous. I answered their questions as best I could, and I tried to make our enterprises sound rather more commercial and less adventurous.

The dinner was all that Mr Blair had expected. First they gave us a beautifully cooked river fish, and this was followed in quick succession by duck with olives, supreme of chicken, oysters, salad and a delicious fruit compote with cream. Mr Blair ate largely in silence, relishing every mouthful. All through the meal the questions from the others continued; to change the subject, I turned to Mr Scott.

"Surely you must have heard enough about blockade running, perhaps you can tell me what it's like running a plantation in wartime, Mr Scott."

"We do not have the same excitements as you, thank God," he said, "our problem is selling the cotton once we have grown it. I can understand the 'King Cotton' policy, but if it goes on like this, there will *be* no plantations when we have won the war."

Colonel Munro was frowning.

"Our government has good reason for the policy, Henry. We need to bring Britain and France onto our side. The 'King Cotton' policy is the best way to do it."

"What do you think Mr Wells?" asked Scott, "you were in London when the policy was introduced, do you think it will work?"

This question put me in an awkward position, as I was inclined to agree with Mr Scott, but I didn't want to find myself in conflict with Colonel Munro. I tried to answer as diplomatically as I could.

"There is no doubt that the 'King Cotton' policy is having its effect. The cotton mills in the north of England are suffering badly, and that's putting pressure on our government."

"You see Henry!" interjected Colonel Munro, "I saw Breckinridge at Shiloh, and he told me the same thing."

"But I think Palmerston finds himself in a quandary," I continued, "he can't be sure which side will win, and he doesn't want to back the wrong horse. It may be easy to see the course of events from this side of the Atlantic, but it isn't so easy in London."

"But after all our victories," shouted Munro, thumping the table, "surely Lord Palmerston must see that the South will win. The Yankees have no generals to match Lee and Jackson. The result is inevitable!"

"We all believe and hope that we will win," said Scott, "and we are giving everything that we can to ensure that it happens. But I am interested to know what our British guest thinks, and maybe that will shed some light on whether the 'King Cotton' policy will work."

I could not help looking at Mr Blair, who had given me such a different view of the war a week previously. He looked down at his plate. Slowly I answered.

"I wish I knew what to think, Mr Scott. I really don't know enough about the campaigns to know how events will unfold. For my part I will do my best to bring munitions and military supplies in on Mr Pembroke's ships, and I fervently hope that the South will prevail."

I paused.

"But perhaps you can give me a little notice of the date of the final victory so I can sell the ships before they lose their value."

They all laughed, even Colonel Munro, and the crisis had passed. The conversation moved on to lighter matters, and soon the evening came to a close.

The following morning was taken up with a service at the local church. I still hadn't had any time alone with Amy except that brief moment in my room. When we were back from church, we all stood in the hall and I went over to her.

"Can we walk down to the river? We saw the landing stage yesterday - wouldn't it be pleasant to sit down there on the riverbank?"

She agreed, and we made our excuses to her parents. We started to walk towards the river. As soon as we were out of sight of the house I put my arm round her waist, and as we walked she turned and looked up into my eyes. Perhaps I should have delayed, but I stopped and turned to her.

"I can't wait any longer to ask you, I love you so much, and I want you to be my wife. I am not a rich man like your father, but I am doing well with the blockade running business. We could get married here, and then you could come and live with me in Nassau until the war is over. My career would take me back to London then, would you like to live there? Will you marry me?"

"Oh Tom," she said, "of course I want to marry you, I have been longing for this moment. If my parents agree, I would love to come to Nassau and then live in London. I want to be where you are."

We kissed and strolled on down to the river, where we sat in complete happiness watching the water go by. I turned to look into Amy's eyes, my heart was filled with love for her, and my head with dreams of our happy future together. But then as we talked about that future we realised that the next hurdle must be crossed. We had to go back to the house to seek Colonel Munro's permission to marry. We walked back up the hill to the plantation house holding hands. We were both worried about Colonel Munro's reaction, but Amy seemed confident that he would put her happiness first. She thought that I had made a good impression on her parents. As we came into the house the colonel was crossing the hall. I asked him if I could have a word with him in private, and he led the way to the library. He sat down at his big desk, and gestured to a chair.

"Take a seat Mr Wells, what would you like to talk to me about?"

I composed myself as best I could.

"Sir, you know that I met Miss Munro in London. We formed an attachment there. We have been writing to each other over the last two years."

He nodded.

"Now that we have seen each other again," I continued, "we have found that our attachment has deepened into love. We have talked about it, and we would like to have your permission to get married."

"I see," said the Colonel, "you have only met twice in your lives, and you are convinced that you want to get married."

"Yes," I said.

"May I ask you some questions?"

"Of course."

"What is your income, and do you have any capital?"

"My salary from Mr Pembroke is five hundred pounds a year, although I receive much more than that at the moment because his ships are doing well. At the end of this voyage I think I will have accumulated capital of some two thousand pounds."

"Do you consider that is enough to support yourself and my daughter?"

"I do," I said.

"May I ask about your family background? Who is your father?"

"My father is dead, but he was a clerk in a timber company in Deptford, just outside London."

"Is your mother alive, and how does she live?"

"My father left her a house in Deptford, and she lives by letting rooms to lodgers. I also support her from my salary."

"If you married Amy, where would you live?"

"We would like to live in Nassau whilst the war lasts, and then Amy wants to come with me to London."

Colonel Munro was silent for a moment, and then he looked at me grimly.

"Mr Wells, my wife and I like you, and we admire your courageous actions on behalf of the Southern Cause, but what you are proposing is impossible."

"You want to marry Amy and take her through a dangerous blockade to Nassau. She would stay there, at risk from the yellow fever, whilst you run back and forth through the same dangerous blockade, making your fortune. Then if all this went well you would go back to London, hoping that your career would continue

119

to prosper. You have no family means, and so there would be risk to Amy there too."

"On top of that," he continued, "there is your social position. Our plans for Amy are that she will marry a Southern gentleman – not an English adventurer. She has had an offer from our cousin Major Hamilton Douglas. He comes from South Carolina. We consider him to be an ideal match for Amy. It is our wish that she should accept him."

He paused, and I started to speak, but he held up his hand to stop me.

"Have you considered *this*?" he went on, with a stern look in his fierce eyes, "Amy has a soft heart, and she wants to help anyone in trouble – to my cost on this plantation I might add! Is that the reason she wants to marry you? Does she feel sorry for you, coming from the background you do? No. What you are asking is quite impossible. My answer is no. You cannot marry Amy, and that is final."

"But Colonel Munro…"

"No," he interrupted, "that is my final answer. Now can you please find my daughter, and ask her to come here and see me. You are still our guest, and I am pleased that you are staying until Monday. I am sorry that my answer is an unhappy one for you. You can be a friend to our family, but that is all."

I was shattered, and I walked in a daze out of the room. Amy was waiting nearby and she came hurrying up. She could see from my face that the interview had not gone well.

"His answer is no?" she asked.

"Yes, and he had his reasons," I said gloomily, "but he wants to tell you them himself. I'll wait for you on the porch."

I walked with her to the library, opened the door for her, and then walked out to the porch. All my dreams had been shattered, and I sat numbly looking out over the plantation. It felt like a bereavement, and I was taken back to the terrible moments when, as a child, I had been told of my father's death. A few minutes later Amy joined me on the porch, and we walked aimlessly towards the river again. She was crying.

"Tom, I tried everything to make him change his mind, but I

could not move him. He explained his reasons, but my love is stronger than those reasons. I so desperately wanted to marry you Tom, despite all the dangers."

"Amy, your father told me that he thought you want to marry me because you feel sorry for me, is this true?"

"No Tom, how can he say that? I wanted to marry you because you are you, and I love you – not for any other reason."

"He says he wants you to marry your cousin, Major Douglas…"

"I won't do it," Amy interrupted in a low determined voice, "I have been to their plantation and I know how he treats his slaves. I could never live like that. Father likes him because he sees him as like-minded, and he's rich too…"

Amy's sweet face had taken on a dark, almost bitter look, and I felt I could ask her no more questions about her cousin.

"Do you think there is any chance your father could change his mind about us?"

"No, I'm afraid not," she said, sadly.

We had reached the river, and we sat down on the edge of the Marion landing stage, looking at the water. There were tears on Amy's cheeks.

"I have never seen my father more definite," she continued, "getting married was a wonderful dream, but I'm afraid we must forget it now. Will you stay my friend Tom?"

"Amy, of course I'll always be your friend, but I just can't accept that I'll never marry you."

She tearfully explained that although she felt the same way towards me, she would never cross her parents on something as serious as this. We went round and round the subject, but the answer was always the same. We agreed that we would go on writing to each other.

"Write to me at my sister's house," she said, "send the letters addressed to her. I will write to you at my uncle's. It's all we can do Tom."

We kissed and clung to each other for a few more moments, and then we went sadly back to the house.

Later that afternoon it was clear that Mrs Munro and Mr Blair knew what had happened, and we all talked bravely during dinner about subjects of no consequence. Eventually the strain proved too much for Amy, who burst into tears and ran up to her room. Her mother followed. We all met again for supper, but the evening broke up in sombre silence.

The following day as Mr Blair and I prepared to get into the buggy, the Munros said their goodbyes. Amy shook my hand tearfully, and in doing so, slipped me a small note. I read it on the cotton barge going back down to Wilmington.

Tom, I will love you always, your Amy.

Mr Blair had settled his business in Fayetteville quickly, and we took our places on the steamboat. The journey back to Wilmington seemed interminable to me. I was a poor companion to Angus Blair, as I spent much of the journey turning over in my mind the events of the last few days. At one moment I had had the sweetness of Amy's acceptance, and then almost immediately the bitterness of her father's rejection of our suit. I wondered what I could have said that would have persuaded Colonel Munro to a different decision. Perhaps he would have thought differently if I had said that we would live in Wilmington or Charleston, or that I would give up blockade running. But there would still have been the objection to my background, and I needed to prove that my financial position would be adequate. Finally I could contain my thoughts no longer, and I posed my questions directly to Angus Blair. We were seated at the table in the saloon, eating the inevitable pork and beans. I opened the conversation as Blair pushed his plate away in disgust.

"Did Colonel Munro tell you that he had forbidden our engagement?"

"He did I am afraid Mr Wells. A most unfortunate outcome for you, I must say."

"And he told you the reasons?"

"Yes he did, my dear fellow. He felt that the life you were offering for Amy posed too much risk, and I suppose you could say that, objectively speaking, he is right. There is also this fellow Hamilton Douglas who keeps renewing his offer for Amy – it seems that he will not accept her rejection of his suit. But I wonder whether perhaps there was another reason. I am sure that Colonel Munro is worried about my sister being left alone at the plantation whilst he's away serving with the army. With the loss of Preston and the worry about Jack, she desperately needs companionship. Did he mention that?"

"No," I said, "I suppose he thought that his other arguments were stronger. Despite everything he said, Amy and I still yearn to get married. I wonder if it would have made any difference if we had offered to live in Wilmington?"

"I really do not think so. Amy spoke to me this morning and she asked the same question – I am afraid I could offer no real comfort. She is unhappy, and I hate to see that ... I did agree to accept her letters for you."

"Thank you" I said.

"I hope and trust that the Munros have no real objection to you just as a friend to Amy. I am sure they must like you. The main problem is the risky life you are offering. My advice is to wait until circumstances change, and that may happen sooner than you think. The war is changing everything ... I can only hope that it changes the wretched food they provide on these boats," he added, with a scowl at his discarded plate.

From Wilmington I took the train back to Charleston. Fortunately most of the troop movements seemed to be in the other direction, and the train was not so crowded. I used my last bottle of brandy to secure a place in the conductor's car, and the journey wasn't too unpleasant. In Charleston I found that the *Clara* had been repaired and loaded. Mansell was anxious to set sail for Nassau.

Our voyage was uneventful, but for me it was taken up with bitter thoughts about my failure to obtain Amy's hand. Colonel Munro's message was clear enough. I would never marry her.

Chapter Nine
A Visit to Herr Kohler

When we arrived back in Nassau in early March 1863 there was a note from Tobias Johnson waiting for me at the hotel. He told me that our office in East Street was ready, and he was hoping to see me. After breakfast I went down there.

Johnson was sitting at his desk in the outer office. He was a quiet man of about thirty, soberly dressed. He was English, and he had moved to Nassau with his family to join a shipping firm, which had then gone bankrupt. He seemed efficient, but unimaginative. He rose to greet me, and I explained the reasons for our delay. He expressed his sympathy for the loss of our two crewmembers. Then we went though all the critical business issues. Finally he gestured to the office.

"I hope you are pleased with the offices, Mr Wells," he said, "Herr Kohler has accomplished all that he promised, and I think it is very satisfactory."

He was eager to show me round, and I was indeed very satisfied with the offices and the rooms above. Our fat Bavarian landlord had met all his commitments. When we got back downstairs again, we sat in the front office to talk.

"I moved into this office two weeks ago," said Johnson, "and all we need now is to find servants to make everything comfortable for you upstairs."

"I'll contact Herr Kohler for that," I responded.

We then continued with the business affairs that had collected whilst I had been away. Johnson had dealt satisfactorily with the more simple matters, but he had been reluctant to tackle any thorny issues. Profits were accumulating rapidly for Mr Pembroke, we were able to send him a very optimistic report on the state of the business. There would now be a period of three weeks before the next runs could be made in moonless conditions. Those weeks would be filled with a multitude of activities from the sale and purchase of cargoes to the repair and maintenance of the ships. I also had to work with the captains on ships' crews and obtaining pilots.

I was glad that the day-to-day responsibility for the *Clara's* crew was not mine whilst they were in port. With their pay jingling in their pockets they were soon getting into trouble, but Mansell was the right man to sort them out. Usually the problem was just drunkenness or women, but some got into fights with the locals and other crews, and one of the *Clara's* firemen was seriously wounded in a knife fight. Mansell frequently had to intervene with the Nassau authorities to keep his crew out of jail.

We wanted to progress our case against our chief engineer, Mr McNab. We were soon disappointed to discover that the Nassau authorities had taken a lenient view of his misdemeanours. They had decided that the evidence against him was slight; they had accepted his undertaking that he would never again take a position on a blockade-running ship, and they settled the matter by expelling him from the islands. He had taken passage on a mail ship for Liverpool. I was annoyed, as I felt that he could still damage us. I wrote to Mr Pembroke telling him of my anxieties, but I realised that there was nothing further I could do about it.

I decided to move immediately into the house in East Street, and Harry Mansell joined me there. A maid and a cook were found. The cook was the less successful of the two, but we were comfortable enough. I resumed my swimming lessons with Harry in the evenings, and we flung ourselves into the feverish social activities in Nassau. The more formal side centred on Government House, but there were also wild nights with other blockade-runners and the merchants who were dealing with us. Ours was a hazardous occupation, and it wasn't always just the ordinary seamen and firemen who drank long into the night. I had arrived in Nassau unaccustomed to liquor, but I'm afraid that soon I was almost an old hand.

We were also continuing with the hard and dangerous voyages we had to undertake – the constant perilous shuttling between Nassau, Charleston and Wilmington. I was still frustrated and sad from my failure to persuade Colonel Munro to allow my engagement to Amy. I didn't undertake every voyage, but when I went to Wilmington I collected letters from her, and posted letters back. Her letters were loving, and even passionate, but they held no comfort that our marriage might be accepted. Colonel Munro was back with Lee on his campaign through Virginia and up into the Northern States. Jack was still incarcerated in Fort Lafayette. Amy had received yet another letter from Major Douglas trying to persuade her to marry him. He was due to visit Fayetteville in May, and he said that he was going to call at Marion. I began to worry that perhaps Amy might eventually be persuaded to change her mind. Even though it seemed that I was not destined to marry her myself, I still could not bear the thought of Amy marrying another.

The Yankee navy was expanding its fleet of blockading vessels, and our task became increasingly difficult. In March 1863 we suffered the loss of the *Granite City* – captured by the USS *Tioga* off Eleuthera Island in the Northeast Providence Channel. The *Granite City* had only achieved two successful runs, but her profits from those two voyages had at least paid for the ship. Under Mansell's command the *Clara* completed successful runs, as did the *Flora* and the *Calypso*. The changing fortunes of our blockade running enterprise increased the challenges of the commercial side of the business. Sometimes we had a surplus of goods shipped out for us from London by Mr Pembroke, and we were auctioning goods, or selling them directly to the agents for other shipowners. Then suddenly the situation would reverse, and we were scrambling to buy. Blair and Somerville handled the trade in Wilmington and Charleston very skilfully, so I tended to concentrate my efforts on Nassau.

At the end of April I had a visit from Herr Kohler at our East Street offices. The weather was warm, and he was sweating heavily.

"Please be seated Herr Kohler," I said, "we are very happy with this house. I apologise for doubting that it would be completed on time. What can I do for you?"

"Ja, Mr Wells, the house is nice. Ze men werked hard und all is good," he answered, mopping his brow, "but I have a request for you. Ziss house is one of five I haff here in Nassau."

He paused to pick up his straw hat and fan his face with it.

"My wife and I, we have decided to leave ze islands. Zere is the

126

sickness in the sommer."

"You mean the yellow fever?"

"Ja. Und my wife she worries so. Ja, we will move back to München, you call it Munich I think."

"How can I help?" I asked. "As you know, we have a contract for three months with extensions and we have just exercised the first one through our lawyer, Mr Dupont. Is that the difficulty?"

"Nein. My question to you is, perhaps you have an interest to buy ze house? I would a good price make for you."

"I would have to think about that," I said, "but we are a shipping business, I doubt whether the owner would wish to invest in houses. If you'll forgive me for saying so, this is all very sudden; we only took the lease of the house three months ago."

Herr Kohler looked down at his boots. Then he looked up again.

"Ja, I understand your question. But my wife and I we haff decided. Tomorrow evening perhaps you would come to my house? We talk more, and maybe I convince you, Ja? My cook he is good, we will a fine evening make."

I started to find reasons why tomorrow evening might be difficult, but he would accept no excuses.

"Nein, you will come, I send my carriage for you at five."

Later in the day, when we were in our sitting room waiting to go out for the evening, I mentioned to Harry Mansell my engagement to visit Herr Kohler the following afternoon.

"If Kohler's cook is as good as he says," Mansell exclaimed, laughing, "perhaps that explains why he's as fat as a pig. You won't regret it; you'll wallow in Bavarian sausage and beer. Frau Kohler is no doubt equally huge. They probably want to get back to Europe while there's a ship strong enough to take them."

"But my evening was already planned," I said, "I can't believe I allowed that Bavarian lump of lard to talk me into going to him for dinner instead."

"No, an evening with Herr Kohler is too good to miss. Perhaps he intends to drug your sausage, and make you sign up to buy all his property. You're in for a fine evening my friend. I envy you. If I wasn't heading for Wilmington on the good ship *Clara* tomorrow, I'd ask to come with you."

The next day was hectic, but there was still time for a swim with Mansell before he left that evening. I was now swimming reasonably well, and we swam quite long distances in the beautiful clear water. We came back from Hog Island to the Nassau quayside, and watched the Negro boys diving for copper coins. Mansell headed for the ship, and I wandered back through the town to East Street, resisting the offers from street sellers eager to sell me anything from fruit to a tarantula in a jar. I was only just changed when Kohler's carriage arrived. A Negro servant opened the door for me, and we set off along the coast to the west. I asked the coachman how far we were travelling.

"Further along a bit, Massa."

It had been a fine day and the drive was beautiful. We were moving towards the late afternoon sun, which bathed the coast in a delicate yellowy orange light. There was a faint breeze, and the temperature was pleasant. As we passed through the residential part of town I was curious to see the wide, low, limestone houses with their piazzas and walled gardens. I also noticed again that none of the houses had chimneys, and I asked the Negro driver about this. He laughed.

"No need for chimneys here, sah! It's warm in the winter."

As the carriage clip-clopped through the shaded, gracious streets, I was feeling soothed and almost somnolent by the time we reached Herr Kohler's house. It was a fine limestone villa overlooking the sea. As we reached the house, Kohler himself came out onto the veranda. He was smiling happily.

"Ah! Mr Wells, velcome. Come inside to meet my wife."

He was smartly dressed in an enormous frock coat. He led the way into the house.

The shutters were partly closed. The room was shady compared to the brilliance of the light outside. I could see the slight, elegant figure of a woman standing at the back of the drawing room. This was not the fat hausfrau I had been expecting.

"Mr Wells, I introduce my wife Frau Kohler. We ver married just three months ago. You are one of our first guests."

"Liebling, this is Mr Wells."

As she came forward I could see shock on her face – she was

Susan from Mrs Dalrymple's. We both stopped and stared at one another.

"Ja, ja, shake hands," said Kohler, "no shyness please."

I recovered myself and walked forward to shake Susan's hand.

"Delighted to make your acquaintance, Frau Kohler," I said, "please forgive me for speaking English, I'm afraid Herr Kohler will have to translate for us."

A grateful look came into Susan's beautiful brown eyes.

"No, no," said Kohler, "she speaks English. She comes from zese islands. Now she will learn German, ja mein Liebling?"

"I am right pleased to meet you Mr Wells," she said in the attractive lilting accent of the islands, "would you like to sit down?"

There was silence in the room for a moment as we settled into comfortable cane chairs. I knew I should be trying to start the conversation, but all I could think about was the delights of the last occasion I had been with her. I pulled myself together and fell back onto the normal social formula.

"What a charming house this is. You must get wonderful views Frau Kohler."

"Yes, we are very lucky," said Susan, with a smile towards her husband, "but can we offer you some refreshmen'?"

Her question took me back to that same evening, and I blushed. Susan saw my confusion, and I could see an amused glint in her eyes under her long lashes. I stood up and walked to the window.

"Yes, I would like something cool. You must see plenty of activity from ships like ours from your house, Herr Kohler."

"Ya, over ze last two years ze traffic is enormous, but it waxes und wanes with ze moon, is that not so Mr Wells? But please to sit."

I came over from the window and took my seat again.

"Yes," I said, "the blockade-runners have their best chance on moonless nights. You'll have seen plenty of ships over the last few days."

"So you're a blockade-runner Mr Wells?" asked Susan.

"Well, I'm an agent for an Englishman who runs ships through the blockade. Sometimes I travel as supercargo on a ship called the

129

Clara."

So the conversation started, and gradually the atmosphere became more comfortable. A servant brought drinks, and we could hear the noise of dinner being prepared. Judging by the delicious aromas coming from the kitchen, we would soon be eating something more exciting than Bavarian sausage. As the sun sank in the sky the room took on a different appearance in the changing light. We could see the beautiful colours of the sunset through the windows on the westerly side of the house. Herr Kohler's admiring eyes looked frequently towards his wife, and I have to admit that she looked lovely as she sat in her chair or as she walked quietly about the room to adjust the shutters. Then there was a discreet knock at the door. A servant asked to speak to Herr Kohler, and he left the room. Susan and I sat in silence for a moment. Then Kohler returned.

"Please forgive me," he said, "zere is a matter with which I must deal. I shall be no longer than halve an hour. We shall eat soon after six, Ja? You will look after our guest my Liebling?"

He bowed and left.

"What calls Herr Kohler away at this hour?" I asked.

"Oh, often he gets call' away in the evening. He must deal with his businesses you see. But we're only just on the edge of town, he'll be back soon."

As she said this, we could hear the sound of the carriage door closing, and the grinding of the carriage wheels on the gravel as it turned out onto the road towards Nassau.

I was wondering how Susan had come to be married to Kohler. Did he know about her exotic past? She was looking at me speculatively.

"Perhaps you are married too? Mrs Dalrymple said that you would be married soon."

She said this with a charming and confidential look. I was surprised at the mention of her old employer, but I felt more comfortable now that Susan's previous life would not be an unspoken secret in our conversation.

"Why did she think that? I suppose my friend Harry Mansell must have said something about it. Well I had hoped so, but now it

130

isn't going to happen."

"You must be very disappointed, Mr Wells."

I found myself telling the story of how I had met Amy, how we had stayed in touch by letter, and the agonising disappointment of Colonel Munro's refusal of our engagement. I could see sympathy in Susan's lovely brown eyes.

"She is always in my thoughts, but now it seems hopeless."

"Always in your thoughts..." said Susan, with an amused smile, "what am I suppose' to think about that?"

I blushed in some confusion. I was wondering why I was the one who was embarrassed. Apart from her initial hesitation, Susan seemed the more relaxed of the two of us.

She leant forward confidentially, and I couldn't help glancing at the swell of her bosom, partly revealed as she moved forward. She smiled as she saw the direction of my glance, but she didn't move back.

"Tom... may I still call you that? Thank you for thinking so quickly when you came in. I was dreading a situation like this. Hans he has tol' you that we mean to move to Munich. It's for me. I can' bear the thought of meeting one of the men who used to know me when I am with dear Hans."

"Yes, I can understand that."

"You are wondering how this all came about, aren't you?"

"Well, yes," I said.

She hesitated.

"Perhaps I shouldn' tell you, but I think I must."

She was looking embarrassed, but she looked charming in her confusion. I felt my blood stirring as it had that night in Mackey Street. Susan looked searchingly into my eyes as she told her story. It was as if she was trying to detect how I was reacting to what she was saying. But she had no need to be concerned. As her story developed I was touched and I felt deep sympathy for her.

"Hans was a bachelor when he came to the islands from Munich. He work hard, and he make money. Perhaps the fac' that he is rather stout, and that... well he isn't English, that didn' help him here. He can be impatient too. People don' see what a nice nature he has, underneath.

"Anyway he want' to marry, but he didn' find anyone. So he start' coming to Mrs Dalrymple. She's expensive, but he is rich now. The other girls they say he was no good in bed. But then he came to me, and he was happy. He was visiting often, and he always ask' for me. Then Mrs Dalrymple she came to me – the night after you came, Tom."

Susan looked up into my eyes with a sad, sweet expression.

"She said 'Mr Kohler, he is crazy about you, he wan' to marry you'. Well, all the girls dream for that. Maybe Hans is not handsome, but he is kind, and he is rich. How could I refuse?"

"Maybe if you had waited, someone younger might have wanted to marry you,"

She smiled.

"Would *you* have married me Tom?"

I looked down in confusion.

"What a question Susan – you know about Amy, how could I?"

"All the young ones have an Amy. I don' blame you Tom, you came for fun, not for marriage."

"So you said yes to Herr Kohler?"

She nodded.

"He pay my debt to Mrs Dalrymple. Hans paid for me to stay in Mrs Dalrymple's own house for a week, and then we marry. It's everything I dream for Tom. Only we can' stay here, surely you can see that?"

"Yes I can see that, and I can understand why you want to move quickly. How long had you been at Mackey Street?"

"You wan' to know how many men could recognise me? You are so polite Tom! Well I hadn' been there long, only a month; twenty men, that was all."

Once again there was silence. I was puzzled as I remembered Mrs Dalrymple saying it had been three months, but I said nothing. This was just one of many questions in my mind. As our talk became more and more confidential, so Susan leaned closer to me, and her attractions were blurring my senses. Her beautiful face shone in the early evening light. As she moved closer the outlines of her sensual body were clear through her long gown. It didn't seem as though she was trying to please me, she was only trying to explain her situation and perhaps make me feel sympathy for her. But the effect was the same – she was still the ravishingly attractive Susan of my night at Mrs Dalrymple's.

She gave me a long quizzical look.

"You wan' to know how I came to be at Mackey Street, don' you Tom?"

"Yes I do," I said, "but I don't see why you should tell me."

She paused again for a moment before she answered me.

"I was born into a happy family Tom, but the yellow fever came. My father he work in an office in Freeport, he was white, but my mother was half Negro. We were poor, but our life was fine. When I was twelve they got sick, I nursed them but they died from the yellow fever – my brother too."

"I'm so sorry, Susan,"

"That was the end of everything, and the priest he sen' me to the orphanage here in Nassau – we had no family in Gran' Bahama. Well at fifteen the girls had to leave and find work. I was sewing shirts in a small tailor's shop, and then the tailor closed and there was no more work. I got into debt trying to pay my rent.

"I know I was pretty, because men used to look at me, and try to take advantage of me. But I didn' let them. Then Mrs Dalrymple saw me in the street one day, and invited me to see her in Mackey Street. I met the other girls, and they tol' me what a good life it was. No more worry; no more hunger, nice clothes and maybe one day one of the clients would take a real fancy to me. Mrs Dalrymple said she would lend me the money to pay my debt. It was so hard to decide Tom."

I nodded.

"Well, that was how it happened. Do you despise me?"

"No," I said, "and if Herr Kohler is as kind as you say, then maybe your story really does have a happy ending."

"He is a wonderful man, and I so want to make him happy. He wan' a child, a son – that's his dream."

She looked at me softly.

"But what about you Tom, are you happy here in Nassau? Are you living at the Royal Victoria?"

"No, we've taken number 10, East Street, it belongs to Herr

Kohler. But I'm busy enough. Sometimes we get quiet periods, but most of the time I'm on board ship or managing the cargoes."

Susan was still looking at me appealingly, as if she was about to say something, but she was hesitating. Then we could hear the sound of a carriage in the distance, and a look of urgency came into her brown eyes.

"Tom…"

"Yes?"

"Could I come and see you in East Street? Would there be anyone else there? I have some business I would like to discuss with you. Tomorrow afternoon?"

I thought for a moment.

"Mansell's away … if you came at four, I could make sure nobody else was there."

"Thank you Tom," she said softly.

We could hear the sound of the carriage pulling up in the drive. Susan and I moved away from each other. We heard Herr Kohler talking to the servants and then he came waddling in through the door.

"Ja, they call me for nothing, but since I am a fool I go anyway. The dinner she is prepared. We eat now, Ja?"

Then the three of us sat down to a gargantuan but delicious dinner. Harry's foreboding of a dinner of sausage and beer was unfounded. The Kohler's cook specialised in dishes using the wonderful fish from the island – turbot, mutton fish and morgate. Susan ate sparingly, but Herr Kohler and I did justice to the fine fare. I was hungry after my long swim, and it seemed that Kohler was always hungry. As we ate, I occasionally caught a confiding affectionate look from Susan.

After dinner Kohler suggested that he and I should smoke a cigar on the terrace before joining Susan in the drawing room, and we walked outside. The sun had now set, it was dark, but the temperature was pleasant. The night sky was a glittering canopy of stars. For a moment we just stood and puffed at our cigars, then Kohler grasped my arm in one of his fat hands.

"Now, you have eaten well, Ja?" he said, "so we talk about my properties in Nassau."

"Herr Kohler," I said, "I have had a wonderful evening, and I am very honoured to have had the chance to meet Frau Kohler. I have thought about your idea, and I am sure that we are the wrong firm to talk to about purchasing your property. It is true that we have made money through blockade running, but when the war ends we will leave Nassau. So will the other blockade-runners, then the Nassau property boom will be over.

"We don't need more property, but there are some other firms that do. I would be happy to introduce you to one or two of my friends who are expanding their businesses and are desperate to find more space."

"So you vill not invest, und that is final?"

"Yes, I'm afraid so."

Herr Kohler laughed, and his whole body shook. Tears streamed down his cheeks, and he mopped his eyes with his handkerchief.

"You are amused at my decision?" I asked.

He pulled himself together, mopping his eyes again.

"Nein, nein, I respect your decision Mr Wells. You have right, buying my houses would not be a good decision for you. I think you vill do well here. But I accept your offer. I have to travel for the next few days, but when I am back, introduce me to your foolish friends who want to buy my property!"

We finished our cigars and went back inside. Soon it was time to leave. It had been a strange evening, but after the initial shock I had been happy to see Susan again. The dinner had been delicious. I told them how grateful I was for an excellent evening.

"Nein, the pleasure was ours, ja mein Liebling?"

"Yes, thank you for coming Mr Wells," said Susan, "I am so please' to meet a business friend of Hans."

She gave me a charming smile.

Herr Kohler called his carriage. Soon his coachman was taking me back towards Nassua. As we clip-clopped our way to East Street I thought about the unexpectedly pleasant evening. I was also fascinated to know what on earth Susan's business proposition could be. No matter how much I speculated, no obvious answer came to mind.

The following morning I was in the office at seven as usual. I had been expecting a quiet day, but there was mail from England, including a letter from Mr Pembroke. It was full of detailed instructions on the business, but most important was a request for me to return to London, taking the mail steamer within the month:

'I have decided to review our operations in Nassau, and I would like you to be present. Of particular interest to me is the type of vessel we should now be employing. Please discuss this with Mansell and the other ships' captains. Also prepare a full statement of our accounts. When our review is complete, I will be asking you to return to Nassau to continue your excellent work.'

It was likely to be anything up to a month before I could sit with Mansell and at least one of the other captains to seek their views, but I calculated that I could take the mail ship by the first week of June. It was already hot and humid in Nassau, and in some ways I was grateful for the prospect of a trip to England to avoid some of the worst of the summer's heat. I spent the rest of the day starting to put together some of the information we would be needing. Regular as clockwork, at half past three, Johnson left to spend the rest of the afternoon with his young family.

I started to put away my papers, and once again I was turning over in my mind Susan's strange request. The more I thought about it, the more pleased I was to have seen Susan, and her attractions seemed to have increased for me over the intervening months. The imminent prospect of seeing her again was beguiling.

At four o'clock there was a knock at the office door. I opened the door myself, and outside there was the veiled figure of a smartly dressed woman.

"May I come in Tom?" It was Susan.

We went through into the inner office. She lifted her veil and looked nervously round. It was a hot day, and she was wearing a lace dress, which clung charmingly to her figure. The slightly nervous look on her face seemed to enhance her appeal. She was looking lovely.

"Will we be disturb'?" she asked.

"No. Our clerk, Mr Johnson, has finished for the day. I share the house with Captain Mansell, but he is on his way to Wilmington. Our two servants are upstairs, and they won't come down here."

"Thank you, Tom."

I was expecting Susan to state what her business was, but she was looking at me speculatively, just as she had the previous evening.

"When do you think you will be leaving New Providence?" I asked, "I shall be sorry to see you go; although I may be gone before you. I have to travel to London at the end of the month."

"Hans has difficulty to sell his houses, but we leave in June I think, or maybe July. He lef' this morning to go to Freeport to settle his businesses there. He will be back in three weeks."

"What can I do for you Susan?" I asked, "what was the business you wanted to discuss with me?"

"Well it wasn't business exactly," she said, looking downwards and moving awkwardly in her chair. With the movement, the curves of her delicious body were outlined through the tight lace of her dress. It was low cut. As she leaned forward to talk more intimately, once again I could see the perfect figure I remembered from our night in Mackey Street and I felt a surge of desire for her.

"It's a very difficult thing. Hans and I have been married for three months now. I tol' you that Hans wan's a child, and so do I of course. But the more he wan's, the less it works with me. You understan'?"

"No, Susan."

"The act of love, it isn't working, and the more he wan' the less it works. He get very frustrated with himself, and with me. I am so worried."

"But what has this got to do with me Susan, I'm not a doctor."

"Hans is a proud man, he won' see a doctor."

She paused again and looked appealingly at me.

"If we had a child, I'm sure he would be fine again, it's because he worries so much … oh Tom, mus' I say it? You can help me, you can father the child and Hans will never know. We will be in Munich and you will be here. You tol' me you cannot marry Amy, please help me!"

"Susan!" I cried, "I can't believe I'm hearing this. You love Hans,

137

surely you don't want to be unfaithful to him?"

"It's the only answer," she said, and looked into my eyes with sweet appeal.

I was stunned. One minute I had been looking at Susan like a child gazing at sweets through a sweetshop window, knowing that they were unobtainable. The next moment I was being invited in to the shop to help myself. But how should I react? I was often accused of taking decisions too quickly, but this time I was faced by a dilemma I found hard to resolve. Susan's request was extremely enticing, and it seemed that no one would be harmed if I were to accept. But I had been brought up to respect the institution of marriage, and adultery was a sin I knew I should not commit. Additionally, although Colonel Munro had forbidden our marriage, I was as much in love with Amy as ever. Surely this would be a betrayal.

As these thoughts turned in my mind I was looking at Susan, and the ironic side of her proposal struck me. I smiled.

"Why are you smiling, Tom?"

"I was thinking that I should ask you to pay me. Then it *would* be a matter of business, and our roles would be completely reversed from the first time we met..."

She smiled too.

"So you'll do it?"

"No Susan, I can't make up my mind in two moments, I think we should both have time to think it over. Can you come at the same time tomorrow? Let's both make our decision then..."

"If you say so Tom."

She stood up slowly and turned as if to go out, and once again the sinuous movements of her body were an invitation to paradise. Then she turned back and smiled alluringly.

"I'll see you tomorrow, Tom. But you *will* help me won' you?"

I was weak. I suppressed my conscience and convinced myself that this temporary liaison with Susan was permissible. Amy seemed sure that her parents would never allow us to marry, and as for Susan, if she were to be believed, I was doing a favour for Hans; and why shouldn't I believe her?

The following day when she called, I told her that I accepted, and over the next three weeks she was a frequent and circumspect late afternoon caller at my East Street bachelor establishment. I confess that my guilt added spice to the affair, and it filled me with sadness when one afternoon as we were making our way into my bedroom, Susan told me that Hans was due back that evening, and she must be at their villa at seven o'clock. This would be the last time we could be together. Our lovemaking was passionate and afterwards we clung to each other for comfort in the sadness of the approaching separation. We fell into a deep sleep. Suddenly I was woken by Susan shaking my arm.

"Tom, Tom, I fell asleep, what time is it?"

It was almost dark in the room, I reached for my pocket watch and I could just see that it was nearly seven.

"Almost seven Susan. Quickly, we can get a cab from in front of the Royal Victoria."

We got dressed hurriedly, rushed out of the house and started walking quickly towards the hotel. Susan was wearing her veil.

"That was wonderful Susan, I shall never forget you. I will think of you often in your new life in Bavaria."

"Thank you Tom. I will think of you too – I hope things will change for you, and you will fin' happiness with Amy. I know we shouldn' have done it, but it was a wonderful time, and maybe it will make my dream come true."

There were barouches waiting outside the hotel, and soon after seven I dropped Susan close to her house. As the cab took me back to East Street I was convinced that this would be the last time I would see or hear from Susan. Despite my love for Amy, this second passionate episode with Susan was filling me with affection for her. Suddenly the thought of never seeing her again made me desperately sad. Her youthful beauty, her gentle trust in me, and her passionate nature made her very enticing. I longed for the chance to see her again, but realistically I knew this was not going to happen.

A few days later I was relieved to see Mansell safely back with the *Clara* after a successful run to Wilmington. We spent a feverish week finalising the accounts for Mr Pembroke, preparing cargoes for the next blockade runs, and discussing ship designs. I told

Johnson that he was to look to Mansell for advice on any difficult issues, and I briefed Harry on what to expect. It was towards the end of May 1863 when I boarded the mail steamer for England.

Chapter Ten
Austin Friars

The voyage across the Atlantic was uneventful, blessed as it was by fine summer weather. At the beginning I was still mourning my lost affair with Susan, but as we drew closer to England I put my thoughts of her to the back of my mind, and I began to enjoy the company of my fellow passengers. I was also looking forward to seeing my friends and family again, and debating with Mr Pembroke the merits of the different ship designs we had been analysing in Nassau.

The mail steamer arrived in Liverpool. I took the train to London and went immediately to my mother in Deptford. I had written to her telling of my plans to come to London, but my arrival that day was unexpected. At first she was speechless, and then:

"Tom! Tom! How you have fluttered my poor heart! How brown you are looking! You have been in the sun too much. Oh come in, come in, I just can't believe you're here. Let me look at you. You're looking stronger and more robust, what have you been doing?"

"I've been swimming, and helping out on our ships, Mother," I said.

We went in and sat down in the parlour. The house seemed smaller than I remembered, but it was wonderful to see my mother surrounded by the old familiar furniture and objects. The room was looking spruce and tidy.

"You are looking well, Mother, and the house is looking very smart."

"It's the money you have been sending Tom. I have put some away, but I have spent money on decoration. I only have one lodger now. But why are you back, Tom? There's no trouble I hope. How long will you be staying?"

I explained the request from Mr Pembroke.

"After we have looked into our business affairs in the Bahamas, he wants me to return straight away to continue to run the office there. I'm not sure how long I'll be here, but I think it will only be a few days."

"Your old room is always ready for you, Tom. Please stay as long as you can."

I spent the rest of the day with my mother, and one or two old friends came round to see us that evening. I had sent a message to the Stringer, Pembroke offices in Austin Friars saying that I would come into the office the following day.

The next morning I took the train from Deptford, and walked in the busy throng of clerks and merchants along the old familiar route over London Bridge to our office in the City of London. It was a cool, misty morning. I could hear shouts from the drivers of cabs and omnibuses, the rattle of wheels and the neighing of horses. The air was thick with the smell of horse dung and the odours of the river. I had only been away from the City for six months, but the adventures and excitements of those months made England feel almost like a foreign country to me.

When I went into the old office, David Hardcastle stood up and ran over to greet me. Soon we were shaking hands, smiling and laughing.

"Wells! Home from your travels! Burnt almost black by the sun and sturdy as a trooper! I have been following your adventures. I wish Mr Pembroke would send me out there you lucky rascal!"

"So you want an early death do you Hardcastle, stretched out and desiccated on a tropical beach, draped in a pirate flag?"

"No," he said, "mountains of gold doubloons and dusky maidens in grass skirts; but more of this later. His lordship awaits, and I think you may find that a certain very elegant gentleman is with him."

Hardcastle was referring to Mr Pembroke's partner Mr Edgar Stringer. Stringer was very much a St. James's street dandy, who had joined the partnership shortly before W.S. Lindsay had left. We were always a little puzzled by Stringer's role in the partnership. He worked much shorter hours than Mr Pembroke, and frequently disappeared to luncheon at one of his West End clubs, or to go to race meetings. We assumed that Mr Stringer was there to provide a fund of family money and contacts. He had an extensive list of wealthy and fashionable friends and acquaintances.

I went through to Mr Pembroke's office, and both of them were there. Mr Pembroke was dressed as always in the familiar outdated frock coat. His bearded face always gave an impression of a man eager to do business. Mr Stringer looked indolent. He was sleekly turned out in a new and extremely elegant coat, with an elaborate buttonhole. He wore his hair fashionably long. A cavalry moustache and side-whiskers added to his aristocratic appearance.

Mr Pembroke was up and out of his chair as soon as I came into the room, and he shook my hand.

"Welcome back, Wells," he said, "it was very good of you to come back so promptly on receipt of my letter. How come you look so well – it must be the sea voyages. How was your passage to Liverpool? Was it agreeable?"

"Yes," I replied, "far more agreeable than my previous passage. No storms, and no attacks from Yankee cruisers!"

"I'm pleased to hear it, pleased to hear it. But you must be wondering why both of us are here for this interview. Stringer has kindly offered to join me in our Southern States enterprise," he smiled towards him, "our profits have finally convinced him that it's a good business!"

"Just so," said Stringer languidly, "not only is Pembroke here making spectacular sums, but so are many of the fellows at the Baltic. You certainly seem to have the golden touch, Wells."

"We've got good ships, good captains and good crews," I said, "and apart from the capture of the *Granite City*, we've had a certain amount of luck. As far as the profits are concerned, I have brought an up-to-date set of accounts, and I think you will be satisfied with what we have done."

I handed a small folio of papers to Mr Pembroke.

"I give a summary on the first page," I said, "but all the details are given in the other sheets."

There was silence as he read the summary; then he began checking some of the details. As Pembroke worked, Mr Stringer lit a cigar and puffed elegantly, with a bored expression on his face.

"Highly satisfactory," said Pembroke eventually, and he turned to Stringer. "This bears out all I have been saying. If it's carefully managed, this is by far the best business available to us today. But you've left it late to come in!"

"We haven't all got your genius for sniffing out the best horses, Pembroke," responded Stringer, "and I have made one or two smaller investments, but I'm pleased you are letting me in."

"Thank you," said Pembroke, smiling. "Wells, with Stringer coming in we want to have another look at what we are doing. We may want to make some changes. I asked you to have a careful look at our ships. Perhaps you could tell us what you might recommend."

This was the question for which I had been preparing. I had discussed it forwards and backwards with Mansell and the others. Now I outlined our views.

"Well sir, it's difficult to avoid stating the obvious, but I'm sure we would all agree that our ships have to be quick and manoeuvrable and they have to have a relatively shallow draft. The other key consideration is their carrying capacity. We went through it all in Nassau. Can I take each point in turn?"

"Go ahead," said Pembroke.

"The Yankees have some fast ships in the blockade now. Some of them are blockade-runners they have captured and then armed. A few months ago I would have said that the fourteen knots we can squeeze out of the *Clara* was enough. I don't think it is now. Twin-screw ships are manoeuvrable, and they have the advantage that the screws are much less obtrusive than paddles, but they are just not fast enough. The *Granite City* was faster than the *Clara*, but even so McEwan got caught by the *Tioga* off Eleuthera. We all feel that paddles are the answer, and the engines should be as powerful as we can afford. Seventeen or even eighteen knots should be our target. The other benefit with paddle ships is that we can go for shallower draft."

"Are you sure that the paddle wheels aren't too vulnerable?" asked Pembroke.

"If they are in the stern they are, so they should be mid-mounted," I said, "the key is to be fast enough to get away. Once you're in range the whole ship is vulnerable, let alone the paddles."

"That's what one of the fellows at the Baltic was saying to me yesterday," said Stringer, with a wave of his cigar.

"As far as manoeuvrability is concerned," I said, "there isn't a huge difference but paddles are definitely better.

"For draft," I continued, "we felt thirteen or possibly fourteen feet is the absolute maximum. Obviously you can get more cargo space if you go deeper, but you're better going for length or breadth. With fourteen feet you can only just squeeze over the bar at Fort Fisher to get up to Wilmington.

"And that brings me onto tonnage. We are seeing more and more steamships in Nassau with a displacement tonnage of five hundred or more. That's nearly double the *Flora* or the *Clara*. The best ships achieve this by being longer, certainly more than two hundred feet. As you know, if they're too long and narrow they become unseaworthy. If you make them too wide it slows them down and they're too much of a target in a stern chase. Our view is that a ratio of length to beam of eight to one is about right."

"Very well, but what would be the ideal dimensions overall?" asked Pembroke.

"We discussed that," I said, "we felt that the best runner would be about two hundred and twenty feet long by twenty-seven in the beam. She would draw thirteen feet, and she would have mid-mounted paddles. It goes without saying that her profile should be as low as possible, and her engines should be as deep in the ship as you can put them. We made some sketches and drew up some specifications. I've got them here."

"How much cargo could she carry?" asked Pembroke.

"I think you would have to go to the shipbuilders for that calculation, but we thought that she would carry at least five hundred tons, maybe even six hundred, twice the capacity of the *Flora*. A ship of that size would only need a slightly bigger crew than the smaller ships we have now. Wages are so high, our profits are squeezed on the smaller ships."

Until then, Mr Stringer had not shown tremendous interest in what I had been saying; now he leant forward and started to do some calculations on a piece of paper. Pembroke and I sat in silence as he scratched away with a pencil in a gold pencil case, which he

145

carried on his watch chain. The chain jingled expensively as he wrote. Eventually he looked up.

"I say, Wells, there is one more thing. What would these little beauties cost?"

"*I'll* answer that," said Pembroke.

"The early runners were costing about twenty thousand each, but they were pioneers, and so the costs were ridiculously high. Only a few shipbuilders were interested. There's a great deal more competition now, so I don't think they'll cost much more, even though they're twice the tonnage. I think you can assume twenty-five thousand to be on the conservative side."

We then got into a much more detailed discussion of ship design, but made little further progress.

"I think it will be best if we call in a marine engineer or a shipbuilder," said Pembroke eventually. "I will do my best to get that arranged for tomorrow.

"Wells," he continued, "we keep reading about the war in the newspapers, what are they saying about it in Wilmington and Charleston? How long is the war going to go on for?"

"That's a good question old fellow," said Stringer, with a puff on his cigar, "we don't want to plunge on a whole lot more ships if it's all going to be over tomorrow! I don't think they'd be worth much for general business. What's going to happen, Wells?"

"I'm not sure I can help, Mr Stringer," I said, "generally speaking the Yankee troops seem to do better in the west, and Lee runs rings around them in the east. I suppose there's a risk that Northern troops will get right down the Mississippi and then work along the coast - closing the Southern ports. If they were able to close Savannah and Charleston they could concentrate the blockade onto Wilmington.

"Both sides are pig-headed enough," I continued, "and neither is going to surrender easily. The South think they are protecting their way of life, Blair thinks it's a matter of pride for them now. He thinks that the best chance for the South to win would be if Lincoln were to be defeated in the elections in sixty-four. It looks as though he'll run against McClellan. If McClellan wins he might settle with the South. Blair thinks that otherwise it will be a long war of attrition, and he is fearful that eventually the North will win."

"My dear fellow, I can't believe that," said Stringer, "Lee and Jackson smashed Hooker at Chancellorsville. *The Times* said that if it hadn't been for Jackson's death the Union Army would have been destroyed."

"Well it's what Blair thinks, sir," I said, "he says that the resources of the North are massive, they could overwhelm the South in the end. I must say that if it means the emancipation of the slaves, I am beginning to feel that a Northern victory is desirable anyway."

It soon became clear to me that stating my reservations about the Southern cause was not what Mr Pembroke wished to hear. But I had witnessed the harsh treatment that the slaves were receiving in the towns and plantations in the Carolinas, and the whole system seemed completely unjust to me. I suppose I could be accused of hypocrisy, as of course I was earning huge sums by our trade with the Southern States. But I was still hoping to marry Amy, and the blockade running business was giving me my chance.

"Your moral qualms are *your* concern," said Pembroke dismissively. "*My* concern is for our business, my partner and our investors. At least it looks as though the war will run for a good while yet. We will just have to adapt our ships to make the most of it."

"Well said!" said Stringer, opening his gold hunter watch. "I'm afraid I must leave you both now. I have a luncheon with a couple of fellows at Brooks's. Let's meet again tomorrow if you can find a shipbuilding expert for us, Pembroke."

We watched Stringer leave the office, and then Mr Pembroke turned to me again.

"That man McNab's a mystery," he said, drumming his desk with his fingers, "I wrote to several shipping companies trying to trace him, but he seems to have disappeared. I've warned my associates in *this* business, so he'll find it hard to be employed on a blockade-runner. I can't see why they didn't lock him up in Nassau. Let's hope we've seen the last of him."

"Would he have gone back to Scotland?"

"Good heavens, Wells, do you suppose I didn't think of that?

No, the Scotch companies have no trace of him either."

With that Mr Pembroke made it clear that the meeting was finished.

Over the next few days we met regularly to continue the discussion. Pembroke and Stringer accepted the outline design that had been put together by the captains and myself. Then they debated how their little fleet should look. In the meanwhile I spent a couple of agreeable evenings with Hardcastle and his friends. Late one night Hardcastle and I were having a final drink on our own, seated in a tiny public house on the edge of the City. It was a cheerful place, full of boisterous young City clerks celebrating the successes of the day. There was a stench of beer intermingled with tobacco smoke and the odour of wet sawdust from the floor. Hardcastle looked at me quizzically.

"Have they reached a decision yet? His lordship has no difficulty making up his mind, but the elegant gentleman takes forever. If he didn't spend so much of his time eating and drinking for England at his clubs, he might get things done a bit quicker."

"I think they're nearly there," I said, "his elegance has got a sniff of easy money, and sees himself in the House of Lords in no time. Mr Pembroke has made a fortune over the last six months; I just hope that his luck doesn't change now. We've had one disaster with the *Granite City* – we don't want any more. She was a good ship too, with a good crew. This blockade running lark isn't all beer and skittles."

"Talking of beer, let's have another one," said Hardcastle.

He picked up our glasses and he went over to the bar on the other side of the small noisy smoke-filled room. Soon he was back.

"I don't want to be pessimistic, but I think it's a bad sign that the elegant gentleman is joining his lordship's enterprise. He's a lazy fellow, and when he comes round to something, it's usually too late."

"Well, at least he's got Mr Pembroke to keep him in order," I said. "Pembroke's no slouch. If *he* still wants to be in the business that's a good sign isn't it?"

"I suppose so."

"But you don't think so?"

Hardcastle took a long pull at his beer.

"Well, put it this way. If his lordship thinks it's such a good thing, why is he bringing in a partner?"

"More finance?" I suggested.

"Well you know his finances better than I do, but he's managed up to now without one, and he's made heaps. I'm sure he could go on alone if he wanted to."

He paused.

"Personally I'm surprised that they want to help the Southern States so much. Don't they worry about supporting slavery?"

Once again the open sore of my concerns about the slavery question had been rubbed, and I wondered how to respond. My only real justification was Amy, and I didn't want to talk to Hardcastle about her, so it took me some time to reply.

"I asked them that myself, and of course it's all to do with money. But when you asked about *them*, I suppose you were probably wondering about *me*?"

Hardcastle nodded.

"Well, I could tell you a lot of nonsense about supporting freedom, and sticking by our friends, but I suppose it comes down to money with me too. Mr Pembroke is offering me my chance, and I mean to take it."

Hardcastle shrugged, and swallowed down the rest of his beer.

I remembered our conversation in the morning, and the question of Stringer's involvement gave me some unease. However, despite Hardcastle's pessimism, that day turned out to be the one when the decisions were made. Pembroke, Stringer and I met in the partners' office. The two of them sat at either end of their partners' desk, and I pulled up a chair alongside.

"You've no doubt been wondering about our conclusions," said Pembroke. "Stringer and I have decided that the template for a ship you gave us is a good one. We intend building ships based on that pattern, but first we want to sell the smaller ships. When you get back to Nassau I want you to put the *Calypso*, the *Flora* and the *Clara* onto the market. You must realise at least twenty thousand pounds for each of them, but I believe that twenty-five or even thirty thousand is possible. You must seek my permission for a price less than twenty-five thousand. Your commission will be two percent up to twenty thousand pounds, and three percent on anything above. I don't believe that it's realistic to make the sale here in London. We could sell a ship that had already been captured by the Union Navy. That would get me into all sorts of trouble."

Stringer laughed, rather as if he thought the idea of his partner getting into trouble was amusing.

"You're as sharp as anything, Pembroke," he said, "I can't believe you'd allow *that* to happen old fellow. It's like this Wells; Pembroke and I have agreed to build three more ships. It may take some time to get the design right, and to choose the builders, but we would hope to have them out to you by October or November at the latest. If the gold keeps flowing, we'll consider more."

"What do we do with the captains and crews in the time between selling our current ships and the new ones arriving?" I asked.

"Keep paying the good ones," said Pembroke, "some of them may want to take leave in England anyway. Do you agree Stringer?"

"If you say so old fellow."

Soon Stringer was on his way to yet another lunch, this time at White's, and Pembroke and I were left alone. There were a number of details I wanted to settle before I returned to Nassau. It soon became clear that Pembroke would be managing our operations, and he didn't feel the need to consult Stringer on anything except investment decisions.

"You will be getting your instructions from me, Wells," he said. "Stringer is quite happy to leave it that way. He also agrees that your salary should increase. Whilst you remain in Nassau you will be receiving eight hundred pounds per annum. You will of course still have the opportunity to take five percent of the cargo capacity of the ships under your management. There will be the usual success payments."

"Thank you, sir," I said, "that's more than generous."

"No, no, I should thank you Wells. I have made a great deal of money from our operations, and you must take a lot of the credit."

He then invited me to lunch with him at the City Club. He had never invited me there before.

"We can't allow Stringer to have all the pleasure, can we?" he asked with a twinkle.

That afternoon I made all the arrangements for my return to Nassau. I would take a train to Liverpool the following day, and the mail ship would leave that evening. I was feeling very satisfied with my week in London. My work was appreciated, my salary had been increased, and I was looking forward to the new challenges. I spent my last evening in London in my mother's house in Deptford. She was grateful that I had stayed longer in London than I had predicted, but it was still a sorrowful parting. Once again I could give no accurate idea of when I might return.

The following day I called into the office on my way to Euston station for the Liverpool train. I was in a light-hearted mood with the excitement of returning to Nassau. I was just saying my goodbyes to Hardcastle when Mr Pembroke came into the general office, looking pale and holding a piece of paper.

"I have just had very bad news," he said, "we have lost the *Clara*."

All my feelings of contentment left me in a second; it was as though they had been kicked out of me. The *Clara* had been my home for many weeks, the crew were almost like a family to me, and Harry Mansell had become my closest friend. For Pembroke it was a financial setback, for me it was a deeply personal tragedy.

"How, sir? What happened? What happened to the crew?"

"We know very little," said Pembroke, "this telegraph is from our agent in Liverpool. All it says is that the *Clara* has been sunk by a Union cruiser off Cape Fear."

Chapter Eleven
The Clara's Fate

As soon as I reached Liverpool I rushed into our agent's office, but they could tell me no more about the fate of the *Clara*. I boarded the mail ship with a heavy heart, and throughout the Atlantic crossing my mind was on the *Clara* and the crew I knew so well. Had they survived, and if they had, were they now locked up in a Northern jail? Harry Mansell was my closest friend, and of course he was foremost in my thoughts. How would Harry, with his carefree, swashbuckling attitude to life, stand up to incarceration?

It was a morning at the end of June when I finally arrived back in Nassau. The crossing had been good, but spoilt for me by my worries about the *Clara*. The weather was hot and steamy. There were barouches waiting at the quayside, and one of them took me straight to the house in East Street. Johnson was there, and he rose to greet me.

"You've heard about the *Clara*?"

"Yes, but only that she was sunk by a Yankee cruiser, what more can you tell me?"

"Well it's true that the *Clara* has been lost, but I wouldn't say that she was sunk exactly. The best person to tell you what happened would be Captain Mansell."

"I'm not going to wait for him to escape from jail in New York to hear his story!" I exclaimed, "tell me now! What happened? Who survived?"

"No, you misunderstand me, Mr Wells; Mansell is here, upstairs, I'm sure he would want to tell you the story himself."

I apologised and rushed upstairs, to discover that Mansell was still in bed. I went into his room, where one open eye showing from under the covers indicated that he was awake.

"Harry! I was told that the *Clara* had been sunk, I imagined that you and the crew had been lost, or you were locked up in New York. I can't tell you how delighted I am to see you here and still alive! Tell me what happened!"

"I'm delighted to see you too Tom," he groaned, "but please don't shout. We had one of those nights at the Victoria last night and my head is hurting. Every time you speak it's like a hot nail being driven into my forehead. Be a good fellow and ask Mary to get me some coffee. In half an hour I may be able to answer your questions."

That was all I could get out of him.

When I went downstairs I was amazed to find Herr Kohler waiting for me in the office. He hardly ever visited us, so it was puzzling. Had he discovered about my guilty liaison with Susan? Would there be angry remonstrations and accusations? Obviously she was still in the Bahamas. Despite my worries about Kohler, I found myself thinking about those delicious May evenings when Susan had lain in my arms. Had she realised her dream? Was she with child? Would I get the chance to see her before they left?

He seemed calm, although he was sweating heavily. He was pale, and his eyes were bloodshot. For a moment I wondered whether he too had spent a night of alcoholic dissipation at the Royal Victoria. I tried to appear as calm and matter of fact as I could.

"How are you Herr Kohler? How is Frau Kohler?"

"She is fine, thank you, fine. But I am not so good. I haff been sick, but today I feel better. I haff come to tell you that zis house it is sold."

I hoped that the relief didn't show on my face.

"Please sit down," I said, "can I get you anything? A glass of water perhaps?"

"Nein. I will sit, but I want nothing, thank you. All my property it is sold, and we leave for Bavaria next week. Only my own villa is not sold. You remember it? Perhaps you have an interest, Ja?"

"I'm afraid not, Herr Kohler. My answer is the same as before, Mr Pembroke is not interested in buying property in Nassau. He is happy to rent."

"Then I leave ze sale with my lawyer after we leave. May I wash my hands please?"

He got up with difficulty, and waddled over towards the back of the house. He was some time in returning.

153

"Are you all right Herr Kohler?" I asked.

"Some small recurrence of my illness. I will leave you now. I wish you well with your business Mr Wells. Perhaps you will come to München, ja? I hope you will visit us there. Here I can be contacted."

He gave me a card with an address in Munich. I saw him to the door.

"May I wish you and Frau Kohler a successful passage home?"

"Thank you," he said. He climbed ponderously into his carriage, which was waiting for him outside.

I looked at my watch and decided I couldn't wait any longer for the news about the *Clara*. I rushed back upstairs again to talk to Harry. He was in the sitting room, drinking coffee and eating some fruit. He looked up.

"Sorry about that old fellow, but you know what those nights at the Victoria are like. I think I may have been the last to leave, and I don't even remember getting back here. I was awake when you came into my room, but I didn't want to move my head."

I tried to smile.

"I feel sorry for you Harry, but please have some compassion for me too! I heard that the *Clara* had been sunk just before I left London, but I couldn't get any details. Ever since then I have been desperately worried about you and the other fellows – and also the *Clara* of course."

"I sent a full report to Mr Pembroke," said Mansell, "but it would have crossed with you on the Atlantic. I knew that's what you would have wanted me to do. It won't have been as ship-shape as your nifty reports, but I explained everything."

"Harry, please don't keep me in suspense, what happened?"

"Yes, all right," said Mansell, with a smile. "We were headed for Wilmington as you know, and it was all to do with the damned pilot. We were loaded with the usual cargo, Enfield rifles, cartridges, uniforms, barrels of salt pork and so on, so the *Clara* was lowish in the water. We had a new pilot, one Dawson by name. The *Clara* was performing well, and we had no trouble on the passage across. We saw a couple of Yankee ships in the distance, but I doubt they saw us, and we soon had the distance of them.

"Our plan was to bull our way through the blockade in the early hours, and pass through the western inlet. The sea was relatively calm. The night had been partly cloudy, but we were able to get an occasional fix on the stars, so I had our position pretty well nailed. Then, just as we were getting into position to make the final run, the cloud thickened up. Not a peep of a star did we get for the rest of the night.

"I turned to Dawson. 'It's up to you now' I said, 'you'll have to get us close to the bar based on casts of the lead'. He looked a bit shifty, but he said he thought he could manage all right."

Mansell sighed.

"Why did I believe him?

"We crept forward, and we were damned lucky not to see a single cruiser or gunboat as we made our approach. Dawson was examining samples of sand as we went forward. With the first cast of the lead we were in fifteen fathoms, but two or three casts later it was only six.

"I said to Dawson that we must be damned close to the bar, but he said no, this was only a shoal and we would be clear of it in a moment. Bloody idiot. Just as he was saying it there was a long heavy scrunching sound. The poor old *Clara* was stuck fast on something, which turned out to be the bar."

"It was still dark?" I asked.

"Yes, it was four in the morning. First light was two hours later. We had planned to show a light at around five, and then be guided in on the two shore lights."

"And still no Yankee ships?"

"I'm coming to that," he said, "it wasn't high tide yet, so I was confident that we would come off eventually, but we couldn't risk being spotted at dawn. I asked the engine room to reverse both engines, but at low power it had no effect whatever. We were stuck like a beached whale.

"It was still calm. I knew that with full power from the engines we were almost certain to be heard by the Yankee blockaders. But if we were going to get off we had to keep increasing the speed of the screws. Then the inevitable happened, up went a rocket from a Yankee gunboat – they had heard us.

"At least then we could see where we were. We were stuck on the western inlet bar, quite close to Fort Caswell at the entrance to the Cape Fear estuary. We were stuck because bloody Dawson had brought us in too close to the fort. The gunboats couldn't risk firing too many rockets, but they had our location pretty well pinned. Soon there was the sound of shells all round us."

Mansell paused to eat some fruit, and take a drink from his coffee cup.

"Now we put the engines onto full power, and the old girl started edging off the bar. That was when the flood tide hit us, and swung us round parallel to the bar, and we were stuck fast again. Not only that, our screws were stuck in the sand, and we could make no movement at all.

"It was a black moment. The *Clara* was rolling like a drunken sailor as the surf tried to push us onto the bar. Shells were dropping all round us like horseflies on a cowpat, and any moment we were bound to take a hit. We told the crew they could take off in the boats if they wanted to, and several did, including that damn fellow Dawson.

"Then we took a couple of hits. One of them ripped up the deck over the after cargo compartment like a tin opener. A fire started, and we could see burning pork barrels through the hole in the deck. We were in a desperate position, and I was wondering whether the rest of us should abandon ship, when three things seemed to happen all at once. The firing stopped. Two large boats full of Yankees crashed alongside, and the *Clara* seemed to free herself from the bar. I guess the flood tide had finished, and the additional water had lifted us off. If that had happened fifteen minutes earlier, we could have got away."

"No light yet?" I asked.

"No, but we could see what was happening close to us by the flames coming from the *Clara's* stern. It was burning as bright as the fiery furnace.

"Then the old girl was swarming with trigger-happy Yankees. They wanted to get her away before the dawn light put them on display for Fort Caswell. They demanded our surrender, and we were in no position to argue. Then I had my stroke of genius.

"A small group of Yankees was heading towards the stern to see what could be done about the fire. I shouted as loud as I could 'watch out there, the cargo in the stern's gunpowder in barrels!' Actually of course it was salt pork destined for Lee's army.

"The effect was instantaneous! Up went the cry 'back to the boats!' Abandoning their prisoners, the Yankees scrambled back into their boats. They were off as fast as they could go. We got steam up again, and pulled away from the bar. The stern was still blazing nicely, but we were down to a skeleton crew and it was as much as we could do to handle the ship. I didn't have anyone free to put out the fire.

"The Yankees could see what we were doing, and soon they were shelling us again. It was full tide. We comfortably cleared the bar in the centre of the channel, but we knew we couldn't go far. We had a choice, either we could handle the ship or we could tackle the fire, and the fire was getting worse by the minute. I decided we had to beach the *Clara* as soon as we could. Fortunately dawn was up, and Fort Caswell was peppering the gunboats. We saw no more of them that day."

"You *are* a genius," I said, laughing, "weren't any of the crew captured?"

"None of them," he replied, "one of the firemen was wounded by a Yankee pistol shot, but no one was captured. We found the ones who had taken off in the ship's boats at Fort Caswell later.

"We ran the *Clara* onto the beach under the fort, and they sent as many men as they could to help us. The stern was very badly burnt, and by the time we got the fire out, the rudder mechanism had been damaged, and the shafts for the propellers had warped. The hull was warped too. But the fire was out, and only the cargo in the two stern compartments was damaged. By the way, the pork burned beautifully and we had the devil's own job to put it out. We were all sick of the smell of it by the end. I don't think I ever want to eat roast pork again."

"How much of the cargo did you manage to salvage?"

"I thought you might be interested in that," he said, smiling, "we got all of the cargo in the bow compartments out first, and that took us nearly all day. Then we started on the stern. The last compartment was hopeless, but we managed to salvage some uniforms and cavalry swords from the other one. Johnson tells me that in terms of value we managed to salvage three-quarters of the cargo. Once it was carted up to Wilmington and sold, we even managed to make a profit. That should please Mr Pembroke."

"You're a marvel, Harry," I said, "but saving the crew is the best part, where are they now? How did you manage to get back so quickly?"

"Well that was lucky too. We had to go into quarantine before we could go up to Wilmington. They're dead scared of another yellow fever outbreak. But we had only been there a couple of days when the *Flora* turned up. We were able to catch a ride with her. She managed to slip through the blockade without a shot being fired. So here I am!"

"What happened to the *Clara*?"

"That wasn't so lucky. By the end of the day she was still beached, and she couldn't move under her own steam – there was too much damage to the propeller shafts and the rudder. We planned to get another steamer down to pull her off the following day, but the Yankees were too quick for us. They must have been watching during the day, and they realised we couldn't get the *Clara* away. That night they came back over the bar in small boats and set light to her. I have to admit it was daring. By the time we got to her it was too late, she was completely burnt out. I was angry, but there was nothing we could do."

"It's sad to think of the poor old girl burnt out on the beach," I said, "but you mustn't blame yourself. It was that damn pilot who put you there. You saved the crew and most of the cargo. The Confederates will be pleased that she didn't end up in the hands of the Yankees. Anyway, you can congratulate yourself as being the first captain to rescue a cargo of roast pork under fire from Union gunboats!"

"I think you have just talked yourself into buying me dinner at the Royal Victoria," said Mansell, "but please don't let me drink champagne cocktails again."

Mansell and I discussed what we should do with the *Clara's* crew. There were one or two of them who Mansell didn't want to keep. They would be paid off, and the others would be offered return passages to England. I wrote to Mr Pembroke giving a further account of the *Clara's* fate, emphasising the brave part taken by Mansell and most of the crew. I suggested that they could be retained and perhaps used to bring the next ship out to Nassau. The weather in the Bahamas was now unpleasantly hot and humid. Most of the crew, including Mansell, decided to take leave in England. Within a week they had gone, either on the mail steamer or on merchantmen.

Now my most important task was to follow Mr Pembroke's instructions, and sell the *Calypso* and the *Flora*. I considered that it would be foolish to sell them at the same time, and I decided to sell the *Calypso* first. If anything, I felt that she might be the more difficult vessel to sell, as she was single screw. But blockade running was still a very profitable business and the level of interest was high. Almost immediately we had a buyer. A few days later we were able to complete the sale. She sold for more than twenty-five thousand pounds, and I felt sure that Mr Pembroke would be pleased. The transaction was completed in our lawyer's office on Parliament Street. On our return to East Street I found a letter waiting for me. It was marked 'URGENT'.

Dear Tom,

   How I hope and pray you are there! Can you please come to see me urgently at the villa. Poor Hans is dead, and I need your help.
   Yours, Susan.

I immediately went to the Royal Victoria and found a barouche to take me to the villa. I was shocked to hear of Kohler's death. He was hardly a friend of mine, but I admired his efficiency and his business skill. He had been kind to Susan and I had been grateful for that too. As the cab made its way to the villa I was speculating about Herr Kohler's death. I had only seen him a couple of days earlier. He had seemed unwell, but not gravely ill. But there seemed little point in speculation, we were nearing the villa, and soon the mystery would be solved. A servant let me into the drawing room. Susan was sitting in one of the armchairs, crying. I

159

went over to her.

"This is terrible news, Susan," I said, "what happened?"

Susan was still sobbing, but somehow she managed to pull herself together.

"It was the yellow fever, Tom. Hans had been ill, but he seemed to recover. He started to work again, and then he was very sick. The doctor he tol' us it was the yellow fever. There was nothing he could do. Then it was all over. Hans turned a horrible yellow colour, and in two days he was dead."

She shuddered.

"It is my fate to lose all those I love to this evil sickness."

Then she was crying again, and it was a few minutes before she could continue.

"Hans was Catholic, and I have spoken to the priest. The funeral will be tomorrow at eleven – you will come, won' you Tom?"

"Of course I'll come. I have to go to Wilmington next week, and I expect to be away for three weeks at least, but before that please let me know what I can do to help."

"Hans, he did everything for the house, the servants, money, everything. I need help with that. Hans tol' me to go to Mr Dupon', but Hans was so sick, he never tol' me who this Mr Dupon' is. How can I pay for the funeral? Can I pay the servants? There is so much to worry about when I ought to be looking after Hans's funeral."

She looked desolate.

I checked in my pockets. I found that I had some twenty pounds in coins, and I gave them to her.

"This will keep you going for a day or two. Tell me if you need more for the funeral."

Susan put the coins in a small heap on a side table, and whilst we continued talking she shuffled them distractedly into different piles.

"As far as Mr Dupont is concerned," I continued, "that's the name of our lawyer, and I was with him this morning. If it's him, I think you ought to see him straight away, and he'll advise you."

She looked into my eyes appealingly.

"Oh thank you Tom, will you come with me?"

"Of course I will. Is there anything else you need to sort out, or shall we go there now?"

"I must write to his family, and I have to decide about his grave, oh an' so many other things, but I think we must see this Mr Dupon' first."

We ordered her carriage, and we went back to the lawyer's office where I had spent the morning. I suggested to Susan that she should wait in the carriage whilst I checked that he was indeed Herr Kohler's lawyer. I was able to speak to him, and he confirmed that he acted for Kohler in his private affairs. I made it clear that I expected him to act fairly with Susan, or he would risk having difficulty with Mr Pembroke's business. Then I showed Susan into Mr Dupont's room. I said that I had some things to deal with at East Street, but that I would return in half an hour.

When I came back, Susan had just left Dupont's office and was waiting for me. I joined her in her carriage. She was looking calmer.

"Tom, Hans has been so kind to me. He has made a will and he has made sure I will be comfortable. He has not left everything to me, but mos' things. He has given money for his family in Munich. I have his paren's address so I can write to them, but I mus' find someone who can write in German. Can you help Tom?"

I said I could, as I was sure that there was a merchant from Hamburg staying at the Royal Victoria.

Gradually we sorted out all the problems and difficulties. Apart from her servants and one or two business associates, she and I were the only mourners at Hans Kohler's funeral. Afterwards we went back to the villa for dinner. I asked Susan what she was intending to do. Would she still go to Munich?

"No, I don' think so Tom. I don' know anyone there. I think I'll stay here in Nassau. But I'll be lonely, I hardly know anyone here either. Will you come and see me sometimes Tom?"

"Of course I will. We leave for Wilmington on the *Flora* on Wednesday, but I'll see you before then. Are you worried about the yellow fever? Do you think you might catch it too?"

"No, Tom. If you grow up here in the islands you don't usually get it – my family was just very unfortunate. *You* should be worried Tom."

"There have been very few cases so far this year," I said, "so I

161

hope I'll be lucky. I have a lot of work to do for the owners, and I must stay here this summer. It's a risk I have to take."

"Well I worry for you Tom, but I'm please' you are going to be here. You have been a wonderful fren' to me, and you have help' me so much," she paused, "it's Saturday tomorrow, can I come and see you at East Street?"

"Yes, we work in the morning, but why don't you come in the afternoon? Please make sure you remember to bring a list of all the things you want me to help you with. I'm afraid I must go back to East Street now. I think we did everything we could for Hans."

"Until tomorrow," she said, "thank you for everything. I will call for the carriage to take you back."

The following day Susan came to see me. First we talked a lot about Herr Kohler. Susan explained that she was very fond of him, but she had seen him as a rescuer rather than a lover. Hans had been very kind to her, more like a father. She had hoped that if they had children they could have had a normal family life. She was looking for the same happy life she had had before her parents died. There was something on my mind to ask her, but I found it difficult. Eventually I found the words.

"I probably shouldn't ask you this Susan, but were you expecting a child at the time of Herr Kohler's death?"

"Tom!" she looked almost shocked, "how can you ask such a question at a time like this?"

Then she smiled apologetically.

"I'm sorry Tom, you have every right to ask. No, I am not."

Then she asked me about Amy.

"Nothing has changed," I said, "I only get news of her when I go to Wilmington, and I visit her uncle. I think our suit is virtually hopeless. Her uncle thinks that the civil war in America may change circumstances so much that we might be able to get married. But I have met her father, and I don't think he's going to change his mind."

"Then we are both alone," and again she was crying.

Chapter Twelve
Wilmington

On a dark night towards the end of June 1863 we slipped safely over the bar by Fort Fisher on the *Flora*, at the entrance to the Cape Fear estuary.

A quarantine station had been set up between Smithville and Wilmington after the yellow fever outbreak in '62. We were in quarantine there for two weeks, under close supervision. As usual we carried ample supplies of food and water so we could be self-sufficient during the quarantine. Then we steamed up to Fort Anderson where our cargo manifest was examined by the Confederate authorities. They were checking that we were carrying no embargoed goods from the Northern States. Having obtained clearance, we followed the Cape Fear River as it narrowed up the fifteen miles to Wilmington. The low-lying riverbanks were thickly wooded, and it was pleasant easy steaming. The pilot took control of the wheel and guided us up the river. The Confederates had placed obstacles and torpedoes in the river, so it was essential to have a competent pilot on board to avoid them.

I always enjoyed my visits to handsome bustling Wilmington. The town had originated as a port to serve the plantations further up the Cape Fear River, but in the 1840s it had become the centre of the web of railway connections to Fayetteville, Richmond, Atlanta, Charleston, Savannah and the points beyond. The new trade had enriched the local merchants and they had built splendid houses on the long hill on the eastern bank of the river. Many of the plantation owners built houses there too. In contrast to crowded Charleston, the houses are well spaced out and have splendid gardens. As I looked up at those great houses, I could see the live oak trees in many of the gardens, with their strange festoons of Spanish moss. Along the riverbank were the docks, wharves and warehouses. This was where we secured the *Flora*.

As we drew close to the town, Amy was constantly on my mind. I immediately made my way to Angus Blair's office. I was desperate for news of her, and I also needed to make the arrangements for the discharge of our cargo, and the purchase of merchandise for our outward voyage.

Before the war, Wilmington had been a gentle and dignified town, but since it had become a centre for blockade running, its character had changed. The outbreak of yellow fever in the town in the late summer and autumn of 1862 had caused many of the more respectable inhabitants to flee the town. Ships like ours brought in rowdy and overpaid crews, and the town was buzzing with merchants and speculators attracted by the rich pickings of the blockade economy. There were troops patrolling the town to keep order, and curfews were in force in the evening to prevent violence.

I made my way on foot in the sweltering July heat from the docks to Market Street. Parties of Negro labourers were passing under the watchful eyes of their white overseers. Many of the Negroes seemed cowed and morose as they went about their tasks. Their eyes were cast down and I found that they would not look me in the eye. Sometimes they would chant sad melodic songs as they worked, but even this did not seem to lift their spirits. It was a grim contrast to the much more independent, cheerful and lively workmen and labourers I was used to in London or Nassau. I found the treatment of the slaves in Wilmington and Charleston a shocking contrast to the treatment of their equivalents in Nassau. It seemed to me that for the Southerners the difference between the races was much more than just a matter of colour. I felt that their white masters viewed their Negro slaves almost as an inferior species. In Nassau the Negroes were treated much more as equal citizens, despite any differences in social position or prosperity. Once again my conscience was jolted at the thought that I was knowingly providing sustenance to a regime that was defending these injustices. For all the South's sacrifice, dash and bravery, they were fighting for a cause that I was finding it increasingly difficult to endorse. I was beginning to understand why Fraser McNab had taken the stance he had, even though he had damaged us.

It was more than two months since I had visited Angus Blair, and so I had heard nothing from Amy in that time. He came over to greet me, but his face was long, and I was fearful of the news he

164

was going to give. Could it be that Amy had finally given in to her mother's wishes, and become engaged or even married to Hamilton Douglas? He gestured for me to sit down. Then he composed himself enough to tell me what had happened.

"Welcome, Mr Wells," he said, "I have several letters for you from my niece, but I have to warn you that the news is not good ... two weeks ago we heard that my nephew Jack died in Fort Lafayette prison. There was another outbreak of typhoid fever, and Jack was one of the victims. Amy and my sister are truly in despair. Not only that, Colonel Munro is still with Lee's army. We have just heard that he was wounded in the leg in Ewell's attack on Winchester. The army has gone on to cross the Potomac into Pennsylvania, but the colonel is recovering in an army hospital in Virginia. He desperately wanted to get back to Marion, but he can't be moved."

"Have you been up to Marion yourself?" I asked.

"Yes, I have just returned. They are in deep mourning. Their neighbours are sympathetic and they are helping as much as they can, but it is a familiar story. So many families have lost two or even three sons."

"It must also be terrible for you."

"Yes, I have to say that Jack was my favourite nephew, I do not think I will ever get over his death."

There was silence for a moment, and I could see that he was close to tears. I tried to think of a tactful way to change the subject.

"I have just been in London as you know, and the papers are full of Lee's amazing victory over Hooker at Chancellorsville. If Lee is over the Potomac and into Pennsylvania, perhaps there's a chance that the war will be over soon?"

"I would just love to think so," said Blair, recovering himself a little, "but Grant, the Yankee general, is working his way down the Mississippi, and threatening Vicksburg. For all Lee's victories in the east, we are still suffering in the west. If Lee were to have an overwhelming victory over Hooker in Pennsylvania, perhaps Lincoln would come to terms, but to be truthful, I doubt it."

I asked about Amy, and I could hardly conceal my delight to learn that she was still unattached. Then we talked about business, and the sale of the *Flora's* cargo. I explained that we had sold the *Calypso*, and that we were also expecting to sell the *Flora*.

"So with the *Clara* gone, Mr Pembroke will have no ships left, is he getting out of the blockade running business, Mr Wells?"

"No. He has taken on a partner, Mr Edgar Stringer, and they have decided to reorganise their ships. Mr Pembroke's smaller ships are being sold, and they are going to invest in larger ones, all of them with side paddles. I think the *Flora* will definitely be sold when we get back to Nassau. I'll get a message to you when I know how the new fleet will look."

"I have two dear friends coming for dinner tomorrow evening," said Blair, "Mr and Mrs Elliott. Please do come and join us, and I can give you Amy's letters. Charles Elliott follows the war very closely, so you may be interested in his views. I should warn you that they lost their son, their only child, early in the war. Can you come at five o'clock? I can promise you some fine Madeira wine – since *you* kindly provided it!"

"I would be delighted," I said.

I went back to the *Flora* and arranged with the captain about the cargo. To take advantage of the moonless conditions, we needed to get it unloaded quickly.

At five o'clock the following evening I was at Mr Blair's substantial house on Second Street, built in the Greek revival style, with a fine pillared piazza at the front. The Elliotts were already in the library. They were an elderly couple. She was very quiet and deferential to her husband. He was a short, stout, red-faced man with a fiery temperament. After I had been introduced, Mr Elliott dived straight into what was clearly his favourite topic of conversation.

"How closely are you following the war, Mr Wells? Do you know that we are on the brink of victory in Pennsylvania?"

"I would have thought we could hardly assume..." interjected Mr Blair.

"Of course we can," said Elliott, with an angry look. "Lee and Jackson thrashed Hooker at Chancellorsville did they not? Everyone says that if it hadn't been for Jackson's death, the war would be over now!"

166

"But Lee without Jackson…" Blair interjected again.

"Lee's a genius," shouted Elliott, "he's got Ewell and Longstreet hasn't he, *and* Hill? *They* will make short work of Hooker, although one of the papers has a rumour that Meade has replaced Hooker. Another of Lincoln's blunders no doubt. They also say that Lee has got between the Yankees and Washington at a place called Gettysburg. Surely this must be the end."

"Yes," said Mr Blair, "and there are even rumours of a big victory there, but it takes ages for our papers to get the full facts."

"Lee has got Hooker where he wants him," said Elliott firmly, "Hooker has to attack or Washington will be threatened. Lee has done it countless times before, and he's going to do it again."

At this moment Mr Blair's Negro butler announced dinner. Blair led the way downstairs to his sombre dining room. There was a long mahogany dining table, with eight or ten chairs round it, but the table was only laid for four. On the walls were dark oil paintings of Mr Blair's forebears, and silver gleamed softly on the sideboards and dining table. Most of the larger Wilmington houses had their dining rooms in the basement so diners would not have to suffer the heat of the upstairs rooms in the sweltering North Carolina summer.

Before we started eating, Blair and Elliott debated Lee's tactics from Fredericksburg to Chancellorsville and back again, with Elliott insisting on Lee's tactical genius and the inevitability of a Southern victory. Then Mr Blair's cook provided an excellent dinner from the limited variety of food available in Wilmington. Admittedly it was supplemented by some delicacies I had sent over from the *Flora*. As we started to eat, Blair turned to me.

"Mr Wells has just been in London. I am sure you have heard enough about our troubles in the war here; what's going on in London? It seems an age since I met you there before all this started. I always think that the best time to be in London is October."

"It's cooler then?" I suggested.

"No, it is the game season, dear fellow. Just to think of pheasant, partridge, grouse, venison – well I mustn't grumble… you were there in June, and I suppose you will have had asparagus, and perhaps the first strawberries?"

"Yes, we did have asparagus," I said, "but London is quite boring compared to what's going on here. The war in America fills the London newspapers these days. There is one thing that might interest you. They've just built an underground railway connecting two of our big London railway stations, Paddington and King's Cross. It opened in January."

"You're joking!" expostulated Mr Elliott, "not with steam trains, how can they travel underground? How do the passengers breathe?"

"I travelled on it, and it seems to work. They have vents to let out the steam and the soot, and let the air in. Your clothes can get a bit dirty, but it's a very quick way to get between the stations. It should have opened last year, but a sewer burst at Farringdon Street and filled the tunnel. It's supposed to be called the Metropolitan Line, but now everyone calls it 'the drain'."

"Nobody takes anything seriously in London," said Mr Elliott.

He had been to London often himself, and he had many questions. The dinner passed quickly. Towards the end a Negro servant came in with a note for Mr Blair.

"Excuse me," he said, "this is from my sister and it is marked 'urgent', do you mind if I read it?"

He scanned the note and turned pale. He looked round as if he was almost frightened to speak.

"This is tragic news. My sister's husband, Colonel Munro, has died. It seems that his wound at Winchester was more serious than they thought. First his leg had to be amputated, and now he has died. Poor fellow. They're bringing his body back to Marion for burial."

"They have lost their two sons too, have they not?" said Elliott. "This is frightful. We are all patriots, but sometimes even I wonder whether our families are making too much of a sacrifice for the Cause. Please give Mrs Munro our deepest condolences."

"Yes," said Mrs Elliott, "we have lost our only child in this war, Mr Wells, and I know what she must be feeling."

Mr Elliott gave his wife a look of heartfelt sympathy.

"Now, now, my dear, John's death is our own personal tragedy.

He wanted to give everything for the Cause, and that is what happened."

There was silence round the table.

"There will be a funeral service at the local church at Marion in three days time," said Blair. "I know my sister and Amy would appreciate you being there Mr Wells. Can you come?"

"Yes," I said, "of course I'll come. How would we travel?"

"By steamboat," he said, "I will arrange it first thing tomorrow morning. I will send a message to you on the *Flora*."

"Thank you, but I'll have to return immediately after the funeral, as the *Flora* must leave within six days and I must be on board. I hope they will understand."

"The important thing is for you to be at the service," he replied.

The party then broke up. Blair made excuses, but said that he must make arrangements for the following day. He said he would offer us the Madeira wine on another occasion. The Elliotts were sympathetic and left. Mr Blair then gave me Amy's letters. I was worried that Mrs Munro wouldn't want to see me at the funeral, and since the Elliotts were gone I felt I could ask Blair.

"Are you sure that I would be welcome at the service?"

"Yes, Mr Wells. My sister is worried about Amy. She has become very sad and depressed after the news of Jack's death, and she thinks it is made worse by Amy's worries about you. I think you should definitely come."

A flicker of hope went through me that Mrs Munro might have changed her mind about me, but I said nothing about it to Mr Blair, who shook my hand, and I left.

That night I read and re-read Amy's letters. The early ones were full of loving messages, but then came the news of Jack's death. She had obviously been devoted to him, and the letters became an outpouring of her grief. They were still affectionate to me, but her feelings had been overwhelmed by her sad love for Jack. She longed to see me as she felt that I could give her comfort, but she was convinced that her parents wouldn't allow it. They were still pressing her to accept Major Douglas's suit, and her steely determination to resist them was all too apparent in the letters.

She also wrote of her worries about me. I had sent her a message saying that I was going to London, but this had obviously not arrived. Her last letters were full of desperate concern for my safety.

The following day Mr Blair himself was at the *Flora* at nine.

"I have secured two passages on a cargo boat leaving for Fayetteville in half an hour," he said, "can you be ready?"

I packed my valise with lightening speed, and we raced to the steamboat. Almost immediately we were on our way. We arrived at Fayetteville very late the following evening. Mr Blair said that it was too late to travel out to Marion and we stayed at the Fayetteville Hotel.

We sent a message saying that we had arrived, and that we would hire a buggy to take us out to Marion in the morning. First thing the next day a message came saying that Mr Scott would pick us up from the hotel. It seemed that Mr Scott's mother lived in a house just behind the hotel. He was collecting her for the funeral, he would pick us up at the same time.

I was nervous about my reception at the Scotts' house, but they were very welcoming. They were all standing in the hall when we arrived. Mrs Munro and Amy were standing together, both wearing black mourning clothes. As I caught Amy's eye there was an immediate flash of understanding between us, and I felt a strong surge of emotion. In that brief look I could see that Amy's feelings for me were equally strong and unchanged, and even in those gloomy circumstances, my heart was filled with light and happiness, but I kept my face solemn.

Mrs Munro hobbled over to me.

"Mr Wells, thank you for coming. I hope you will be able to stay with us at Marion after the service."

I expressed my condolences.

"Thank you for inviting me to stay, Mrs Munro. I'm afraid that I have to return to Wilmington early tomorrow morning, but I would be pleased to stay tonight."

Then Amy joined us. She was pale and had obviously been crying.

"Thank you Tom, it is so wonderful to see you. The last three weeks have been terrible, but it is so good to see you alive, and looking so handsome and strong. At least that is one thing I do not have to worry about."

"I was devastated to hear the news of Jack," I said, "it seems so cruel after Preston's death. And now Colonel Munro – it's a terrible burden for you all to bear."

I wanted to say more, but Mrs Munro was standing beside us. I felt that I couldn't express my feelings for Amy without upsetting her mother.

Soon we were making our way to the church. It was small and filled with the Munros' friends and acquaintances. The service was simple and moving. I was not able to be close to Amy, as she stood between her sister and her mother, but I could see that she was crying throughout the service. My heart went out to her, and I longed to comfort her.

Then we all went to the small cemetery close to Marion for the burial. Afterwards the family and a few close friends came to an early dinner at Sandy Plains. The meal was sombre, and the neighbours left shortly afterwards with only the close family remaining. Louise Scott said that she had some questions to ask me, and we went upstairs to a sitting room. We sat on a small sofa, and Louise was leaning towards me confidentially as we talked.

"How is your husband?" I asked.

"We have been fortunate so far," she said, "our son Henry was born in April, and James was granted furlough. It was at the same time as the battle at Chancellorsville, so he missed that. He was in the latest battle in Pennsylvania, but I have just heard that he is safe. Pray God there is no more fighting for a while yet."

"You wanted to ask me something?"

"No, I wanted to get you alone to talk about you and Amy. You can see how Amy has suffered over the last few weeks and months. Of course she was worrying about Jack and Father, but she has been worrying about you too. Now she is going to need you more than ever."

"But what can I do about it? Your parents didn't approve of me. I'm not sure that I can trust myself to hope that Mrs Munro will change her mind so soon after your father's death. I will talk to Amy if your mother allows it, but I'm afraid that our position is hopeless."

"Amy *must* have hope, Mr Wells," said Louise firmly, "she gets so depressed and frightened at Marion. We have all suffered terribly, but somehow it seems to have affected Amy the worst."

"Why is she frightened?"

"We are all worried about the Yankees getting into North Carolina, and of course they are already on the coast at New Bern. But Amy is always concerned for the safety of herself and Mother at Marion. Did you hear about what happened to Mrs Witherspoon at Society Hill in South Carolina?"

"No, what was that?"

"Mrs Witherspoon was murdered by her Negro slaves for the money and clothes she kept in her room at their plantation. Amy has always been nervous about the slaves at Marion, and the murder at Society Hill has made it worse."

"I hope I'll get the chance to talk to Amy at Marion," I said, "unfortunately I have to leave for Wilmington tomorrow morning – my ship, the *Flora*, has to get back to Nassau as soon as possible, and I must be on board."

At that moment a Negro servant came to find us, as Mrs Munro wanted to return to Marion. As we went downstairs Louise whispered to me.

"Good luck Mr Wells! Do not despair, all will come right."

Mrs Munro suggested that Amy should travel in the Scotts' buggy with her uncle, and that I should be with her in her carriage. It became clear that she wanted to have a confidential talk. Secretly I was hoping that she might give some indication of a change of heart. I could not have been more wrong. After we had exchanged some remarks of no consequence, she came to the point.

"When you were last at Marion," she said, "I know that my husband told you that he did not think you were an appropriate suitor for Amy. He was worried about the dangerous life you lead, and the risks to Amy if she were to join you. I so appreciate you coming to the service today, but I must tell you that nothing has changed. I must respect my husband's wishes."

"My feelings are unchanged," I said, "my dearest wish is to marry Miss Munro, and I hope with all my heart that you can

172

eventually accept that. I haven't been able to speak to her yet, but I believe she feels the same."

"Yes, I think she does," said Mrs Munro, "and it is hard for me to disappoint you both, but I am sure Colonel Munro was right, and I do not intend to go against his wishes. Amy's cousin Hamilton Douglas was here in May, and it was my husband's wish that Amy should marry him. I still would like Amy to respect his wishes. I will allow you to write to one another, but that is the limit."

"I'm grateful Mrs Munro, but where does that leave us? Can you see any circumstances under which you might approve our suit?"

"No, Mr Wells, it is out of the question," she said, looking at me firmly in the eyes, "Colonel Munro was convinced that you are not the right person for Amy, and of course I will respect his wishes."

Gently I tried to convince her that she might reconsider her position, but she was adamant.

"I would like Amy to marry Hamilton Douglas," she said, "and I am not prepared to consider anything else. Colonel Munro wanted Amy to marry a Southern gentleman, and so do I. As I have said, he was also concerned about the dangers you would bring to Amy if she were to marry you. No, you must forget it, and content yourself with being her friend."

That evening Mrs Munro and her brother wanted to discuss family matters on their own, so I was left alone with Amy. It had been a hot and humid day, and even the downstairs rooms at the plantation house were unpleasantly warm and close. It was now cooler outside and there was a slight breeze. We decided to go out onto the veranda to talk. Although Amy was looking pale and troubled in her dark mourning clothes, she was more appealing to me than ever. Somehow her sadness and vulnerability enhanced her attraction. All my old feelings of love for her overwhelmed me again.

At first Amy only wanted to talk about Jack and her father, but then she leant towards me.

"What is going to happen to you, Tom? Will you still be running the blockade? Might you not be safer staying in Nassau or Wilmington?"

173

"Our business is changing, Amy," I replied, "Mr Pembroke has sold nearly all his ships. His last one is the *Flora*. I will be going back to Nassau with her. Then she will be sold too. He wants to have bigger ships, and those will be coming out to Nassau in the autumn. It will be quiet for me until then."

"Could you not stay in Wilmington, Tom?" she asked eagerly.

"No, unfortunately I have to go back to complete the sale, and Mr Pembroke has asked me to stay in Nassau. I don't think I'll be out again until September at the earliest. I'm so sorry Amy."

She looked at me bravely.

"At least I will know that you are safe, but please write to me as often as you can. When do you have to leave for Wilmington?"

I explained that I had to take the steamboat the following morning.

"Oh Tom, I was hoping that you could stay a few days at least, surely you can stay a day or two more?" she asked tearfully.

I put my arm round her and explained why I had no choice but to get back to Nassau as soon as possible; gradually she accepted it.

"At least your mother is allowing us to write to each other," I said, "I pressed her to consider our engagement, but she was completely against it. I'm afraid she gave no hope whatever."

"Yes Tom," she said, "I'm afraid it is hopeless. How can I go against my mother's wishes at a time like this? But perhaps I could see you in Wilmington sometimes, even if I can't marry you."

Then that steely look came into her eyes.

"Mother wants me to marry that pompous idiot Hamilton Douglas, I *won't* do it."

I heard the words, but somehow I didn't find them convincing. Amy would be alone with her mother at Marion and I was sure that the pressure from Mrs Munro would become unbearable. I was going to be away for several months, and I felt a pang of doom that during that time this beautiful girl would slip through my fingers. I questioned Amy repeatedly, and she was adamant that she would never marry Major Douglas.

"How can I convince you?" she kept asking.

That night as I was preparing to go to bed, there was a soft knock on my bedroom door. It was Amy; she slipped inside. She was wearing a pale yellow silk dressing gown, and her long soft brown hair was over her shoulders. She was looking adorable.

"I dare not stay more than a second," she said, "I wanted to kiss you goodbye properly before you go tomorrow."

Before I could say anything, she was in my arms and kissing me passionately on the lips. My arms were round her; I could feel the soft curves of her beautiful body. We clung to each other for a few moments, and then she broke away.

"I love you Tom, and it is forever," she whispered, and in a moment she was gone.

I travelled alone from Fayetteville to Wilmington, as Mr Blair had agreed to stay a few more days with his sister. The boat was cramped and full of tobacco chewing passengers. I tried to shut out the discomforts, and my thoughts were all about Amy. I turned Mrs Munro's words over and over in my mind, but the prospect of marrying Amy was still not even a distant dream. Our love was as deep as ever, but it seemed doomed to be frustrated. I was angry about the approach Mrs Munro was taking, but in her present tragic circumstances there seemed to be little or nothing I could do about it.

The news had now reached Wilmington that the battle at Gettysburg had been a disastrous defeat for the Confederates. The atmosphere in the town was gloomy. The *Flora* was ready to sail when I arrived. She was loaded almost entirely with cotton, and if we could get to Nassau we would make a very handsome profit on the run. The weather was calm, and the Atlantic swells were gentle. We broke through the blockade successfully during the night, but in the morning there was a Yankee cruiser on the horizon behind us. They were clearly in pursuit.

A curious incident followed. We still had some anthracite coal left over from our inward voyage. Even though the *Flora* was at virtually maximum speed, we could see that the cruiser was very gradually gaining on us. The weight of our cargo was holding us back, but we were reluctant to jettison it. The captain told me that he thought we were close to the area where the Gulf Stream made its way through this part of the Atlantic. He said that another captain had told him that a distinctive ripple showed the edge of the Gulf Stream. If we could get to the far side of that ripple it would give us another two or three knots. We scanned the sea with our telescopes. Eventually we found the ripple about three miles to the east, and we turned to steam towards it. As soon as we crossed over we turned north and our speed increased perceptibly. We could see that the additional few knots were enough to allow us to pull away from the cruiser. Although the cruiser eventually also crossed into the Gulf Stream it was too late. She fired a few desultory shots with her Parrott gun, but soon it was dusk and we were clear away. Gradually we swung south again.

At dawn two days later we steamed into Nassau.

Chapter Thirteen
A Tender Interlude

We arrived back in Nassau on the *Flora* on a morning late in July of 1863. Although it was early in the day, it was already hot and humid. I walked down the companionway to the quay. The limestone buildings of the town gleamed and shimmered in the sweltering conditions. Negro street vendors in brightly coloured clothes moved lazily as they offered their wares, little boys ran up to ask me to throw them copper coins. It was far too hot to walk to East Street, so I took a barouche.

When I reached the office I sent a message to Susan saying that I had arrived safely, then I talked to Johnson about the sale of the *Flora*.

"Have you heard from Donald MacGregor?" I asked.

"Yes I have, Mr Wells. They've had great misfortune on their first voyage with the *Calypso*. Apparently they were carrying iron plating for Confederate ships as part of their cargo. Maybe that slowed her down. A fast Yankee cruiser, the *Florida* I think, caught her as she was going through the Old Inlet at Cape Fear. But you will be happy to know that MacGregor still wants to buy the *Flora*."

"Do we know what happened to the crew of the *Calypso*?"

"Captured and locked up I'm afraid."

"I feel bad about it," I said, "she had seven successful runs for Mr Pembroke, and then as soon as we sell her…"

"The crew had the choice not to transfer to the new owner, Mr Wells," Johnson replied, "and that will be the same for the *Flora*. Don't forget that we lost the *Granite City*, and she hadn't even got as far as Cape Fear. I think they all recognise that it's the luck of the game."

"You're right," I said gloomily, "we must go ahead."

That same afternoon we completed the sale of the *Flora* in Mr Dupont's offices, and her crew chose to pass to the new owner. It was a strange moment for me. At one point I had been managing a fleet of five ships for Mr Pembroke. The sale of the *Giraffe* and the capture of the *Granite City* had cut the number to three. The loss of the *Clara* and the sale of the *Calypso* and the *Flora* now reduced the fleet to nothing. In a recent letter Mr Pembroke said that he didn't expect the new ships to arrive until October at the earliest, but that he was looking for an opportunity to find a new ship as a stopgap. If he were successful he would send her out to Nassau with Harry Mansell and the remainder of the *Clara's* crew. He asked me to remain in the Bahamas for the moment.

I had to face up to the fact that I was now looking at a period of idleness possibly lasting as much as four or five months. There were stocks of Mr Pembroke's goods lying in Henry Adderly's warehouses, and these would have to be sold. Johnson and I would perhaps do some trading of goods for other blockade-runners, but I was not looking forward to such a peaceful life. I was used to a life where every moment was filled with excitement and tension – running the blockade, dodging Yankee cruisers and gunboats, buying and selling cargoes and even selling ships. I also had the prospect of a separation from Amy lasting several months. I still had friends in Nassau, but Harry Mansell, my closest friend, was in London. My other friends from the *Clara* were away too. When I returned home to our rooms above the East Street offices late that afternoon I was feeling sorry for myself.

I had only been lounging in our sitting room for a moment, when our maid, Mary, knocked at the door.

"Dere's a lady to see you, sah," she said, "shall I show her up?"

I nodded. I hoped it was Susan, but I thought it was unlikely. She was usually so discreet in her visits. Up until now she had first made sure that our servants would not see her.

A few moments later the maid showed a slim, smartly dressed, veiled lady into the room. It was unmistakably Susan. I asked Mary to bring tea, and cool drinks.

"Yes, sah," she said, and left the room.

Susan lifted her veil. She was looking lovely. Her beautiful brown eyes were sad, but she was looking more attractive and charming than ever.

"Oh Tom, I have been waiting for this moment all day. As soon as I got your note I knew I had to come. I have been lonely an' sad an' worried, but now I know that you are safely home – it's so wonderful to see you."

She rushed forward and almost flung herself into my arms. We were holding each other tightly. Then she broke away and we sat side by side on a small sofa. I was holding both of her hands.

"You're looking so much better, how have you been since I left?"

"It's been one of the loneliest, saddest times of my life, Tom. But how are you? You are so brown from your travels. Don' you worry about being lock' up in Wilmington as a runaway slave?"

"They would miss getting their guns and silk if they locked *me* up," I said, "but there's no risk for the next few months. We sold the *Flora* this afternoon, and I don't have any more ships to manage. I was worrying about how bored I was going to get – and then you called. It's wonderful to see you."

"I mustn' stay long," she said, "I had to see you, but if I'm going to stay in Nassau I have to be a bit respectable. I'll leave after we've had some tea. But it's Sunday in two days. The servants are away. Please come and see me, and stay for dinner. It will only be cold food, but I promise it will be nice. I would love to have your company, dear Tom."

"Of course, Susan, I would be delighted to come on Sunday, and to think how I used to dread Sundays as a child!"

"Me too, Tom. All those sorrowful hymns, and lots of praying, when all I wanted was to be outside with my frien's. But how was your voyage Tom? Did you see Amy?"

Her face became more solemn as she asked me.

"Our voyage went well, and we made plenty of money for Mr Pembroke. I did see Amy, but under very sad circumstances. Her father was wounded in a battle in Virginia, and he died of his wounds. I went to his funeral near their plantation. I was only there for a day."

"How was Amy?"

"Very sad and distressed. Her mother still forbids our marriage, and our prospects are as distant as ever."

"I am so sorry, Tom," there was a gleam of soft sympathy in her eyes as she said this.

At the same moment we could hear Mary coming down the corridor with the tea. I got up and moved to another chair. Mary arranged the tea things on a table, and left us. Soon Susan left too, and I stayed at home that evening, full of self-pity.

On Sunday I walked down Parliament Street to Bay Street. All around there were throngs of smartly dressed churchgoers, and I could hear the sound of hymns being sung in one of the churches. There was an empty barouche on Bay Street. Soon the rather shabbily dressed Negro driver in his battered top hat was flicking the horse with his whip. I was on my way to Susan's villa. It was the height of summer. Although it was only just past ten in the morning, the day was already very hot. I was as lightly dressed as respectability would allow, and I was wearing a straw hat to protect my head from the sun.

The drive was pleasant, and the movement of the barouche provided a cooling breeze. The palm trees along the streets gave some shade, and many of the houses had their piazzas decorated with brightly coloured tropical flowers. But my mind was on Susan. I wanted to be supportive to her in her tragic circumstances, at the same time I felt a strong physical attraction to her. She had made no hint of any possible liaison; all that she seemed to be asking for was comfort and consolation in her despair and loneliness. I wanted to be loyal to Amy, and I made up my mind that I would stay as a support and protector for Susan. I would give no hint of the allure she still held for me.

She welcomed me at her front door; then she led the way through to the terrace at the back of the house. There we could sit in the shade of the piazza, looking over a quiet and secluded garden. We sipped cool drinks, and we talked about her business affairs, and the various matters where she needed my advice.

She was wearing a black silk mourning dress, but to cope with the heat I could see that she was not wearing her corset or the fashionable heavy petticoats of the day. Every time she moved, her charming figure was outlined, and I found it difficult to keep my eyes away. We were discussing a technical point to do with Hans's estate, when she paused and looked up at me with a quizzical expression in her brown eyes.

"What is it Tom?" she asked with a charming smile, "you seem distracted."

Blushing, I looked down in confusion at the glass I was holding.

"I'm sorry Susan. I don't know whether it's the heat, or this beautiful garden or what it is, but I don't seem to be able to concentrate."

She gave me an amused glance.

"Don' you wan' to help me Tom? Are you thinking about your ships, or your life in London?"

"No, Susan."

"What is it?" she asked softly.

"Susan, it's you. I want to be thinking about investments and money transfers, and all that, but all I can think about is those magical times we've had together. Please forgive me."

Susan stood up, and I stood too. I was expecting her to ask me to leave, but she stood looking at me with a shy smile.

"I'm afraid I've been thinking about that too."

Suddenly I was in her arms and we were kissing passionately. Then she pulled away and a teasing look came into her eyes.

"Take me upstairs, Tom, I don't think you've ever seen the view from my bedroom."

I suppose I should have hesitated and thought of my loyalty to Amy, but Susan was looking so alluring and delicious that I picked her up in my arms and started to carry her into the house.

"Are you sure this is what you want to do?" I asked.

"Yes Tom. I just want to forget everything and be with you. Am I too heavy for you?" she giggled, "don't tire yourself out jus' yet."

We woke up in each other's arms early in the afternoon. Susan went down to the kitchen to fetch some fruit and cold food. We sat at a small table in her room and ate some delicious cold meat, fish, salad, pineapples and mangoes, and we drank a little wine, chilled with ice from her icehouse. I lifted the blinds. Then we could see the spectacular view across the ocean towards Eleuthera Island, and I wondered if Sunday could ever have been spent in a more pleasant fashion. I had pangs of guilt that I had given way to my desire so easily, but Susan seemed to feel the same way I did. I thought of Amy, but I convinced myself that since our engagement was forbidden, somehow a liaison with Susan was permissible. I imagined that no one was being damaged and I let myself drift into a lagoon of pleasure.

"This is wonderful Susan," I said, "it seems like an amazing dream. I'm terrified that I shall wake up and find that it never happened."

"Whilst you were dreaming, and snoring like a hog, I was thinking."

"What about, Susan?" I asked.

"Why don' you come and live here with me?"

"How could that work? What about your reputation on the island? As a blockade-runner I have very little reputation to lose, but what about you?"

She looked at me seriously.

"I'm lonely here. I can only see you sometimes, and then I'm alone with servan's for the res' of the time. You could be here."

"How Susan?"

"I have one maid who I really trus'. I'll sen' the other servants away. She can look after us. I can get a cleaner to come during the week. If I need a carriage, I sen' the gardener for it, there are stables not far away."

"What will you say to the servants?"

"I'll say that I don' have enough money to keep them."

"Is that true?"

"No. Hans was rich, but they don' know that. Come back to bed an' think about it there."

We lay in each other's arms. I know it sounds selfish, but I couldn't help thinking how bored I was going to be over the next few months, and what a wonderful opportunity this was to change all that. The contours of Susan's body pressing against me made the prospect almost irresistible, but I hesitated.

"I know what you're thinking Tom, but don't worry about it. I know you are not going to marry me, and that you want to marry Amy. But why can't we be happy, even if it's only for a short while?"

"Can you really accept that, Susan?"

"Yes," she said.

I had already taken the first steps downwards, and the others came easily. I know now that my decision was wrong, and indeed it led to consequences that caused much anguish and bitterness, but I was weak.

"Then let's do it," I said.

Before I could say any more she was kissing me passionately again.

"Oh Tom, please move here as soon as you can."

"Yes, Susan, but I think I should still have my base in my rooms at East Street. I'll spend most of the time here, and I will leave some clothes, but I think that if we are going to protect your reputation, I won't move here completely."

"Yes, if that's what you wan' Tom," she said.

Within a few days Susan had made the arrangements, and I moved into her villa. I could walk to our offices in the morning when it was still relatively cool, and in the afternoon or the evening, I would take a barouche back from Bay Street or the Royal Victoria. Sometimes I went to the receptions and gatherings at Government House, or parties organised by my blockade-running friends, but afterwards I would go home to Susan. We still had our servants at East Street, and they looked after us in the office.

My conscience troubled me. I was ashamed that instead of being Susan's guardian and advisor I had become her lover. I was very fond of her, and passionately enjoyed being with her, but I was still in love with Amy. Amy was writing to me, and I wrote her long letters in reply, smuggled into Wilmington through the kind efforts of my friends. I should have been honest with Amy, and confessed to my sins, but I thought that I could walk on water in those days. I convinced myself that I could hold the distant prospect of marriage to Amy in one hand, whilst holding Susan with the other, and no evil would come of it. Well our sins catch up with us eventually.

At the end of August a letter came from Edward Pembroke telling me that he was in the process of buying a small steamship called the *Heroine,* and that his new ships would be delayed. The *Heroine* did not fit the pattern that he had agreed with Mr Stringer, but it would be an opportunity for Mansell and the remainder of his crew to return to Nassau. Johnson and I were excited at the prospect of the work the *Heroine* would bring, but three weeks later another letter came to say that the *Heroine* was already sold to Henry Coffey. We were able to provide some assistance to her, but now it seemed that it would be November or even December before we could expect the first new ship, the *Isabella*.

For most of the time Susan and I lived harmoniously. Our affair was passionate and sweet, and we got on well together. I wondered whether she would get bored during the days when I was at the office, but I had so little to do that my days there were short. Susan seemed to be happy enough enjoying the house, helping the maid to prepare our food, and making shopping expeditions into the town. On one occasion I came to the villa unexpectedly, to find Susan in close conversation with a handsome Spanish visitor, but she explained that he had business to conduct to do with Hans Kohler's estate. I had a momentary pang of jealousy, which she soon soothed away. Then in November everything changed.

One evening I was invited to a dinner in the Royal Victoria. Several of the fleet of blockade-runners were in port, and my friend Thomas Taylor had just returned from a successful trip on the *Banshee*. He wanted to celebrate. First we drank champagne cocktails in one of the saloons, then some twenty of us went to a private dining room for dinner. The meal was gargantuan, and we drank champagne throughout. Afterwards the evening became rowdy, with songs being sung, games played, and even fights breaking out. Some were still drinking champagne, but brandy bottles were also being passed round. After the tension and danger of running the blockade it was no surprise that those involved wanted to release the tension by drunken revelry. The hotel staff were tolerant, they were earning huge sums from us.

I had decided to sleep that night at East Street, and late in the evening came the time to make my way there. I walked round to Thomas Taylor to thank him, and I made my way towards the door, followed by shouts.

"Which house are you going to, Wells?" … "Is it the Dalrymple?" … "Have you got a girl somewhere Tom?"

I almost sleepwalked up the stairs at East Street and into our sitting room.

"Hallo old fellow, do you remember Harry Mansell?" came a cheerful voice, "I heard you were at the Victoria, so I decided to wait up for you."

There he was, springing out of one of our armchairs, and coming over to shake my hand vigorously.

"Harry! You've given me the surprise of my life. How did you get here so quickly? Did you bring the *Isabella*?"

"She was ready quicker than Pembroke expected, so he decided to send her straight out. There was no point in writing to warn you. I have a bundle of letters and documents for you downstairs. He gives you such detailed instructions, I'm surprised he doesn't come out here and run the show himself! Mary says that you don't spend much time here, what have you been doing?"

This was awkward. I had never told Harry about Susan, and although our servants knew something, I had asked them for discretion. Only Johnson knew where to contact me in an emergency. Mansell went to fetch a bottle of brandy, then we sat down in easy chairs to talk. Perhaps the alcohol loosened my tongue, but I found myself mentioning Susan.

"I have been visiting a friend who lives further along the coast. She is the widow of poor Kohler, who died of yellow fever in June."

Mansell frowned.

"Mrs Kohler? Forgive me Tom, but I'm almost sure I've heard something about her. I think Mrs Dalrymple mentioned her to me, wasn't she at Mackey Street for a while?"

I wondered how to answer his question.

"She hasn't talked about her past much to me," I muttered.

"Yes," continued Mansell, "isn't she the clever little minx who tricked that fat Bavarian into marrying her?"

Now it was my turn to frown.

"Harry, it may be true that she was at Mackey Street, but she has been through a very difficult time. I often stay at the villa to keep her company. She has no friends here, and she has been very lonely since her husband died. I would be grateful if you didn't speak of her in that way."

"Sorry old chap, I didn't realise she was such a friend of yours," said Mansell, "I shall say no more and leave you to your secret assignations. Get the cork out of that bottle again, would you Tom."

Harry's arrival transformed everything. Mr Pembroke gave notice in his letters of the commissioning of two more ships, the *Index* and the *Nutfield*. These were to be expected in January. We could now work in earnest to assemble the cargo for the *Isabella*. Harry took me down to see her the following day. She was a magnificent ship, designed to the template we had determined. She was two hundred and twenty-five feet long by twenty-eight in the beam, she drew only twelve and a half feet. She was iron hulled, and driven by side paddles. We talked as we went round the ship.

"You wait 'til you see her move," said Mansell, with an excited gesture, "I'm sure she can outrun any Yankee cruiser. She's nippy too – I've heard that the blockade ships are as thick as fleas on a dog's back now, and we'll need every ounce of speed and manoeuvrability we can muster. The ideal time for the next run will be the end of this week, can you get her cargo ready by then old fellow?"

"How much can she carry?"

"The shipbuilders calculate on five hundred and fifty tons, but I'm sure you'll want to squeeze on more than that! Shall we say six hundred? Any more, and she may get caught like the *Granite City*."

"I think I can undertake to get her loaded by Friday night," I said, "it'll be Wilmington. Charleston's too risky now that the Yankees have taken Fort Wagner. I'll come with you if I may."

We went and sat in Mansell's cabin.

"What's the news of Miss Munro?" he asked, with a smile.

"A letter from her came through last week, she still sounded rather low. They had some terrible family tragedies in the summer. She lost her brother Jack to typhoid fever in a Yankee prison, and her father died just before the big Confederate defeat at Gettysburg. She gets nervous being at the plantation just with her mother. They have a manager, but he is an elderly man, and he doesn't live in the plantation house. On top of all that, all the plantations are struggling because they can't sell enough cotton."

"Sounds pretty gloomy. Is there any progress on your suit? Will her mother allow your engagement?"

"No, nothing has really changed in that direction. Mrs Munro forbids us to get engaged, but at least we can write to each other. But I need to get to Wilmington for business reasons too. We've put no cargoes in there since June, and I must see Angus Blair. I did let him know that there was a new ship coming, although I couldn't tell him when. I think he'll be impressed when he sees this ship, and he'll be happy to hear about the *Nutfield* and the *Index*."

Late that afternoon I went back to Susan's house. We were sitting on a cane sofa on her veranda when I explained about the arrival of the *Isabella*, and the fact that we were going to be leaving for Wilmington on Friday evening.

A sad expression came over Susan's face.

"I suppose it had to happen, Tom, do you really have to go? Couldn't you stay here?"

Her arms were round me as she pleaded with me, and a tear trickled down her cheek.

"No, Susan, I'd love to stay, but I must get to Wilmington. Mr Pembroke is sending out two more ships, and I need to get everything ready."

"Will you see Amy, Tom?" she asked in a low voice.

"I doubt it, Susan, you know that her mother has forbidden our marriage."

"I see," she said thoughtfully.

We spent a quiet nostalgic evening together, and I agreed to spend Thursday evening with her too. For four months Susan and I had been seeing each other almost every day and our parting came as a desperate wrench. I think we were both wondering whether our relationship would be the same when I returned. As I started to leave, late that Thursday evening, Susan was in tears. I found it hard to comfort her.

Chapter Fourteen
The Isabella

We left early the following morning. The *Isabella* had been built on a more generous scale than the *Clara*, and was much more comfortable. I had a cabin to myself, which I considered luxury indeed. There were no Northern cruisers lurking outside the harbour, and we saw none before we were through the Channel. Then the trouble started. As Mansell had warned, the Atlantic between Nassau and Wilmington was now swarming with Yankee ships. Fortunately, Pembroke and Stringer had invested their money well. The *Isabella* performed beautifully. Her profile was low, and her grey colouring made her difficult for the Yankees to see. She was very fast, and she could turn in the water as quickly as a hansom cab in Piccadilly. Mansell had Nigel Fenton as his first officer and Rowland was his chief engineer. We had been fortunate to secure a very experienced Cape Fear pilot.

There was a strong easterly breeze blowing, generating a heavy swell. Our lookouts were constantly finding new Northern ships on the horizon, but Mansell managed to dodge them during the first two days. On the third day he called the ship's officers together, and we discussed the tactics for getting through the blockade cordon at Cape Fear. He decided that it was too dangerous to take the coastal route, as gunboats and cruisers tended to lurk along the surf line. Many blockade-runners had been trapped. We decided that our best chance was to try to slip through the cordon during the early part of the night, and aim to be at the bar in the New Inlet as the moon was rising.

The plan was a fine one. But as was so often the case, events conspired against us. There seemed to be Northern ships everywhere, and we had to twist and turn to avoid them. Eventually Mansell announced that it was now too dangerous to attempt the Cape Fear entrance that night. Soon it would be daylight, and we were certain to be trapped by the blockade cordon, so we steamed north, and hid out along the coast. As we lurked along the sea shore some twenty miles north east of Fort Fisher, a Yankee gunboat dropped anchor not more than three hundred yards from us in the early dawn light, but our grey colour and low profile protected us. To our relief, two hours later they upped anchor and steamed away.

That evening we made our second attempt, and this time the *Isabella's* speed and Mansell's skill brought us safely through the cordon. We had a brief encounter with a Yankee gunboat, and received a broadside as we passed, but fortunately the shots passed over us. By midnight we were safe at anchorage at Smithville.

We were informed that we must go into quarantine, so I sent a message to Angus Blair at Wilmington giving details of our cargo. I enclosed a letter for Amy, and I asked him to try to get it quickly to her at Marion. Despite my long idyll with Susan, I was still as eager as ever to see Amy and try to renew my suit. I was deeply in love with her, and fiercely jealous of Hamilton Douglas.

We had no yellow fever cases, and after two weeks we steamed into Wilmington.

My intention had been to go immediately to Angus Blair's office, but a surprise was waiting for me. Amongst the crowd on the quay I could see Mr Blair's carriage, and a young girl was leaning out of it eagerly scanning the ship. As we got closer I could see to my surprise and delight that the young lady was Amy. She had a young Negro servant girl with her.

Breathlessly I told Mansell that Amy was there, and I was the first off the companionway after we tied up.

"Amy! What a wonderful surprise! What are you doing here in Wilmington? How did you know that we were arriving today?"

The warmth of her smile showed me that she was just as thrilled and excited as I was.

"Mother has sent me down to Wilmington to stay with Uncle Angus, and he gave me your letter. Well we knew you that would have to be in quarantine, and so it would be at least two weeks before you could get up here. I'm afraid that I asked my uncle if one of his servants could wait on the riverbank below the town. He was happy to do it as he's trying to get money to help his mother. As soon as he saw the *Isabella* he ran to the house, and I came straight down here. This is Rosa who came with me."

She smiled at the young Negro maid.

"It's nice to meet you Rosa," I said, "is this your first visit to Wilmington?"

"It sure is, Mr Wells. I've never been away from the plantation before," she said, and she gave an excited smile, "I'm here to look after Miss Amy."

"Rosa thought the boat trip from Fayetteville was very exciting," said Amy, "and she loves staying at my uncle's house. But how was your voyage Tom? Did you have any trouble?"

"As you can see, we came through the blockade unscathed. This is Mr Pembroke's latest ship and she's a beauty. Would you like to see on board? Harry Mansell's the captain, and I would like to introduce you."

We made our way onto the *Isabella*. I showed Amy and her maid my cabin first.

"It's very small," said Amy, as she glanced round the cabin, "how on earth do you manage to sleep here?"

"It's great luxury I can assure you compared to my cabin on the poor old *Clara*. There I had to share with the first officer, and the cabin was even smaller than this. But let's go to the wheelhouse, I think Harry Mansell will be there."

We went back out onto the deck, and round to the wheelhouse. Harry was talking to one of the Wilmington harbour officials. He made his excuses and came over to us.

I introduced them.

"I feel that I know you already," said Harry, "Tom has never stopped talking about you from the moment I first met him in London. Now that I've met you, I can understand why."

He bowed and smiled.

"But I hope you will excuse me; unless I can get all the permissions from Mr Elphinstone, we'll have to go back to Smithville. Can I hope that I'll see you again in Wilmington?"

"There is a ball tonight at the Elliotts – they are friends of my uncle. It is in aid of the Southern Cause. I was hoping that Mr Wells would come. Shall I try to get an invitation for you as well Captain Mansell?"

"I would be delighted, Miss Munro," said Harry.

We left the *Isabella* and we were taken in the carriage towards Angus Blair's office. Amy said that there were so many rough types in the area of the docks that Blair had insisted that Amy and her maid came in his carriage. Amy and I had so much to talk about that we almost forgot that Rosa was with us; but Rosa spent much of the time looking at the sights of Wilmington through the carriage windows.

"It was the most wonderful surprise to see you," I said, "I never dreamt that you would be here in Wilmington. Is your mother here? Has she changed her mind about me?"

"No, Tom," said Amy sadly, and she glanced quickly at Rosa. But Rosa seemed totally absorbed by the street activities.

"Mother stayed at Marion to help with the management of the plantation. She sent me here because she says I'm making trouble for her with the Negroes. Why can't she see that all I'm doing is looking after their health, which surely helps us?" she frowned as she said this, and looked appealingly at me, "but anyway she sent me to Uncle Angus telling me that if you were here, I could only see you as a friend. She has also sent poor Uncle Angus very detailed instructions about me."

Then she smiled, leaned over to me and whispered excitedly in my ear.

"But of course although I can strictly forbid you to talk about marriage, I know you pirates can be very wilful."

We both smiled.

"How is Mrs Munro?"

"Louise and little Henry are staying with her whilst I am away, so she has some distraction, but she is still deeply depressed by the deaths of Father and my two brothers."

Amy's beautiful eyes were cast down, and she clenched her little hands round her handkerchief in her lap. Finally she turned to me again.

"You *will* see me as often as you can in Wilmington, won't you Tom?"

I smiled. It was an easy promise to make.

Then I broached a subject that perhaps I should have waited to ask about. What was the position with Hamilton Douglas?

"Oh Tom, you didn't trust me did you?" said Amy with an amused smile, "perhaps my charms are not so wonderful as you both seemed to think! Major Douglas is engaged to marry a girl from Savannah. It seems that the everlasting love he spoke about was a little short lived…"

I'm afraid I couldn't hide my delight despite the presence of Rosa in the carriage.

We made our way out of the dock area. There were sinister, scruffily-dressed figures lounging against walls, and making their way furtively, or sometimes brazenly around the streets close to the river. There were soldiers too, trying to ensure that order was kept. As we progressed towards Mr Blair's office the streets became more civilised, and more respectably dressed citizens were to be seen. When we reached her uncle's office, Amy explained to him that she wanted to arrange for invitations for Harry and myself for the ball that night. Then with a smile to me, she left with Rosa. Mr Blair invited me to sit down. He seemed genuinely pleased to see me.

"I am sure that Mrs Elliott will be delighted to invite two young blockade runners to her ball, if I can vouch for your respectability. So many of the young men from Wilmington are with the army now, and our young ladies are desperate for eligible dancing partners. How was your voyage on the *Isabella*?"

"It's getting more and more difficult. Fortunately she's a very well built ship and we managed to dodge the Yankees in the end."

Mr Blair sat for a moment fidgeting with the papers on his desk. Finally he looked up at me with a troubled expression.

"My sister has put me in a very difficult position, Mr Wells. She says that Amy may see you if you are here in Wilmington, but she is determined that there should be no talk of marriage or engagement between you. But how can I act as a chaperone at one moment, your host at another, and your agent for the rest of the time? I am afraid that my beautiful niece knows only too well how to bend me to her will. I just hope that you can help me.

"My sister has sent Amy to me in the hope that I can get her to spend more time with people of her own age and social position. It seems that at Marion she spends most of her time trying to help the

Negroes. I am delighted that she's going to the Elliotts' ball, and I am happy that you are going too, but please can you help me to fulfil my undertaking to my sister?"

"I'll do my best," I said, "I know how close Amy is to her family, and I have no intention of causing any estrangement. If Mrs Munro continues to forbid our engagement, you have my word that I will respect that. I will not cause you any embarrassment if I can help it."

"I am grateful to you, sir," he said. "I think my sister is wrong. Her objection to you is mainly the danger of your occupation, but that is the time we are going through. If Jack or Preston had wanted to become engaged I do not think there would have been any objection. But I must respect my sister's wishes."

We then moved on to discuss the disposal of the *Isabella's* current cargo, and the purchase of cotton and tobacco for her return voyage.

"You will be pleased to know that we now have a cotton compress at Eagles Island," said Blair, "the steam presses can compact those five hundred pound bales. I imagine that will mean that you should be able to restrict the cotton on deck for your return voyage."

This was excellent news. The extra capacity of the *Isabella*, together with the compacted bales, would mean much increased profitability for each trip. Once our business discussions were complete, I told Mr Blair that I hoped to see him later that day before the Elliotts' ball.

"I think you can be sure," he said, "that there will be invitations for you and Captain Mansell. I should warn you that they will be raising money at the ball, and there will be ladies selling all sorts of nonsense at the stalls. I would be more than delighted if you and Captain Mansell would come to my house at four this evening for dinner. I think I can promise you something nice. Then we can go on to the Elliotts' house together in my carriage. Perhaps both of you can spend the night at my house afterwards. I will need to get you passes for the curfew."

I accepted on behalf of Harry and myself, and I asked Mr Blair for the Elliotts' address. I said that I would send them something from the *Isabella* to be sold at one of the stalls. Then I returned to the ship. Harry was in his cabin and I explained the arrangements I had made.

"Excellent," said Harry, "but I won't be able to spend the night there – it's our first night in port, and I need to be here to sweep up any trouble the crew might get into. I'll make my way back here from the ball. I have no dress coat on board, do you think they would accept me in my naval uniform?"

"Mr Blair tells me that the young ladies of Wilmington are desperate for eligible young men. If you're in uniform, I think there'll be a stampede. You might be sensible to wear your sword so you can fight them off."

"That's the kind of fighting I've been looking for," he said, "surrender could never be so sweet. I just hope they allow me to surrender to them one at a time."

We presented ourselves at Mr Blair's house at four. Harry was looking very dashing in his naval dress uniform, and I was respectable in my London tailcoat. Amy was still in half-mourning for her father and her brother, but although she was wearing grey she was looking lovely. She apologised that the dress had been adapted from one that her mother had worn years ago, and it was hardly fashionable. It seemed beautiful to me. As she led the way downstairs to the dining room, she and her uncle told us more about the ball.

"Mrs Elliott was thrilled," said Amy, "that we are bringing two handsome blockade-running pirates to her ball. She has asked us to come early. She has her sister Mrs Pierce staying in the house, and Mrs Pierce's two daughters, Charlotte and Virginia. I have met them, and they are very beautiful. She wants to introduce you both before the others all arrive."

"You told us that the ball is in aid of the Southern Cause," said Harry, "what does that signify?"

"It is a fund raising event," Mr Blair replied, "the invitations have to be bought, but only certain families in Wilmington have the opportunity. During the ball there will be a bazaar and various other ways to raise money. I hope you have brought some with you!"

Harry jingled his pockets.

"Surely no self-respecting pirate would go out without his pieces of eight."

Soon we were on our way to the Elliotts' house in Market Street, ten minutes away in the carriage. It was a small mansion with the customary white-pillared piazza. It had a ballroom on the top floor. The house was looking tired on the outside, and seemed in want of paint and loving care. But the inside was filled with flowers, and stalls had been set up in the downstairs rooms. Although we were virtually the first to arrive, the house was already humming with activity. The ladies running the stalls were scurrying about, making last minute preparations, and Rosebud, the Negro band, was tuning up its fiddles, and they were practicing on their banjos, mandolins and dulcimers. A Negro butler led us through to the drawing room where Mrs Elliott was waiting with her sister and her nieces. Mr Blair introduced us.

"Of course I remember Mr Wells," said Mrs Elliott. "Captain Mansell, we are so pleased that you are able to come, and Mr Wells, thank you so much for the contraband you sent over from your ship. One of the cases will be sold in the bazaar, and I'm afraid that we have decided to use the other to bolster the wine cup."

"Do tell us what your contraband was Mr Wells," asked Charlotte, "everything is so drab here now – it is thrilling to be benefiting from the treasures of your pirate ship."

"We sent over two cases of champagne," I said, "the Yankees failed to capture them on the way over, so it's only fair to donate them to the cause."

Charlotte and Virginia were twins, and just as beautiful as Amy had described. Both were tall and vivacious, but Charlotte was fair and Virginia dark. I could see that Mansell was rapidly becoming bewitched by both of them.

"Do come up and see the ballroom," exclaimed Virginia, "aunt Miranda has made it so beautiful with the autumn flowers. We must go and see how the band look in their corner."

"I have to stay here to receive," said Mrs Elliott, "but please do go upstairs and make sure that everything is set up properly. Charles is in charge up there, but he may need helping. The band is very excited to be out after the curfew."

We went upstairs with the twins, but Mr Blair stayed downstairs with Mrs Elliott. Soon the ballroom started to fill up with the other guests. There were more ladies than men, and nearly all the young men were in uniform. Some of them showed signs of injuries received in the recent battles – eye patches and empty sleeves were only too prevalent. The war had taken its toll of the dancers' clothing too. The ladies' dresses were much repaired, and the men's uniforms were patched and darned. But they all seemed proud, happy and determined to enjoy the evening. The guest of honour was the dashing Colonel Lamb, commander of Fort Fisher. He had brought with him his beautiful wife, who came from the North, but had now taken up the Southern Cause. Mrs Lamb had refused all offers to live in the safety of Wilmington, and insisted on living in a small cottage close to the fort. I had met both of them on my visits to Fort Fisher

As the guests arrived the band played a medley of the popular tunes of the day – *Dixie's Land, Darling Nellie Grey* and *The Girl I Left Behind Me*. Soon the dancing started in earnest.

Etiquette only allowed me to ask Amy for two dances, and I asked her to reserve both waltzes for me. The first dance was a waltz, and we were in each other's arms spinning around the dance floor.

"It is a dream to be dancing here with you Tom, and not to be surrounded by the gloom of Marion."

"It's a dream for me too to be dancing with the most beautiful girl in the world, instead of dodging Yankee ships on the Atlantic. But surely you love Marion, haven't you told me in your letters that you think it the most wonderful place in the world?"

"Yes, in my childhood it was the most wonderful, happy place, but all that has changed. Let's not talk about that now, we must enjoy today. Your friend Harry Mansell is dancing with Charlotte Pierce, how did he choose between them?"

"I think he would have danced with both of them simultaneously if he could. The choice was easier for me…"

All too quickly the dance was over, and I had to return Amy to Mrs Elliott who was acting as her chaperone for the evening. The waltz was followed by a polka. Amy told me that I must dance all the dances, and she introduced me to her friends and cousins as the evening went on. I even managed to secure a dance with Mrs Lamb, despite her popularity. The champagne in the wine cup heightened the spirits of the dancers, and the evening became increasingly gay and light-hearted. The ballroom was buzzing with excitement as we danced the Lancers, the Gallop and the Virginia Reel. Most of the dances I knew from London and Nassau, but I had to learn some of them from patient partners. At ten o'clock there was a break for supper, and we went down to a table reserved for Mr and Mrs Elliott and their party. Mr Blair and Mr Elliott had not danced. They had been playing cards downstairs with some of the other more elderly gentlemen. Mr Elliott turned to me.

"I trust you have been doing your duty and dancing all the dances Mr Wells?"

"Yes, Miss Munro has instructed me in my duty, and I have been enjoying it. It's wonderful that people can have such an interlude of pleasure in these dark times."

"How does it compare to London, Captain Mansell?" asked Mr Blair, "I believe you have just returned from there."

"The girls are much prettier here," he replied, smiling at Charlotte and Virginia Pierce, "but otherwise it's much the same. I've seldom enjoyed an evening so much. How are the stalls going Mrs Elliott? I hope that we are making a good contribution to the Southern Cause?"

"Your champagne is the most popular item!" she replied, "we are selling the bottles individually, and they all sold in the first hour. I cannot thank you enough."

"Can you give us any encouragement about Britain's attitude to the war Captain Mansell?" asked Mr Elliott, "will she go on sitting on the fence? I cannot understand it. It is clearly in your interest to come in on the Southern side, what are you waiting for?"

"I'm sure Captain Mansell doesn't want to talk about politics, Charles," said his wife, tugging at his sleeve.

"It is not just politics my dear, it is life and death for the South!" he replied angrily.

"Well at least we're not slipping into Mexico," said Mansell, "and trying to grab it under your noses like the French. But I don't think Palmerston's going to change his policy now. The cotton famine might have brought him in earlier in the war, but we're getting more cotton from India and Egypt now."

"Damn the fellow," said Elliott, "I guess we will just have to do it on our own. We certainly licked the Yankees at Chickamauga, and I have to admit that damn fellow Bragg did well there, but now…"

Mr Elliott fulminated on about the war, and soon he was launching a tirade against General Bragg. His face took on a darker shade of red as he talked.

"After his success at Chickamauga, I refused to listen to criticism of him," he said, "but now I can see what they mean. He never makes a decision. What stopped him attacking at Chattanooga? He had the Yankees at his mercy! Now that damn fellow Grant is making a fool of him and he is retreating again!"

"Have you heard what they are saying about him?" asked Blair, "they say that Bragg could never get into heaven. Even if he was invited in, he would fall back."

"It is no laughing matter," said Elliott, "if he hadn't sent Longstreet to chase Burnside into Knoxville, he could have smashed Rosecrans at Chattanooga, and then Atlanta would be protected."

"Atlanta!" exclaimed Amy, "surely the Yankees could not get there could they, Mr Elliott?"

"If Bragg is still in charge they might," grumbled Elliott, "but I cannot believe that Davis will still support him after Chattanooga. I think the army really would mutiny this time. What else did you bring in on your ship Mr Wells? I trust it was not *only* champagne."

"No, our cargo was mainly military, but we do have one or two luxuries on board. I hope that you will all come and visit the *Isabella.* What do you say Harry? Shall we arrange a dinner on the ship? We have a very good cook on board."

"An excellent idea Tom. How about Saturday at three?" he looked eagerly round the table, "Mrs Pierce, will you and your daughters still be in Wilmington then?"

"Oh please Mama! I have never been on a pirate ship," said

Virginia.

"Well if your aunt will allow us to stay one more day," said her mother, looking at Mrs Elliott, "but I don't think you should be describing poor Captain Mansell as a pirate."

"No," said Harry, "far too risky. There'll be a hint of cold steel at your throat, up anchor, and we'll have you in the Bahamas in no time."

There was laughter around the table.

"Of course you may stay until Saturday," said Mrs Elliott, "we accept your invitation to the *Isabella*, Captain Mansell. I am also most excited to be visiting a genuine blockade-runner."

After supper the band lured the dancers upstairs by playing more of their favourite tunes. Soon we could hear *The Bonny Blue Flag* and *When Johnny Comes Marching Home*. We made our way up to the ballroom again. My happiness and excitement at being with Amy had been enhanced by the knowledge that my rival, Hamilton Douglas, was no longer a threat. I was longing for my next dance with her, but I had to wait until the end of the evening for the waltz. After the last dance, Mansell went back to the *Isabella*, and I travelled with Amy and Mr Blair in his carriage back to his house in Second Street. Amy and I sat side by side opposite her uncle. Soon I could feel Amy's soft little gloved hand searching for mine between us, and we sat holding hands as the carriage made its way back towards the house through the quiet streets

It was two o'clock in the morning when we reached Mr Blair's house. As we got down from the carriage, the night was chilly and we could see the steam coming from the horses' nostrils. We pulled our coats round us, and hurried into the house. As soon as we were inside we went our separate ways to bed. As I got into my night things I went over in my mind the magical evening we had just spent. I was more in love with Amy than ever, and just sitting next to her holding her hand in the carriage had been a moment of ecstasy for me. I only had to close my eyes to feel myself waltzing round the Elliott's ballroom with Amy in her lovely grey dress. I could experience again the feeling of being so close to the person I loved most in the world. Susan was a charming companion, but Amy was the love of my life. I got into bed and was I sitting up, about to blow out my candle, when there was a gentle knock at my bedroom door. Amy slipped inside.

She was wearing the same yellow silk dressing gown I had seen at Marion; without her crinoline I could see her beautiful slim figure. She came over and kissed me on the lips, then she sat down on the bed. Her body was pressed against my legs under the covers, and she rested her right hand gently on my knee.

"Mother would kill me if she knew I was here," she whispered, with her dark eyes looking seriously into mine, "I don't think Uncle Angus would, but he would send me straight back to Marion in disgrace. Oh Tom, it has been five months, and I have thought about you every minute. What are we going to do?"

"I've promised Mr Blair that I wouldn't mention marriage or engagement, Amy," I replied, "but I'm afraid those are the only things on my mind at the moment. How long are you going to be staying here?"

"At least another week I think, but I'll certainly stay as long as you do. When does the *Isabella* have to leave?"

"Very soon, I'm afraid. I have to go back with her, as Mr Pembroke is sending out two more ships. How I wish I could stay longer, you are more beautiful than ever. I was so proud to be waltzing with you in your lovely grey dress. I knew every man in the room was envying me."

"Oh Tom, you know that dress looked awful, but thank you. You were very smart and handsome in your tail coat – how did you know to bring it?"

"Harry says that a gentleman should always be prepared for all contingencies, although I think I was more prepared than he was. What did you think of him?"

"He is very dashing and makes a very convincing pirate. He seems to have fallen for the Pierce twins, and I think that Charlotte is very taken with him."

As we spoke, the candle on my bedside table was burning very low; now it started to flicker.

"I must not stay," said Amy, but she showed no sign of leaving.

In the flickering light she came closer to me until the urge to kiss became irresistible. As we kissed the candle finally burnt out, and we were left in darkness. She lay down on the bed beside me. She lay on her side with her left arm around me, I lay back, and we kissed again. She shivered.

"What's the matter Amy?"

"It's so cold in your room, Tom."

She snuggled against me with the covers in between us and I pulled a blanket over her to keep her warm. Even through the covers I could feel her soft body against me. We lay blissfully, just holding each other.

"Will we ever marry, Amy?" I asked, in a whisper.

There was a long silence.

"Mother is against it, and no matter how much I argue with her, she will not change her mind. It is making us both miserable. I told you that I was sent down to Wilmington because Mother thinks that I'm making trouble for her with the slaves. Well it was more than just that. We found ourselves arguing all the time, and I think she could not bear it any longer."

"But where does it leave us, Amy?"

She kissed me, and she was stroking my arm through the covers.

"I'm going to marry you, Tom," she said in a quiet determined voice, "and nothing Mother can say is going to stop me. We are going to get married at Marion, and I'm going to convince Mother."

"Amy, that's wonderful, it seems an age since you agreed to marry me, and then your parents forbade it. I can't tell you how much I have longed to hear those words again, but when? We can't wait forever…"

"I don't know, Tom. But I love you, and it is going to happen."

"How are you going to persuade her? Surely some of the things that they held against me are gone. I am becoming a rich man, and I think she will have no objections there. I admit that blockade running is dangerous, but so is the army, or almost anything here at the moment. Let's pray that she listens to reason. But if she goes on refusing … would you consider eloping with me?"

"My mother has been through so much, I don't know, Tom."

She sighed.

"But we *will* get married, I promise you we will!"

We had one more long passionate kiss, and I hugged her to me.

Then she slipped out of my arms and tiptoed to the door. She peeped outside, and she was gone.

I lay in bed with my mind in turmoil. I thought about Amy, and her promise to marry me, and I thought about Susan and our long, passionate affair. I had justified my actions with Susan because Amy said she could never marry me. Now everything had changed, and I had to review my actions. The more I thought about it, the more the conclusion was blaring at me.

I had to tell Susan that our affair was over. The liaison wasn't fair to her, and it wasn't fair to Amy. My mind was made up. Finally I could get some rest.

Chapter Fifteen
The Nutfield

We had three more days before we sailed for Nassau. I moved back on board, and I only saw Amy once more before our departure, and that was when Mr Blair, Amy, the Elliotts and the Pierces came for dinner on the *Isabella* that Saturday afternoon. Harry continued to press his attentions on Charlotte Pierce, and I managed to have five minutes on my own with Amy. I promised her that I would be back in Wilmington as soon as I could. Amy undertook to do her best to persuade her mother to give her permission for us to marry. Our farewells were sweet.

On Monday morning I sat on my bunk thinking about Amy as the *Isabella's* boilers were fired up, and it was only when the ship pulled away from her moorings that I went to join Harry in the wheelhouse. He had just worked out the course with the Cape Fear River pilot. First we would go to the smoking station to check for runaway slaves, before we could head for Smithville and the estuary. Harry and I went up to the flying bridge on our own, as the pilot took control of the ship.

"Sad to be leaving Wilmington?" Harry asked.

"Yes. I wish I knew when I would be back here. But at least we had nearly a week. How were your farewells from the beautiful Miss Pierce?"

"Charlotte is leaving for their plantation just north of here – it's by the coast at Hampstead. But don't distract me with that old fellow, or we'll strike one of those damned torpedoes in the river; then our goodbyes would be a bit more permanent."

Although the pilot was in charge of the ship, Harry's eyes were everywhere as we moved carefully down river.

"She'd have to have an adventurous spirit to cope with you Harry – or a will of iron. Perhaps she could turn you into a farmer."

"No, not here," replied Harry. "I'm a supporter of the South, but not slavery. Maybe she could tempt me with a kangaroo farm at Ballarat. But what about you Tom, any progress with the beautiful

Miss Munro?"

"Well I feel the same as you do about slavery, and if it wasn't for Amy I think I might give up blockade running. Mrs Munro still forbids our marriage; Amy promises that it *will* happen, but I don't know when. It may take years for her to persuade her mother."

"So it's back to Mrs Kohler?"

"Harry! I feel guilty when you mention her name. It's true that there is a strong attachment between us, but Amy knows nothing about her, and I hope she never will. When we get back I have decided I must finish it."

"Well Charlotte knows nothing about the delights of Mrs Dalrymple's establishment, but I can't say I'm going to finish with *those* ladies just yet."

He paused.

"I have got to know Mrs Dalrymple quite well over the last year or so, Tom."

"Your secret is safe with me," I said, smiling.

"It's not that ... Mrs Dalrymple knows about your liaison with Mrs Kohler, and she's worried about it."

"Does she think I've been unfair to Susan by staying with her? It was Susan who suggested it..."

"No. It's something quite different. She says that Mrs Kohler was the most artful of any of the girls who worked for her. She had an incredible ability to enthral her clients, and you can't do that without being both clever and devious. She thinks that Mrs Kohler may be more scheming than you realise. How much do you know about her background?"

I was stung by Mansell's remarks.

"Look Harry, Susan has been nothing but sweet to me. There has never been any hint of anything else. I know that my own actions are hardly very creditable, but Susan has never made any unreasonable demands of me, and she has been more than candid about her sad past. I really don't want to hear any more criticism of her."

"Fair enough, old fellow, I'm only passing on old Dalrymple's comments. I just thought you should know what she said."

As we were talking, the smoking station came into view. Our

cargo was cotton, but we were also carrying tobacco and turpentine. My corner of the cargo consisted entirely of cotton, purchased through Mr Blair. Despite the new cotton press, we had several cotton bales piled on the deck as well as stowed in the cargo holds.

Four men came on board with smoking machines and applied these to the whole cargo. At first it appeared that the exercise was quite pointless, but suddenly a poor Negro wretch appeared from between two of the cotton bales secured on deck. He was put in chains and dragged away. The supervisor then entered into a debate with Mansell as to whether the *Isabella* should be detained for attempting to smuggle the escaped slave out of the Confederacy. He was persuaded to see sense, but this episode cast a cloud over our departure. We wondered about the fate of our poor attempted escapee.

We reached Smithville at dusk. Mansell called the ship's officers with the pilot and myself into his cabin to review the options for our passage through the blockade. He was sitting at his desk and was looking at us intently.

"It's the same story," he said, "either the coastal route or straight through the middle of the blockade. At least going out we have an exact starting position, and once we are over the bar we can head straight out to sea. I propose that we take the chance to leave as soon as it's dark and head straight through the blockade using the Old Inlet, under Fort Caswell. There's no point in risking the shoals along the coast. It will be dark at eight and we'll leave then."

The ship was prepared as well as possible. With the cotton bales on deck, we must have been a strange sight, but they were well secured, and Mansell made sure that no lights were showing. Our only frustration was that we had run our coal stocks low on the voyage in. We had enough anthracite coal for a few hours steaming, but we would have to use poor quality local coal purchased in Wilmington after that.

At eight o'clock steam was up, and we started our voyage. First we had to manoeuvre to get the lights in line, and then we began to steam out towards the blockade. On the flying bridge we peered anxiously into the darkness for Yankee ships.

Mansell ordered full speed, and the *Isabella* surged forward into the gloom. It was a reasonably calm night, and the motion of the ship was gentle.

The cruisers themselves were stationed well out to sea, out of range of the guns of Fort Caswell, but we soon discovered that one of them had managed to station a rowing boat under the fort as a lookout for blockade-runners. Since it was a moonless night they must have been confident that escapes would be attempted. As we shot past Fort Caswell suddenly rockets were fired from just ahead of us and the sea was lit up.

"Boat straight ahead!" shouted one of the lookouts on the bow.

Mansell altered course to avoid the rowing boat, and one of their rockets suddenly lit up the whole scene. Although we did our best to avoid the boat, we came so close that we brushed against their oars, and capsized them.

"That'll give them something to keep them occupied," muttered Mansell, as we swept past, "but now the Yankees know we're here."

Soon I could hear shots being fired quite close to us, and the whine of shells passing overhead. It was a confused picture. Occasional rockets lit up the sea, but fortunately the night was so dark that it must have been difficult for the Yankee ships to see us. Mansell altered course several times, but he was always taking us out towards the southeast. I spent my time searching the inky seas for ships, but usually the others found them first.

After an hour of fast steaming I became more confident that we had broken out of the blockade. I began to relax. We still kept a sharp lookout, but we seemed to be clear of the cruisers. Eventually I went to my cabin to try to get some sleep, but I slept fitfully. The dawn light woke me, and I went back out on deck.

As the dawn came up we were steaming south towards Nassau. There was a light haze, but it cleared at about nine o'clock. We scanned the horizon anxiously. We had used up our anthracite coal by going so fast through the blockade, and now we were using the poorer quality coal we had taken on in Wilmington. Black smoke was coming from our funnel, which would make us more visible to Northern ships. All too soon we discovered that there was a large paddle-wheel cruiser about six or seven miles astern of us. Simultaneously it seemed that she had spotted us, as she altered course to chase us. Mansell ordered full steam and changed course to the east, hoping that by heading into the wind we would disadvantage the cruiser, but although at first it was almost imperceptible, we were horrified to discover that she was gradually gaining on us.

"The *Isabella's* not giving us full speed," said Mansell. "Fenton, can you go down to the engine room and find out what's happening. We'll be in range of their guns in a couple of hours."

Fenton was back in a moment.

"It's the coal we took on in Wilmington, Captain," he said, "Rowland says it just can't give us the power we get from the anthracite coal, it's losing us at least three knots."

"Damn it!" cried Mansell, and he looked astern to where the cruiser was gradually creeping up on us. The tension built up as she edged closer. Those of the crew not engaged with managing the ship gathered at the stern to watch. All of us were once more agonised by the thought of possible capture, or even death if we were to be damaged or sunk. By midday the cruiser had opened fire with the Parrott gun on her bow, but fortunately the shots fell well short.

"It won't be long now though," said Mansell, "any ideas gentlemen?"

An obvious course was to jettison some of the cargo, but all us of felt that this should be the last resort. Finally Fenton turned to Mansell.

"Is there any way we can spike the fuel to give the engines extra power? How about the turpentine?"

Mansell summoned Rowland to the flying bridge.

"We are going to be in range of the cruiser soon," said Mansell, looking intently at Rowland. "Fenton thinks we should try spiking the Wilmington coal with turpentine, do you think it could work? How much extra speed could we get?"

Rowland was a short pugnacious Yorkshireman who thought slowly, but then gave very definite opinions. He scratched his head.

"No. You'd destroy the furnaces Captain."

"But what can we do?" asked Mansell urgently.

Once again Rowland was plunged into thought.

"Well, maybe it's worth a try," he muttered.

"What?" cried Mansell.

"I heard at Nassau that they've tried soaking cotton with turpentine, and adding that to the coal."

"Right, let's try it!" cried Mansell.

One of the cotton bales was quickly pulled to pieces, and the wads of cotton were soaked in turpentine. Soon the firemen were shovelling in the cotton wads with the coal. The effect was dramatic. The *Isabella* seemed to take a deep breath and leap forward; our funnel belched black and oily smoke. We turned our telescopes on the cruiser.

"I think we're holding her, aren't we?" I asked anxiously. But the cruiser fired her parrot gun again, and the splashes were still ominously close to the *Isabella*.

"Let's hope so," said Mansell, "or all that swimming we've been doing may come in handy…"

All afternoon we raced the cruiser. Sometimes she seemed to be gaining on us, and sometimes we seemed to pull away. We checked periodically with the engine room that no damage was being done, but the *Isabella's* furnaces and engines had been well made, and they held out. When the second bale was pulled out a surprise greeted us. A Negro runaway had been squeezed between the bales, and now came to light. The smoking machines at Wilmington had blackened his clothes, so it was a totally black figure that reeled out onto the deck. He had almost suffocated, and he couldn't stand.

Mansell shouted to one of the seamen to take him below and Fenton followed.

"Do what you can, Fenton," called Mansell.

Finally dusk fell with the cruiser still following us, and firing occasional shots. As soon as she was hidden by the gloom Mansell changed course, and that was the last we saw of her.

Later that evening Mansell asked me what we should do with our runaway.

"They won't like it in Wilmington," I said, "and there's no point in hiding it. Either we return him on our next trip, or we'll have to

208

pay compensation. I'll go below and check how he is."

So I went down to find that Fenton had managed to revive the stowaway, and he was half sitting and half lying on a bunk. As I came in he tried to sit up, but Fenton made him lie back again.

"How are you?" I asked.

He seemed very nervous, and although he answered my questions, he was shaking, and turning his eyes away.

"Well Massa, I'm feeling pretty good thank you."

"Who are you?"

"I'ze a house slave in Wilmington, Massa. I'ze a cook, but there's mighty little to cook in Wilmington right now."

He rolled his eyes piteously, "What are you folks going to do with me?"

His name was Sam Thomas, and he seemed a polite and helpful fellow. He claimed that he had been ill treated, and with the food shortages, practically starved. Certainly he seemed painfully thin. Fenton told me later that his body was covered in scars and contusions from numerous beatings.

"We'll see what happens when we get to Nassau, Sam," I said, "in the meanwhile you can help our cook here on the *Isabella* once you've got your strength back."

Once Sam had some of the *Isabella's* good food inside him his health improved rapidly. Soon he was able to help in the galley, and he proved to be an excellent cook. We decided to pay the compensation on our next visit to Wilmington, and Sam replaced the indifferent cook we had at East Street.

Two days later we steamed into Nassau. We had lost two bales of cotton from our cargo, and a barrel of turpentine, but this was a very small price to pay for saving the ship and the cargo, let alone our freedom or even our lives. When all the costs of the voyage had been taken into account I calculated that Mr Pembroke had made a clear profit in excess of fifteen thousand pounds, well over half the cost of building the *Isabella*. Pembroke and Stringer would be delighted.

I now had to make the break with Susan that I had promised myself, but I found it agonisingly hard to set about it. I didn't write to tell her that I had arrived back in Nassau, and I prevaricated for over a week. It was a letter from Mr Pembroke that compelled me to action. He told me of the imminent despatch of two new steamships, the *Index* and the *Nutfield*. The *Index* would arrive in February, but he told me that the *Nutfield* was due in Bermuda during January. He asked me to take the next mail steamer to St. George's to meet her there. He said that he was reluctant to use Bermuda, as there had been inexplicably high losses of blockade runners from that island in recent months, but he had medical stores warehoused in St. George's that were urgently needed by the Confederacy. The *Nutfield* would be carrying a purser. Mr Pembroke wanted me to sail with them to Wilmington, introduce the purser to Mr Blair, and provide guidance on current trading conditions.

I checked the steamship timetables, and the next mail steamer left for Bermuda in two days. With a heavy heart I sent a note to Susan saying that I was back in Nassau, and that I would come and see her the following day.

Early that morning I took a barouche out towards her villa. It was late in December. The weather was perfect; it was sunny but a very pleasant temperature. I thought of all those days when I had hurried to Susan from the office or from an evening in Nassau, longing to be with her. Now the journey was torture to me with the anticipation of an emotional reception of my decision to end our relationship. I knew she was deeply fond of me; indeed I was sure that she loved me. Now her world was going to fall apart.

I asked the driver to let me down a few hundred yards away, and I walked slowly to her house, wondering if this would be the last time I would be there. The maid let me in. Before I could say anything, Susan was in my arms, kissing me, and smiling with delight at seeing me. It was a stake through my heart.

"Tom, Tom, I thought you would never come back. It's been so long, did you have trouble? I was so worried."

"No, Susan, we had a good voyage. We had the usual clashes with the blockade fleet, but we came through safely."

"How long can you stay, it's Christmas in a week and I have such a nice presen' for you. You will be here won' you?"

The maid was standing at the back of Susan's drawing room

waiting to see if we needed anything. I knew that I couldn't tell Susan about my decision until the maid had left the room.

"Let's sit down Susan. Do you think Anna could bring us some coffee?"

Susan gave me a searching look.

"Of course Tom. Anna, did you hear Mr Wells? Bring us some coffee please."

"I won't be here for Christmas Susan," I said.

I still couldn't bring myself to break the news to her.

"Mr Pembroke wants me to take the mail steamer to Bermuda tomorrow. I'll be meeting one of his ships, and I'll sail with her to Wilmington."

"How long will you be away Tom?" she responded in a small voice.

"A month, two months, I can't be sure Susan, but ... well ... there is more I should tell you..." but she interrupted me.

"Months? You could be away for months, and you have only been with me for a day? Oh Tom, I can't bear it. It's too much. I have been so lonely an' sad, an' there's so much on my min'..."

With that, tears started down her cheeks, and she threw herself into my arms again for comfort. I held her to me, and once again I found it impossible to tell her what was in my mind. Finally she composed herself, and dabbed at her eyes with her handkerchief.

"How awful I must look, Tom, and I wanted to look so pretty for you."

"But you are looking beautiful Susan,"

As I looked at her she did indeed seem lovelier than ever.

"Thank you, Tom, but if you are going away, there is something I must tell you. It was going to be your Christmas presen', but I'll tell you now. You see, Tom ... you, you are going to be a father..." at first this came out hesitantly, but the rest came in a rush, "I've been to the doctor and he says that we will have our chil' in June, are you happy, Tom?"

I was stunned, and I started pacing about the room. How could I tell her now that I intended to end our affair? The consequences of what she was saying were washing though me like an ice-cold tidal wave; Christ, a child in June, me a father; must I take responsibility

211

for it? What would happen between Amy and me? I did the mental calculations; surely Susan must have known before I had left for Wilmington on my last voyage. I came to a stand still in front of her.

"Susan! You must have known in November, why didn't you tell me? Didn't I have the right to know?"

"The right … what right? We are not married. I suppose you mean your right as the father…"

"Are you absolutely sure? Could there be a mistake?"

"I saw the doctor again last week, Tom. There's no mistake. Our chil' will be born in June."

"But I'm leaving for Bermuda tomorrow; couldn't you have let me know before?"

Susan started crying again.

"Don't bully me Tom. Why didn't you come and see me? I heard that the *Isabella* was back over a week ago. I would have tol' you then. But now, as you're going away, an' … an'…"

Then she was crying again in earnest. She was looking so sad and appealing that I sat down again to comfort her. Gradually she got her composure back, and she looked at me again with that sad entreaty in her eyes.

"Don't answer me now Tom, but I wan' you to marry me. I don't want our chil' to be, to be … think about it Tom, and when you're back…"

My dilemma was terrible. I was fond of Susan, but I loved Amy. Susan's pregnancy made me feel a guilty duty to her, so I said nothing about ending our affair, and I spent the rest of the morning at the villa. Now that she had told me her secret, she was sweet and charming to me. She made no further suggestions of marriage. As we sat talking I remembered all those happy magical times we had spent together during my idleness of the late summer and autumn. The prospect of life with Susan seemed more attractive as I thought about it, but I made no commitment. My only promise was that I would return as soon as possible, and give her my decision then. I stayed far longer than I had expected to, and I had to hurry back to Nassau to complete my preparations for joining the *Nutfield*.

All the way on the mail steamer to Bermuda I wrestled with the problem. Every way I looked at it, I knew now that my duty was to marry Susan and I felt increasingly compelled to take that ultimate step. It meant the end of my hopes for Amy, and there would be some difficult explanations for my mother and our relations, but I knew it was what I should do. It was the right course and it was bitter. To use that old expression, I had made my bed and now I must lie in it.

I arrived in Bermuda in advance of the *Nutfield*, and I had a few days to wait. When I landed at St. George's I went to see our agent, George Murchison. He found me accommodation at a hotel. In those weary days I wandered around the town in an attempt at distraction from my problems.

I found that the island didn't have the same tropical feeling as Nassau. The houses were more like Cornish cottages, except for their limestone-tiled roofs. But in one thing St. George's and Nassau were alike. St. George's was filled with drunken, lawless sailors from blockade-running ships, spending their inflated wages and making a nuisance of themselves. My dilemma over Susan and Amy made me depressed and I found the atmosphere in the town unpleasant. I was eager for the *Nutfield* to arrive.

Three weeks later she came, and letters from Mr Pembroke informed me that her cargo was already complete, apart from the medical stores. He wanted her to sail for Wilmington as soon as possible. Her purser told me that she had a mixed cargo. The main items were some Whitworth rifled cannons, a large quantity of pig lead and some muskets. Apparently the weight of the cannons and the pig lead deep in her hold caused the *Nutfield* to lie quite low in the water, but although her heavy cargo made her stiff and jerky in her movements, it had caused no problems for the Atlantic crossing. The captain was anxious to sail as soon as possible to take advantage of the favourable lunar conditions.

I went to George Murchison's office to make the final arrangements and I was almost knocked over by a small black-bearded figure who was leaving the office in a hurry just as I arrived.

Murchison was standing close by.

"Who was that?" I asked as I recovered myself.

Murchison was a lean, efficient, jovial man who spoke like a fusillade of rifle shots.

"Donald Hay, joined us six months ago, very good man. What he doesn't know about steamers… bumped into you did he? You'll recover."

He laughed.

"Grabbed a piece of paper, said it was needed on board somewhere. Whoosht! Next second he was gone."

For a moment I failed to see why Murchison should be so amused, as I rubbed my arm where Hay had bumped into it. Then I smiled too.

"I thought the office must be on fire. Does he do all his business like the overnight express?"

"Well you'll find out. Dealing with the Nutfield. Damned efficient I must say. You'll have no complaints."

I made the arrangements with Murchison for taking on fresh coal and supplies, and I was grateful to have no more encounters with the energetic Mr Hay in Murchison's office. Three days later, on 1 February 1864, the *Nutfield* pulled away from the quayside at St. George's. Murchison was standing there. As we pulled away he was joined by the same bearded figure who had bumped into me in his office. As I looked at him, he turned away, but in that brief moment I was sure I recognised him. Try as I could, I failed to place him.

The *Nutfield* was a fine ship, built by James Ash in Millwall on the Thames. She was a classic blockade-runner of the period, two hundred and twenty-five feet long by twenty-six in the beam. She was iron-hulled, with side paddles and drew only twelve and a half feet unladen. She was a superb piece of shipbuilding, and the crew were very proud of her. I was looking forward to becoming acquainted with the ship's company.

As we steamed towards Wilmington we could soon see the sails of a distant ship that seemed to be following us. Our captain increased speed to the maximum, and tried changing course, but somehow we failed to shake them off. It was frustrating, but they were so distant that in the end we just ignored them.

Early in the voyage I spent most of my time with the *Nutfield's* purser, explaining the intricacies of the blockade running business, and current commercial developments. He was an experienced man, but he had only worked in Europe and the Indian trade. He needed to understand about cotton certificates, embargoed goods and the feverish market that now existed for imported goods in Wilmington and Charleston. He learned quickly, and I was looking forward to introducing him to Angus Blair. He told me that Mr Pembroke was already planning an additional ship.

At nightfall on the third day of our voyage we reached the blockade cordon at Cape Fear, and somehow the mystery ship was still following us. We could see her signalling to other ships, and then our troubles started. Despite constant manoeuvring we just could not penetrate the blockade. With dawn approaching our captain decided to turn north-eastwards, hoping to shake off our pursuers, and lie up during the day close to the shore. As the dawn rose we sat down to breakfast in the saloon. It had been a long night, and it was pleasant to sit down and relax. Most of us had been on the flying bridge for the whole night, and the effort of staring out into the blackness for Yankee cruisers had exhausted us.

The *Nutfield's* cook did us proud. They had brought ham and tinned food from England, and this had been supplemented in Bermuda by wonderful pork, chicken, fish and fruit. As we ate we talked about the progress of the Civil War, and the changes in ship design that the war had brought about. Since I had been involved in blockade-running longer than any of them, I was more than capable of contributing to the technicalities of the discussion.

We were just debating the relative merits of side-wheels over propellers when there was a cry from the lookout at the masthead. He could see the smoke of yet another ship astern of us. We abandoned our meal and went up to the flying bridge. Soon we could see that the ship was a Yankee cruiser.

Our pursuer was small, probably less than a thousand tons, but it almost immediately became clear that she was fast. I later discovered that she was the USS *Sassacus* , commissioned in Boston the previous October. We put on maximum speed, but she was gradually catching us as the extra weight of our cargo was slowing us down. Now we discovered the disadvantage of the heaviest part of the cargo being stowed lowest in the ship, since it was hard to jettison anything that would make an appreciable difference to our progress. The captain decided that we just had to take our chance, and hope that the cruiser would not be able to maintain her speed. Unluckily for us the *Sassacus* had been recently commissioned and her engines were in excellent condition.

All morning we toiled along the coast, with our boilers at maximum pressure. There was a strong wind and a rough sea. On the flying bridge we tried to fix our telescopes on the Yankee cruiser, which belched smoke, and crept gradually nearer. At first all we could see was a blurred outline, but gradually the details of the ship became clear, and we could even distinguish the features of her crew.

By noon the cruiser was in range, and she opened fire with her bow-chaser. Both ships were pitching and tossing in the heavy seas and it was hard to see where her shells were falling. We weren't hit, but it was obvious that it was only a matter of time. We discussed every possible stratagem to avoid her, but it seemed hopeless. She was faster than us, and just as nimble. It became clear that we would either have to surrender or abandon ship. This was particularly bitter, as it was the *Nutfield's* maiden run.

We concluded that we would rather give ourselves the best chance to avoid a Yankee prison, and we didn't want our cargo to fall into Northern hands. The decision was made to spin the wheel and head towards the long thin series of spits and islands stretching along that section of the coast. We would then take to the boats, and hope to escape capture. We would just have to risk the heavy sea, and take our chance. So we turned northwest and headed for the coast.

The *Nutfield* was designed to draw less than thirteen feet, but with the weight of her heavy cargo she was probably drawing more than fifteen. The captain took her at full speed towards the beach. We gripped the rails tightly, waiting for the shock as the *Nutfield* would ground on the nearest obstruction. In the end she took a long slow lurch onto a sand bank at least four hundred yards off shore. We decided to keep the engines running, to keep her as stable as possible. Then we set fire to the ship and manned the boats. As I came through the saloon with my papers I could see the sad remains of our breakfast still on the table.

The *Nutfield* was lying hard on the sand bank, but she was heaving and lurching in the very heavy swell. I had been party to the decision to abandon the ship, but now the reality of what we had decided really hit me. I was gripped by fear as I saw the massive swells round the ship turning into monstrous breakers as they approached the beach. The captain shouted for the ship's company to man the boats, and he divided us into two parties, one for each of the boats. There were some sixteen or seventeen of us in each of them. I was in the first boat with the purser, two of the ship's officers and a mixture of seamen and firemen. It was lowered on the port side of the ship, and we scrambled into it without loss. The captain followed in the second boat on the starboard side.

In our boat the first officer detailed the seamen to take the oars. The first few minutes seemed to last forever. The boat was difficult to handle in the heavy seas, but gradually we inched forward with the boat pitching and tossing violently. As we pulled clear of the *Nutfield* we could see smoke pouring out of her hatches, and then we could see the other ship's boat pulling for the shore on the far side. As we fought our way nearer to the shore so the swells turned into breakers.

We had only rowed about fifty yards when one of the huge breakers lifted us up, and turned us sideways to the beach. My muscles tensed and my stomach seemed to leave me as our bow lurched high into the air. I was in the stern, and I clung as tightly as I could to the side of the boat as the rowers started to fall towards me. Then the boat turned violently onto its side, I lost my grip, all of us were flung out and we had to swim for it. The water was bitter cold, and as I went in I swallowed what seemed like a gallon of it. I came up coughing and choking. I looked round to see if the boat was near me, but it seemed to have disappeared. I could hear the shouts and screams of the survivors, but a compulsion gripped me to swim desperately for the shore. I took in rasping painful breaths as I swam through the surf as strongly as I could.

Hardly a moment had gone by when another huge breaker lifted me up and flung me towards the beach. As it subsided I swam feverishly towards the shore, but I could feel the water inexorably sucking me back. No matter how frantically I swam, the current was stronger, and I could feel myself being dragged back towards the breakers again. This happened seven or eight times. Each time I was flung forwards, sometimes being pushed under water in the process, and then sucked backwards, even though I fought as hard as I could. I grew weaker and weaker. I kept telling myself that I should look out for the others, even though it was gradually dawning on me that I didn't have the strength even to save myself.

Soon I began to realise that try as I might, I was not going to reach the shore. As I got weaker, my thoughts started to drift. I thought of Amy. How soon would she learn that I was dead? Would she marry someone else? I thought of Susan, her unborn child, and my guilt at not being married to her. Then my mind drifted back to Deptford, my old home and my mother waiting for me. As I thought of all those things that meant so much to me I continued to struggle, but despair was gripping me.

Then the biggest breaker of all lifted me up. As I went up I saw that I was alongside the dead body of one of the firemen. I had the horror of seeing his dead, black-bearded, staring face, and then we were both being propelled at great speed towards the shore, but this time the wave seemed to be taking us higher and further in than before.

We raced forwards and as we did so, the sight of that bearded face suddenly triggered in my mind the identity of the black-bearded figure who had bumped into me in Murchison's office in Bermuda, and whom I had seen on the quayside.

Donald Hay was Fraser McNab, the clean-shaven chief engineer on the *Clara*, who had given away our position to the Northern navy off Madeira. He must have been working under another name at St. George's, and he had done the same thing again to the *Nutfield*.

He had taken his promised revenge.

I cursed him bitterly as the breaker shot me forwards and then flung me against something extremely hard.

I seemed to go backwards down a long dark tunnel. Then I knew no more.

Chapter Sixteen
The Myrtle Dunes Plantation

How can I describe the horror of coming gradually into consciousness to discover myself bandaged so tightly that I was unable to move or speak. I was in great pain and I was being fed through a tube. Only the soothing voices of those nursing me gave me some hope. I had no idea where I was, or how long I had been there. As my memories of the *Nutfield* catastrophe came slowly back to me, so I became desperate for news of the survivors. It was many days before my bandages could be removed sufficiently for me to be able to communicate with my rescuers.

It seemed that I had been found unconscious by a party of Confederate soldiers on the beach close to Hampstead, about twenty-five miles north east of Wilmington. I had been carried to the house of the local doctor. That saintly man had judged that my injuries were too great for me to be moved, so he and his wife nursed me in their house. For over a month I had lingered close to death, drifting in and out of consciousness. My head had been badly battered, there was a long cut in my forehead and my jaw was broken. My head was swathed in bandages. One of my legs was very badly broken, and so were both of my arms. It was only after two months, in late March of 1864, that I was able to communicate with my hosts, but I could learn little. It turned out that they lived close to Myrtle Dunes, the Pierce plantation. The Pierces offered to take me in. As soon as I was well enough, I was moved there. I was put in the room usually occupied by Mansell on his visits to pursue his interest in Charlotte Pierce.

I was still frantic with worry about the fate of the Nutfield's crew, and the troubles I had left behind me in Nassau. I was also eager to inform Mr Murchison and the Bermuda authorities of the true identity of 'Donald Hay'. Mrs Pierce sent a message to Angus Blair saying that I was alive, and asking him to get the same communication to Harry Mansell, Tobias Johnson in Nassau and to the Munros. In the same message I urged Mansell and Johnson to write to the Bermuda authorities about McNab.

I was still in a very weak state, and the Pierces and their Negro servants looked after me. Major Pierce was with the army, as was their son, but I was fortunate to have Mrs Pierce and her beautiful twin daughters as my nurses. I was in an upstairs room looking out over the plantation towards the sea. It was a large handsome room, furnished in much the same way as my room had been at Marion. One morning the dark haired Virginia Pierce was in my room, and she had been helping me with my struggle to eat a late breakfast. I had been asking her whether they had heard any news from Angus Blair, when there was the noise of a buggy drawing up outside the house. Moments later we heard urgent footsteps on the stairs. Harry Mansell burst into the room.

"What are you doing in my room Tom? This is where I stay when I'm here! But it's wonderful to see you old fellow. Good morning Miss Pierce, my apologies for not seeing you there."

He came over and put his hand on my shoulder, and then he brought up another chair and sat next to Virginia.

"Harry, what are you doing here?"

I managed to mumble weakly from under my bandages.

"Good Heavens Tom, it's like talking to one of the mummies in the British Museum. I was in Blair's office when he got Mrs Pierce's letter. I was on fire to get down here. I just can't believe you survived the wreck; it's a miracle. But how are you old fellow? You look a bit of a mess, but at least you're still breathing!"

"Cuts and bruises and a couple of breaks. The doctor says I may be up and about in a month."

"And a cracked skull," said Virginia, "he is supposed to keep still and not get excited. A fine chance he'll have with you bounding in here like a buffalo."

"Sorry old fellow, but I had to see you. Anyway, Miss Pierce, I'm not sure I've ever seen Tom quiet for more than two minutes together. Don't blame me!"

"What about the *Nutfield*?" I asked as urgently as I could, "what happened? How many survived?"

A serious expression came over Mansell's face.

"It's a grim story Tom; I heard most of it from Jenkins. He was the only ship's officer to survive. I'll tell you…"

Virginia Pierce clasped Mansell's arm to interrupt him.

"Mr Wells is tired, Captain Mansell. Couldn't you tell him another day?"

But I was desperately anxious to hear what had happened, so I begged him to continue.

"Well Jenkins was in the boat on the starboard side with the captain. You were on the port side weren't you?" I nodded, "a huge breaker almost capsized their boat, and they lost three men, including the captain. They saw your boat go over, but then they had trouble enough of their own, so there wasn't anything they could do to help you."

"Can't you get on with the story?" asked Virginia, "Mr Wells knows perfectly well what happened to his boat, Captain Mansell."

"You see what I've got to deal with here, Tom? One twin's no better than the other. I *am* getting on with it aren't I? … Anyway by good fortune they spotted a channel through the spit, and they rowed like hell for it. They had some tricky moments, but they made it through."

"Did they see the captain, or the other two?" I asked despondently.

"It was hopeless. The boat was being thrown about like a shuttlecock. They kept an eye out, but Jenkins took the view that the only way to save the lives of the boat's crew was to take them through that channel.

"When they were through they ran back to the ocean beach, and they tried to find survivors from both of the boats, but not a single living soul did they find. They recovered the bodies of two dead firemen, poor fellows, but eventually they had to conclude that everyone else had drowned. It was a heavy swell as you know Tom, not much of a chance in that."

"He knows it was a heavy swell Captain Mansell," said Virginia, "goodness, you only have to look at him to see that…"

"Tom asked me to tell him what I knew didn't he? Now I've lost my thread … well Jenkins decided to stay on the spit. He half hoped survivors might be washed up, and he wanted to see what would happen to the *Nutfield*. I think he had some crazy idea that

221

the Yankees might abandon their prey, and he could row back out again! That didn't happen of course. The boats from the Yankee cruiser got alongside the *Nutfield*, and they put the fire out. Jenkins could see them salvaging some of the cargo, and trying to get her re-floated. In the end they gave up, and used her for target practice. I'm afraid *she'll* never see the Thames again."

"How did the crew get to Wilmington?" I asked.

"Well eventually they rowed down the sound behind the spit until they found the Gatlin Battery. They were fortunate that the quarantine wasn't in force, and they were taken by boat straight to Wilmington."

"Were any of them injured?"

"No, it looks as though you were the only one with any serious injuries, but over half the crew were killed. One of the seamen in Jenkins' boat thought he saw the Yankees pulling someone out of the water, but he couldn't tell whether they were alive or dead. Jenkins wrote a report, and sent it to Mr Pembroke when he got to Nassau. You were reported as drowned."

Whilst we were talking, Mrs Pierce and Charlotte came into the room. Mansell and Virginia both stood up, and they all gathered around my bed. Virginia was looking anxiously at me.

"Mother," she said, "I think we have been tiring Mr Wells. The doctor says he needs to stay as quiet as possible. Should we not leave him to get some rest?"

"Yes," Mrs Pierce replied, "I will call a servant to get those breakfast things cleared away. We will leave Mr Wells in peace."

"Harry, how long will you be staying?" I asked.

"I have to leave again today," he said, "the *Isabella* must leave tomorrow, but I thought I had to dash out here to see you."

I asked Harry to stay for a moment after the others had left. Virginia gave Mansell a stern instruction to keep our conversation short.

"Goodness, Tom, that girl's stricter than a sergeant-major, and Charlotte's little better. If those two were in the Confederate army, Lincoln wouldn't stand a chance."

Then he looked at me affectionately.

"Great Heavens, it's wonderful to see you alive, but what is it

Tom, what's bothering you?"

I summoned up as much energy as I could to address what was on my mind.

"Well firstly Harry, I wanted to thank you for teaching me to swim. I could never have survived if it hadn't been for that."

"Well I hoped you wouldn't need it," he replied, "often it makes no difference, it can even prolong the agony if you're out at sea, but I've always been more comfortable knowing I can swim. How much have you lost with the *Nutfield*?"

"I feel almost guilty about that. The cargo was complete when she came to Bermuda and I didn't get the opportunity to add anything of my own. I only lost my clothes and some money."

"We are much the same size," he said, "and I guessed you might have that problem. I've left some of my own things for you. Mr Blair says that he will provide any funds you may need."

"Thank you Harry. I need to write some instructions for Johnson, and I must write to Mr Pembroke and my mother. Can you wait until I've done that?"

"No, Tom. You're not writing anything with a broken arm. This is where I'm going to act as your doctor. Don't worry yourself with any of that, I'll take care of it. Mr Pembroke will know your mother's address won't he? Everyone will be delighted to know that you're alive, and their only concern will be that you should make a complete recovery. Mr Blair has told me about some new Confederate laws affecting our cargoes in and out of Wilmington and Charleston, but I'll speak to Johnson about that, and include it in my letter to Mr Pembroke … What about Mrs Kohler?"

Harry had a mischievous look in his eye as he asked this.

"You may think it's funny, but she will be worrying about me. Could you do me a great favour and call on her? She has a particular reason to know that I'm alive, please tell her that I will get to Nassau to see her as soon as I can."

"Yes, I'll do that for you. In fact I called on her after we heard that the *Nutfield* had been lost – Johnson gave me the address. She was devastated to hear about it," he hesitated, and then with that same mischievous look he continued, "are there any other ladies who will be missing you in Nassau?"

This time I could only laugh, and immediately I began to regret it as various parts of my body started to complain in unison.

"Sorry old fellow, I couldn't resist asking. You're a dark horse. Just remember, Charlotte's off limits. I've told her that if you give any trouble she's to get the doctor to wrap you up a bit tighter. I've told them to put you onto ground peas if you misbehave. Those are what we call peanuts. They grow them here - funny looking things, a bit like large pieces of chicken dung, and they taste rather like it too. They used to grow them to feed the pigs, but now the army's eating them. Cutting out the middleman I suppose."

Soon Harry was off, and I was left with my thoughts. Mr Pembroke had now lost three of his ships, the *Granite City*, the *Clara* and the *Nutfield*, but the latest disaster had been by far the worst. The total loss of the *Nutfield's* cargo and the loss of well over half her crew was a savage blow, and I wondered how Mr Pembroke and his partner would react. I reviewed in my mind my own part in what had happened. I felt guilty that I had not been able to help any of the crew, particularly those who couldn't swim. But the more I thought about it, the more I came to the realisation that there was little I could have done.

But uppermost in my thoughts was Susan. She would be seven months pregnant by now, and she would be more anxious than ever to get married. I knew it was my duty to get back to Nassau as quickly as possible. The honourable course was to marry her, and that was the course I was going to take.

I wondered how Amy and her mother would react to the news. My decision to marry Susan made the speculation pointless, but I wondered whether Mrs Munro would be sympathetic to my current plight.

As I thought about Amy, so I drifted off to sleep again.

Ten days later Mr Blair came to see me. I was still in bed, but feeling much stronger. He apologised for the delay, but he had felt unable to cancel an important visit to Richmond. He told me that he had been in touch with Amy, to tell her that I had survived the wreck of the *Nutfield*. He brought a letter from her, which he allowed me to read immediately. It told of her relief and delight that I was alive and it was filled with love and affection. She longed to visit me at Myrtle Dunes, but her mother wouldn't allow it. Contrary to what I had hoped, Mrs Munro was taking the stance that the wreck of the *Nutfield* was yet another example of the hazardous nature of my work, and therefore of my unsuitability. She had allowed Amy to write this one letter, but there would be no more.

"I am sorry to have to tell you that Amy is now kept almost locked up at Marion," said Blair. "My sister fears that she may try to make her way to Myrtle Dunes to see you, and *that* she will not allow. Amy can only leave Marion if my sister is with her."

My own circumstances with Susan hardly put me in a position to argue the point, so with a heavy heart I turned to business matters. I asked Mr Blair about the changes to the Confederate import and export laws that Mansell had mentioned.

"It was for that I had to go to Richmond," he replied, "the government has recently passed the new laws, and I think you may be a little shocked at what they do.

"In essence it is three things. They forbid the import of unnecessary goods – no more champagne and perfume I am afraid. Express permission from President Davis is needed for the export of cotton, tobacco, rice and the other Southern crops. But worst of all, every ship must offer half of their cargo capacity to the government, both for imports and exports... I must say I will miss the tea, coffee and chocolate you have been bringing in for me," he added wistfully.

I was stunned.

"I can hardly believe it, why on earth are they doing it? Aren't we blockade-runners critical to the supply of the Confederacy? Don't they realise that this may stop us from running our ships?"

"I can understand your reaction," he answered, "but think of it from the point of view of the government. As far as exports are concerned they are recognising that the 'King Cotton' policy is dead. Britain is not going to come in on the Southern side. But they want to control the export of our staple products. For imports they are desperate for supplies for the army, and they want to make sure that the blockade-runners only bring in critical goods."

"I can understand both of those arguments," I said, "but what about taking control of half our cargoes? That strikes at the very profitability that makes the risks of running the blockade worthwhile!"

"You may not like it, but the profitability you mention is one of the reasons why they want to do it. It will be a way in which they can finance the Confederacy. Also they think that blockade-runners are making excessive profits out of the South's misfortunes."

"But surely they must be worried about people like Mr Pembroke and his partner no longer wanting to take the risk of running the blockade?"

"They have made their calculations," said Blair, "and they reckon that it will still be worthwhile. Maybe not quite so many new ships will be built, but they are sure that it will still be profitable to run the existing ones."

I started to make some mental calculations.

"On what basis will they charter the fifty percent they're taking?"

"All they are saying is that *they* will determine the rates."

I continued with my mental gymnastics.

"Assuming that they pay standard international rates, I suppose it will be worthwhile for the bigger ships. That's based on a ship successfully completing about six round trips, and then being captured or sunk. But with the blockade getting tougher all the time, how many shipowners will calculate on six trips?"

"Time will tell," he replied, "I can only imagine that the government will adjust the charter rates if they get into trouble."

"What are they saying in Richmond about the war?"

Blair looked gloomy and shifted in his chair.

"Up until now there have always been plenty of optimists in the government, but I did not find any this time. Lincoln has chosen two generals in Grant and Sherman who know their trade. In fact Grant is working his way down towards Richmond at this very minute, and Sherman is threatening Atlanta. They may not be as skilled as Lee or Johnston, but our generals respect them. Privately many in Richmond are conceding that the war is virtually lost. Some are saying that we are only fighting for honour now."

"So you're saying that it's only a matter of time. How long have we got?"

"I suppose our only hope is that we can inflict so many losses on the Yankees over the summer that Lincoln loses the election in November. McClellan might settle. Otherwise I can't see the war lasting beyond the end of this year, or maybe into 1865."

"That's a grim prospect – let's hope you're wrong!"

Mr Blair left later that day, and I didn't see him again until I passed through Wilmington on my way to Nassau two months later.

The next month began to have the desired effect on my health, I started taking short walks and eventually I was able to accompany Mr Stuart, the Pierces' overseer, as he supervised the slaves working on the peanut crop and looking after the pigs and chickens. My distaste for slavery increased, not helped by seeing how the slaves were driven and bullied by Mr Stuart and his Negro foreman. However this did not affect my gratitude to Mrs Pierce and her daughters for their hospitality and care for me. I was convinced that I owed my life and my health to them and to their doctor. I longed to be able to repay them in some way, but they would hear of no such thing. They were the finest possible example of Southern hospitality.

By May, if it hadn't have been for my dilemma over Susan and Amy, I would have been eager to get back to Nassau and start working again. Although I had made the decision to marry Susan, I knew I would do so with deep regret. But early that month brought another lightening visit from Mansell and some news that promised to change everything. Mansell and I walked slowly down to the sand banks that looked out over the grey Atlantic to talk. The weather was fine and dry, and we sat on a dune looking out at the breakers dashing themselves against the sand spits. Mansell was looking solemn. First he asked me about my health, and then:

"You want to know about Mrs Kohler, don't you?"

"Yes of course Harry, I'm desperate to know how she is. How did she react to knowing that I'd survived?"

"It's not like that Tom. After I saw you in April, we sailed for Nassau. We had a few problems en route, but that's usual, as you know. As soon as we got there I did as you asked. I called on her villa. It was empty. The neighbours said that Mrs Kohler had sold the villa, and she had left for Europe three weeks previously."

"Jesus, Harry, I can't believe it! Did they know where she went?"

"No, Tom, and I had the devil's own job finding out what had happened. It was Mrs Dalrymple who told me. It seems that she and Mrs Kohler were still in contact. Mrs Kohler was expecting a child, did you know that?"

I nodded.

"After she heard that you had died – sounds strange doesn't it? – she decided that she wanted her child to be born in Europe, and she took a steamer for Hamburg. I'm afraid old Dalrymple didn't know where she was going after that."

"How on earth will I find her?" I asked.

I lowered my voice, "you know that the child she's expecting is mine, don't you?"

"Yes, Tom, Mrs Dalrymple told me. But there's something else you ought to know. Mrs Kohler wasn't travelling alone. Before she joined the Dalrymple establishment she had been living with some Spanish fellow, Lopez or Gomez or something, and it seems that they have got together again. In fact old Dalrymple suspects that they never really separated completely…"

I was stunned. There had been virtually nothing in my relationship with Susan that had suggested to me anything duplicitous in her nature. I remembered one Spanish visitor who had been there when I had arrived unexpectedly, but Susan had given a convincing explanation.

"I can't believe it Harry, she just wasn't like that."

"Don't take my word for it old fellow, ask Dalrymple. I did take the opportunity to check with the shipping line, I know them pretty well. It seems that Mrs Kohler and her companion were travelling as man and wife…"

Harry could see the shock and dismay in my face.

"Look here Tom, Dalrymple always told me that there was more to Susan than met the eye, and I tried to warn you didn't I? Look at it this way, old Kohler's death made her rich, and now she's quite a catch for this Lopez, or whatever his name is. You weren't thinking of marrying her were you?"

I nodded shamefacedly.

"Well you're best off out of it. At least one good thing has come from the poor old *Nutfield*."

He was going to say more, but I motioned him to silence. I must have sat saying nothing for almost quarter of an hour as I numbly thought through the consequences of what he had been saying. The suggestion of Susan's duplicity had indeed shocked me. She had been so sweet to me that I really found it hard to believe what Mansell had been saying. I felt that I should take my own steps to make sure that he was right. This news did seem to release me to renew my attempts to marry Amy, but if Mr Blair's information was correct, that would now be an almost impossible task. These thoughts pursued each other round my head as I sat rigidly gazing out over the ocean. Finally the leg that had been broken began to trouble me, and I moved.

Mansell had been watching me anxiously.

"All right old fellow? This must have come as a thunderbolt."

"Yes, I'm fine Harry, it just takes some getting used to."

I decided to change the subject.

"But we've talked enough about my problems, have you heard any news of the *Index*?"

"She left for Nassau a week ago. There's no news of any ship being captured or sunk in the last few days, so let's hope she got there safely. Did I tell you about the *Pevensey*?"

"It's not bad news I hope. If we had another disaster like the *Nutfield* I think Mr Pembroke might give the game up."

"No, it's nothing like that old fellow, or I would have told you. Mr Pembroke has come to an arrangement with the Confederates. He's chartered her to them. Once the profits of the charter have paid off her purchase price, they take ownership."

"So we have no hand in the management of her?"

"No, and she's operating out of Bermuda, now that McNab's gone. Not only that, they're changing her name to the *Kangaroo*. That name makes hardly any more sense to me than the previous one. Why on earth did Pembroke call the two sister ships *Nutfield* and *Pevensey*? Until now, nearly all of his ships have had girls' names."

"I can give you half an answer to that," I said, "I don't think it was Pembroke. Edgar Stringer lives in a village called Nutfield. Maybe he has a holiday house in Pevensey…"

"Well I call it damn silly. I know they can call their ships whatever they like – there are probably a hundred *Carolines* ploughing the seas – but I'm not so keen on place names. Let's hope that the *Pevensey* has better luck than the *Nutfield*."

"Well it could hardly be worse," I said gloomily, "and you can't really attribute *that* disaster to bad luck. What happened to McNab anyway? Did they lock him up in St. George's?"

Mansell frowned.

"He has the luck of the bloody devil. He must have realised that you were going to recognise him. Murchison tells me that by the time he got the message, McNab was gone. Took passage to Glasgow. I've written to Mr Pembroke, but let's face it, McNab is too fly for us, damn it. By the time Donald Hay gets back to Glasgow, he'll be Malcolm McTavish."

Mansell told me that he was short handed on the *Isabella*, and he could only stay one night at Myrtle Dunes. He planned to sail for Nassau in ten days, and he hoped I would be well enough to sail with him.

My time at Myrtle Dunes had been quiet, and my recuperation slow and painful, but I was now reasonably confident that another ten days would make me strong enough to undertake the voyage back to Nassau. I was disappointed, but not surprised to receive no more letters from Amy. I had now virtually convinced myself that my association with Susan was over, and I longed to see Amy, but I had to be content with the company of the Pierce twins and their mother.

Then one day, about a week after Mansell had left, I was sitting reading in the Pierces' drawing room, when their Negro butler came to tell me that there was a man in the hall asking for me. This turned out to be a middle aged white man, who was clearly a groom. He looked at me respectfully.

"You Mr Wells?"

"Yes."

"I have a note for you, could you read it now, sir?"

I took it from him. The envelope was not addressed, but when I opened the note I could see that it was in Amy's handwriting, and my heart leapt. It read:

'Please accompany this man, say nothing to anyone, Amy'

"We must be quick!" exclaimed the groom.

We were alone in the hall, as the butler had gone back down to the basement. The groom beckoned me to follow him. We went down the front steps of the plantation house, and soon I was following this unknown man up the drive and along the road towards Wilmington. He was walking at a brisk pace. As I was still limping from my injuries, I had some difficulty in keeping up with him. The road bent round to the left, and there was a small track leading towards the dunes. There was a buggy partly concealed in the track, and I was thrilled to see that seated in the buggy was Amy. The groom gestured to the buggy, and then sat down at the entrance to the track.

I hurried over. Amy sprang down into my arms, and then we were kissing and hugging one another. Finally I handed Amy back up into the buggy and climbed up to sit alongside her. We were smiling, holding hands, and gazing into each other's eyes, and then as Amy looked at me, there was sympathy and shock expressed on her dear face.

"Oh your poor forehead Tom, how did you get that terrible scar?"

"I'm afraid that wasn't the worst of my injuries, but I'm almost back to full strength now. I limp a bit, but otherwise…"

She squeezed my hands, but there was a worried look on her face.

"It took forever to get out here, Tom, so I've only got a few minutes. I can't tell you how difficult it's been over the last few weeks. First I thought you were dead … and then when we got the wonderful news, Mother wouldn't let me see you or even write to you – except that one letter…"

"It's so marvellous to see you, Amy," I cried, "but how did you manage to escape? Your uncle told me that you're a virtual prisoner at Marion. Has your mother changed her mind?"

"No, Tom, or I wouldn't be hiding here. But I was going to see you, whatever she said."

A grim, determined look came over her sweet face.

"She had to come down to Wilmington about the plantation, and she didn't dare leave me behind. She is visiting our cousins out at Currie today, and she was too ashamed to take me, for fear of what I might say to them. She left Uncle Angus in charge of me. Well I just told him that I was going to see you, and that nothing he could say would stop me. I hired this buggy, but I did promise him I would be back by five.

"Oh, Tom, I must leave in a minute. How are you, how long will you be staying at Myrtle Dunes?"

"I'll be leaving in three days to go back with Harry to Nassau, can I try to see you in Wilmington?"

"No, Tom," she said softly, "Mother has finished her business, and we travel back to Marion tomorrow, but I just had to see you."

As she made this last remark, we could see the groom standing up and signalling that she had to leave. He started to walk towards us.

We flung ourselves into another feverish embrace, then Amy pulled herself away.

"Goodbye dear Tom, we will get married I promise, somehow I'll get mother to see reason. Write to me at Uncle Angus's, and I'll try to get letters to you there…"

The groom was now ready to whip up the horse, so I had to jump down. I ran after the buggy to the road, and I stood waving to Amy until the buggy disappeared in a dusty cloud round one of the many twists and turns of the road. I walked soulfully back to Myrtle Dunes.

Two days later I was saying my goodbyes to the Pierces, and thanking them again and again for their incredible hospitality. They kindly sent me in their carriage to the *Isabella*, and after four more days, at the beginning of June 1864, I was back in Nassau.

There were letters waiting for me from my mother, Mr Pembroke and many others. There was delight that I had survived the loss of the *Nutfield*, but pleas from my mother for me to return to London. I felt sympathy for her wishes, but despite the dramas of the wreck, I felt that there was too much unfinished business for me to leave now, and in some ways the *Nutfield* catastrophe had hardened me to the dangers.

My first actions in Nassau were to investigate what had happened to Susan and our child. I wanted to challenge Mansell's interpretation of her actions, but everything I learned reinforced his story. Questioning the girls who had known Susan at Mackey Street, I found that Susan's account of her life to me had been less than accurate. It seemed that she had been living as the mistress of a man called Lopez before she had joined Mrs Dalrymple's establishment. She had resumed her relationship with him even whilst Kohler was alive, and only broke with him when I went to live with her. Soon after she had been told that I had been lost with the *Nutfield*, they were together again. I was sad and distressed to learn of her true nature, but I felt released from any obligation to her.

My investigations had caused some delay in catching up with our shipping business, but almost as soon as I was back I learned that the *Pevensey* had been chased ashore by Union ships and destroyed whilst still under charter to the Confederates. Stringer and Pembroke were still operating the *Isabella* and the *Index*, and the *Charlotte* was expected in August. They were considering commissioning one more ship. Times were difficult, but there was still money to be made. All of our runs were now to Wilmington. In July and August I was still recuperating from my injuries, but in September I made the run to Wilmington in the *Charlotte*. I had hoped that I might see Amy, but she was still incarcerated with her mother at Marion. I wrote to her saying how much I wanted to see her, but no reply came before we set off back to Nassau.

Mansell arrived back in Nassau on the *Isabella*, three weeks after the *Charlotte*, and he brought a letter from Angus Blair, but no letter from Amy. With a heavy heart I turned to Mr Blair's letter. He was pleading with us to undertake a voyage to Charleston. He recognised the difficulties, but so did the Confederate Government. The rewards would be much higher than for a run to Wilmington.

Isaac Jones was no longer available, so Blair suggested that Mansell and I should meet a Charleston pilot in Nassau called Bill Feaney. Apparently he had undertaken a number of recent trips in and out of Charleston. He could help us to assess the risks. That evening I met Mansell for dinner in the Victoria, and as we walked home to East Street we talked over Blair's Charleston proposal. As usual the streets were thronged with drunken sailors, louts and prostitutes. Mansell told me that it reminded him of Portsmouth on a Saturday night when the fleet was in.

"Only the fellows here have got more money, dammit. Look at that chap!" he exclaimed, pointing to a sailor who was dead drunk and lying in the gutter, "thank God he's not one of ours. The sooner we get the *Isabella* out onto the Atlantic the better."

"Agreed! But what do you feel about the run to Charleston? None of our ships has done it for months, what have you heard?"

"Now that it's under siege, the risks are much higher than for Wilmington..."

There was a tall, finely dressed Negro standing in our way, trying to persuade us to come into a rough-looking pothouse, but we pushed our way past.

"I suppose we'll just have to try to calculate the rewards, and see if it's worth it," I said, "there's no good reason for me to go to Wilmington at the moment. Amy has told me that her mother keeps her locked up at Marion."

"The old bitch," said Mansell, "that woman's a danger to society. If all mothers were like that, civilization would die out."

"Don't tell me..." was my sad response.

The following day a letter arrived on the mail steamer from Mr Pembroke. He said that he and Mr Stringer had been reviewing the performance of the *Isabella* and the *Index* and they had decided that the *Index* was too small to make sufficient income in the new circumstances. His letter told me that she was provisionally sold to a London shipowner, and the sale would go through with my confirmation that she had arrived back in Nassau safely. His letter also gave me instructions to hand her over to the agents for the new owner.

This would have seemed negative but for the fact that his letter also informed me that we would keep the *Isabella* and the *Charlotte,* and that the *Maude Campbell* was currently on order. She would replace the *Index* . We could expect her early in 1865.

He told me that he and Stringer were committed to the *Maude Campbell*, but they were beginning to get concerned that the war was entering its final stage. He urged me to work the ships as hard as I could whilst the opportunities were still there. This made me all the more eager to explore the possibilities of a run to Charleston. We contacted Bill Feaney, and he came to the East Street office that afternoon.

Feaney was roughly dressed, and smoked a foul pipe. He looked to be in his fifties, and his grey hair was tucked under a grimy nautical cap. He sat and looked at us both with a quizzical look in his sharp little eyes, and he only opened his mouth to put his revolting pipe into it. Mansell broke the silence.

"Mr Blair of Wilmington tells me that you're the right man to get us into Charleston."

Feaney nodded, said nothing, but looked at us acutely.

"Can you do it?"

Feaney took his pipe out of his mouth.

"Yup," was all he said.

"How does it compare to Wilmington now?" asked Mansell, "how great are the risks?" .

Feaney put his pipe on my desk, and looked hard at Mansell.

"If you're the Captain Mansell I've heard about, you'll know as well as I do … it's ten times as difficult."

He put his pipe back into his mouth. I could see that Mansell was getting frustrated with the curt and unhelpful answers he was getting. But he kept his patience.

"Look here Feaney, we have to try to compare the risks between Wilmington and Charleston. We don't *have* to go to Charleston, but we're told that they're desperate for munitions, and the Confederate Government wants us to get in if we can. For us it's a matter of balancing the risks against the rewards, but we also have the lives of the crew to worry about, not to mention our own."

Feaney knocked out his pipe, and put it in his pocket. Then he looked slowly up at Mansell.

"Let's put it like this, Captain Mansell," he said, "Cape Fear River's got two entrances, the old and the new inlets. Our troops man *all* the forts at the mouth of the river. Charleston only has one entrance. You know that. Yankees hold the southern side. *And* - they've sunk ships to block the channels. New channels have opened up, but they're difficult to find. If you run aground on a mud bank they can knock you to pieces with the artillery they've got at Fort Wagner. It won't be easy."

There was an awkward silence.

"But can you do it?" I asked.

Now Feaney turned his uncomfortable gaze onto me.

"Yup, I told you I can. You'll have to pay me plenty. I want to get back to Charleston, and there's precious few ships going there now. I live on Sullivan's Island, and I know those channels. I can get you in, and I'll get you back out to the island. Then you'll be on your own."

"Sullivan's Island is just outside the harbour isn't it?" asked Mansell.

Feaney nodded.

"The *Isabella* can do seventeen knots and she draws thirteen feet with a big cargo. What are our chances?"

"Last I heard, they were losing one runner in three," said Feaney.

He paused.

"With a fast ship and a top pilot the odds are maybe better than that. But not much."

"Are you a top pilot?" I asked.

"Reckon so."

Mansell and I looked at one another. Mansell raised his eyebrows and shrugged. He turned to Feaney.

"Thank you. We'll make our minds up quickly, and get back in contact."

Feaney shambled to his feet, touched his cap, and slouched out of the office.

Mansell smiled.

"D'you know, it's a strange thing," he said, "for all Feaney's disgusting appearance and execrable manners, I trust him. I've heard good things about him too. If we're going to go to Charleston, let's do it with him."

And in the end, that was what we decided to do.

The next few days were feverishly busy. We completed the sale of the *Index*, and shortly afterwards the *Charlotte* arrived back from Wilmington after another successful round trip. Harry confessed to me that he had written to Mr Pembroke asking for his latest ship to be named after Charlotte Pierce; but he didn't ask to transfer to her. The *Charlotte* would return to Wilmington almost immediately. Johnson and I worked hard with Heyliger to complete her cargo. We finished the work just in time for her to catch the period of dark nights at Cape Fear.

In the meanwhile the *Isabella* was loaded with munitions for Charleston. Feaney told us that it was critical to enter the harbour when moonless nights coincided with high tides. Two days later, towards the end of October 1864, we slipped out of Nassau and headed towards Charleston.

Chapter Seventeen
Charleston under Siege

The conditions at sea were reasonable on that late October day in 1864 when we left Nassau. They remained fair for the whole of our voyage. Despite this, by the time we had evaded two persistent Union cruisers, it took us over three days to reach a position some fifty miles off Charleston. It was early evening. Mansell asked Feaney to meet him in his cabin. At my own request I sat in on their conversation.

During our short voyage we had seen little of Feaney. He had joined us for meals in the saloon, but said very little. At other times he was mainly in his cabin, but despite the time he spent there, somehow the rank odour of his pipe seemed to pervade the *Isabella*. Inevitably his pipe was clenched in his teeth when he joined us in Mansell's cabin. He brought with him a bundle of grimy charts, which he spread out on the table. Harry welcomed Feaney and pointed to our current position on one of his charts.

"That's where we are now, Feaney," he said, "there will be virtually no moon tonight, and I think you said that high tide will be at about eight in the morning. How do you think we should make our approach?"

We were standing looking down at the charts on the table. Feaney leant forward towards the charts. As he puffed at his pipe, little pieces of burnt tobacco fluttered down onto the paper. Feaney slid one of the charts towards him. He pointed to the southern side of the entrance to the harbour.

"Morris Island," he said abruptly, "Yankees took it summer last year. They've got artillery at Fort Wagner right there at the entrance. That makes the two channels on that side too risky."

He brushed some tobacco flakes away with his hand, and pointed to a large channel clearly marked on the chart.

"Main Channel. There'll be blockaders there. Can't use that one. We'll take Sullivan's Channel on the northern side."

"Won't the Yankees be expecting that?" asked Mansell.

"Yup. That's why we'll make our approach at dawn."

He pointed at a spot about eight miles from the entrance.

"Get me there at six. I'll do the rest. Put a good man at the wheel. That channel's very tricky."

"Is it possible to navigate the channel in the dark, using casts of the lead?" asked Mansell.

Feaney looked him in the eye.

"Nope. She draws too much. I must have some light," Feaney spoke these words as if there could be no argument. Then he looked down at the charts again.

"Yankees are based there at Port Royal. The blockade ships come from the south. My advice is, make your approach from the north."

With these cryptic words Feaney started to roll the charts up as if he felt the meeting was over.

"Wait," said Mansell, "can you leave me the charts, I'd like to study them whilst we're making our approach."

Feaney nodded, and let the charts unroll again.

"You mentioned that the channels are shifting," Mansell continued, "something to do with ships being deliberately sunk in them by the Yankees. How will that affect us?"

"That was at the beginning of the war."

Somehow Feaney managed to utter these words with his pipe still between his teeth, but the movement of his pipe caused a shower of ash to fall onto the charts. Mansell bent down to blow the ash onto his cabin floor.

"I've not been to Charleston for three months," said Feaney, "but I don't expect changes. Will you have me called at five Captain Mansell?"

With that, Feaney touched his filthy cap and slouched out of Mansell's cabin.

Mansell and I stood staring at each other.

"What do you think Tom?" asked Mansell, "can we trust him?"

"Well it's his life as well as ours," I said, "we'll all be sitting on five hundred tons of explosives. He knows that as well as we do. He comes recommended by Blair and Heyliger, I think we have to go ahead."

"I guess you're right Tom, but I'm not sure I like it," he turned towards the charts, "anyway, we'll provide some entertainment for the good burghers of Charleston if it all goes wrong. It's a pity it won't be the Fourth of July."

At six the following morning Mansell, Feaney, Fenton and I were grouped on the flying bridge. Mansell had successfully conned the ship to the point Feaney had indicated on the chart, and we were at the entrance to Sullivan's Channel. In the faint light of the dawn we could see the earthworks of Sullivan's Island, and the outline of Fort Beauregard. For the moment we could see no sign of the blockade ships, but as Mansell pointed out, the dawn light would help them rather than us. There was a man at the bow making casts of the lead and softly calling out the depths.

Feaney now seemed to give a different impression to the one we were used to. Although he was still shabbily dressed, he looked alert, and he kept requesting small changes to our course. With his sharp nose he seemed to be almost sniffing out the channel. He kept muttering incomprehensible words and phrases like 'Swash' and 'that's Drunken Dick', but we were making slow steady progress.

It was now half past six. Just as we were getting close to Fort Beauregard, the leadsman called out urgently that we were only in three fathoms. Mansell looked anxiously at Feaney.

"Reverse engines and hard to port!" Feaney called. But he was too late. Almost as soon as he had uttered these words we were all thrown forward as the *Isabella* slid onto some hidden obstruction and stopped dead.

"Damn!" said Feaney, "I'm a fool, it *has* shifted! We must get off as fast as we can, Captain Mansell. It won't be long before they see us. Then we'll be a sitting duck."

With these reassuring words he bent to relight his pipe. Mansell snatched it out of his mouth.

"Don't show a light Feaney!" he snapped, "concentrate on where we go if we can get off."

Our paddles were in reverse, but despite putting them onto full power this seemed to have no effect on our situation. Then Mansell had the crew running from side to side of the *Isabella*. When this

240

failed to work he had us running from bow to stern. But nothing we did seemed to shift us. All the time the dawn light was getting stronger, and we felt that at any minute we would be spotted.

Mansell called me up to the flying bridge.

"It's getting desperate Tom. We may get some help from the tide, but every second is vital. We don't have any choice; we *must* start jettisoning cargo. We'll start with the forward cargo compartment."

Fenton and I rushed forward and helped the crew to remove the main hatch cover. Then with heavy hearts we started manhandling barrels of gunpowder and cases of shells out of the hold and over the side. Fenton insisted that all of it went over the starboard side to avoid the splashes being visible to the blockaders or to Fort Wagner. At first our precautions seemed to be working. As the light improved we could see the shadowy outlines of blockading ships, but they didn't see us. Then a rocket went up.

"We'll have to work faster now!" shouted Fenton.

Sure enough the Union cruisers turned towards us like hounds scenting a fox. There were three of them, and they were in the main channel. As we worked on the cargo, Fenton told me in short bursts what was happening.

"Straight for us at the moment…"

"Only training their bow chasers on us…"

"It won't be long before they turn. We'll get their broadsides then…"

"Damn, I think that's Fort Wagner starting up."

Now we could hear almost continuous gunfire and we could see the splashes of their shells around the ship, getting closer all the time. We worked frantically, and despite the chill of the morning we were soon soaked with sweat, and covered with grime from the cargo.

Whilst we worked the *Isabella's* paddles churned the water as Mansell tried to break us free. The Confederates were doing their best to help us with their guns from the Sullivan Island forts, but it didn't seem to make much difference. I paused for a moment to look at the Yankee cruisers. The Main Channel was taking them round and soon they would be parallel to us. My heart sank; surely it would all be over then, and we would have to abandon ship. The smoke created by the gunfire from the forts and the blockaders was beginning to drift over the water. Unfortunately this was not enough to give us any protection. As the blockaders approached, the noise of gunfire was becoming louder and more pervasive.

Then, just as four of us were rolling a barrel of gunpowder across the deck, suddenly there was the scream of a shell and a huge explosion from the *Isabella's* bow. Pieces of metal flew high into the air and the *Isabella* lurched. We had the greatest difficulty keeping hold of the barrel. There was a moment's pause and then the *Isabella* started to move slowly and jerkily astern. Mansell shouted for everyone on deck to run to the stern, and this seemed to free us from the mud. We shot backwards.

"Fenton, check the damage to the bow!" shouted Mansell, "can you get that barrel over the side, Tom, and get the cover fixed back on?"

Fenton ran forward, and I helped with the barrel and hatch cover before going back onto the flying bridge.

The *Isabella* was now moving forwards at about ten knots. Feaney was concentrating fiercely on the channel, and he was talking to the helmsman and Mansell at the same time,

"*Two points to starboard* ... you can increase your speed a little captain ... *two to port* ... increase again if you want to ... may I have that pipe, can't think without it ... *one to port*..."

Mansell laughed, and handed him his pipe.

"I'll give you ten new ones if you can get us out of this. In fact you can have them anyway, and some fresh tobacco."

He turned to me.

"How much cargo have we lost Tom?"

"Only about five tons. Let's hope we can persuade the Confederates that it all came out of *their* half!"

At this point Fenton climbed up to the flying bridge to give his report on the damage to the bow. Mansell cut him short.

"Are we taking in water Fenton?"

"No Captain, the damage is well above the water line. It would only affect us in heavy seas."

"Very well. We'll have a look at it later."

As all of this was going on, the blockade fleet and Fort Wagner were still shooting at us. Fortunately we only took a couple more hits, one winged the stern of one of our boats; the other hit the rigging. The damage was slight. Gradually we worked our way along Sullivan's Channel.

"Ten more minutes," said Feaney, anxiously. Even as he said this, the fire from the cruisers seemed to slacken. They clearly didn't want to risk getting too close to the Confederate forts on the north side of the harbour mouth.

Time seemed to crawl, but eventually we came through the entrance, and out into the open area of Charleston Harbour. The blockade ships drew off, and we were safe. Mansell turned to Feaney:

"Thank you," he said, "you've earned your new pipes."

Feaney looked embarrassed.

"I ... it's never happened to me before, Captain. Going aground like that I mean. It's been expensive for you. I'm sorry."

He looked down at his feet.

"You can make amends by getting us out again safely," said Harry, clapping him on the back, "let's say no more about it. One thing you can tell me."

He pointed to what looked like an island of rubble in the entrance to the harbour.

"I know that's Fort Sumter, but what's happened to the walls and parapets and things?"

Feaney took a pull at his pipe, and stood up straighter.

"It did have walls, Captain. They've been blasting it from Fort Wagner and the Swamp Angel battery for more than a year. But our guns are still firing. Those damn Yankees'll never take Fort Sumter."

When we were in the harbour we found that we still needed Feaney's help to avoid the underwater obstructions and torpedoes. Fortunately he knew his business and we made good progress towards the docks on the eastern side.

I was sad to see what had happened to Charleston since my last visit. The southern part of the city had been under artillery fire for over a year, first from Morris Island, and then from the other

Yankee batteries around the southern side of the harbour. It was a sad sight that greeted us. The beautiful Battery walk on the eastern bank of the Charleston peninsula had been dug up. Heavy guns, including an English Blakely twelve pounder, were sited there. Many of the fine houses had been damaged or burned. From the harbour they looked almost derelict.

We pressed on to the docks. When we reached our destination we were amazed to see a crowd of local citizens shouting and waving their arms in greeting. It seemed that they had witnessed our dramatic entry to the harbour, and they were thrilled to see us shake off our Yankee pursuers.

Mr Blair had told me to get in contact with his agent George Somerville, who could be found at his office at the upper end of Meeting Street. This proved unnecessary, as almost the first person to come on board was Somerville himself. With his tall and massive build, he was soon towering above everyone on the ship. I remembered him from my last visit as being very much the polite and urbane Southern gentleman, but fortunately for us he was also highly energetic and efficient. Mansell, Somerville and I sat in chairs in Mansell's cabin. I was pleased to see Somerville sitting down carefully; the chair creaked but survived. Even so he made it look tiny with his tremendous bulk.

"I am delighted to welcome you gentlemen to Charleston," he said, "as you can see from that fine demonstration on the quayside, we are all most impressed and invigorated by your dashing entry into the harbour. Since we heard of the fall of Atlanta, we have been in desperate need of good news. By the look of your bow you probably had more difficulty than we could see from the city. Is that so Captain Mansell?"

Harry described our problems at the harbour entrance. When he came to describe the Yankee shell freeing us from the mud, Somerville looked delighted.

"God damn it sir, if that is not the finest thing I ever heard! Freed by a Yankee shell! The whole city shall hear of it. Let me take your hand sir, and yours Mr Wells."

With that he heaved himself out of his chair and insisted on shaking us both by the hand.

Mansell continued with his story. Somerville was now seated again, and he looked more and more delighted. Finally the tale was finished.

"My congratulations gentlemen," he said, "a magnificent story, and one of which you can be truly proud. Something to tell your grandchildren too I fancy! I certainly was surprised to hear of your problems with the pilot. He's a strange fellow, but I genuinely believe him to be one of our finest. You were most unfortunate, most unfortunate. Where is he? I would like to talk to him."

"He has just left the ship," I said, "he requested time to visit his family. But tell us about Atlanta. We heard that it had been lost when we were in Nassau, but it's hard to believe that fine generals like Johnston or Hood could have been defeated there."

"Johnston was replaced by General Hood, Mr Wells," replied Somerville, with a depressed look on his face, "but that story is for another day. To business gentlemen! You need to get your cargo unloaded, and then you must get your ship repaired. Pray allow me to help you with both of those tasks."

It was then that we saw Somerville in action. It seemed that with a single click of his fingers he could summon up Negro slaves to unload our cargo. Then with impressive speed he arranged for the *Isabella* to be moved to a shipyard further up the peninsula for the repairs to our bow and to the ship's boat. Despite the yard being frantically busy with navy work, Somerville somehow managed to persuade them to make the work on our ship a priority.

Our first days in the city were completely occupied with the sale of our cargo, arrangements for the new cargo, and organising the repairs to the ship. I was able to deal directly with Somerville for the private half of the cargo, but I had to deal with Confederate Government agents for their part. Throughout the process Mr Somerville smoothed all paths and opened all doors. When the *Isabella* moved to the shipyard the whole ship's company had to leave the ship and move into hotels and rooming houses. On Mr Somerville's recommendation, Harry and I moved to a small hotel in the north of the city. It was not as well known as the Mills House or the Charleston, but it was situated further away from the Yankee guns. As Somerville put it, we were less likely to be disturbed by uninvited explosive visitors.

On the financial side, everything that Blair had promised seemed to have come to fruition. Even after the cost of our repairs and the loss of a small part of our cargo, our profit on the voyage seemed destined to exceed my wildest expectations – as long as we could get out again.

It was now the middle of November, but our repairs would not be finished until the end of the month. I had a few matters to settle with Somerville, so I walked to his Meeting Street office. His room was on the first floor, looking over the street. He invited me to take a seat, and first we sorted out our business. Then Somerville offered me a cigar, and we moved to armchairs either side of the fireplace.

"I fear I have been very inhospitable during your visit," he said, "we have a small property at Flat Rock in North Carolina, and my wife and daughters are there at the moment. I entertain very little when my wife is away. You wanted to hear about the fall of Atlanta. My son Charles was there and can tell you the full story. We would both be truly delighted if you and Captain Mansell would care to have dinner with us tomorrow. Charlie is with Signal Corps, but he will be at home tomorrow in the evening. My house is at the bottom end of Church Street. If you don't mind dodging a few more Yankee shells, please do join us at five tomorrow evening. Charlie likes to stay close to his post, so if you would like to meet him, I'm afraid that does involve some risk. I should tell you that in these hard times we live very simply."

I told him that I would be delighted to come, and that I was sure that Mansell would join us. I felt very pleased and honoured to be invited. I knew that Somerville had a very prominent position in Charleston society, and apart from the dinner with General Beauregard on my first visit to the city, I had only met him on a business basis. I was also looking forward to meeting Somerville's son, who was probably close to my own age. Charleston was a city virtually under siege, and evening entertainments were limited. As in Wilmington, the blockade-running business had attracted many unsavoury characters to the city – speculators, prostitutes and the like – who thronged the northern section of the town. They kept away from the battered southern part. Supplies of food and alcohol were very limited, but there was no shortage of tobacco. Certainly the eating-houses and taverns of Charleston were a big disappointment in comparison with Nassau.

The following evening, carrying wine and brandy from the *Isabella*, Mansell and I made our way down to the Somervilles' house in Church Street. It was probably less than a mile from our hotel, but as we walked down we were shocked at the change to the quality of the city. The area around the Mills House Hotel was still showing evidence of the fire in '61. As we walked further on, the streets were virtually empty and there was grass growing between the cobbles. Houses which had clearly once been fine and elegant were now damaged, shabby and abandoned. We even saw a fox in one of the gardens. There was plentiful evidence of shell damage as we walked southwards. There were holes in walls and roofs, and in some cases major sections of a house had been destroyed. The majority of houses were boarded up, but we noticed that sometimes the boarding had been ripped down as if to force an entry. At first we were commenting on the sights we saw, but eventually the prospect was so depressing that we walked in silence. Occasionally we could hear the high-pitched whine of shells from the Yankee artillery as they screeched over the city, and landed with thuds and explosions.

There were signs of life at the Somervilles' house. It was a three-storey house with a three-level piazza running the full height and width of the southern side. It too was shabby-looking, and partly damaged, but lights were showing, and it was clearly occupied. An elderly Negro servant opened the door.

"Welcome. I'm the butler *and* the cook," he said with a smile, "Mist' Somerville, he's in the dining room, please come this way."

The dining room was big, but it was crowded with furniture. There was a dining table and chairs at one end, and armchairs grouped round a fire at the other. There were also two big desks, littered with papers. The walls were lined with ancient portraits, but on one wall there was a massive map of America, with the southern portion covered with small pins and flags.

"Come and join me gentlemen!" said Somerville, rising from an armchair to greet us, "this is virtually the only habitable room in the house. We have bedchambers upstairs, but Charlie and I live here in this room most of the time. He'll be here in a minute."

"I hope you can accept these small tokens from the *Isabella*," I said, handing over the wine and brandy, "I can't thank you enough for the trouble you have taken to help us in Charleston."

"Ordinarily I could never accept such wonderful generosity," Somerville responded, "but I think I can persuade myself that today is different. Thank you. It will certainly make our evening more convivial. Pray be seated gentlemen. What was your impression of this part of the city?"

We looked at each other. Finally it was Harry who replied. Normally he was hardly known for his tact, but now he surprised me.

"You can see why Charleston has such a reputation for the beauty and elegance of its buildings Mr Somerville, but it must be sad to see all the damage. The Yankee guns have taken their toll. Let's hope she will be like the phoenix, and will rise again just as beautiful as before."

"I like your poetic image sir, but I am afraid that it is not just the Yankees who are doing the damage. Our own citizens – even our soldiers – have been looting and vandalising the houses here. It is a disgrace. Charlie and I stay here to protect our property. Fortunately we have suffered very little damage as yet."

We could hear the clatter of someone else arriving in the house, and we could hear voices from the hall.

"Hello Mose, what's for dinner? I'm starving."

"You'll see Mr Charles," came the solemn response.

Then a tall slim figure in a shabby grey uniform burst into the room.

"Am I late Father? Oh, how d'you do, I *am* late. Sorry gentleman."

"Have you seen a charging rhinoceros, Captain Mansell? Let me introduce you and Mr Wells to my son Charles."

We stood up, and Charles Somerville bounded forward to shake our hands.

"At last!" he almost shouted, "I have been pleading with Father to let me meet the famous blockade-runners. I hope you will tell me everything about your run into Charleston. Everyone is talking about it. Is that wine I see there Father? How did you get it – we haven't seen any in months. Out with the corks!"

His father smiled

"It is from our guests Charlie, but I think we might broach a bottle."

He gestured for us to sit down again, and he pulled a bell rope. When the butler appeared he asked him to open two of the bottles we had brought. We sat in the armchairs grouped round the fire.

I turned to Charles Somerville.

"We were hoping you would tell us about Atlanta, sir. I gather you were there. Your father said that the loss of Atlanta may have had something to do with Hood replacing Johnston."

"Now you are on our favourite topic!" Charlie replied. He pointed to the map of America on the wall. "Father and I follow every step of every campaign, and there are the flags to prove it. Yes, I was in Atlanta for a few days when the railway was still open, but I wasn't there when it fell. But you can't blame Hood, Father!"

"And pray why not?" his father responded, "Joe Johnston was brilliant on the retreat from the Kennesaw Mountains, but President Davis has his favourites, like Bragg and Hood. As soon as he appointed Hood, Atlanta fell."

"It was going to fall anyway Father; we were outflanked, outgunned and outnumbered. Even Johnston couldn't have saved us."

"What will Sherman do now?" Mansell asked. A worried look came over both of their faces.

"The rumour is that he is heading for Savannah," said Mr Somerville, "but we can't be sure. Hood has tried to lure him into Tennessee, but it seems that Sherman has called his bluff and is heading south. He is trampling on Georgia as he goes. There are refugees here now from southern Georgia and even Savannah. Some of them are living in boxcars, I am ashamed to say."

"Well they'd hardly want to live here and be shelled Father, would they?"

"No I suppose not. Anyway, we were worried that Sherman

might turn east towards Flat Rock and Columbia. But it seems that Savannah is what he wants."

There was a knock at the door. Two Negro servants came into the room, carrying trays. The table was already laid, and they started to put the food onto a sideboard.

We moved with our glasses to the table. The main dish was chicken, which Mr Somerville said had been sent down from his plantation.

"You have killed the fatted chicken Father!" exclaimed Charlie cheerfully, "and quite right too! We have not had a meal like this for weeks. Here's to the blockade-runners!"

He raised his glass in a mock toast. We all laughed.

"Why do you think Sherman's going for Savannah?" asked Mansell.

"We don't know, do we Father?" said Charlie, "Father thinks Sherman has a chance of finishing the war if he turns to join forces with Grant in the east. I think Sherman has a problem with his supplies, and he wants to link up with the Yankee navy."

"Well, whichever it is," said Somerville, "at least Flat Rock and Charleston are not in his sights at the moment. The problem is…"

There was the scream of a shell seemingly heading straight for the house. We all ducked, but the shell seemed to pass straight over us. There was silence, then the sound of an explosion well to the north.

"Where will that have landed, Charlie?" asked Somerville, he turned to Mansell, "I should have told you that most days and alternate nights Charlie is up the steeple of St. Michael's church in Meeting Street, just round the corner. He is in the Signal Corps, and it is his job to spot the shells as they come over – *if* he can stay awake that is."

This was said with a sharp look at Charlie, who laughed.

"Damn dangerous work it is too," Somerville continued, "St. Michael's is always a target, but it hasn't been hit yet. Who is up there tonight, is it Augustine?"

"No, Gus is still on furlough father. It's Benti and John. I think the Yanks may have a new gun; they can't usually shoot that far north. But that's enough about us. I want to hear about blockade running. The nearest I have got to it was serving on the *Palmetto State* in Charleston Harbour."

"That's one of your ironclads isn't it?" asked Mansell, "I've only seen them from a distance. Usually they've been Yankee ones, and they've been firing at us. What's she like? Can you describe her to us?"

"I can do better than that. I think I can get you on board if you'd like to."

"I'd give my right arm for it!" exclaimed Mansell.

"I don't think that would be necessary Captain Mansell," said Mr Somerville wryly, "but why have you come to Charleston this time? I'm told that Wilmington is your usual destination."

"We really did it as a favour to Angus Blair," I said, "but if we get out safely the owners will be delighted with the profits. They are worried that the war is reaching a critical stage."

"You mean they think we may lose it!" said Charlie with a grin.

"I'm afraid you're right. That's what they're worried about. Isn't there a chance that the Yankees may try to strangle your army by shutting off Wilmington or Charleston?"

"Wilmington is the greater risk for us," said Mr Somerville, "hardly any blockade-runners get through to Charleston these days. My fear is that Wilmington's poorly defended. I am told that the garrison is only two thousand men. General Whiting is a good man, but now Davis has replaced him with another of his favourites – Bragg. We all know what a poor general he is."

"Do you think the Yankees *will* attack Wilmington?" asked Mansell.

"I am afraid so Captain Mansell," said Somerville grimly, "Wilmington is our last viable port since the Yankees shut Mobile in August. If they can close Wilmington, where will the army get its supplies? I am amazed it has not happened already. I think your owners should make the most of things whilst they can Mr Wells, before your namesake sends his navy to Wilmington. If he does, I hope we shall have the pleasure of seeing you gentlemen here again."

Whilst we talked about the intricacies of the Wilmington defences the chicken was cleared away, and we started to eat some

251

fruit compote. I was anxious to learn more precisely how the closure of Wilmington would affect the progress of the war, but I found it hard to get a clear opinion.

"If they close Wilmington, how long can the Confederacy last?" I asked.

"Father and I both think that now Lincoln's been re-elected things look pretty grim for us," said Charlie, "if that idiot McClellan had got in we might have had a better chance."

"I hate to say it," said his father, "but Lincoln is a typical lawyer, all politics and hopeless at running things; but he has finally found two generals in Sherman and Grant who he can trust. Grant has got Lee tied down at Petersburg, and now he has lost Fort Harrison. Lee made a nuisance of himself with Early in Shenandoah, but Sheridan overwhelmed him in the end. No, gentlemen, I am afraid we are stuck in the east, and things look worse here. If our military supplies are cut off we will be in a very serious situation."

"It's hard to believe that a genius like Lee could find himself bogged down like that," said Mansell.

"It all started with Gettysburg," responded Somerville.

He got up to pour the remnants of the second bottle of wine. Then he sat down again.

"Lee's army was fatally weakened, and we do not have the resources to build it up again. Every battle Lee fights gives him the same problem, and Grant knows it. His attack on Lee at Cold Harbour was suicidal, and thank God Lee was too strong for him, but we had losses we simply could not afford. The Yankees seem to have an endless supply of men and materials."

"You certainly paint a gloomy picture," said Harry quietly. "Lee outnumbered and pinned down in the east, and Sherman rampant in the west. Every voyage we make we can see how strong the Yankee navy is. Your navy doesn't seem to be able to do anything about it. Is there any hope for the Confederacy?"

Mr Somerville and his son looked at each other as if wondering who should reply. Eventually it was Somerville himself.

"This is where Charlie and I tend to disagree Captain Mansell. He is more optimistic than I. He thinks Lee could conjure up some more magic in the east, or Hood could prove us wrong here. He even thinks that England could come in on our side. But sadly I feel that it is just a matter of time. Certainly the closure of Wilmington would be the beginning of the end. Maybe Lee can hold out for another six months in the east, but there is nothing to stop Sherman. If he turns east he will roll the Carolinas up like a rug."

This struck home for me as I thought of Amy and her family at Marion.

"I have friends close to Fayetteville in North Carolina, will they be at risk?" I asked.

"I am afraid they will certainly be at risk, everything will be at risk. What they need to worry about is that Fayetteville is a centre for our munitions. Sherman will know that, and I am afraid it is bound to be a target."

He paused.

"Do you think we should try some of the *Isabella's* brandy, gentlemen?"

He walked over to the sideboard to collect the bottle. As he did so we heard the scream of another shell. Once again we all flinched, but this time the scream ended with a massive explosion either in or very close to the house. The whole house shook and trembled. There was the sound of breaking glass and damaged masonry, and then the patter of falling dust and plaster.

Mr Somerville spun round remarkably quickly for a man of his bulk.

"Damn Yankees!" he shouted, "why can't they let us drink our brandy in peace? Follow me gentlemen!" and he raced for the door.

When we got into the hall there was the smell of plaster dust, but no obvious sign of damage. Then one of the Negro servants ran in.

"It's next door!" he shouted, "they'ze on fire!"

We ran outside, and then we could see that one of the buildings in the garden of the house next door had been badly damaged and was burning.

"Is there anyone living there?" shouted Mansell.

"It's their kitchens, but the house is empty!" called out Charlie, "Benti will be on to it, he will have the fire brigade here in a moment, but there's no time to lose!"

It seemed that the Somervilles were well prepared for an event of this kind. There were buckets in one of their outbuildings, and one of the Negroes manned the pump. Soon we were forming a chain to do our best to put the fire out. One or two others joined us, and then one of the engines from the Charleston Fire Brigade. It was ten o'clock before the fire was finally out, and we were able to go back into the Somervilles' house. Then we could have the brandy we had been promised, and tales were told of Atlanta and running the blockade. Finally Mr Somerville recommended that we should be on our way.

"I am afraid it is dangerous at night here gentlemen," he said, "there are two of you, so there should be no difficulty, but it is during the night that we get most of the problems with looting. I hate to seem inhospitable, but I suggest that you would be wise to return to your hotel."

That evening proved to be the start of a much more sociable time for Mansell and me. Two days later Charlie insisted that we should join him and his friends for an evening in Meeting Street in a house close to St. Michael's church. It was then that Charlie asked us to meet him at the docks two days later for a visit to the Confederate ironclad, *Palmetto State*.

We were at the docks punctually, but we found Charlie talking excitedly to a young handsome Negro, who was dressed in naval uniform.

"Gentlemen, can I introduce Joe McNeil?" asked Charlie, hurriedly, "Joe, this is Captain Mansell and Mr Wells. I've been called to an interview with General Beauregard about a post I have been seeking on active service. Joe and I served on the *Palmetto* together, would you mind if he showed you round. Now I must run."

With a wave of his hand he was sprinting off down the dockside.

"That's just like Charlie," said Joe McNeil, "zip, zap, zip, and he's gone. Life is never dull when he's around. We certainly miss him on the *Palmetto*. You've probably seen her anchored in the Channel. There's a boat just here to take us across."

When we talked about it afterwards, Mansell and I confessed to

254

being equally astonished to be in the company of such a well-spoken Negro, who was obviously a free man. When we asked Charlie, he said that Joe was certainly not unique. He was one of many free Negroes in Charleston, some in the services - mainly cooks or cleaners - and others in the fire brigade.

We followed Joe into the boat, and soon we were approaching the *Palmetto State*. All we could see was a long flat iron deck about one hundred and eighty feet long, and only rising a foot out of the water. Welded to the deck was an angular sloped black hump some eight feet high by a hundred feet long, which turned out to be the casement. Guns poked out of it on all sides, and there was a funnel on the casement's flat top. Mansell was bombarding McNeil with questions.

"What's she built out of, Mr McNeil, and what does she draw?"

"Well she's built out of oak and pine some twenty inches thick but she's got four inches of iron covering the casement, and two inches on the deck. She draws twelve feet, but as you'll know Captain Mansell, that's quite a lot in this harbour."

"How is she powered?"

"She's a screw ship of course, and we got her engines out of another steamer. She's a bit underpowered, but we can get six knots out of her on a good day."

"How many crew?"

Joe McNeil looked at Mansell with a twinkle in his eyes.

"How many more questions have you got Captain Mansell? I'm beginning to worry about my ability to answer them... anyway there's about a hundred and twenty of us. It's manning the guns that really brings the numbers up."

"I'm sorry Mr McNeil," said Mansell, "but I was in the British Navy in the recent war in the Crimea, and your ship fascinates me. Our ironclads were primitive affairs compared to the *Palmetto*. May I ask you what guns she carries?"

"I'll show you when we get on board, but they're Brookes and Dahlgrens."

Now it was my turn to be inquisitive, but I could see Mansell looking a bit astonished at the naivety of my question.

"Why do you need both wood and iron? Surely she could just be built of iron?"

"Well iron is good for deflecting shells off the deck and the casement, but it's not so good for direct hits. The wood underneath supports the iron."

Now we had reached the *Palmetto State*, and Joe McNeil showed us round. First we climbed over the iron hull and the casement, and he showed us the spar torpedo projecting from the bow. Then we clambered through the hatch into the interior. It was pretty dark inside, but fortunately it was cool. Joe told us that in the summer it could be unbearably hot in the casement, particularly when the guns were firing. During our tour Mansell continued with his questions. Eventually Joe came to describe General Beauregard's attempt in January 1863 to use the *Palmetto State* and her sister ship the *Chicora* to help break the blockade. He was amused to learn that on the *Clara* we had run into the blockade ships that they had chased out of the harbour mouth.

"I'm sorry, gentlemen!" said Joe, "but at least we did some damage to their ships and ours were untouched. They stood well out of the harbour after that."

When the tour was complete, Joe McNeil took us back to the Charleston docks again. We were full of gratitude for his hospitality, and we invited him to visit us on the *Isabella* when our repairs were complete. This was our incentive to give a big dinner on board to return the generous hospitality we had received whilst we were in Charleston. The Somervilles came, some of Charlie's friends from the Signal Corps, and Joe McNeil from the *Palmetto State*. Liquor and fine foods were short commodities in Charleston, and the evening was convivial to the point of riotousness. Our hilarity was heightened by news just coming in that Colonel Colcock had defeated a large Union force at Honey Hill, as the Yankees tried to sever the Charleston and Savannah Railroad.

Despite the conviviality of the evening, there was the unspoken thought that Charleston and Wilmington were threatened, and that the blockade was tighter than ever. It was with some sadness and apprehension that we viewed our imminent return to Nassau.

Chapter Eighteen
Mansell's Advice

Our cargo was exclusively cotton. Every hold was tightly crammed, with some bales secured on deck. Feaney had returned from visiting his family, and we sat in the saloon to discuss how to make our exit from Charleston on that chilly day in early December 1864. Ever since the *Isabella* had gone aground in Sullivan's Channel, Feaney had taken a more cooperative tone with us, so the discussion was more comfortable. Mansell, Fenton, Feaney and I were seated round one side of the saloon table, with charts spread out in front of us. I was pleased to see Feaney smoking a new pipe, and his tobacco seemed less offensive.

"How's the pipe Feaney?" I asked.

He smiled.

"It'll take a lot of getting used to. I was fond of the old one, but Mrs Feaney agrees I should change."

"I should think she does!" exclaimed Mansell, "if *we* were being poisoned on the *Isabella*, what about your poor family?"

Feaney laughed.

"I have to admit, they're pleased."

"What do you think we should do about leaving Charleston?" asked Mansell, "we've got favourable lunar conditions at the moment. We want to get back to Nassau quickly, but we want to get there in one piece."

"It's the same as before," he said, "as soon as we get to the harbour mouth we'll be in danger from Fort Wagner and the Yankee ships. But if we use Sullivan's Channel I must have some light to con the ship."

"How about the Main Channel?"

"Well that would be easier, but we'd have to dodge the blockaders. And how would you get me back to the island? You agreed to do that Captain Mansell."

"One thing at a time," responded Harry, "if we were going to use the Main Channel, how would we do it?"

"We'd take the *Isabella* up to the harbour end of Sullivan's Island. That would have to be in daylight to avoid the torpedoes. We'd lay up 'til dark. Even in the dark I think I could con us to the Main Channel from there. Then we would take our chance through the Yankee blockade ships. I could take us up the channel on the compass. It's wide enough."

"How about this," said Mansell, "we do as you say, and we lay up at the western end of the island. When it's pitch black you con us to the Main Channel and we go out on that. If they don't see us, we can cut round to Sullivan's Channel straightaway, and put you ashore in one of the boats. If they do spot us, we'll have to shake them off in the dark. The *Isabella* can do seventeen knots even with this lot on board. As soon as we lose them, we swing back to the other end of the island. That helps both of us. You get back to the island, and we take a route that we can navigate in the dark."

There was silence as Feaney took a long pull at his pipe. Then he looked hard at Mansell.

"It might work. The most risky part will be getting to the Main Channel ... well, I'll do it. When do you want to go?"

"Tonight," said Mansell.

A few hours later we had worked our way to the western end of Sullivan's Island, passing the *Palmetto State* on our way. We were waiting for darkness to fall. The harbour was relatively calm, and even out to sea the conditions were favourable. We could see the city of Charleston in the distance. Every so often the Yankee guns fired in the direction of the city, and I thought of Charlie Somerville perched up in his eyrie at the top of the St. Michael's steeple. I had been up there once to see him. There was almost a party atmosphere during the day. At the time of my visit, there were two others fellows there and I understood that he even had visits from some of the Charleston ladies. The Signal Corps had to plot where the Yankee shells landed, and get the Fire Brigade out if fires started. They also checked ship and troop movements, so I was sure that he would have seen us making our way across the harbour.

As darkness fell Feaney was standing up on the flying bridge with Mansell, and I joined them there. They were talking in low tones.

"We'll have to go dead slow, Captain," Feaney was saying, "and I must have a good man on the lead. We'll be feeling our way to the Main Channel."

"Do you need a light?"

"Yes, I must be able to see the compass."

"I'll have a shaded light put there. When should we start?"

"As soon as possible. It's almost high tide now. We can't risk getting stuck when it's falling."

"Right. In quarter of an hour."

Mansell went down onto the main deck to make the final arrangements. I was tense. The *Isabella's* cargo represented a huge profit to Pembroke and Stringer, and also to me. I was more anxious than ever to get it out. In my anxiety my fingers were drumming the rail.

"Nervous, Mr Wells?" asked Feaney.

"Yes, I suppose this is one of the most hazardous moments we've had on this ship."

Feaney puffed on his pipe. I felt the need for distraction.

"Do you live on Sullivan's Island, Feaney?"

"Used to. My house is there. Many of them have been knocked down to help our gunners. I'm told mine is still there, and I want to see it."

"Where are your family?"

"Little way up the Cooper, with my Pa."

Feaney told me that his father had been a deep-sea fisherman but he had suffered injuries when his boat had capsized in the Atlantic, close to the Charleston coast. His life had been saved by his crew, but his fishing days were over.

"We moved north of Charleston on the Cooper," he continued, "but the sea was in my blood by then, and I couldn't wait to get back."

After this unusual burst of candour from Feaney we were both silent. My mind was on the dangers to come. Feaney seemed unperturbed and he resumed his rhythmic sucking on his pipe. After a couple of minutes Mansell reappeared.

"We're fired up," he said, "shall we cast off?"

On this occasion Feaney showed us his true expertise. The

weather remained calm and the *Isabella* was conned slowly towards the Main Channel through the darkness. It was clearly painstaking work, with Feaney making frequent minute changes to our course. Once there was a slight shuddering as the ship brushed over a small underwater obstruction, but gradually the depths called by the leadsman increased, and finally Feaney was able to announce that we were in the Main Channel. At first the channel ran south-south east, but then it gradually swung full south. Feaney was looking more and more confident as time went by. The atmosphere on the flying bridge became less tense. Fenton had joined us and we were all searching the horizon.

"You can douse that light now captain," said Feaney.

We were steaming at low speed in an attempt to be as silent as possible. At first we saw no sign of any of the blockade ships, but then we saw the lights of a cruiser ahead. Mansell altered course slightly, and we slipped past. We were still using good quality anthracite coal from Nassau, but at this point the *Isabella* chose to send a shower of sparks up her funnel. We were beyond the cruiser, but she hailed us.

"Full speed ahead!" Mansell shouted.

The *Isabella* leapt forward. A rocket went up from the cruiser.

"*She'll* never catch us," said Fenton, "but how many friends has she got?"

We saw ships and rockets in the distance, but the Yankees gave us no trouble. Mansell steamed south at full speed for two hours, and then began the sweep round which would take us back to the eastern end of Sullivan's Island. It was three in the morning when we crept in, and Feaney prepared to take his place in one of the *Isabella's* boats.

We all thanked him, and wished him well. I paid him, and then he was on his way to the island. We waited anxiously for the boat to return, and then Mansell set his course for Nassau.

Three days later we arrived safely. We found that the *Charlotte* had already returned to Nassau. She had loaded a new cargo, and she had set off for Wilmington again.

I needed to take stock. With the *Index* sold, and the loss of the *Pevensey*, our little fleet was down to two. The *Charlotte* was on her way to Wilmington, and with luck, this voyage or the next one would see her paid for. After that, apart from her running expenses, all would be for profit. The *Isabella* was already highly profitable for the partners, and our run to Charleston had made a massive contribution. If the Somervilles were right, we needed to capture as much profit as we could in the next few months. The risks were increasing all the time, as the blockade concentrated on Charleston and Wilmington. Even if the war didn't end with the closure of the ports, it would be the end for us. I was happy that our Charleston gamble had paid off, and I was sure that Pembroke and Stringer would be delighted. Their new ship the *Maude Campbell* was expected in Bermuda late in January, would there still be work for her to do?

I had put Susan to the back of my mind, and my thoughts were on Amy. How would I get to see her again? I was depressed, but fortunately there was plenty in Nassau to occupy me. We worked on a new cargo for the *Isabella*, and we made preparations for the return of the *Charlotte*. Harry had determined that the best moment for the *Isabella's* next run to Cape Fear would be just before Christmas.

Even at this late stage of the war, Nassau was still seething with blockade-runners. The hotels and bars were full of drunken, swaggering sailors, most of them British. The risks of making each run were increasing. Everyone used the time they had in Nassau as a release of tension before and after their dangerous voyages. It was unsafe to walk on your own late at night, and the taverns reminded me of the worst pothouses in the East End of London. Drunken sailors and red-faced prostitutes mixed with the riff-raff of the town. It was through this bedlam that Harry and I walked late one afternoon from the *Isabella* to the Royal Victoria Hotel. We were due to sail the following day. That evening we had dinner together at the Victoria. We had numerous cocktails before dinner, and we drank champagne with it. Towards the end of the meal Harry was looking serious despite the large quantity of alcohol he had absorbed.

"Come on Harry, out with it, what's on your mind?" I asked.

"You've noticed haven't you? Yes, there's been something on

my mind that I've wanted to say for a while. Now I am going to say it."

He drained his champagne glass and looked down at the table, which was littered with the debris of a splendid dinner.

"Christ!" he exclaimed, "we better get someone to take away all these bottles and things. How can I be serious looking at those dead cigars?"

He paused, looked round in vain for a waiter, and then continued slowly.

"You and I have been pals since you first came on board the *Clara*. I didn't quite know what to make of you then, you were a quiet fellow, a bit straight laced, but I took to you. You're honest, and I know I can rely on you in a crisis. You threw yourself into the work on that first voyage, and you've always been the same since. When there's trouble, or work to do, there you are at hand. I wouldn't have guessed it when I first met you, but now I must give you the credit for it."

"You're making me nervous," I said, "too many compliments – what's coming?"

Harry didn't answer my question.

"In two years you've had more experience of the world than most men have had in their lifetime. You've run the business here – I know how difficult that is – and you've seen more action onboard ship than many navy fellows. It's made a man of you, and I admire you. You used to get a bit nervous when you first joined us, but you're as cool as any sailor now, in fact cooler than most."

"That was the *Nutfield*," I said, "I felt that if I could get through that, then I could face anything."

Mansell nodded, as if what I'd said underlined something in his own experience.

"You told me about Amy when we first met, and it was a romantic story. He's young, I thought, and it won't last. But I was wrong. You've been in love with that girl for years. I've met her, and I have to admit you've made a great choice.

"I take the blame for your escapade with Mrs Kohler," he continued, "I shouldn't have dragged you along to Mrs Dalrymple's. Most of us have had similar episodes in our lives, we're a little ashamed of them, but secretly we would make the same mistakes again if we had the chance. I suppose you've learned something about women of her sort and luckily for you, the lesson hasn't been too expensive."

"I'm not sure where this is leading," I said, "but I think I may need the comfort of a glass of port before you go on."

Harry laughed. He looked round, finally found a waiter, and called him over. Then he continued.

"If there's a Yankee cruiser on the horizon, you're as cool as an icicle. Look at the advice you gave to poor Donald off Madeira. He was thinking of surrender, and you advised him to tough it out. He admired you for that."

"You never told me."

"Would have given you a swollen head. It's been the same all along. You've made hard quick decisions. You may take them too quickly, and sometimes you're wrong, but that can't be helped. You're decisive, except for one thing."

I could feel the blow coming but I couldn't guess where it was going to fall. Was he worried about Wilmington closing? Did he want me to sell the *Isabella* rather than setting sail for Cape Fear? I was concerned myself, but I had concluded that we should go on making money if we could. Our ships would be pretty useless for any other purpose.

"Are you thinking we should close our operations here?" I asked, "don't keep me in suspense, tell me!"

"No Tom, you're completely on the wrong tack. It's Miss Munro. You ought to marry her."

"But Christ Harry, it's the thing I most want in the world; you don't have to tell me that!"

"Yes, but what are you doing about it? You have been in love with each other for three years…"

"Four," I muttered.

"…and you're allowing that mother of hers to keep you apart. Miss Munro's not going to marry anyone else, and nor are you. Are you going to wait until you're both fifty?"

"That's not fair, Harry, Mrs Munro's concerns are real. There are genuine risks for Amy if she were to marry me. She'd have to run the blockade with us, and then there's the yellow fever…"

"Nonsense!" he almost shouted, "do you want to marry that girl or not? You don't have to stay in Nassau, if that's what you're worried about, you could go back to England. Besides, are the risks any less at Marion? They're losing the war, Tom. Somerville told us that Sherman is grinding Georgia under his boots, and he thinks the Carolinas will be next. Sherman's rumoured to be almost at Savannah now. Would it be any more risky to take the run to Nassau than to be at the mercy of Sherman's troops? If you brought her here, there's virtually no risk of yellow fever in the winter, and anyway you could head straight for England."

We sat looking at each other across the table. I said nothing, but the more I thought about it, the more logical his arguments sounded.

"Well, that's what I wanted to say," he said with a grin, "you probably think it's the drunken ramblings of an idiot."

"So you want me to shoot Mrs Munro, and carry Amy away from Marion over my shoulder?"

"Yes," he said, "let's have another glass of port and get back on board the *Isabella*. We have an early start ahead of us."

"Wait a second. Supposing I do what you suggest, kidnap Amy and carry her off down to Wilmington. Then we set sail and run the blockade. If we're under the guns of a Yankee cruiser, and I ask you to surrender, would you do it?"

"Yes, Tom, if that's what you asked me to do, I'd do it."

There was something else on my mind, but I wondered how should I express it. Despite his inebriation, Mansell noticed, and waited patiently.

"Harry," I said finally, "what should I say to Amy about Susan? If there had been no child, I suppose I could talk myself into saying nothing, but now…"

"Tom, don't be an idiot, that episode is gone, dead, defunct! How can it possibly profit Amy to know anything about it? It would only be an open wound in your marriage to be mentioned every time you had the slightest disagreement. Take my advice old fellow; say nothing! You'll only regret it if you spill the beans. Mrs Kohler has gone, and the best thing you can do is to forget her."

I struggled with my conscience as I thought about Harry's words, but I said nothing further about it as we finished our port, and walked through the noisy town to the *Isabella*.

Chapter Nineteen
The Last Chance

Mansell had planned to leave with the *Isabella* on the nineteenth of December, but we woke up to a howling tempest, so he decided to delay our departure. When we set off the following day there were still heavy seas and visibility was poor, but the wind had abated. The motion of the ship was very uncomfortable. When we passed through the Northeast Providence Channel the weather was worse, but Mansell thought that he could detect positive signs, so we pressed on. One advantage of the poor visibility was that we saw no Yankee cruisers for the first two days of the voyage. They would have had equal difficulty in seeing us, and any vessels at sea would have had enough work just to stay afloat.

On the third day the weather improved, and then we began to see considerable activity from the Northern navy. Mansell's plan was to reach the blockade cordon around midnight, and to make our attempt on the New Inlet in the early hours. We spent the afternoon dodging Yankee cruisers, but we managed to work our way towards Cape Fear. After we had taken evasive action for the fifth time, Mansell gathered the ship's officers, the pilot and myself together in the wheelhouse, and we stood round the chart of the Cape Fear estuary.

"I don't remember ever seeing so many Yankee ships," he said, "something unusual is going on, or maybe we've just been unlucky. I still intend to stick to our plan, unless you have any objections, Tom? Do you feel there's unnecessary risk to the ship and the cargo?"

"It's the business we're in, Harry," I replied, "they must be desperate for the munitions; I think we just have to take the risk."

"I guessed that's what you'd say," responded Harry with a grin. He pointed to our location on the chart, "that's where we are as near as we can figure it. We'll keep going. As you can see, all this weaving about has taken us a bit further north than we'd hoped. When it's dusk we'll turn southwest and work our way towards the

New Inlet."

When night fell he changed course. All lights on the ship were extinguished, and we steamed slowly. I was standing with Fenton on the flying bridge and Harry was pacing nervously about as the *Isabella* pitched and rolled in the heavy seas. Finally he came over to Fenton and me.

"It's after midnight fellows, so it's Christmas Eve. Any chance of a star from the east to guide us to Christmas Day in Smithville?"

"Of all the places to spend Christmas Day, Smithville – what a hell-hole," said Fenton.

Mansell was still scanning round the ship with nervous intensity.

"Am I starting at shadows?" he asked, "or can I see the silhouettes of two cruisers keeping pace with us to port?"

"I hate to say it," said Fenton quietly, "but now you mention it I think I can just see one to starboard through the spray."

"We'll drop back," and as Harry said this he leant down to the engine room speaking tube and ordered slow speed.

"It's strange," he said, "you'd have thought they would have seen us, but there was no reaction. Has peace broken out?"

"We'll find out at Smithville," I replied, "five hundred cases of Enfield rifles may move a little slowly in peacetime. Fifty cases of cavalry swords may not be too popular either."

"Ploughshares perhaps?" asked Harry.

We fell back, but soon we thought we saw other shadows, always travelling in the same direction – towards the New Inlet.

"It's almost as though we're in the middle of a fleet," said Harry, "I'm not sure that there's any point in manoeuvring. We'll stay on the same course. Maybe they think we're one of them."

We were now almost opposite Fort Fisher. The Yankee ships turned, and made their way towards the fort. We worked our way gradually out of the fleet towards the New Inlet.

"I think that's the last of them," said Fenton.

Almost as he said this, there was a huge and deafening explosion, and the sky lit up. The explosion was close to the fort, and for a moment we could see Fort Fisher brilliantly illuminated. We could also see a huge Armada of Northern ships heading towards the fort. A confusion of thoughts ran through my mind, what was the explosion? Was it an attack on Fort Fisher, or had they trapped another blockade-runner and blown her up? Would they have seen us in that dazzling flash of light? I turned to Mansell, but he was obviously thinking along the same lines.

"Christ!" he exclaimed, "it looks as though the Yankees are really having a go at the fort."

He ordered full speed ahead, and we raced towards the New Inlet. It soon became obvious that the flash from the explosion had revealed us to the nearby cruisers, and one of them turned in pursuit. We were already half a mile away, and the *Isabella* was the faster ship. The cruiser opened fire with her bow chaser, but the heavy seas made us a difficult target. Gradually we pulled away, and soon we were able to slip over the bar at the entrance to the river. We reached Smithville early in the morning, and tried to find out what had been happening. Information was scarce.

Around midday we could hear the sound of heavy gunfire. The Yankee fleet had opened fire on Fort Fisher, and Colonel Lamb was replying in kind. Now we were told that the Northern admiral had sent a powder ship as close to Fort Fisher as he could, and that it had been blown up during the night. This was the huge explosion we had witnessed. The Yankees had waited to see the extent of the damage. They had thought they were going to destroy the whole fort, but apparently the damage had been minimal. The plan had been a fiasco. Now they were trying to remedy their failure with their ships' guns.

Harry called a council of war of the ship's officers and myself in his cabin.

"This seems to be the long expected attempt to close the Cape Fear River," he said, "we have to decide whether we continue to Wilmington, or discharge our cargo here and try to escape back to Nassau. We might have a chance of getting through now, but we have several tons of explosives on board, and I want them unloaded before we try to get back through the fleet. Tom, what's your view as the owners' representative?"

"If we discharge our cargo here," I said, "it could take two days and since it's Christmas, maybe even longer. Then we have all the costs of taking it in wagons to Wilmington. How long do you think it'll be before we know the outcome of the attack?"

"Haven't any idea," said Harry, "maybe this is just an attempt to destroy Fort Fisher from the sea, and they'll land troops later. But I don't believe that. They won't give General Whiting a chance to reinforce the fort. My guess is that they will land troops today, or tomorrow at the latest. These kinds of engagement are usually over quickly."

"So we have three choices," I said, "start unloading, wait, or steam to Wilmington. If we start unloading here there's a good chance that the river will be shut even before we finish. If we wait, what do we gain? Either the attack will fail, and we will wish we'd set off for Wilmington, or it will succeed, and we're shut in anyway. I vote that we steam to Wilmington, discharge our cargo and wait to see what happens. If the Yankee attack fails we can load our next cargo and take our chance."

"Before we toss that three sided coin," Harry added, "there's one other point. If the attack succeeds quickly, the Yankees will take their gunboats through the New Inlet to Smithville and we risk being caught at our moorings whilst we're discharging the cargo."

We argued the points backwards and forwards and eventually concluded that our best course of action was to steam to Wilmington. We were fortunately out of the quarantine season, so after we had obtained our pratique, we could steam directly there. As we made our way up river I discussed my plans with Harry. The pilot was in control of the ship, so we sat in Mansell's cabin

"I'm going to take your advice," I said, "I'm going to go to Marion and beard the gorgon in her lair. Somehow I'm going to persuade her to let me marry Amy. If the Yankee attack on Fort Fisher fails, I'll try to persuade Amy to run the blockade with us to Nassau. If it succeeds, we'll have to escape to England some other way – maybe through Charleston, or through the North. Assuming the Cape Fear estuary is still open, will you wait with the *Isabella* until I get back? ... but first I'll stay in Wilmington to see which way the cat's going to jump before I leave for Fayetteville."

"Which cat?" asked Harry, "Mrs Munro or the Yankee army? But I'm delighted, should I come with you to Marion?"

"No, but thank you. This is something I have to do on my own, and you'll be needed with the ship. What about Charlotte? Will you try to get her out too?"

"It's not going to work, old fellow," Mansell replied, "Charlotte and I cannot agree about our future. She will only marry me if I'll settle down, either here or in England, and I can't agree to do that. No, there'll only be one female passenger on this ship if you bring Miss Munro. But I haven't answered your question. I *will* wait for you, but we can't wait forever. Even if this attack fails, they're bound to attack again. We owe it to the owners and the crew to get out again quickly. I'll work out the longest we can decently wait, and then you'll know how much time you've got."

This was reasonable. Even if I couldn't take passage with them this time, there would always be a chance that I could travel with the *Isabella* or the *Charlotte* on a later voyage.

When we arrived in Wilmington the result of the Yankee attack was still in the balance. Mr Blair told us that the *Charlotte* had arrived successfully two weeks ago, and had probably made her way out through the attacking fleet as we came in. We might even have passed her on our approach to Cape Fear.

Over the next two days it became clear that the attack on Fort Fisher had failed, and the town was ablaze with excitement and celebration. Colonel Lamb was the hero of the hour, but again General Bragg was criticised. It seemed that he had failed to attack the Union soldiers as they tried to evacuate. Only some 2,500 Union troops had landed and Bragg's force was now more like 3,500. Many of the townspeople were puzzled by Bragg's actions. But at least the outcome filled everyone with delight. The Yankee troops had re-embarked and the Northern fleet had slunk off with its tail between its legs. The die was cast and now I could make my way to Marion.

First I called on Mr Blair. He had been amazed that we had successfully come through the Northern fleet, and he had been delighted with our cargo of arms and munitions. Now he agreed that our next cargo should be assembled and loaded as quickly as possible. He too was concerned that another Yankee attack would come soon. Then I told him that I was going to Marion. I did not tell him of my plan for Amy, but I told him that this might be my last chance to see her before Wilmington was finally closed to shipping.

"My sister will not welcome your visit," he said, "would you like me to send a message to her first?"

"No, I'll take my chance. Time's short and I can't wait for messages to go backwards and forwards."

Blair nodded. "I understand."

Over the next two days we completed the arrangements for the *Isabella's* cargo. I was now free to make my trip to Fayetteville, and I consulted Mansell on the timing. He was in his cabin and he told me that he had made his calculations. He said that the *Isabella* should be fully laden by the fifth of January, and that we should leave no later than the tenth. This gave me twelve days to complete my mission.

"I really would prefer to leave before that," he said, "but the tenth is the absolute latest. If you're not here by ten o'clock on the morning of tenth of January, the *Isabella* will leave without you. So get going, and good luck!"

I packed my portmanteau, and made my way to the steamer for Fayetteville. I arrived in the town late on New Year's Eve, and found a room in the Fayetteville Hotel. Celebrations of the New Year were muted, with the war having reached a deeply depressing stage. The news had just come through that Sherman had captured Savannah. General Thomas had virtually destroyed Hood's Confederate army at Nashville, and now there were hardly any Southern troops available to defend the Carolinas. The residents of Fayetteville were worried that soon they would be in the path of Sherman's brutal army. The hotel was nearly full of refugees from Georgia, and there were even one or two families from South Carolina who were moving north to relatives further away from danger. Many of the refugees were rough types and the atmosphere in the town was unpleasant.

New Year's Day was a Sunday, and that morning I sent a message to Mrs Munro at Marion saying that I was staying in Fayetteville, and that I intended to call on them at twelve noon that day. I didn't leave her sufficient time to send me a message in reply. With some difficulty I hired a buggy to drive me, and I asked

271

the driver to drop me at the gates to Marion.

At noon I was walking down the drive to the plantation house.

When I had first visited Marion the property had been beautifully cared for, and the fields had been white with cotton. Now there was a feeling of desolation and neglect. The drive was untidy, and many of the fields had clearly remained unplanted. As I walked up the drive I tried to work out my tactics to secure Amy. I had been wrestling with the problem ever since Mansell had convinced me to try, and no great Napoleonic plan had come to mind. All I could work out was that the risks for Amy of staying were now as great as the risks of leaving. The choice was now about me. How could I convince Mrs Munro that Amy should marry me? I hoped that I still had Amy's love, but there had been no letters waiting for me with her uncle.

I walked with some sadness to the front door. If Amy and I could not convince her mother, or if Amy would not go against her mother's wishes, this was probably the last time I would ever be at Marion.

The elderly butler met me at the door.

"Mrs Munro, she's expecting you."

He led the way to the drawing room.

She was in a far corner of the room. She was seated, with her stick beside her. She did not try to get up.

"I hope you will forgive me Mr Wells if I do not get up to greet you," she gestured to her stick, "pray be seated. Your visit is unexpected, and if I may say so, you come uninvited. Amy will join us shortly. Would you mind telling me what your visit is about?"

Her manner was cool, but polite.

"I'm sure you can probably guess why I'm here, Mrs Munro. We have just come through the blockade. We passed through a large fleet of Yankee ships, and they were attempting to capture Fort Fisher. You probably know already that their attack failed, but everyone in Wilmington is convinced that another attack is not far off. Next time it's highly likely that they will close off Wilmington as they have closed New Orleans, Savannah and Mobile. My ship leaves for Nassau on the tenth of January. Getting out of Charleston's virtually impossible, so this may be the last opportunity to leave the South by sea. I'm as much in love with Amy as ever, and I think she still loves me too. I want to marry her and take her to Nassau on my ship. Sherman's army…"

Mrs Munro reached for her stick and tried to stand, but fell back into her chair.

"Mr Wells, I must protest…"

I held up my hand and cut her short.

"Please let me finish, Mrs Munro. Sherman has marched through Georgia and has captured Savannah. The only general who could stop him was Hood, and his army has been annihilated at Nashville. Sherman can now be supported by sea, so he's bound to attack the Carolinas, and there's no one here who can stop him.

"I love Amy," I continued, "and I can't bear the thought of her being at the mercy of Sherman and his rascals. You were worried about the dangers of the blockade and yellow fever at Nassau. I think the dangers are worse here. If you will let Amy marry me, I will take her straight to Nassau. There is no yellow fever in the Bahamas in the winter. Then I will take her directly on to London. She will be away from all the horrors of this war."

"May I speak now, Mr Wells?" asked Mrs Munro in icy tones, "I am sure you mean well, but please consider this from our point of view. I admit that there are dangers here, and that it may not be in my power to protect Amy. But why should I hand her over to an adventurer like you? I will be honest with you. Colonel Munro did not think that you would be a suitable husband for Amy. You were not brought up as a gentleman, and he felt that your means and your prospects were too slender to support Amy."

"As far as that is concerned," I replied, "I may not have been born a gentleman, but I am now a relatively wealthy man. I have accumulated capital of some twenty thousand pounds, and I have the written assurance from my employers that they will offer me a good position when I return to London. I can expect a partnership within the next five years. If our current voyage is successful, my capital will increase again."

"That may be so, Mr Wells…"

At this point Amy burst into the room and ran over to take my hands. I rose to greet her. From the happy look in her eyes there seemed no doubt of her continuing love for me.

"Mr Wells, thank you so much for coming, I couldn't wait any longer to see you."

She sat down on the sofa beside me.

"Mr Wells has come here to renew his suit, Amy," said Mrs Munro glacially, "he wants to marry you and take you out through the blockade to Nassau. His opinion is that there may not be another chance before the Yankees close Wilmington for good. He is worried that you are in greater danger here than you would be running the blockade in his ship. Have I stated all this fairly Mr Wells?"

I nodded.

"Of course what he is saying is nonsense," she continued, "I need you here, and if Sherman comes, I can take you to Wilmington or Richmond. I have told Mr Wells that Colonel Munro considered him to be an adventurer, and not a suitable husband for you. That is my opinion too. I am not prepared to give my consent."

In desperation I turned towards Amy.

"Miss Munro, I have explained to your mother that I am now quite wealthy, and that my prospects in London are good. I am sure that your uncle will confirm that I am a reliable man of business, and that I have earned considerable sums over the last two years. I am not trying to marry you for your money, if that is what Mrs Munro is implying. I have more than enough for the two of us."

"Anyway, Mother," said Amy, "lots of people in Georgia have lost everything when Sherman's army came through, the same could happen to us."

"May I talk to Miss Munro alone?" I asked.

"No you may not!" exclaimed Mrs Munro, angrily, "anything you have to say, you must say with me present."

I turned towards Amy again, and looked into her eyes.

"Miss Munro, this is what I wanted to say. I would have preferred to say it to you alone, but your mother will not permit it. I love you, and I want to marry you. It's what I've always wanted ever since I first met you, and I want it more than ever now. This may be our last chance. My ship has to leave by the tenth of January. As your mother explained, everyone in Wilmington is convinced that this may be the last time a ship can leave before the Yankees seal up Cape Fear. After that it could be years before I could see you again. If you want to marry me, please marry me now."

"This is disgraceful..." began Mrs Munro.

"Please," I said firmly, "you are present, but this is a conversation between myself and Miss Munro. I think I am entitled to hear her reply."

Mrs Munro gave me a furious look, but remained silent. Amy never looked more attractive to me than she did at that moment. Her eyes were open wide with anxiety as she looked between us, and I could see that she was torn in her love for both of us. It took her a long time to say anything but finally she responded.

"Oh this is not fair. You know I love you Tom, and I want to marry you. But my mother is almost helpless here, how can I leave her alone?"

"I wish I knew the answer to that," I said, "but Sherman is coming, and then you may both be trapped. I could take you both down to Wilmington, and perhaps your mother could stay with Mr Blair?"

"Is that not a possibility, Mother?"

"I do not see why Mr Wells should organise my life," said Mrs Munro, "I will not leave Marion until I have to."

"Would you consider staying with Mrs Scott at Sandy Plains?" I asked.

"I will not discuss this with you, Mr Wells," she said, "this conversation must now cease. I need time to talk all of this through with Amy. I must ask you to return to Fayetteville. We will give you our reply tomorrow, but do not hold out any false hopes, my advice to Amy will not change."

"Yes, Mr Wells," said Amy, "this is all so sudden, let me talk it through with Mother. Come to Marion tomorrow morning, and stay for dinner. How did you get here? Can we send you back in the buggy? Come with me, and I will organise it."

Before Mrs Munro could protest, Amy had led the way out into the hall.

"Dixon," she said to the butler, "can you arrange for the buggy to take Mr Wells to Fayetteville? We will wait out on the veranda."

We walked outside. It was a cool breezy day. Tall pine trees bending and flickering in the wind framed the view down to the river across the tired-looking cotton fields. It was a sad and somewhat desolate vista. Amy shivered and drew close to me.

"Put your arm around me, Tom. I can hardly believe that you're here. You are more like the Pirate King than ever, dashing in to seize the poor maiden from her home! When your message came, Mother was angry, but I persuaded her she must see you. It is all so sudden, one minute I was worried that I would never see you again, and the next you want to whisk me off in a quarter of an hour."

"I'm sorry Amy, but it really is now or never. Please think about it – and say yes! Do you think your mother would consider living at Sandy Plains with Louise?"

"I'll do my best to persuade her. Mr Scott is very worried about his mother in Fayetteville, and he's hoping to persuade *her* to move to the plantation too. Louise told me that he'll be visiting her again today. I'll try everything, dear Tom."

She turned away from the view and slipped her arms round my waist and we kissed passionately. Soon we could hear the sound of the buggy coming, and Amy broke away.

"Until tomorrow," she said, with a sweet smile, "let's pray that all will go well."

As I travelled back to Fayetteville I pondered over the difficult discussion in the drawing room at Marion. I was annoyed with myself that I had upset Mrs Munro, but I couldn't see how it could have been avoided. I knew that she would influence Amy against me, and I could think of no way to put my arguments any better than I had.

It was early afternoon, and there were slaves working in the fields. They worked sulkily, urged on by their Negro foremen. They were being watched closely, as at this late stage in the war many slaves were trying to escape and make their way to the Union lines. There were Home Guard patrols looking for runaways, but also for deserters and spies. For a moment I was distracted by the thought of what would happen if Sherman were to come through with his army. What would happen to the slaves, where would they go and how would they live? How would the plantation owners manage without their slaves? Would the plantations still be viable? I could imagine huge difficulties for the Munros, the Scotts and all their friends. The Yankees would be solving the slavery problem, but they would be creating almost as many problems as they were solving. But this distraction only lasted for a few moments, and my mind turned back to my own immediate prospects.

Finally we reached my hotel. I went to my room, which was at the back of the hotel on the first floor. It looked out over a small street of modest houses. It was mid afternoon, and I sat in a chair racking my brains to find a way out of my difficulties. Occasionally I would glance out into the quiet street. I could see people going about their business, and I was sure that my problems must be far worse than any they could have. I envied them their gentle lives, even though I knew that Sherman's maelstrom would probably engulf them in the end. Then I was back to thinking about Amy again. Those precious minutes with her on the veranda and our passionate embrace had heightened my love and desire for her. I was desperate to find a solution.

At first my love for Amy had largely been an overwhelming physical attraction, although her sweet and caring nature had been a big part of her charm for me. Now the many hours I had spent with her at Marion and Wilmington had taken our love to a higher level. Every time I saw her or even thought about her I felt the same surge of love, and it was almost like a drug. I was addicted, and this was an addiction that I longed to have forever. As I thought about Amy in that room in the Fayetteville Hotel, I found it impossible to imagine the rest of my life without her. I knew that somehow I had to find a way to marry her but I was depressed at the thought that I would probably only have one chance, and that would be tomorrow. If I failed, life would lose its meaning for me. Certainly I could see no point in continuing to support slavery and the Confederacy, I might just as well go back to London.

My little room was making me more depressed, so I decided to walk down to the river and watch the boats at the busy little port. At least it would be some distraction from my gloomy thoughts. I walked with my head down, hardly noticing the other pedestrians and the wagons, buggies and carriages thronging the main street. Fayetteville was critical to the Confederate war effort in the Carolinas and beyond, and the activity was frenetic.

Suddenly I was dragged out of my sad trance by a voice calling out my name, and eventually a hand tugging at my sleeve.

"Mr Wells, Mr Wells, are you all right? What are you doing here?"

I looked up, and I could see that it was Mr Scott, Louise's father-in-law. He had climbed down from a carriage, and it was he who was trying to pull me out of my morose reverie. He signalled to his Negro coachman to keep the carriage still and he was looking at me with a worried expression on his face.

"I'm staying at the Fayetteville Hotel," I said eventually.

"Have you been visiting Marion?"

"Yes. I was there earlier this afternoon, and I will be calling again tomorrow."

"I see," he said sympathetically, "and Mrs Munro has not invited you to stay there?"

I nodded.

"Well, that's at least one thing I can put right. Go and collect your things from the hotel, Mr Wells, you are coming to stay at Sandy Plains, I insist upon it. Never let it be said that we are lacking in hospitality in North Carolina."

"Mr Scott, are you sure…?"

"Certainly!" he interrupted, "I absolutely insist. You will collect your things now, and I will wait with the carriage outside the hotel."

A quarter of an hour later I was in his carriage on the way to Sandy Plains, and Mr Scott was explaining that he had been visiting his elderly mother to try to persuade her to move to the plantation house. He was concerned that the town was becoming rough and dangerous, and eventually it might be threatened by Sherman's troops, but his mother had refused to move. I started to explain my own situation, but Mr Scott held up his hand.

"My dear fellow, there is no need to explain. You have been renewing your suit for young Miss Amy, have you not?"

"Well, yes."

"And Mrs Munro has refused?"

"She says that she will discuss it further with Miss Munro, but she has certainly indicated that I should not expect a positive result."

"I am sorry to hear it, sorry to hear it. She seems to forget that our world is crumbling. Half the young men she thinks would be so suitable for her daughter have died or will die in this terrible war, and our farms and plantations are on the verge of ruin. I really believe that if Colonel Munro were still alive he would have allowed your engagement. He may have been a proud man, but he was a realist. He surely would have seen that you could provide the life and security that Amy needs.

"I'm sorry," he continued, "and I hate to say it, but Mrs Munro is a stubborn woman, it takes an earthquake to shift her views."

When we arrived at Sandy Plains we discovered that Louise and her mother-in-law were out, but when they returned we all had dinner together. They were sympathetic to my cause, but they offered me no real hope. They told me that by chance they had visited Marion that day, and they had found Mrs Munro adamant in her decision to refuse the marriage. That night I slept badly, and as I tossed and turned in my bed, I thought of Mr Scott's words about Mrs Munro in the carriage, and I despaired.

Chapter Twenty
The Threshold

The following morning I was almost as nervous as I had been on the *Clara* in our first encounter with a Union cruiser. My whole life was in the balance, and my mind ran in circles like a frightened rabbit as I prepared myself for another difficult interview with Mrs Munro. I had left her angry, and she had revealed her most telling objection against me. I had been stung by her criticism that I was not a gentleman, but how could I argue against it? Her previous objections, lack of funds and the danger of my occupation, I could now virtually dismiss. But how could I remove an objection to my social status? The conundrum seemed impenetrable. Crossing the Atlantic or evading the blockade seemed simple by comparison.

When I came into the hall to take the Scotts' carriage to Marion, Louise was standing there, waiting to see me off.

"I wish you success with your mission Mr Wells," she said. "I am just dying to know what is going to happen. We are assuming that you will be coming back here after dinner, and I hope you will tell me everything then."

In my nervousness I hardly knew how to reply.

To save the Scotts embarrassment, I asked their coachman to drop me at the gates. When I arrived, Mrs Munro received me alone in the library. She was looking tense and solemn. My depression deepened. This was hardly the expression of someone who was about to greet a future son-in-law. She was standing, leaning on her stick.

She greeted me, and we exchanged the usual polite remarks. I waited for Mrs Munro to open the topic that was foremost in both of our minds. Finally she gave a half smile.

"Mr Wells, firstly I owe you an apology. I said some things yesterday that I regret. I just hope you can forget that I ever said them. I suggested that you were not a gentleman, but I have to say that your behaviour here and with Amy has always been punctilious. My accusation was quite unfounded."

I was puzzled by her remarks, but I said that I accepted what she had said, and that I would endeavour to put it to the back of my mind. Mrs Munro thanked me and continued.

"You can imagine, Mr Wells that I have given a great deal of thought to what you said yesterday. I have also discussed it with Amy, and I have even taken the advice of Louise and Mrs Scott. I wanted to be absolutely sure that I was making the correct decision."

She hesitated, and once again a sense of doom was going through me. Surely if Louise and her mother had managed to change Mrs Munro's opinion, they would have told me.

"I have thought about it all last night, and I am now convinced that I have been mistaken in my views. Louise has also told me that she feels that I have misunderstood both you and the depth of your attachment to Amy. She is convinced that I ought to agree to your marriage. Amy also insists that she will never marry anyone else."

A slightly bitter look came over her face as she made this last remark, and I could sense that there must have been yet another battle of words between Amy and her mother. Then Mrs Munro composed herself and continued.

"I have thought long and hard about it and I have changed my mind. I give you my consent. I would like to welcome you into our family."

I was stunned; I could hardly believe what I was hearing. I had prepared myself for a hard fought battle at best, and for rejection as the most likely outcome. I could not restrain myself. I was grinning like a lunatic, and I went over to kiss my prospective mother-in-law.

"Thank you Mrs Munro. I promise I will take the greatest possible care of Amy, and I want to make her the happiest woman in the world."

"Well I suggest you tell her just that, Mr Wells. I think you will find her waiting outside."

I rushed over to the door, and there was Amy. We clung to each other, hardly believing that our dreams were about to come true. Amy was crying with happiness and we were both almost speechless with the emotion of the moment.

Was this the time when I should have made my confessions about Susan? Should I have given Amy the chance to judge my actions before she made the final commitment to marry me? I even thought of doing so, but how could I spoil such a beautiful and happy moment with those sordid echoes of my past? I shirked the task, and having made the decision, I continued to find it easy to do so, and nothing was said. Amy brushed away her happy tears, and we turned and went back into the library to discuss the wedding.

Mrs Munro was determined that the wedding should be a proper one, and she had already discussed it with the minister of their local church, who lived close by. The wedding would be on Saturday, and there was no shaking her from that date. In order to be on the *Isabella* on the morning of the tenth of January, which would be the following Tuesday, we would have to take a boat on Sunday from Fayetteville. This made me nervous. I turned it over in my mind, and finally I responded.

"My closest friend is Harry Mansell, and I want him to be my best man. He is the captain of the *Isabella*, and he's at Wilmington. If the boat schedules allow it, I will travel back down, collect him, and bring him back. We have some cases of champagne and some fine food from Nassau. I'll bring them too."

At first Mrs Munro would not hear of me contributing to the wedding feast, but then she admitted that such luxuries were scarce, and I persuaded her to accept. I said that I needed to leave that night to be sure of finding Mansell. It was always possible that he might be visiting Charlotte Pierce at Myrtle Dunes. A servant was despatched to Sandy Plains to collect my portmanteau, and to invite the Scotts to join us for dinner.

An hour later we were all assembled in the drawing room. The Scotts expressed their delight that Mrs Munro had come round to giving her consent. I thanked Louise again and again for her efforts on our behalf.

"May I call you Tom now?" she asked, "you are fortunate in one thing. By going back down to Wilmington you will avoid all the wedding preparations, and discussions on wedding dresses, trousseaus and all of that feminine nonsense. We are also fortunate that you will not be here to stop us from any of the foolishness we

282

will want to get up to!"

Dinner was a festive occasion, but much of it was taken up with discussion about the wedding – who should be invited, bridesmaids, the wedding feast and so on. They asked me to try to persuade Mr Blair to come up from Wilmington. The Scotts invited Harry Mansell and me to stay with them for the night before the wedding. Finally the dinner was over, and Amy and I could get away to a quiet sitting room. It was wonderful to be alone together. First we kissed and clung to each other in the happiness of finally knowing that we could spend our lives together. Then we sat holding hands on a small sofa to talk.

"I am amazed that your mother gave her consent so easily," I said, "when I left here yesterday she seemed totally against it. I still can't really believe what has happened."

"Yes, she was angry and upset," Amy replied. "When you left, I told her that I had made up my mind that whatever she said I was going to go away with you and marry you anyway…"

"Amy! Surely you wouldn't have done that?"

"Yes I would! I felt that this was my one chance for true happiness in my life. I love you Tom with all my heart. I know it is hard on Mother, but she has Louise and little Henry so close by. She could see how serious I was. Then Louise and Mrs Scott called, and they said that they were convinced that you are the right person for me. This morning she told me that she had changed her mind – something she hardly ever does! So I hope you are proud of me…"

There was only one answer for that; I kissed Amy again.

"She admires you Tom for making your way so successfully in the world, and for your loyalty and love for me."

The word loyalty shot a pang through me as I thought of Susan, but again I said nothing.

"She will find it hard, but she accepts it totally now. Besides, our family tree was so boring before. All farmers and soldiers – not a single adventurer…"

We sat smiling, chatting and holding hands until finally there was a knock at the door. Mr Scott said that the steamer was due at the Marion landing stage in half an hour, and I needed to get down there. Amy and I embraced happily, knowing that in just a few days we would be married. Then she saw me off on the boat.

The steamer stopped at several plantations on its journey down, and I arrived on Wednesday morning. I went straight to the *Isabella*, and there, to my great relief, was Harry Mansell. He was in his cabin.

"Good heavens, Tom, you're back quickly. Where is Amy? What's happened?"

I explained the events of the last few days.

"So I want you to be my best man, Harry, will you do it?"

"Congratulations Tom. This is wonderful news. Of course she has made a terrible choice, but I'm sure she'll make the best of it! As far as being your best man is concerned, it's awkward. I really ought to stay here and complete loading the *Isabella's* cargo. But ... dammit ... Fenton can do that. Yes, I'll come. When do we have to leave?"

"Tomorrow morning. Then we'll be up at Marion on Friday afternoon, and we can go and stay at the Scotts on Friday evening. If we leave on Sunday evening, we can be back here on the ninth. You said we must leave by the morning of the tenth, so we just have time."

"If there's a boat on Saturday evening," said Harry, "I'll come down on that. I'll want to make sure that everything's ready."

Then I went to see Amy's uncle. I was touched at how pleased he seemed to be that we finally had his sister's consent. He was determined to come to the wedding, and he said that he would come up to Marion with us the following morning.

All went smoothly. We reached Marion early on Friday afternoon. We brought several cases of champagne, smoked hams and tins of fish and vegetables from the *Isabella*. The coachman from Marion was waiting for us at the landing stage, and he took us up to the plantation house. The introductions were made, then the whole party went to the little church for a rehearsal of the wedding ceremony. That night the Scotts gave a splendid dinner for us. One or two neighbours came, and the dinner was given in what Mr Scott described as 'the old style'. The table was groaning with fine silver. Times were difficult in the South, some slaves had run away,

284

and others had been impressed into state service, but the Scotts seemed to have plenty of Negro servants to wait on us. The food was abundant, and the wine flowed. We had contributed champagne and brandy; it was an evening to remember.

The next day passed in a wave of happiness for me. Amy, Louise and Mrs Munro had achieved miracles in the short time available to them. Amy was wearing Louise's wedding dress, and dresses had been found for the bridesmaids. Harry was wearing his naval uniform, and I was wearing my smartest London frock coat, which had fortunately not been with me on the *Nutfield*. Angus Blair gave Amy away. The wedding ceremony was in the morning at the little local church, which was gay with flowers. As Amy and I stood at the altar to make our vows our arms were touching, and an electric thrill went through me as we sealed our purpose to be together for the rest of our lives. Then Amy turned to me and lifted her veil. We kissed and my heart was filled with love for her.

It was a chilly January day, and the wedding feast was held indoors at Marion. The big drawing room had been emptied of its usual furniture; two long tables had been placed there for the wedding guests. The whole room had been decorated with flowers, and the Negro servants kept the tables loaded with food and wine – much of it from the *Isabella*. Harry Mansell and Angus Blair both made speeches, and then I stood up. My words were few and spoken nervously, but I can remember them now.

"Mrs Munro, Louise, dear friends and neighbours. How can I thank you enough for letting me take away one of North Carolina's dearest possessions, my beautiful Amy? All I can say is that I will love and cherish her, and I want her to be the happiest girl in the world. We hope to be in London soon, and it is our fondest wish that you will come and visit us there when times are easier.

"We feel sad to be leaving you at this difficult time, but with General Lee in charge, and with your brave and audacious soldiers, surely the South must win in the end.

"Amy has asked me to say a special thanks to all those at Marion who have made her life so happy and worthwhile. But knowing Amy as we do, surely we can imagine that she will be sorely missed too, especially amongst those who have ever needed her special care, and her understanding heart."

This last remark of mine was greeted by thunderous applause, and I could go no further. I could see that many of the Negro servants were openly crying. It was obvious that she would indeed be sadly missed by Marion's slaves and servants.

Harry left late in the afternoon to take the steamer to Wilmington. Gradually the party broke up, and the last guests made their way home. As a sign of the times there was no dance in the evening. Instead there was a small family supper. Finally the supper ended, and Amy and I were able to go upstairs to her bedroom.

All day I had been looking forward to this moment. Amy had been looking so wonderful in her wedding dress, and every so often we had managed to sneak away from the festivities for a kiss and an embrace. Now we were alone together in her room. Amy looked at me shyly.

"Louise told me that there are thirty buttons down the back of this dress. I hope you can be patient enough to undo them, none of your pirate tricks please! Don't tear it – Louise will never forgive me!"

"I've waited for four years," I said, "so I hope I can wait for another few minutes. I can't tell you how beautiful you look in that dress, but I know you're going to be even more beautiful without it."

She giggled and turned her back to me, and I started to undo the buttons. I lifted her dress off carefully.

"Louise would be proud of me – not a single rip or tear. Am I allowed to rip off your petticoat?"

"No Tom! You have no idea how hard it is to get these things now."

She carefully took it off. Now she was standing in her corset. She blushed.

"I am afraid I must ask you to help me with this too, normally Rosa does it, and I just cannot do it on my own."

"When I give up piracy I'm going to be a ladies underwear manufacturer," I said, as I helped her to undo the strings, "it must be a wonderful business. You're wrapped up like a gorgeous parcel, with each layer of the wrapping more beautiful and exotic than the last."

"Well I am just not going to be married to an underwear manufacturer, Tom, so you are going to have to be satisfied with the present inside the parcel," she said, giggling again.

Her corset was off, and now her beautiful figure was deliciously revealed as she stood in her chemise and drawers.

"No," I said, "I can see that I'm not going to be disappointed."

I stepped forward to hold her in my arms and kiss her again, but she dodged away.

"I am not going to kiss you in your tail coat, you must take your clothes off too."

She went round behind me to help me off with my coat. Now it was my turn to be helped with my buttons, studs and links. Finally I was just in my shirt.

"Shall we get into bed?" she said in a small, determined voice, "can you turn your back please?"

I could hear her taking off her chemise and her drawers.

"Shall I put my nightdress on?" she asked in the same small voice.

"No, Amy. I think I've done enough unwrapping for one night."

She giggled nervously, and I could hear her slipping in between the sheets on her bed. Then the room went dark. She had blown out the lamp on her bedside table. I took off my shirt and slipped into bed beside her.

That night was the culmination of my hopes and dreams. My guilt about Susan was forgotten, and finally the person I loved most in the world was in my arms, and the night was filled with sweetness, whispered love and undiluted pleasure. At last we fell asleep in each other's arms. We slept late, but I was woken by a loving voice.

"Tom, Tom, you have slept too long, and you are snoring like a hippopotamus. We ought to get up soon…"

Although the curtains were still drawn, there was light coming into the room. Amy was smiling, and as I gazed at her beautiful face on the pillow I was thinking that now this wonderful girl was finally mine, and I could look forward to a future full of delight and love.

Eventually we went down for breakfast, and we had to face up to the reality of the day. Amy had to decide what to take with her on the steamer to Wilmington, and everything had to be ready for the boat that afternoon. Her mother had given her some of the family jewellery. Although it was going to be risky to take it through the blockade, Mrs Munro recognised that it was perhaps even more risky to leave it at Marion.

Angus Blair was travelling down to Wilmington with us. The steamboat normally travelled directly from Fayetteville to Wilmington, but Blair had some influence with the steamship company, and he had persuaded them to pick us up from the landing stage at Marion. Mrs Munro, Louise, Mr and Mrs Scott, and even little Henry, were all there to see us off. Amy's trunks were loaded onto the steamboat, and then there were tears of farewell. They knew that if we could get through the blockade successfully we would then go on to London. It might be years before she could see her family again. Amy was worried about Sherman's army coming through North Carolina and she was imploring Mr Scott to look after her mother and sister. Then the steamboat blew its whistle and pulled away into the river. Amy's eyes were filled with tears as the plantation disappeared into the distance.

"What does the future hold for Marion, Tom?" she asked, with a catch in her throat.

"Maybe Sherman has exhausted his destructive powers on Georgia," I said, "and anyway, only part of Georgia really suffered. There must be a good chance that Marion will come to no harm."

But as I said this I knew in my heart that the future in the South was going to be hard and dangerous. I could see from the expression on her face that Amy knew it too.

We arrived in Wilmington late on Monday afternoon. The steamboat came into the same area of the port as the *Isabella*. A small party of our seamen carried Amy's trunks to the ship, and we stowed them away below decks. Harry greeted us as we came on board. He was looking grave.

"I've put you in my cabin," he said, "you'll be more comfortable there. But I'm afraid the news is bad. There are rumours in the town that the Yankee fleet has left Beaufort again, and it's heading down the coast – although apparently General Bragg denies it. I want to leave immediately. Now that you're on board I'll contact the authorities, and we should be under weigh within the hour."

"I'm sorry if we've held you up," I said.

"No, that's fine, as long as we can get away now. We should have plenty of time."

We went along to Harry's cabin and we could see that he had made a huge effort to turn it into a comfortable bedroom for the two of us. Amy was delighted, and very grateful. We installed ourselves, and then we went back up on deck to say goodbye to Mr Blair. He and I had discussed our business affairs in great detail on the journey down. We both assumed that this might well be the last voyage that the *Isabella* could make into Wilmington, and our business was as settled as it could be. Our cargo of cotton had been paid for by the cargo of arms and munitions we had just discharged, and the balance we were carrying in gold. All that was left was to say our goodbyes and to wish him well over the difficult times to come. He was anxious about our journey through the blockade, but he tried not to show it to Amy.

Then Harry came on board, and we cast off. As he manoeuvred the *Isabella* out of her berth we could see that another blockade-runner was coming into the port. Harry blew the *Isabella's* whistle urgently.

"It's the *Kite*, and she's travelling fast," said Mansell anxiously, "unless she gets her engines reversed she's going to come devilish close. With the *Isabella* like this we can't get out of *her* way."

As he said this we could hear anxious cries from the other ship. Their paddlewheels went into reverse, but it was too late. She tried to swing away from us, but she clipped our port paddle box as she came round. The air was blue with Mansell's curses. We could hear our paddles grinding against the box. Mansell called for the engines to stop, and finally the noise ceased.

"That's torn it," exclaimed Harry bitterly.

We drifted towards our berth again. As we got close our seamen threw ropes to the men on the quay, and soon we were tied up. Harry's face was grim with foreboding as he leant to the speaking tube to call up the chief engineer. Rowland was with us moments later. Harry turned to him.

"Let's have a look at the damage."

Chapter Twenty One
Our Final Run

Rowland was joined by Torrance, the chief engineer from the *Kite*. They spent two hours assessing the damage, then they came to the wheelhouse to report.

"The news is bad, Captain Mansell," said Rowland, "the *Isabella* won't move without extensive repairs I'm afraid. The damage to the paddles is the worst. There are fourteen paddles on each wheel, and six of them are damaged on the port paddlewheel. The paddlewheel box itself is severely dented and the wheel is out of shape. The only good news is that as far as we can see the drive shaft is not out of line."

"We're looking for good news," said Harry, "with the Yankee fleet heading for Cape Fear. Tell us the worst, Chief, can it be repaired, and how long is it going to take?"

"Well it could have been worse," said Rowland, "if the drive shaft had been out of line, it could have taken a week or more. We have three spare paddles, and the other ship has two. Yes, and before you ask the question Captain Mansell, they're as near the same as makes no odds. I think I can either hammer or force the wheel into shape, and the box doesn't matter too much."

"You said there were six broken paddles, what about the other one?" I asked.

"I think we can patch up one of the broken ones. The wheel won't be perfect, but it'll get us back to Nassau."

"And how long will the repairs take?" asked Harry.

"I wish I could tell you exactly," said Rowland, "two days, three at the most. That's assuming that we work round the clock, and that we get virtually no help from the town. There's little hope of that, most of the dockworkers have left Wilmington now. John here has offered all his engineers to help."

He nodded at the engineer from the *Kite*.

"It's the least we can do," said Torrance.

Mansell turned to him and gripped his arm in thanks, then he turned back to Rowland with a determined look.

"You'll have to try to do it in two days, Chief, even that may be too long. But don't let me hold you up – get going! … No, wait a moment. You said that the wheel won't be perfect. Does that mean it'll slow us down?"

"It's hard to say," responded Rowland, "we'll only know that when we're under weigh. It might shave a knot or two off our speed, captain."

"Very well. Please let me know of anything you need, day or night. There will be a two hundred pound bonus for each engineer if you're finished by Thursday morning at six o'clock."

The two engineers left the wheelhouse. Mansell turned to me.

"I don't think there's any point in you and Mrs Wells staying on board, Tom. They'll be hammering and clattering all through the night. Why don't you stay with Angus Blair? Come and visit us when you can – we may need your influence to get a few things done."

Amy and I moved to her uncle's house. He was planning to leave Wilmington himself, and he was packing up the house. He would be travelling to Marion as soon as we rejoined the *Isabella*. As in Fayetteville, there were refugees passing through Wilmington, but they were mainly from the coastal plantations. Rumours of a new Yankee invasion fleet were widespread now, and many people were abandoning their houses to move inland. This was no honeymoon for Amy and me. It was wonderful to be together, but we had the constant anxiety about the *Isabella's* repairs. Would she be ready in time to escape through Cape Fear? I visited the ship frequently, and did my best to help. I could do nothing to assist with the physical work, but I could sometimes help to procure the materials they needed.

Rowland and his team worked with hardly a break. The most difficult task turned out to be the repair to the wheel structure. It was not until Wednesday evening that they managed to get it into a state that Rowland could accept. Then they worked all night to fit the paddles. Finally on Thursday morning all of the paddles were in place, and they took the *Isabella* on a short trial round the port area. After some small adjustments they declared to Mansell that they were ready to fit the paddlewheel box.

"How long will that take?" asked Mansell.

"A couple of hours, Captain," said Rowland.

"It's two hours we don't have," Mansell replied, "we've missed the deadline, and another two hours would take us until midday. The latest news is that they can see the Yankee fleet off the coast just east of here. They'll be at Cape Fear tonight. Can you fit the box as we move down the river?"

"I suppose we'll just have to," said Rowland, "but all the pieces are spread out over the quay. You'll have to give me thirty minutes to get it all on board."

"Be as quick as you can. We'll leave in thirty minutes - or before if possible. And please thank the engineers from the *Kite*."

We knew that the *Kite* had discharged her cargo, and was now laden with cotton. They were desperate to leave, but had kindly waited until they knew that our repairs were complete. Five minutes later we saw them slip out of the port and head towards Cape Fear.

In the meanwhile Rowland and his team were still working flat out. Everyone was either on board or helping to move sections of the box onto the *Isabella*. Amy was in our cabin, and I went to talk to her. I knew that I had to offer her the option of staying in Wilmington, but I was hoping and praying that she would want to run the blockade.

"It's going to be very tight, my darling," I said, "we have to make our run tonight, and we may be doing it through the Yankee fleet. The repair to the wheel is done, but there's no guarantee that we'll be able to make our usual speed. It's very risky. You could still go with your uncle to Marion if you wanted."

"What will you do Tom? If I went back to Marion, would you come with me?"

"Of course I would."

"But would you do it if I was not here at all?"

"I'd go with the *Isabella*."

"Then that is what I want to do. You do not know what it is like … waiting for Sherman's army. My cousin Mary was in Georgia," she shivered, "the stories were terrible. No. Can we take our chance with the *Isabella* please Tom?"

We kissed, and I went back on deck.

A few minutes later all the sections of the paddlewheel box were on board, and the *Isabella* was under weigh. We had a pilot from Cape Fear who took us round the various obstructions on the river. A couple of times we had to stop, as it was too dangerous to fit some of the paddlewheel box sections with the wheel in motion. Then we reached the smoking station. I had sent a message requesting a speedy search for runaways. The check was cursory, and no runaway slaves were found. We reached Smithville at dusk. The pilot left the ship to go back to his home and while Mansell went ashore to find out the latest information on the Northern fleet, Rowland completed his work on the paddlewheel box. When Harry returned he called the ship's officers into the wheelhouse. His first question was to Rowland.

"What's the news Chief? Is there any more work to be done?"

"The box is fitted, captain, and there's nothing more we can do. We've been watching the wheel as we came down river, and I think it'll hold up. We haven't tried it at full speed yet, but I'm afraid that even at half speed I can hear a vibration I'm not too happy about."

"Will she get us to Nassau?"

"Yes captain, I think so. But we must avoid making too much of the journey at anything close to full speed. The wheel could fail, and then we would have to continue under sail … I recognise that would make us very vulnerable."

"This vibration," said Harry, "is it damaging the wheel or the drive shaft?"

"I wish I could say," Rowland replied, "it didn't seem to get any worse as we came down. I say we can chance it."

Harry turned to the rest of us.

"They still expect the Yankee fleet to arrive tonight. So it's now or never. Our best chance is to go through the Old Inlet by Fort Caswell – as far away from the fleet as possible. High water is at one in the morning. I calculate that we can get over the bar at eleven. That means getting under weigh in an hour. Tom, what do you think about it?"

"Our cargo's valueless if we stay here, and so's the ship," I said, "we must take our chance. I'm worried about Amy, but she still wants to come with us. I'll ask her once again, but I'm sure her answer will be the same."

As I had expected, Amy was determined that she wanted to take her chances with the ship. I could see that she was nervous – as we all were – but I couldn't shake her resolve.

"We are so close now, Tom. I know you are worried for me, but I just want to be away from all that horror. If we stay here we only have the prospect of being chased from one place to another. If we can get through the blockade we can be free."

An hour later steam was up and we started to move towards the bar. There was nearly always a swell in winter, but that night it was relatively gentle. It was cloudy, but some light was being given through the cloud by a quarter moon. At eleven we crossed the bar, and at first everything went well. As soon as he could, Mansell turned southwest, and we slow steamed parallel to the coast – away from Fort Fisher and the Yankee fleet. When we were about three miles from Fort Caswell Mansell increased our speed, and then we became aware of a continuous clanking sound coming from the port paddlewheel, varying in intensity with our speed. It made us nervous, but it didn't seem to deteriorate as we steamed along the coast in the darkness. The wind was stronger now, and the motion of the ship was unpleasant. I went to our cabin. Amy was lying on the bunk looking green.

"It is a long time since I was at sea," she said, nervously, "I was like this for the first two days when we crossed the Atlantic. There is nothing you can do for me, Tom, would you like to go back up to help? But before you go, please tell me, have you seen any Yankee ships yet?"

"We saw a gunboat in the distance, but they didn't see us," I said, "if you really think there's nothing I can do, I'll go back up to the bridge. Mansell needs all the lookouts he can get. I'll come back in half an hour."

I kissed her and tucked her up in the bunk, then I went back outside. I was no longer nervous for myself – the *Nutfield* had cured that – but my skin crawled with the thought of Amy being captured by the Yankees. I was determined to do everything in my power to prevent it.

All through the night we could occasionally see the shadows of Northern ships, mainly sailing in the direction of Fort Fisher. We steamed on; they couldn't have seen us, as none of them turned to follow us. I checked on Amy periodically, but she had fallen asleep. At the first light of dawn Mansell decided to turn the ship southwards onto our course for Nassau.

"Friday the thirteenth," he said, "some say it's unlucky. I'd be a lot happier if we were fifty miles south of this."

From far away in the distance we could hear the rumble of heavy gunfire astern of us.

"It sounds as though Fort Fisher's catching it," he said, "maybe we just squeaked out of Cape Fear in time."

We steamed on in the dawn light. We were constantly reminded of the risk to the port paddlewheel by the continuous clanking sound. There was still a light swell, and the wind was gentle. We were just beginning to congratulate ourselves on a lucky escape from the Yankee fleet, when there was a cry from the masthead. The lookout shouted that he could see two Yankee cruisers, one on either side of us. At first we couldn't see them from the bridge, but as the light improved there they were, one of them two miles to starboard, and the other about the same distance to port.

"Now we'll have to test that wheel," said Mansell, and leaning down to the speaking tube he ordered full speed ahead. As our speed increased, so did the vibration from the port paddlewheel. It was a monotonous sound, distinctly audible above the other noises of the ship. It could have been that, or perhaps the light of the dawn, but something woke Amy, and she came up to the flying bridge. She was looking better.

"Am I a nuisance here?" she asked, "would you rather I stayed in my cabin Captain Mansell?"

"No, please stay," he said, "we need something decorative to distract us. You're looking well, are you feeling better?"

"Much better, thank you. Are we going faster? The engines seem to be louder."

"If you look there, you can see a Yankee cruiser," said Mansell, "and I'm afraid there's another one on the port side. We're at full speed, trying to get away from them. I think we'll be in range in about half an hour as they move to intercept us, but if we can maintain this speed we'll get away eventually. Let's hope there isn't another one ahead of us, then we'll be in trouble."

"I'm going to go and see Rowland in the engine room," he continued, "shall I put you in charge of the ship Mrs Wells?"

Amy laughed as Harry went below.

"When he says we will be in range, does that mean they will be firing at us?" she asked, with a tremor in her voice. She slipped her hand into mine.

"Yes I think so. Since they're sailing towards us they'll only be able to use their bow chasers. We'd be unlucky to get a lot of damage. The movement of their ships in this swell won't make it easy for them. The crew's quarters are below decks. You'll be safer there when they get in range."

"Oh, Tom, I have so often wondered what it was like for you on your blockade runs. Will you be with me… or please can I stay with you here?"

"You're very brave my darling, but I think I'd go out of my mind with worry if you were up here. I don't think Harry would be too happy either."

As we talked, the cruisers appeared increasingly menacing as they crept gradually nearer, trying to get into range. They had been roughly parallel with us when we first saw them, but as they got closer, so they gradually fell behind.

"How far can their guns fire?" asked Amy.

"Fenton will know, Nigel, what's the range of a Parrott gun?"

"About a mile and a half. But they wouldn't hit us at that range, and I doubt if they'd even try. I think they'll begin firing when they're about a mile away. If the dear old *Isabella* can keep up this speed they'll be in range in about a quarter of an hour, but then we should be able to pull away. They'll probably have half an hour to do some damage."

At this point Harry Mansell reappeared on deck, looking worried.

"Rowland says we're not getting full speed. He thinks that fifteen knots will be our maximum. He's still concerned about that vibration. He's not sure whether it's the paddles, the wheel or the drive shaft. If it's the shaft we could be in real trouble. Mrs Wells, when the firing starts, can I ask you to go to the crew's quarters? Our steward will look after you."

"Might I not stay here with Tom, Captain Mansell?"

"I'm afraid not, Captain's orders. How can we poor sailors concentrate on dodging the Yankee navy with all this beauty on the bridge? It wouldn't be fair."

Amy started to say something.

"No argument now," Mansell continued, "or I'll clap you in irons."

Amy laughed,

"You may have to, Captain Mansell."

The wind was from the west, and the cruiser on our port side was closing in on us the fastest. The cruiser on the starboard side was coming directly into the wind, and at first she was under bare poles, but as she gradually turned southwards to follow us, her sails went up too. We had crammed on all sail, but we relied mainly on our powerful engines for our speed.

Then we could see puffs of smoke from the portside cruiser, and we could hear the report of her Parrott gun. We could see no splashes round us as yet, but we knew there would be soon. There were grim faces on the flying bridge. Mansell looked at Amy.

"I'm afraid, Mrs Wells…"

"You do not have to put me under armed escort," said Amy, smiling bravely.

I took her down below, and asked the steward, Ames, to take good care of her.

"Stay here in the centre of the ship, my darling," I said, "I'll come down when I can to see you. If anyone can get us through this, Harry can."

We kissed and embraced, and reluctantly I went back up onto the bridge again.

In another ten minutes both cruisers had opened fire, and now we were beginning to see some of the shots coming quite close to us. Harry altered course periodically to distract the aim of the Yankee gunners. The cruisers were virtually astern of us now, and both were under full sail. The *Isabella* was still steaming fast, so we were gradually pulling away. I began to feel more confident.

Then there was a tremendous explosion from behind us. One of the cruisers had scored a direct hit close to the base of the mainmast. The mast crashed down onto the afterdeck, and the spar dangled over the side. The *Isabella* slowed perceptibly.

Fenton and I rushed down to the afterdeck. One of the seamen had been wounded in the explosion, and was sitting in a pool of blood, holding his head. Another was trapped under the mast. Fenton went to the wounded man, and I went to the broken mast. Three other seamen were already trying to cut away the rigging. When that was done we lifted the mast, and dragged the seaman out from under it. He too was injured, and couldn't move. I went over to Fenton, who was binding up the head of the man he had been helping.

"Phelps is injured too," I said.

"Can you get the men to carry Martin down?" he cried, "his head is badly cut, but otherwise he's pretty sound. I'll have a look at Phelps."

Martin was carried away, but soon the men were back on deck again. Fenton was examining Phelps.

"What do we do with the mast Nigel?" I shouted.

"Keep it on deck if you can, and secure it to the rail," he shouted back, "and get that spar out of the water."

We dragged the spar back on deck, and somehow got the sails away from the mast. Then we used part of the rigging to secure the mast to the rails on the starboard side. We heard another crash as something hit the *Isabella*, but it seemed to make no difference to the movement of the ship, so we carried on working.

"Give us a hand with this man," shouted Fenton, "he's broken both of his legs. We'll have to carry him carefully down."

All five of us carried him. He screamed with pain as we moved him, but finally he was down in the crew's quarters. Then we could see that Amy was tending to Martin. She had blood on her clothes, but she was working away at cleaning his head.

"He is going to need stitches, Mr Fenton," she said.

"Could you do that?" he asked, "if Ames could hold the skin

together, could you do the sewing? I must try to put poor Phelps's legs into splints, or he'll suffer the agonies of the damned every time the ship moves. Everyone else is needed on deck."

I went over to Amy.

"Are you sure you're all right?"

"Yes, Tom, you get back to work. Anyway you seem to be a magnet for danger, we certainly do not want Yankee shells coming in here!"

The seamen and I were smiling at what she had said as we went back up on deck. I went directly to the bridge to explain to Harry what had happened.

"Well now that spar's out of the water," he said, "we're gaining on them again. Did you hear that crash when you were working on the mast?"

"Yes," I said, "what was it?"

"I think they've put a shell into the dry provisions store in the stern, right underneath where you were working. Can you take a look?"

I went quickly to the stern, and went down the hatchway. Sure enough a shell had come through the side of the ship, but fortunately well above the waterline. It had passed straight through the iron hull at an angle, and had put a tremendous dent in the compartment wall separating the store from the engine room. By a miracle it had not exploded. I noticed that it had damaged one of Amy's steel trunks as it passed through.

I went back up to Mansell to report.

"The hull will have to be patched," he said, "if this sea gets any worse we'll ship water through that hole. Get Albert onto it old fellow, and that shell must go overboard."

I went to find the carpenter, and took him down to see the damage. He seemed confident that he could solve the problem. After we had manhandled the shell over the side, I went back onto the bridge.

"We're almost out of range now," said Harry, "they're not firing so often. It was damn lucky that shell hit Mrs Wells' trunk. If it hadn't, it could have gone through the engine room wall!"

"I'm not sure that Amy will see it quite that way," I said.

Mansell was right. We had pulled away, and soon there was a good two miles separating us from the cruisers. We could see signalling going on between them, and eventually one of them turned away and headed towards Cape Fear. There was still the ominous shadow of the other cruiser following us. I went down to see Amy and Fenton.

He was full of Amy's praises. It seemed that she had made an excellent job of stitching up Martin's head. He had suffered tremendously from the pain, but had finally fainted from the loss of blood. Then she could finish her work more easily. Fenton had completed the splints on Phelps's legs.

"Can I leave you in charge Mrs Wells?" Fenton asked, "you'll need to get a change of clothes I'm afraid. Maybe Tom can help you?"

"I would, if that cruiser hadn't put a hole in your trunk," I said, "it's been damaged, but it may have saved the ship by protecting the engine room."

"Please do not worry about that now," said Amy with a smile, "I have a change of clothes in our cabin. I shall have a strong word with Captain Mansell later. Is it usual to use a lady's trunk to protect the ship?"

We all laughed, and Fenton and I went back on deck. As we walked towards the flying bridge Fenton put his hand on my arm and I turned to him to see what he wanted. He smiled.

"You've got a great girl there, if I may say so Tom."

"You don't have to tell me that, but I'm hoping that I won't be needing her nursing skills too often."

Harry asked Fenton to go and check on the repair to the ship's hull; then he spoke to Rowland in the engine room and asked him to come up onto the bridge. When Rowland appeared, Harry asked him how the paddlewheel was holding up.

"That vibration's getting worse captain," he said, "I think the wheel would get us to Nassau if we could reduce speed, but I'm worried that something could give if we have to go on like this."

"We have no choice," said Harry, "if we slow down now the cruiser will catch us, and then we can all look forward to a holiday in New York. Do you have any idea what the problem is?"

"I can't be certain, but I think one of the paddles may be coming loose. Possibly the one we repaired. I don't think it could happen to the ones we replaced. Is there any chance of stopping to have a look?"

"No," said Mansell, "we'll just have to take our chance. What we'll do is try to get the mainmast up again. That would help if the wheel failed."

Rowland went back down to the engine room. Mansell asked me to fetch Fenton and the ship's carpenter. When I brought them back Albert was able to report that he had patched up the hole, and he was pretty confident that it would keep most of the water out.

Harry asked him about the mast. He said that he had already looked at it. It had been severed about five feet from the deck. He was convinced that he could rig up the remaining section, secured to the stump. The mast would be at least six feet shorter. If the rigging was put up again and the sail was reefed Mansell felt that we could get most of our sail area back. He put Fenton in charge of the repair, and he got a party of seamen onto it.

Then Rowland reappeared on the bridge.

"That vibration's getting worse, captain," he said, "I'm going to have to reduce speed."

Harry looked astern at the cruiser. It was now about eight miles behind us.

"Very well," he said, "you can slow the engines down a bit. I think the cruiser's doing about ten knots. Slow us to that and see what happens. It's two o'clock now. At eight o'clock it'll be dark. Let's hope the wheel can hold out 'til then."

At first the reduced speed did the trick. The vibration reduced, and we seemed to be keeping pace with the ugly shadow of the cruiser. By five o'clock Fenton's party had rigged up the shortened mainmast, and the sails were helping us.

Then there was an ominous crash from the port paddlewheel box, and a grinding and clattering sound. The engines stopped. Mansell and I could see Rowland rushing up on deck and starting to wrench off a section of the box.

"Go and see what's happening," said Mansell, "I must stay here and manage the ship."

As I got to the box, Rowland was just lifting off a section of the cover. The wheel was rotating with the speed of the ship. We could see that one of the paddles had half come away and was grinding and scraping against the box.

"I can see what the problem is," said Rowland, "and I think I can repair it. But we'll have to lock the paddles, and that will slow the ship. Can you tell the captain?"

"How long will the repair take?"

"Half an hour at most. Maybe twenty minutes."

"Get going!" I said, and I ran up to the bridge.

I explained what was happening to Mansell. He did some calculations.

"In half an hour we'll be surrendering to the cruiser," he said, "tell Rowland he's got fifteen minutes. I'm sorry Tom, this is damn bad luck. To get caught on what's probably our last run… it makes me wild, curse it!"

With a heavy heart I gave Mansell's message to Rowland, then I went down to see Amy. She was ministering to one of the injured sailors. A lock of her hair was falling free over her face, and there were still bloodstains on her clothes, but there was a sweet expression on her face, and she looked utterly charming. Even in this perilous situation my heart lifted. Gently I told her what was happening. She looked solemn.

"Thank you for telling me Tom. If we do have to surrender, please make sure you are with me."

"Of course I'll be here, my darling, but let's hope it won't come to that."

We kissed lingeringly, then I went back on deck. At first I went to watch Rowland and his team working, but I could see that I was only an irritation to him. I went back up onto the flying bridge. Harry was looking at his watch, and then to the cruiser. Black smoke was billowing out of her funnels as she put on all speed to catch us.

"Let's hope she blows up," said Harry, "they must be burning their boats to make all that smoke. The Parrott gun will be banging away in a minute."

Soon we could see the familiar puffs of smoke, and then there were splashes astern of us.

"It won't be long now. Go and see how Rowland's getting on," said Harry, "unless he can be finished in the next five minutes, we're done. I shall have to prepare to surrender."

When I got there, Rowland and his team were still working frantically. Rowland himself was purple in the face with exertion. He looked up and saw me, and when I saw the expression on his face I could see it was pointless giving him Mansell's message. All I could do was wait, sick with worry for Amy and everyone on the ship.

Suddenly Rowland was climbing off the wheel through the hole in the paddlewheel box.

"That's it," he said, and he sprinted for the engine room. Soon we could hear the engines back in action again, and the paddlewheels started to turn. Our speed gradually increased. There were still splashes round us, but after five minutes we were holding our own against the cruiser. Then we began to pull away. The vibration noise had disappeared. After ten minutes Rowland came onto the bridge.

"It was one of the paddles we didn't repair, Captain," he said, "it must have been weakened by the collision, and we didn't spot it. I think she'll get us to Nassau now."

Mansell stepped over and shook his hand.

"In ten minutes we should be free of her," he said. "I doubt one engineer in a thousand could have done it. Your boys have earned their bonuses now. Go and tell Florence Nightingale, Tom; and please thank her for the wonderful work she did with those sailors."

Fenton and I went back down to the makeshift hospital. Both of the injured men were now in an exhausted sleep. Amy was tidying up some of the mess of bandages and splints.

"I'll take over now," said Fenton, "Tom will tell you what's happening, but we're almost clear of that cruiser. I'm pretty sure we're out of range. It'll be dark soon, and that should be the last we'll see of her. Please accept my heartfelt thanks, Mrs Wells."

Amy was exhausted. I took her back to our cabin, and persuaded her to lie down. I told her how much Fenton and

Mansell admired what she had been doing.

"You're a wife in a million, and I don't deserve you. But I'm going to thank my luck every day of my life." I kissed her. "I'll come back again as soon as I can."

I went back up to see Harry. We were well clear of the cruiser, and Mansell was looking relieved.

"We've done it Tom," he said, "and as long as that wheel holds up we've got the legs of any Yankee cruiser. But you don't look too happy, what's on your mind?"

"I'm thinking about the *Charlotte*, she must be due for her next blockade run, and she won't know what the Yankees are doing at Cape Fear. I can't imagine that Colonel Lamb can hold out a second time. When can we be back in Nassau?"

"Two days should do it. I'll keep the *Isabella* going at the best speed I can. Friday the thirteenth of January. I never thought I would ever be thankful on that date. What do you say Tom? If we get back safely to London, this time next year let's meet again, you, the beautiful Mrs Wells and me. If anything ever deserved a celebration, this would be it."

We shook hands, and we stayed on deck until the light failed. Then I said that I was going to turn in. I went back to our cabin.

"Are we safe now?" came a sleepy voice.

"Yes, I don't think she'll catch us now."

"Come to bed, Tom."

We had no more trouble from Northern cruisers, and the paddlewheel behaved perfectly. On the fifteenth of January 1865 we steamed into Nassau. We found ourselves making fast next to the *Kite*, which had also made her escape. I was hoping to see the *Charlotte* still tied up in port, but she was gone. Johnson informed me that she had left for Wilmington the previous day. All we could do was pray that either Colonel Lamb could repel the Yankee attack, or that the *Charlotte* would realise that Cape Fear was in Northern hands.

Amy and I moved into the rooms in East Street whilst we waited to hear what had happened at Cape Fear. Sadly our worst fears for the *Charlotte* were realised. The Yankees under General Terry had quickly captured Fort Fisher, largely due to the incompetence of

General Bragg. Colonel Lamb had been severely wounded, and the unfortunate General Whiting had been killed. Admiral Porter then took his gunboats through to the Cape Fear River, and they took possession of the passage to Wilmington. Porter set up the signal lights in the New Inlet as if nothing had happened. A number of blockade-runners were lured into his trap, including the *Charlotte*. The crew and passengers were captured, and the ship and cargo seized.

Once we had heard this news I determined to shut down our operations in Nassau. With all the Southern ports now closed, it would have been pointless to continue. We prepared the *Isabella* for her return across the Atlantic. We carried with us some of the blockade goods we could not easily sell in Nassau. I closed the office. I offered to take Johnson and his family back to London, but he was determined to stay, and he took Sam and Mary into his employ. He was paid off generously, and I told him that I would recommend to Mr Pembroke that he should be offered the post of our agent in Nassau.

Early in February we sailed for London and so we missed the last desperate days of the Confederacy. With the closure of the Cape Fear River, the flow of arms and munitions dried up, putting a stranglehold on the Confederate Army. April 1865 saw the close of the Civil War. At the beginning of that month Lee evacuated Richmond. He was pursued by Grant, and surrendered to him on the ninth. The fourteenth was the day of Lincoln's tragic assassination in Washington. Lee had reappointed Joe Johnston as the commanding general in the west, finally replacing Hood. But Johnston failed to prevent Sherman's progress through the Carolinas. On 26 April, Johnston surrendered to Sherman, and the war was effectively over.

By then Amy and I were settled in London. I was a proud man. My commercial skills and my courage had been tested in the most difficult circumstances. I had survived and flourished, and I had accumulated the grand sum of twenty-five thousand pounds. Best of all, I had married the beautiful daughter of a distinguished Southern family. The fates had been kind to me.

Chapter Twenty Two
Our First Caller

When Amy and I arrived back in London, we stayed with my mother in Deptford. It was a small house, but my mother gave notice to her only lodger, and soon we were comfortably installed. Then in May 1865 we made the happy discovery that Amy was expecting our first child, and we decided to set up our own establishment. We took the lease of a house not far from my mother in Vanbrugh Terrace, Blackheath. As a youngster, Blackheath had seemed to me the epitome of grandeur and gentility, so I was delighted to be moving to such a fashionable area. It was particularly popular for people working in the City of London, as it is situated well above the London smoke and smells, yet there is only a fifteen-minute train journey to the City. It was an expensive house but we could comfortably afford it. Mr Pembroke had fulfilled his promise to me by giving me an important, well paid position in his firm.

I look back on those early months of our marriage as one of the happiest times of my life. There was the excitement of decorating and furnishing our new home, I was renewing old friendships, and we had the thrill of the anticipated arrival of our new baby. The only cloud on the horizon seemed to be the tragic course of events in the Southern States, as the North imposed its iron will. Amy followed those events sadly from letters and newspapers.

My life in Stringer, Pembroke was quiet compared to the dangers and excitements of blockade running, but at first I found the novelty stimulating. Hardcastle and I were given the task of selling our two remaining blockade-running ships, the faithful *Isabella* and the *Maude Campbell*. These specialised ships were hard to sell, so after a couple of months I was thankful when Mr Pembroke shifted me onto our business in the Antipodes. The Australian gold rush was pulling men and materials into Melbourne, and business there was booming.

Amy and I moved into our new house at the end of June. Mr

Pembroke gave me a day's leave of absence. We worked all morning, and by the afternoon the furniture was close to being arranged to our satisfaction, and some of the pictures were hung. We were seated in our new drawing room. I was admiring the view over the sunlit Heath, and Amy was trying to find the right place for an elegant little what-not we had found in a local furniture store. I think we were both feeling happy and almost smug to be sitting in that splendid room in proud possession of our new home. From downstairs in the basement kitchen there was the delicious smell of cakes being baked by our new cook. Soon we could expect the housemaid with all the accoutrements of tea on a silver tray.

"There Tom, in the corner next to the bookcase."

"Yes, Amy."

"You're not looking - concentrate! If those china dogs were on the shelves…"

I dragged myself back from my peaceful contemplation of our view.

"But then they'd be next to that picture of the cat, we don't want fights breaking out."

She giggled.

"I give up, if you're not going to be serious, I'll just put it there and I won't give you the choice. Let's see what Louise says in her letter."

Amy had opened a letter from Sandy Plains, which she hadn't yet read. She sat down on our new sofa. Soon I was hearing snippets of news.

"She says that more of their old slaves have left, and they are finding it hard to get labour for the plantation … good heavens, Mr Scott is considering turning some of the fields back to woodland … listen to this, 'it was little Henry's second birthday last week,' … can you believe it? … 'and we spent it with Mama at Marion. He is saying his first words now. A week ago he could only say Ma, but now he is saying Papa, and doggy too."

I could see that her eyes were bright with suppressed emotion.

"You could go out there if you wanted to. I must get myself re-established in the firm, but you could go. There are passenger ships going into Wilmington now."

308

"Thank you Tom, but no. Our child is due in five months," she glanced down at the bulge in her gown, "no ... my life is here with you. Who would you like to be our first caller? Do you think your mother..."

Her sentence was interrupted by the sound of our front door knocker.

"...well, we shall soon find out," she continued, "but are we expecting anybody?"

I shook my head. We could hear the footsteps of our housemaid Anna, and then her light knock at the drawing room door.

"Please Mrs Wells, there's a caller for Mr Wells, but she won't give her name."

Amy and I looked at each other in surprise.

"Well show the lady in, Anna," said Amy.

Then she turned back to me.

"Do you have a secret admirer Tom? I hope I'm not going to have any rivalry from one of our new neighbours."

We both smiled. The door opened again, and a slim veiled lady was ushered in. Amy glanced at me conspiratorially and lifted one eyebrow. When Anna left, the visitor raised her veil.

It was Susan.

It was a moment of utter horror. In the happiness of those early days of our marriage, I had put Susan right to the back of my mind. My last news of her had been that she was travelling on a steamer to Hamburg as the wife of her lover Lopez. I had imagined that she had disappeared from my life completely. I had been too ashamed to mention her to Amy, and now my past sins were threatening to submerge me in an avalanche of disaster. In my shock I slumped back in my chair, and I must have blanched. Amy was looking at me anxiously.

"Are you all right, Tom?" she turned to Susan, "I'm sorry, but my husband seems to be unwell for a moment."

Susan was looking at me quizzically. She was smartly dressed, but somehow her olive skin with its hint of Negro blood seemed both conspicuous and out of place in our Blackheath drawing room. Through the infinite agony of that moment, I couldn't help noticing that her face and figure still had the bewitching allure I remembered so well from Nassau.

I staggered to my feet and tried to recover myself.

"Forgive me, it was the suddenness of seeing you so unexpectedly, Mrs Kohler. Dearest, this is a lady I used to be acquainted with in New Providence. She was married to our landlord in Nassau. The poor fellow died of yellow fever in the summer of sixty-three, and Mrs Kohler was widowed. I heard that you had moved to Germany. What brings you to London?"

Amy was on her feet and moving forward to shake Susan's hand.

"How delightful to meet you, Mrs Kohler, I hope you will join us for some tea? I will ring and ask them to bring it. It was clever of you to find us, we only moved in here yesterday. Please sit down."

Amy tugged at the bell pull, and as we sat, Susan was smiling at Amy.

"I am so please' to meet you too, Mrs Wells. Tom has tol' me so much about you."

With Susan's use of my Christian name, Amy stiffened and looked warily at her.

"Did you know my husband well in Nassau?"

"Oh yes, after poor Hans died, Tom was so helpful to me ... he help' me with the house, an' money matters ... all sorts of things. Then I heard he had been los' on one of his ships," a look of concern came over her pretty face, "I was so sad an' unhappy..."

The frankness of Susan's responses to Amy's questions was horrifying me. Not only that, my mind was in turmoil as I tortured myself with every possible reason for her visit. Although I was looking at Susan, out of the corner of my eye I could see that Amy's face was increasingly pale and suspicious. Somehow I had to move Susan onto safer ground.

"Mrs Kohler, when I came back to Nassau last June I called to see you, but I was told that you had left the islands for Hamburg. I understood that you were travelling with your friend Mr Lopez. Have you been living in Germany?"

Susan looked down demurely at her lap as she answered my question.

"I had a reason to go to Germany, as you know Tom. I could'n

310

stay in Nassau. Mr Lopez, he kin'ly came with me, but now he's back in Nassau."

As Susan looked up at me again, there seemed to be a calculating look in her fine dark brown eyes. Then she turned to Amy.

"I have a business matter to discuss with your husban' Mrs Wells, could I speak to him in private?"

Amy's face was white and rigid. She was staring at me, almost as if she could see right through me. Now, without looking at Susan, she gave a tiny shake of her head.

"No, Mrs Kohler, continue with what you were saying."

Susan gave a sly half smile.

"If that's what you wan'" she paused. Then she took a sharp breath as if to brace herself to say something difficult, "you see, when I lef' Nassau I was carrying Tom's chil'…"

Amy gave a small groan, and she buried her face in her hands. Then her shoulders were shaking with what seemed to be despair. I sat paralysed, not knowing how to respond. Finally Amy straightened herself and looked up at me again. There were tears in her eyes, but there was a pleading look too. Her voice was almost reduced to a whisper.

"Tell me this isn't true, Tom. It can't be true."

How could I deny it? It was clear that Susan knew me well, and that our friendship had been a close one. The scandal was out and I could feel myself flushing with shame but no words would come. Whatever light and hope there had been in Amy's face was now gone completely. Still with tears in her eyes, but with a set, grim face she turned to Susan.

"Go on," she whispered.

Susan seemed unaffected by the cataclysm she was creating. Still smiling, she went calmly on with her revelations.

"When I heard Tom had died, I knew I had to leave Nassau. You see, I thought he would marry me, but how could I stay there with no husban'? So I wen' to Germany and our son Hans-Peter, he was born in Hamburg."

There was a harsh silence in the room. Susan, now that she had thrown her bomb, sat quietly in her chair, but clearly she had more to say. Finally it was Amy who broke the silence. Her tone was bitter and her voice stronger.

"Well Tom, don't you want to know more about your son?"

Still I could say nothing. It was Susan who replied.

"He is here in London, Tom, and he is nearly ten months old. I have taken rooms in Kensington. Hans-Peter, he is with the nurse there."

Although I was still in shock, and desperate with remorse for the mortification I was causing Amy, questions about Susan were still chasing each other round in my mind. Both Susan and Amy were looking at me, waiting for me to react. Finally I found my tongue.

"Look Susan, Amy knows nothing about all this, and I'm deeply ashamed that I never told her. I don't want to make excuses, but when I was wrecked on the *Nutfield* I was unconscious for nearly two months."

I pointed to the big scar running across my forehead.

"When I came to, I could tell them who I was, and get a message to our agent in Wilmington. My first visitor was Harry Mansell. I asked him to see you in Nassau, but you were gone. I heard you were travelling with Mr Lopez, and I assumed everything was over between us."

I turned to Amy.

"That was when I was convinced that there was no obstacle to our marriage."

She was silent, but there was a sad, bitter look on her face. She was quietly twisting an envelope in her fingers.

"But why are you visiting us?" I asked Susan, "is it to do with the child?"

"Yes Tom. It's for Hans-Peter. You see I have met someone who wan' to marry me, but I can' tell him about the chil'. At first I thought Hans-Peter must go to an orphanage, and then I thought of your mother."

Another chill went through me as a new vista of horror opened up.

"My mother? Have you been to see her?"

"Yes, I have just come from her. I saw her address on a letter you had at my villa. You see I thought you were dead, an' you tol' me you were her only chil'. I wondered if she…"

"You didn't tell her…" I asked despairingly.

Susan looked almost contrite.

"No. You see she tol' me that you were still alive, and she tol' me where you were. No I didn' say anything to her."

Now Amy stuffed the twisted wreckage of the envelope into a pocket in her gown, and stood up.

"I must ask you to leave, Mrs Kohler," she said coldly, "I think we understand what you want. We must find and pay for an orphanage, or take the child ourselves. Is that right?"

Susan nodded.

"Very well. Tell us your address and we will call on you tomorrow. I think my husband would like to see his child, and we will give you our answer then."

"Did you come by train?" I asked, "can I walk you to the station?"

"No, Tom. Mrs Kohler will find her own way."

For the rest of that day and for most of the night I found myself telling Amy everything about my relationship with Susan. I tried to explain why I had behaved as I did, my reasons for saying nothing about Susan, and why I had felt that our marriage could take place. I apologised repeatedly for failing to give her a true picture of my past. Both of us knew that many men had transgressed as I had, but it was my knowledge of Susan's pregnancy that distressed Amy the most.

The following day we visited Susan in her rooms in Kensington, and we started to make the arrangements to adopt Hans-Peter. Amy's one condition was that if we agreed to do so, Susan must be out of our lives forever. This, I'm afraid to say, she readily accepted.

The months that followed were terrible ones. All the happy trust between us was gone, and there was a coldness that threatened to destroy our marriage. Sadly Hans-Peter's presence was a constant reminder of our problems. Even the birth of our own child in November failed to lift the gloom.

In the distraction of those dreadful times I had lost contact with Mansell, but one day in the office, early in January 1866, a note

313

came to me from Harry reminding me that we were due to meet on the thirteenth. This would be our promised reunion on the anniversary of our escape from Wilmington. I consulted Amy and we agreed to invite Mansell to our house in Blackheath. Amy preferred to stay at home following the birth of our child. The thirteenth was a Saturday. I wrote to Mansell suggesting that he should come for luncheon and I offered to meet the midday train at Blackheath station.

It was a chilly day. I stood on the platform waiting; then I could see his tall spare figure springing down from the train. He was wearing his naval uniform partly concealed by a thick Navy greatcoat. He waved cheerfully as he came towards me.

"Thomas Wells!" he exclaimed, shaking my hand, and examining me closely, "what a respectable figure you've become, but you're looking a little solemn, are you not pleased to see your old chum?"

"Of course, Harry," I said.

In truth my mind was burdened with a promise I had made to Amy that I would tell Mansell of the problems that had beset us. But I delayed.

"Why the uniform?"

"I'm in the Navy, and we work on Saturdays at the Admiralty – not like you slackers in the City!"

We started walking up the hill towards the Heath.

"So do we," I said, "but I thought our reunion was more important. So did Mr Pembroke, and he may call in on his way back from the office later. He moved to Blackheath a couple of years ago, he lives just round the corner from us in Vanbrugh Park"

"So you've moved to Blackheath to be close to your chief have you?"

"We visited Mr Pembroke when we first came back, and we liked the area. It's only a few minutes from the City by train, and up on the top here the air is fresh. We don't get the London smog."

Soon we reached the Heath, and we started to walk across it to the house in Vanbrugh Terrace. I still couldn't bring myself to talk about our troubles.

"What about you Harry, it's hard to believe that you're working in London."

"Yes, I'm back in the Navy, but it's a desk I'm sailing, not a ship. I thought about resigning, but the Admiralty wanted to use my experience from the Civil War. They were particularly interested in what I had learned from the *Palmetto State*."

"What are you doing?" I asked.

"I can't say much about it, but it's to do with the new ironclad ships we're building. Everything moves at the speed of an arthritic snail here. Mr Pembroke can get a ship built in four or five months, but it can take five years to build an ironclad for the Navy. The *Northumberland* was laid down in 'sixty-one, but she's not even launched yet, and we don't expect her to be commissioned until next year at the earliest."

"What's your involvement?"

"Well the Civil War changed everything. Our old wooden battleships are about as much use as a sleigh in the desert. You know that as well as I do. It's all happening at once. Sails are being replaced by steam, wood by iron, paddles by propellers, muzzle-loaders by breach-loaders, smooth bore by rifle, and God knows what. Then there are submersibles and torpedoes. Soon someone will come up with a way to make a battleship fly. There are crackpots bombarding the Navy with crazy ideas, Watts, Admiral Walker, Coles and dozens of others. I'm in a team trying to make sense of it all, and there's damn little sense to be found."

"But I thought that the Navy had already built plenty of ironclads?"

"We were panicked into it. The French built the *Gloire* in 'sixty, and we rushed the *Warrior* through in 'sixty-one. Then the Civil War came and we tried to learn from that, and that's where I came in. We changed the design to the Minotaur class, and now it's been changed again to the Audacious class. It's not surprising that the government's getting fed up with the Admiralty asking for more and more money. I'm sick and tired of the politics of it and I've asked for a transfer – ideally to a ship. It can be clad in concrete for all I care!"

"But what about you, Tom?" he looked at me quizzically, "you've been listening to me rattling on, but you haven't said much. What's been going on old fellow?"

"I won't hide it from you Harry, it hasn't been plain sailing. We lost some money investing in railway shares, but that's the least of my worries."

"Well, out with it, nobody's ill I trust?"

So now, as we walked slowly across the Heath, I found myself telling Harry the whole disastrous story, from the knock on our new front door, to our visit to Susan in Kensington.

"When we were in her rooms, she told us she had met a young architect in Kensington Gardens. They had both been looking at that memorial of Prince Albert the Queen is building. Well you can guess the rest of it. Soon Susan had him bewitched, but she decided that our child was something she would rather not have to explain, it's too obvious that he was conceived long after poor Kohler died."

"Great Heavens, Tom, it's like something out of a nightmare. I remember once saying to you at the Victoria that you'd bought your experience with Mrs Kohler on the cheap. How wrong could I be?"

As we were talking, so we were walking slower and slower, and now we came to a standstill in the middle of the Heath. Harry's face was registering deep concern, and he was gripping my shoulder as if to give me comfort. People were looking at us strangely as they hurried past us in the winter chill.

"Go on Tom, tell me the rest of the catastrophe."

"Well that same day we agreed to adopt the child. We decided to bring him up as if he was our own son, and we shortened his name to Peter. That was the easy part. But you can imagine the problem of explaining Peter to our friends and relations. It was then that we decided to go back to North Carolina. We will be moving there in April."

"And how about Amy?" asked Mansell softly.

"Well I can't say it has ruined our marriage, she's too sweet for that, but I doubt she'll ever trust me again. If I travel, or call on friends on my own, there's always that questioning look in her eyes. It's torture to both of us. But at least she now has our own son Harry to distract her. He was born last November."

Then we walked in silence to our house. I let Harry and myself in with my key, and in a moment Amy joined us in the hall. She looked towards me questioningly, and I nodded, signifying that I had told Mansell of our secret. Then she turned to him.

"Captain Mansell, it really is wonderful to see you, welcome to our home. You know that we now have Peter with us, but has Tom told you about our son Harry?"

"Yes indeed, but why the strange name?"

"I plead guilty to that," I said, with an apologetic look to Amy, "but perhaps I can make amends. The reason we called him Harry is that we'd like you to stand as godfather to him. Can you agree?"

Smilingly, Mansell consented.

There was no further mention of Peter, but throughout our sombre luncheon he was the spectre at the feast. Harry tried to entertain us with recollections of our adventures together and he had news of many of our friends from the *Isabella*. He said he had visited Nigel Fenton in the splendid house he had bought close to Portsmouth

"Did I tell you I came across McNab?"

"What?" I cried, "that scoundrel! Where was he, what happened?"

"Good Heavens, Tom, we can put all that behind us now. He had his views and we had ours, and in some ways they weren't that far apart. He was standing on a box outside a church in Piccadilly. It seems he's dropped his quest on slavery, and this time he was telling a handful of bored-looking idlers about some East End preacher called Booth who wants to save criminals and prostitutes. As far as the criminals are concerned, he'll have had plenty of experience with that."

"You're right;" I said bitterly, "what he did to the *Nutfield* was little short of murder."

"I suppose you *could* say that, but the captain could have surrendered…"

Harry turned to Amy with an anxious look.

"How is everything at Marion, Mrs Wells?"

Amy sadly related the devastation brought by Sherman as he came through the Carolinas. She told of the survival of the plantation houses at Marion and Sandy Plains, and how Amy's mother and the Scotts were struggling to make the plantations pay.

"In mother's last letter she begged Tom and me to consider coming out to Marion to help with the plantation. James and Henry Scott do what they can, but she doubts whether she can keep Marion going without our help. We have agreed to go. We are trying to persuade Tom's mother to come with us."

Harry pleaded urgent Navy business, leaving soon after luncheon. He wished us well with our move to North Carolina, and promised to visit when he could, perhaps coinciding with January the thirteenth. Amy asked him whether he had any marriage plans.

"My mother tells me that Charlotte Pierce is still unmarried, what are you waiting for?"

"It would have been my dearest wish," he said, "but Miss Charlotte could see that I'm a hopeless case. Perhaps one day I can convince her that a kangaroo farm in the Australian bush or ostrich breeding in the Cape wouldn't be such crazy ventures…"

And with that he was gone.

Back at Marion we have retreated into our own small world. Times are hard, and our neighbours find it difficult enough to run their farms and plantations. They have little time for the social world they enjoyed so much before the war. I have plunged myself into the task of making our property viable. We have converted many of our fields back to forest, and gradually Marion has become profitable again.

Our move to North Carolina seems to have stabilised our marriage and our little family has expanded. Peter has proved to be a charming child, and we have both become devoted to him. One day I shall have to tell him of his true origin, and then no doubt he will wish to find out what has happened to his real mother. For myself, I am just content that Susan has kept to her word. She has never tried to contact us.

We are expecting visitors. Trees block our view to the river now, but soon we will hear the steam whistle as the riverboat delivers its cargo. My mother has finally decided to come to live with us, and her journey has coincided with a visit from Harry Mansell. Amy is resigned to listening to our endless reminiscences of our adventures on the *Clara* and the *Isabella*.

Acknowledgements

In 2005 I was researching the life of my great grandfather Edward Pembroke. I knew that he had been a highly successful ship owner and broker, but his obituaries revealed that he had also been Chairman of the Chamber of Shipping. I contacted them, and hey-presto, out came the evidence of Pembroke's extraordinary involvement in the American Civil War. So my first thanks go to David Asprey for revealing wonderfully detailed information of this somewhat disreputable start to Pembroke's stellar career. Perhaps unsurprisingly, it had been brushed under the carpet in the obituaries.

Having stumbled upon Edward Pembroke's involvement in blockade running, I started researching this fascinating corner of the American Civil War. *Blockade Runner* is the result. I delved into many of the histories and archives of the period, but there are two contemporary accounts which I found particularly fascinating, *Running the Blockade* by Thomas Taylor and *Never Caught* by Captain Roberts (the pseudonym of Augustus Hobart-Hampden, who was a captain in the Royal Navy, and subsequently became an admiral in the Turkish navy). I have drawn widely on these two accounts to try to capture the atmosphere of the period.

I visited Wilmington, Charleston and Fayetteville, and explored the areas around them. Thanks to Jack and Sandra Burnett, I was introduced to the South Carolina Historical Society in Charleston. There I met Mike Coker, who now works at the Old Exchange Building. Mike has been incredibly helpful with this book, reading the manuscripts, providing a wealth of unpublished information from the SCHS archives and making many suggestions. I cannot thank Mike and the SCHS enough for all their help. In North Carolina it was Beverly Tetterton from the New Hanover County Library who helped me with my Wilmington research, and put me in touch with others who could assist me.

Also from America, I would also like to thank Kevin Foster, Ed Smoake and Bob Cooke. From the Bahamas I would like to acknowledge the assistance of Stephen Araha.

In the UK I was helped by many people, but in particular I would like to thank Rachel Caldin for her unstinting support and guidance. Jill and David Hughes were very helpful, as was Josie Stapleton.

Finally I would like to thank the team at Pen and Sword Books for their help and tolerance.

In thanking all of those above, and many others who helped me, I must state that any errors in the research are mine. I have done my utmost to make the background to this novel as convincing as possible, but I know that there are thousands (if not millions) of experts on the history of the American Civil War, and it would be a miracle if no faults were to be found!